A COOL DIP
IN THE BARREN SAHARAN CRICK
& OTHER PLAYS

A Cool Dip in the Barren Saharan Crick

Light Raise the Roof

Tap the Leopard

And an essay

By

Kia Corthron

With a preface by Michael John Garcés
And an interview by Kara Lee Corthron

NoPassport Press
Dreaming the Americas Series

A Cool Dip... and other Plays (and an essay)

Volume Copyright 2011.

Light Raise the Roof © 2004 by Kia Corthron
A Cool Dip in the Barren Saharan Crick © 2010 by Kia Corthron
Tap the Leopard © 2007 by Kia Corthron
"Plunder, Plantation, Peace: Two Weeks in Postwar Liberia © 2011 by Kia Corthron
"Playing Corthron" © 2011 by Michael John Garcés
"An Interview with Kia Corthron" © 2010 by Kara Lee Corthron

NoPassport Press Dreaming the Americas Series, First edition 2011 by NoPassport Press, PO Box 1786, South Gate, CA 90280 USA; NoPassportPress@aol.com, www.nopassport.org, ISBN: 978-0-578-09749-7

Book Design and Formatting:

Kia Corthron
Mead K. Hunter
Otis Ramsey-Zoe
Stephen Squibb
Caridad Svich
Ariane Zaytzeff

Line Editors for this volume:

Stephen Squibb
Caridad Svich

A COOL DIP
IN THE BARREN SAHARAN CRICK
& OTHER PLAYS

A Cool Dip in the Barren Saharan Crick

Light Raise the Roof

Tap the Leopard

And an essay

By

Kia Corthron

**With a preface by Michael John Garcés
And an interview by Kara Lee Corthron**

Acknowledgments

I fretted over this, as probably every writer does, knowing I will forget someone, probably many people, who were instrumental in the research and development of these plays and the essay, as well as the compilation of this anthology. So my apologies at the outset for anyone I may have inadvertently omitted.

First and foremost I'd like to thank Caridad Svich and NoPassport Press. In addition: Nancee Bright; the Bush Foundation; Kara Lee Corthron; Peg Denithorne and the New York State Summer School of the Arts; Professor James Dopoe of Cuttington University; Michael Bigelow Dixon and staff at the Guthrie Theater; Rachel and John Fay; Mogana, Angeline and Augustus Flomo and the Flomo family; Flomo Theatre; Michael John Garcés, Seth Glewen and Gersh Agency; Dr. Joseph Saye Guannu, Ph.D.; the Hermitage Artists Retreat, especially Patricia Caswell, Sharyn Lonsdale and Bruce Rodgers; Joanne Jacobson; Melanie Joseph and the Foundry Theatre's trip to Nairobi for the World Social Forum, 2007; Cecelia Kpangbala; Beth Lincks; Kate Loewald and the staff of The Play Company; Michael Loftin and Broadway Housing; Professor Naame of Cuttington University; Jim Nicola and the staff of New York Theatre Workshop; Kennedy Odede; Wynfred Russell; Tim Sanford and the staff of Playwrights Horizons; Talking Drum Theatre; Theatre for Peace; Wilton Sankawulo; Cori Thomas; Time Warner commission; Virginia Center for the Creative Arts Wachtmeister Award; 'Wright On!; Chay Yew; James Yougie.

Playing Corthron

"Silence does not mean consent or surrender."

-Mernissi, "Beyond the Veil"

Always silence.

The plays open into a lived moment, dynamic with noise. They emerge as if from a great welling of sound, a swell of song or raucous urban dissonance, family bickering or some societal disturbance, but at the core of the opening is someone creating for themselves a private space, a home, a refuge. Trying, and perhaps momentarily succeeding, to lose the self in the swirl of water, the careful assemblage of materials, the stirring of a pot. A mediation, repetition: a calm, a pause inevitably and abruptly broken.

One of my first conversations with Kia Corthron was about places to write, sanctuary spaces in the midst of the New York hustle to think, contemplate and dream. We sat in a very noisy café on tenth avenue, wrestling with the production we were collaborating on, director and writer, tense allies, breaking down the thorny difficulties of rehearsals, actors, production: the fraught challenge of partnering to embody the imagined as we worked towards what playwright Dan O'Brien memorably calls the "fitful victories of production." At best. Engaged in conversation about dramatic tension, passion and obstacle, suddenly we found ourselves musing on the notion of calm. Had been for a while. I don't know that we ever got back to talking about the practical issues at hand. But I learned more about her and the play in that conversation than any other we had over the course of that process.

Facts, figures, names. The characters become distinct, slowly, from a chaos, always, as language swirls and eddies around them. They speak, and are swept up. But they are always searching, desperately for the silent place from whence they came. How to really find it, how to conjure it, how to create it. The abundance of flowing water, how does that become something tangible, real, not simply a resource wasted, but a part of lives lived well? How to make a safe space in a brutal urban environment, where one might repose? How to live outside the savage flow of history, how to make a dignified domesticity in the midst of unspeakable degradation? The characters long to extend these personal, private and ephemeral pauses into actual, lived peace. To make it real. Silence is home.

Quiet is a kind of action. A way of asserting truth to power that is sometimes, often, more tangible than words. A truth less likely to be diminished than the spoken. Remaining mute in the face of the unspeakable. Witnessing, waiting, until it can be told. Silence allows for dreaming, for the possibility of the imagined becoming actual. Silence is hope.

Silence is resistance. Characters retreat into the stronghold of their quiet. They hunker down.

They are battered, terribly, but forces greater than themselves. They are damaged. But, at their core, they do not give in.

And silence is also a weapon.

How to play a character who speaks out of a desire for silence?

"My God, Joe - the world is supposed to be for all of us."
-Clifford Odets, *Waiting for Lefty*

The plays are political. Yes, of course. Whatever that means. The author is making the private public intentionally, so as to spark and provoke discourse. It is a theater of engagement. Yes.

Of course, anyone who thinks the play they are writing, seeing or reading is not making a political statement of one kind or another is delusional. The critical conceit that plays should be "above" or "outside" of the political, that somehow plays that do not focus on upper middle class angst are "not art," of lesser worth, is simply a blunt instrument of power, and of passive acceptance of a social order. It is a political statement.

Kia makes another one, over and over in her plays, as incredibly varied as are the voices and themes, characters and subject matter. The great drama in the world, the one we are obligated to engage, the necessary human theater, is that which takes as its subject power. Which only exists insofar as it is exercised. Be it personal or impersonal, active or passive. Which implies by it's nature an imbalance, an inequality, a hierarchy. Which becomes abuse. The human costs of that abuse.

The only drama, really. What is a play without power? Absent abuse? Where is the tension if everyone's equal? So, of course.

It becomes "political" when the writer is intentional in that exploration as a public dialectic.

Liberia, Ethiopia. Water, homelessness, exploitation. Kia sends me a play, I read it and have to laugh. Because it is so fucking good. Because there is no reason to believe that any American producer will invest in making this play happen. Will have the guts to really risk. This play that will not please their subscribers. This play without a happy, or even properly tragic, ending. This play that is not the February programming they are looking for. This play that challenges conventional notions of structure and momentum. This difficult, epic, expensive play that's about shit no one wants to think about after work on their night out, for god's sake. But they do. They make the brave choice. I'm wrong. They do because they have integrity, because they want to do good work. Sure. But, also. Really? They do because it is so fucking good.

Again, place. Power seeks to consolidate. If you're not making money, you're losing money. There is no stasis. Power controls space. Where to go? The characters try to move outside the scope of power - Africa? Underground? The characters move inward, but power encroaches even there. The characters struggle to accommodate. Edward

Bond said that "...free people are corrupted by accepting their masters' description of freedom." I would say that in Kia's plays people are subverted by accepting notions of safety, stability and dignity. By trying to adjust the given structure, or adjust to it, or by replicating the structure elsewhere. But power cannot be accommodated.

The plays disturb, create a sense of unease. They do not properly end, and certainly do not satisfy. They are unresolved, like the lives they portray. They are impeccably crafted and come to a close, but they do not end. The questions are unanswered but they are activated. And we are engaged.

They disrupt like beauty does, shock the mind into thinking, considering, questioning. They remind me how beautiful people are, in the context of their un-heroic lives, how gorgeous our awkward striving. There is nothing pretty about the plays but their juxtapositions and structure are beautiful as only the best plays are.

Of course, that's not true. The gentle exchanges and joyous outpourings of celebration resound with melody, and the carefully composed syntax of the language spoken by her characters are a marvel of rhythm and nuance. There is a lot that is overtly pleasing in the work. Not to mention the humor.

The responsibility of the performer, which can feel overwhelming, is to address the private authentically, creating detailed and authentic characters while actively participating in crafting the performance to be unbearably intimate and intentionally public, and to find the perfectly balanced style to serve that seeming contradiction.

"The man does not remember the hand that struck him, the darkness that frightened him, as a child; nevertheless, the hand and the darkness remain with him, indivisible from himself forever, part of the passion that drives him wherever he thinks to take flight."
– James Baldwin, "Many Thousands Gone"

The mystery at the heart of it. Why does the character do or say what she does or says? Why is he so happy? Why is she so angry? What is the cause?

Actors would ask Kia these questions, I'd ask Kia these questions, and she'd smile. And we'd go back to the language, the situation, the fact of what the characters were saying, how they were saying it, and under what circumstances. And it would slowly start to make sense, in action. Doing it, instead of talking about it. She wasn't smiling because she was willfully withholding some fact, or because it was a stupid question (or at least I don't think she was). She was smiling because she didn't know. She knew that's what they said or did. And she was right. But why?

The mystery at the heart of the plays, at the heart of the lives of the characters, why they speak they way they speak, why they are silent when they are silent. It is there, in what cannot be articulated, that they art and terrible beauty of her work resides. Why they are not "simply" political. Why they resonate beyond "subject."

I don't know why Cole builds, why Lika reads, why Abebe laughs. I mean, I do, I guess, on some surface level that I can converse about if need be. But not why them. Specifically. And not someone else. And not everyone. Or, to look at it differently, why do they not simply give in like everyone else. Does everyone else? It would seem so. What makes them different? There is no back story, not really, and they aren't "special", not geniuses, not chosen by fate. They're just people. The answer is in the speech. Listen to how they talk, the words they use, the order in which they are used. The music. It's in there, somewhere. Why is Kia writing these plays, not someone else? Why are they so specific, different? Ah. There.

The plays require commitment, trust. The actor has to fully activate the language in the voice and body. She has to work extremely hard to effectively sing language that requires a high level of virtuosity to perform, and seem utterly natural. She must be willing to commit to pain without indulging in it. She must care passionately, intellectually, about why she is doing the play, and then let that go, and allow that passion to become the character's passion. Forgo the safety of understanding.

If the center of the character's lives are not a mystery, and do not react and speak out of that mystery, than the play becomes a lie. And these plays are not lies.

Working on her plays always scares the hell out of me.

"Love is a constant interrogation."
-Milan Kundera,
"The Book of Laughter and Forgetting"

Kia laughs easily, delights in corny jokes, gets excited about the small victories, the daily-ness of life. Her enthusiasm is infectious. And that is reflected in her plays. Her characters are playful, the dialogue is funny. The plays entertain, and celebrate the ways in which people care for and love each other. They are deeply and complicatedly human. There is a great deal of light in her plays, sometimes bright, sometime diffuse, but always present. The darkness always promises to abate.

If her work is approached or performed with heaviness it fails to spark. It's lifeless. The main work of the actor is to explore where the joy of the characters live. How they laugh. The moments they forgive each other, and themselves. The ways in which they learn to accept what they cannot change. Their delight in learning and creating. That is truly what is necessary to make the plays sing. The plays are deeply serious, even sad, and often they limn the tragic, but they are *light*.

And in the end they are emphatically not tragedies. They end in hope. Not easy hope, and with a clear eyed understanding that victories are ephemeral. They conclude with a vision of a possible future. She knows that that the goal is not a fixed point, that salvation, so to speak, is in the journey. In motion. In persevering, and believing.

Her plays end with an image that is both an affirmation and a question.

Kia and I when working, talk a lot (both of us talk *a lot*), but our collaboration really started to make sense when we learned how to be quiet together. To let time pass. To consider, to relax. That's when I think I began to really understand how to approach her work.

The plays really happen when no one is speaking.

Silence, always.

Michael John Garcés
Artistic Director, Cornerstone Theatre
Los Angeles, January 2011

Kia Corthron
interviewed by Kara Lee Corthron

*[Bathroom. ABEBE stands, staring at the toilet from the
other side of the room for several moments. Then HE
quietly walks toward the john, kneels before it, and
flushes it, staring into the bowl: fascination . . . ABEBE
stares with wonder into the running water of the toilet.]*

**Kara Lee Corthron: I have some knowledge about
this, but can you talk about what led you to write
A Cool Dip in the Barren Saharan Crick?**

Kia Corthron: In January of 2007 I was invited by
Melanie Joseph and the Foundry Theatre to travel
with about twenty-five theatre artists to the World
Social Forum in Nairobi. The Foundry partnered
with Ma-Yi Theater and Hip-Hip Theater Festival
for the trip. Sixty-six thousand activists descended
upon the Kenyan capital, where literally thousands
of sociopolitical sessions were presented, and I was
most drawn to the ones focusing on water.
   During the opening ceremonies parade,
Katy Savard, one of my fellow travelers, befriended
Kennedy Odede, a man in his early 20s from
Kibera, the enormous slum on the edge of Nairobi.
A handful of us took a matatu (minibus – the
public transportation, except they were technically
private) to the area. Of course there was no
running water or electricity in the neighborhood of
endless shacks. Kennedy ran a community center
in Kibera; a youth theatre was part of its programs.
When he and his partner, the youth theatre

16

director, came to visit us in our central Nairobi hotel, they joked about bathing in the fountain outside. Kennedy spent the night in one of our rooms, marveling that turning a spigot in the shower would, dependably, produce a stream of clean water. This was the beginning of *A Cool Dip* before I knew there would be *A Cool Dip*.

That fall I was in Sewanee, Tennessee, just starting the first draft. At that time Sewanee's neighbor Monteagle was buying water from Sewanee; Monteagle's reservoir had run dry. The South*east?* Such scarcity is expected in cities erected in deserts: Phoenix, Las Vegas, Los Angeles – not to mention Dubai – but the moist, humid South*east?*

To avoid the long answer, when people have asked me what the play's about, I have tended to just reply "water." Which inevitably causes my questioner to pause, then ask, "You mean the diversion of Mono Lake in California?" "You mean the struggle over states' ownership of Great Lakes water?" "You mean the poor quality of water on Indian reservations because of government dumping or neglect?" No No No. Or – sort of sort of sort of. It's a *huge* topic and every state in the nation and every nation in the world has its own unique water issues. I just drop a tiny stone in a large lake – and hope the reverberating circles the stone makes get a little wider and wider. (Is that mixing too many metaphors?)

KLC: Nope. Those metaphors work together perfectly. You and I saw a brilliant, inspiring

exhibit at the American Museum of Natural History a few years ago called "Water: H₂O=Life." Was this exhibit the springboard for you to begin thinking critically about water?

KC: Yes Yes Yes! I *loved* that show! One particular display became a part of my play though I won't address it here cuz it gives some of the story away. But it was a brilliant exhibit encompassing such an amazing gamut of water issues.

KLC: What was the most challenging aspect of writing this play?

KC: It would have to be the last scene of Act 1, which I can't detail here cuz it gives too much away, but ends in a huge crescendo – literally. I'm still honing it, and it's going to be challenging in tech as well because there is a requirement of offstage voices that need to be pre-recorded. So, with very little rehearsal (2 ½ weeks 'til tech, three weeks total 'til first preview!), we've got to record these voices from the *climax* of the first act – meaning having the actors tape this part of a hugely emotional scene long before they would regularly be at the emotional place in rehearsal to be ready for it – and then to plug in these voices in the midst of live actors – and pray there are no bumps in the recording!

Come to think of it, and related to this – it was a challenge in my writing, for the first time, to limit my characters to less than what I instinctually wanted to write. For a few years I was writing these bigass plays with nine actors, ten actors, eleven actors... and getting produced! And then one day, it all seemed to come to a screeching halt. And with theatres' economic intimidations since the financial crash? So there's a child in Act 1 and my impulse was to bring him back as a teenager in Act 2 given the time passage between the acts – but, as that would require another actor, I didn't do it. The flip side: the challenge/limitation led me to creatively figure another way out of the problem, and I love my solution.

KLC: What was the most enjoyable?

KC: The same scene! (End of Act 1.) And also the very last scene of the play because it goes to a world unseen before in the play.

KLC: What I really love about your work is that, as you say, you always begin with a political impetus, but you also always have a *personal* impetus. How soon do characters and character relationships figure into your writing process and are your characters often based on people you've come across in your research?

KC: Because, yes, I always do start with a political impetus, it means mountains of research before I ever get to the writing. Matter of fact, I finally have to make myself *stop* researching and *start* writing, or the research could go on forever. Somewhere in all that a personal story strikes me, and I start flying with that.

There's a lot of autobiography in *A Cool Dip*. Maybe the last piece I wrote that was so autobiographical was *Digging Eleven*, which was produced by Hartford Stage way back in '99. I gave the grandmother in that play many stories of my own grandmother, the little girl many of my own habits as a child.

The only time I remember basing characters on a real person outside of my personal world – Well, in *Life by Asphyxiation* – the shorter version that at Playwrights was part of an evening of one-acts – was a fictionalized Nat Turner. (In the longer version there was also a fictionalized Crazy Horse.) But the only other time where I remember fashioning a character after a real person, albeit *loosely,* was the Professor in *Seeking the Genesis* that was produced by the Goodman and Manhattan Theatre Club. He was (*loosely!*) based on Peter Kramer, the author of that ludicrous (to my mind) book *Listening to Prozac.*

KLC: As much as folks have talked about/written about your work over the years, few people remark on your sense of humor. There's some funny, funny stuff in Kia Corthron plays! This might be a crazy question, but have you considered writing a political comedy?

KC: Yes! But it hasn't happened yet. Yes, there's funny parts in many of my plays but to write a full-blown comedy – I guess the better word for what I'm thinking of is "satire" – that I've considered but haven't yet done. Of course at some point the clowning would turn around and things would suddenly be *not* funny. The point of the humor would be to make people, who may be sympathetic but rather desensitized, see the whole issue new and differently.

I should say something here. I very much have a political *point of view*. I am not in the camp of throwing out issues and then sitting on the fence about them. What I write is not agit-prop; I do encourage an audience to think for itself. But you *will* know where I'm coming from. If, for example, you leave *Life by Asphyxiation* having no idea that the playwright is anti- death penalty, then I've failed.

KLC: As you've mentioned, this isn't your first production at Playwrights Horizons. Back in 2001, your gang-girl story of pain and redemption, *Breath, Boom* premiered at the old PH space. Can you remember how you felt when you began that rehearsal process and how does that compare to how you're feeling now?

KC: *Breath, Boom* had already been done in London at the Royal Court. It was the Royal Court's commission and was chosen to be the play to open the Court's renovated upstairs space after they'd been "slumming" on the West End for years. I was thrilled to be at the Court, had a lovely time with a wonderful cast – but *Breath, Boom* takes place in the Bronx: It's a New York play, and I really wanted to see it done in New York with New York actors and a New York audience. So I was ecstatic when

Playwrights committed to producing it! And, interestingly, just as it had opened the Royal Court's renovated upstairs space, it *closed* Playwrights Horizons old upstairs space before *they* underwent renovations.

In the sense of setting, *A Cool Dip* is the opposite experience of *Breath, Boom*: It [*A Cool Dip*] takes place in a small town, not unlike our* own small town – Cumberland, Maryland. Like I said, there are plenty of autobiographical elements – the good and the bad of living in such a town as a minority, and some stories come out of my growing up. All to say, there wasn't so much the longing desire that this play *must* be done in New York – except for the fact that New York is my home now, and has been for twenty years.

And Playwrights Horizons is a home for me. *Life by Asphyxiation*, my little meditation on the death penalty that I alluded to earlier, was produced at Playwrights before *Breath, Boom*, so *A Cool Dip* is my third production here. I've known Tim Sanford (artistic director) for many, many years, and really trust his vision. And Chay Yew (director) is also a longtime friend, though this is the first time we've worked together. So – this is starting to sound *too* corny! – but to get all sentimental about it, it all really has a feeling of coming home.

[This interview originally appeared in The Brooklyn Rail, and is reprinted with Kara Lee Corthron's permission.]

A COOL DIP IN THE

BARREN SAHARAN CRICK

Script History: *A Cool Dip in the Barren Sahran Crick* was commissioned by Playwrights Horizons through its Time Warner commissioning program.

A Cool Dip in the Barren Saharan Crick received its world premiere at Playwrights Horizons in New York City in 2010, in a co-production with The Play Company and the Culture Project under the direction of Chay Yew with scenic design by Kris Stone, costume design by Anita Yavich, lighting design by Ben Stanton, sound design by Darron L. West, & production stage management by Kasey Ostopchuck. The cast was (in alphabetical order):

Seyoum/Tich.................Keith Eric Chappelle
Abebe.....................William Jackson Harper
Tay...Joshua King
H.J. ....Kianné Muschett
Pickle..........................Myra Lucretia Taylor

CHARACTERS

(in order of appearance)

ABEBE – an Ethiopian man, 20, 27, 28

PICKLE – a black American woman, 42, 50

H.J. – Pickle's daughter, 17, 25

TAY – a white American boy, 9

SEYOUM – an Ethiopian man, 34

TICH – a black American man, late 20s to 30

THREE HEADS

ABEBE is ever-positive, cheerful, always working to maintain this exterior.

Music: John Lee Hooker, Beethoven's Ninth. Regarding the latter, the playwright is partial to the recording of Eugene Normandy conducting the Philadelphia Orchestra with the Mormon Tabernacle Choir.

Place: The U.S. and Ethiopia.

Time: 2006, then seven years later, then a year after that.

Act One

Scene One

> (Bathroom. ABEBE stands, staring at
> the toilet from the other side of the room
> for several moments. Then HE quietly
> walks toward the john, kneels before it,
> and flushes it, staring into the bowl:
> fascination. The flush over, HE sits back
> on HIS heels, gratified.
>
> But the temptation strikes
> again. HE glances around (as if to
> ensure HE is not being watched), then
> slowly (as if such delicacy would
> somehow diminish the volume of the
> flush) pulls the handle. It is this second
> flush that provokes an offstage reaction.
> Slash marks indicate the interruption
> points.)

H.J.: *(Off, yelling.)* Abebe! Did you flush a/gain?

PICKLE: *(Off, yelling.)* Abebe! There's a drought on, don't for/get!

H.J.: *(Off, yelling.)* Abebe! If it's yellow let it mellow if it's clear don't touch it, fool!

PICKLE: *(Off, yelling.)* Abebe! Remember we must conserve!

> (ABEBE, still staring into the toilet,
> flushes a third time. As THEIR steps are
> heard getting nearer.)

H.J.: *(Off, yelling.)* ABEBE, GET THE HECK AWAY FROM THAT TOI/LET!

PICKLE: *(Off, yelling.)* ABEBE, THE COMMODE IS NOT A TOY!

> *(Now a jiggling at the locked doorknob, followed by banging on the door, the yelling uninterrupted.*
>
> *The following indented speeches are spoken simultaneously:)*

H.J: Abebe, you know there's a water shortage! You come from Africa, I'm sure you understand the preciousness of H_2O! Don't think just because you're in America waste is a privilege, we have bills! And limitations, the dang reservoir's dry, boy!

PICKLE: Abebe, I know you're new here but the drought has left us in a crisis! It may be hard to comprehend when water is in the pipes every time you turn them, but this may not go on indefinitely! Water is a finite commodity, we have to be aware!

> *(ABEBE, seemingly oblivious to the WOMEN, stares with wonder into the running water of the toilet.)*

Scene Two

> *(Half kitchen, half dining room. Sliding glass door to the outside. In the dining area an old console stereo with*

turntable. ABEBE stands holding a
Bible, giving a sermon. PICKLE sits in
a chair pulled from the table and facing
ABEBE, holding a Bible. H.J. sits,
chomping on a fat sandwich.)

ABEBE: God assures us in Leviticus: "I will give you rain in due season, and the land shall yield her increase, and the trees of the field shall yield their fruit."

PICKLE: *(Long A.)* A-men!

ABEBE: How many days?

PICKLE: Fifty-seven!

ABEBE: Fifty-seven without rain. And now having to buy water from Seton, our reservoir dry.

PICKLE: Cuz the *crick*'s nearly dry!

ABEBE: Why?

PICKLE: Sin!

H.J.: Are you studying to be an ecologist or a preacher?

PICKLE: Abebe's a freshman, H.J., he doe'n't have to declare his major yet.

ABEBE: I like to think of myself as an e-God-ogist. *(Laughs heartily.)*

H.J.: *(To PICKLE.)* But isn't that how you got the college to sponsor him? Water major?

PICKLE: Just a suggestion because of his interest in water. Let's see. There was classes on wetlands and wells and waterway well-being –

H.J.: *(To ABEBE.)* And what are you taking?

ABEBE: Early Christian Monasticism, English 101, Intro to the Gospel of John, Intro to Calculus, Seminar: Jesus on the Silver Screen.

H.J.: Sounds like there's a drought in your studies.

ABEBE: I write an ecology column for the school paper, next semester I shall take Wetland Management.

PICKLE: I *like* playin' Congregation. Someday Abebe be a real preacher, I say "I knew him when." Preach!

ABEBE: *(Back to preacher.)* What sin has caused our water shortage?

PICKLE: Waste!

H.J.: You oughta know. STOP FLUSHING THE DANG TOILET!

ABEBE: *(Laughs heartily.)* I shall cease immediately!

H.J.: You said that when you got here a month ago.

PICKLE: Well he *did* stop!

H.J.: And just started again. I know indoor plumbing's a fascination for you but we *are* in a crisis.

PICKLE: I think this is exciting. Drought: little hardship, turn off our water three hours a day, *nothin'*. In Orme, (pronounced "Orm") Tennessee, population one hundred forty-five water turned *on* just three hours a day! Six to nine, people rushed home from work to take a shower, do the dishes the laundry. And CNN dot com too discreet to mention that other: flush the commode.

(The doorbell rings.)

PICKLE: That's it! *(Rushes off.)*

ABEBE: Indoor plumbing may still be a novelty as I am a village boy, but I did *not* have to come to America to witness it. Plenty for the city people, Addis Ababa. When your mother invited me to lunch at her hotel, I saw the fountains outside and wanted to dive in: a shower! *(Hearty laughter.)*

> *(PICKLE returns with the mail: letters and a flat package, about a foot square.)*

PICKLE: Knew it come today, just had a feelin'!

> *(PICKLE pulls out of the package an old record album, the cover a bit yellowed with age but in good shape.)*

PICKLE: John Lee Hooker!

ABEBE: I must hear it!

H.J.: *(Finished sandwich.)* I gotta brush my teeth. *(Exits.)*

(PICKLE putting the record on the turntable. It is in very good condition.)

PICKLE: See that? Way he hammers it on, pulls it off. *(Briefly air-guitars.)* And the tempo he change on a dime. No way they could add backin' tracks, instead ask him while he's singin' to stomp on wood, there's the percussion.

ABEBE: Pickle, how do you know so much about music?

PICKLE: My daddy taught me, blues music he loved. That record he used to play for my sister and me when we was tykes. John Lee was my daddy's favorite. John Lee from Mississipp', like us!

ABEBE: *(A question.)* But H.J. was born here. Maryland.

PICKLE: *(Nods.)* Married Hal, followed him here, his hometown. Both my babies born and raised here. Marylanders. *(PICKLE enjoying the music again.)*

ABEBE: *(Holds out Bible to indicate.)* Church?

PICKLE: *(Reminded.)* Church! Hey! You preach the sermon, then I pick the hymn.

ABEBE: Okay!

PICKLE: Don't never lift the needle off middle of a song, ruins the vinyl.

(PICKLE turns the record player volume down, muting the sound.)

PICKLE: Ready!

ABEBE: *(Preparing to preach.)* God –

PICKLE: My daddy loved the blues, he used to get in big hollerin' matches with my husband who on the other hand lean more toward jazz, classical. Like one's better 'n the other. I remember singin' hymns in the shower, one day I'm beltin' out Joyful, Joyful –

(Sings.) Melt the clouds of sin and sadness

Drive the dark of doubt away. Giver of

Hal come flyin' into the bathroom! "Hit it right, Pick!" My husband say, "Beethoven wrote it with syncopation!" then he take it away!

(Sings.) Melt the clouds of sin and sadness

Drive the dark of doubt away – Giver" hear that? *"Giv/er"* Beethoven threw in a little zinger, not everything so symmetrical, blow out your expectations! Just like in the original: three instrumental movements, then don't he pitch the world a curve ball, bring in a chorus the final round! *(Laughs.)* I used to love singin' that song to H.J. and Carve.

(ABEBE smiles.)

ABEBE: Church?

PICKLE: *(Reminded.)* Church!

ABEBE: *(Preparing to preach.)* God –

PICKLE: You gonna make a wonderful preacher, Abebe. Poise, you never talk down to people. And knowledge, for a tour assistant, you educated my church group 'bout the holy lands ten times better 'n the man runnin' the show.

ABEBE: Thank you, Pickle.

PICKLE: You know about my grief. H.J.'s and my grief, year ago. Then I saw this ad for an Ethiopian Christian tour. . . . What I needed.

ABEBE: I am sorry for your loss, Pickle.

PICKLE: *Or* ecologist! You choose that over preacher, you make a good one.

ABEBE: I owe you so much, Pickle. Thank you, Pickle. Is "Pickle" a common American name?

PICKLE: My daddy called me that, baby up. You think I'm a dill or a sweet?

ABEBE: Sweet!

PICKLE: You too! Let's sing!
(Singing.) Shall we gather at the river
Where bright angel feet have trod
With its crystal tide forever
Flowing by the throne of God? here comes the chorus!

> *(As PICKLE continues, ABEBE cheerily fakes singing this hymn HE doesn't know. H.J. returns while THEY are singing.*

*The following indented speeches are
spoken [sung] simultaneously:)*

PICKLE: *Yes, we'll gather at the river,*

ABEBE: *Aaaaaaaaaaaaaaah*

PICKLE: *The beautiful, beautiful river,*

ABEBE: *Aaaaaaaaaaaaaaah*

PICKLE: *Gather with the saints at the river –*

ABEBE: *Aaaaaaaaaaaaaaah*

> *(PICKLE suddenly breaks into
> uncontrollable laughter.)*

PICKLE: *(To ABEBE.)* I can't believe you still do
that! Remember when you were little, I'd turn on
the car radio, if you didn't know the words –

> *(H.J. sharply turns to PICKLE. ABEBE
> is confused. PICKLE, startled by H.J.'s
> look, is silenced.)*

PICKLE: Sorry, Abebe, mixin' you up with
somebody else. *(Beat.)* Nothin', common mistake. I
see a movie with two blond women, I spend resta
the film confusin' 'em. *(Chuckles nervously.)*

ABEBE: Did I tell you about my interesting
opportunity to witness last evening? *(PICKLE, still
unsettled, shakes HER head no.)* The shop was slow,
so I began rearranging the front table display when
Mary Jean behind the register speaks: "That's him!"
I look out into the mall corridor, and Mary Jean

admonishes me for looking where she implied to look. I see a little white boy. A sad little white boy, I think he is alone, that the man seated next to him is a stranger, but every so often the man says something to the boy and the boy responds by nodding. Mary Jean says, "That's the people took him in, fosters. That boy don't speak."

PICKLE: Wait, I know what you gonna say. That's the boy his daddy taken that shotgun, killed his mama, his brothers and sister and lastly himself.

ABEBE: Correct! But this boy on that fateful night his father could not locate, so small he balled himself in a corner under the bed and was unseen. Now a woman carrying shopping bags joins the boy and man, and they stand and walk toward our shop. "He'd like a pair of tennas," the foster father says to me, so I walk the boy to the children's shelf, indicating the styles to see if any are to his fancy. The Adidas? He nods. The New Balance? He nods. These exceptionally hideous Nikes? He nods. The boy carries an old shoebox tied with a string. I ask him to sit. He does, and sets the shoebox on the chair next to him. I take my shoehorn out of my hip pocket and slip the shoes onto his feet. Do they feel good? He nods. Can you walk around in them? He does. How do they feel? A trick to make him speak! He stares. Mary Jean offers to ring them up, an opportunity for her to interrogate the woman, who has pulled her credit card from her wallet. I put my shoehorn back in my hip pocket, and alone with the boy, I kneel beside his chair and tell him that God is always with us, that God will never desert us. He nods. I tell him the people we love will never desert us either, even those in heaven watching us, still loving us, always loving us. He stares at me. I tell him that people make mistakes but that does not mean they do not go to heaven. I lean in close, and I say quietly, "Everyone has a bad day. What we need to remember are all the days of love." *(Smiles.)*

PICKLE: Then?

ABEBE: Then he stands. Walks around me, behind me, he takes the shoehorn from my hip pocket, he puts it into *his* hip pocket. I do not know if this is anger, a robbery and a dare that I not challenge it, or if this is something he is giving me. A closeness. His foster parents did not see, Mary Jean did not see. Then his foster parents lead him out of the shop, and I wonder whether I have sinned in allowing the theft to occur, not to have reported it. But I weigh my offense, taking all the factors into consideration, and in this reflection I remember: The shop has many shoehorns.

(ABEBE turns to PICKLE, smiling.)

ABEBE: Now I would like to hear the entire album. John Lee Hooker has a new fan!

PICKLE: Knew it! *(Turns up the record volume.)* Pretty good condition, huh? "Almost mint," what the seller said. But what we hear today: never again. Next time a bit different – little pop on track two, bump the middle a five. "Dialectics," some ol' Greek called it, change: You can't cross the same river twice. What makes what we have now so precious: Fleeting.

Scene Three

> *(Playground. TAY sits alone at a picnic table, HIS lunch box on the table, eating a peanut butter and jelly sandwich without enthusiasm. HE wears a big plastic backpack, brightly decorated with a cartoon. On the table next to HIS lunch is a worn shoebox, tied shut. ABEBE enters with HIS own packed lunch, sits beside TAY.)*

ABEBE: Hello Tay. Do you remember me from the shoe shop? *(TAY nods.)* They told you I was coming? *(TAY nods.)* Do you know my name? *(TAY nods.)* Can you say it? *(TAY stares.)* Abebe. *(TAY stares.)* All alone. You don't like to sit with the other children? *(TAY nods. ABEBE smiles.)* I'm your lunch buddy. Every Thursday we shall eat lunch together. Okay? *(TAY nods.)* It seems your foster mother noticed that we were having a nice chat, because she came back to the shoe shop the day after you and I met. I was off that day so she came again the next day and I was working, and she told me she thought I might be a friend to you. Then your vice-principal called me. *(Beat.)* As lunch buddies, we will talk. Okay? *(TAY nods.)* Would you like to tell me something about yourself? *(TAY stares.)* Would you like me to tell you something about myself? *(TAY nods.)* Okay. I am from Ethiopia. Do you know where that is? *(TAY nods.)*

Africa? *(TAY nods.)* Correct! There is much much much much water in Africa. Unfortunately sometimes it is not in the right places. Or the dry season becomes drier. Or the water is unclean. This can mean sickness, diarrhea and measles and meningitis, and these can mean death. They meant my mother's death, and my father's death, and my brother's death, and my older sisters' deaths, and my twin infant sisters' deaths. For some reason I was the only one Death overlooked, so I am an orphan: no more family. *(Meaningfully.)* Do you understand? *(TAY stares.)* Another family took me in but I was aware of the burden. Rain came and we rejoiced. I had been going to school but stopped to help out the women with the farming at home. Women may go to school but few do because the task of fetching water requires several hours in a day. I was able to continue my education through occasional odd jobs in the tourist trade and this would allow me access to the internet. I learned of Rajendra Singh, a man who developed a primitive dam system to capitalize on rainwater, thousands of these small dams he brought to his poor, rural countrymen in India, and I felt this could be done in my village. So with the help of my fellow villagers, for most wondrous about this project is that it requires the community to work together, we were also successful with this dam. It provided a bulwark against drought, it allowed a few of our girls to go to school. On one of the Christian tours a kind American woman, interested in my background and asking many questions, was very impressed with my dam project. "How old are you?" she asked. "Nineteen," I replied. Now I am twenty. She brought me to the States to further my education so that I might take my knowledge home to serve my people, to save my people, and I will. *(Beat.)* But first I have another task to accomplish. I will share a secret with you, Tay. My work is the Lord's. When I was offered a trip to America, I saw an opportunity to spread God's word. I am a missionary here, America is not saving *me*, I am here to save *America! (A school bell rings.)* Yours is the second bell. Correct?

> *(TAY nods. ABEBE takes a cupcake out of HIS lunch, offers.)*

ABEBE: You like chocolate?

> *(TAY takes the cupcake, puts it into HIS lunchbox. Then unties the shoebox string, opens the shoebox. Pushes it toward ABEBE. ABEBE is surprised. ABEBE looks into the box. Pulls out a photograph.)*

ABEBE: Your family? *(TAY nods.)* Everyone? *(TAY nods.)* Very beautiful. Except your brother's eyes closed. *(Smiles.)*

> *(TAY indicates the box again. ABEBE pulls out a naked Barbie doll.)*

ABEBE: What is your doll's name? *(TAY points to the picture.)* Your sister's doll?

> *(TAY nods. A reality dawns upon ABEBE.)*

ABEBE: These are all your family's things? What is left to you?

> (TAY takes a roller skate out of the box, the kind that can be attached to the bottom of a sneaker.)

ABEBE: Where is your other skate? (TAY stares.) You could find only one?

> (TAY nods. ABEBE reaches in without looking, pulls out the shoehorn. TAY, instantly mortified, snatches it, hides it in HIS arms.)

ABEBE: No, yours! Okay okay? You keep! I don't need the shoehorn back.

> (TAY stares at HIM several moments. Then pulls out of the shoebox a flag. The flagpole is about eight inches long, such as those given out at parades. It is wrapped around its pole and rubber-banded so that it can't be identified, though red, white and blue may be evident. TAY points to the photo.)

ABEBE: Your father's? (TAY nods. Offers the flag to ABEBE.) Me? (TAY continues offering.) No! you don't have to give me because I gave you.

> (TAY reaches into the box, pulls out an identical rubber-banded flag. Again indicates for ABEBE to take the first flag.)

ABEBE: I see! We can wave the flags together! *(TAY nods.) That* I would like. Together!

> *(ABEBE takes both flags, removes the bands, hands one back to TAY. THEY unfurl them. They are Confederate flags. ABEBE and TAY begin to wave them together. TAY nearly smiles.)*

ABEBE: Together! *(Waving.)* Together! *(Waving.)* Together!

> *(The second bell rings. THEY are still smiling and waving.)*

Scene Four

> *(Bathroom. ABEBE stands, holding HIS Bible, mouthing a silent prayer. H.J. enters wearing a shower cap and HER bathing suit. Over the suit is a long overshirt, perhaps a nightshirt, hanging to HER knees or lower.)*

H.J.: *(Fingering the quote marks.)* I've seen those Baptism "robes," thin as rice paper, not me. Baptism's nothin' but a wet T-shirt contest.

ABEBE: Seven hundred gallons of water to grow enough cotton for one T-shirt!

H.J.: Someday when you get your church, guess every sermon be your Eleventh Commandment: "Thou shalt not waste."

ABEBE: There is sin in godlessness and sin in waste. Waste *is* godlessness. I do not separate.

> *(H.J. steps into the tub, filled with water.)*

H.J.: I still don't see how this helps you. Baptizing a heathen, cuz I know that's what you think of me.

ABEBE: Someday I will witness to someone who will accept the Lord and want immediate baptism in the faith! It might happen next year, it might happen tomorrow! I must practice, I must be ready!

H.J.: Ready.

> *(ABEBE speaks, the Bible verses HE has memorized.)*

ABEBE: Luke writes that the soldiers asked John the Baptist: "what shall we do? And he said… Do violence to no man… (A)nd all men mused…whether he were the Christ… John answered… I indeed baptize you with water; but one mightier than I cometh…: he shall baptize you with the Holy Ghost and with fire."

> *(ABEBE has marked the Bible to the correct page, and holds it out to H.J.)*

ABEBE: Now you read Matthew please.

H.J.: *(Reads.)* "Then cometh Jesus from Galilee to Jordan unto John, to be baptized – "

*(In one fell swoop ABEBE snatches the
Bible back and splashes H.J. SHE
sputters.)*

ABEBE: Dunk! *(Laughing heartily and in good nature.)*

H.J.: I quit! *(Getting out of the tub.)*

ABEBE: Please! I must practice!

H.J.: Yeah I'm doing you a favor, look what *I* got!

ABEBE: Very sorry! I shall make reparations!
Tonight your dishwashing turn becomes mine!

(H.J. considers.)

H.J.: It wouldn't affect the rest of the schedule.
Tomorrow's still your turn.

ABEBE: Of course!

*(H.J. considers, then steps back into the
tub.)*

H.J.: Do it again it's all over. "There are wrongs
which even the grave does not bury."

ABEBE: I have made a deal, a Christian never
welches! *(Beat.)* "There are wrongs . . . ?"

H.J.: Harriet Jacobs. Who I'm named after, didn't
you ever wonder what H.J. stood for? Penned a
page-turner about her escape, so well written the
whites didn't believe a black authored it, and I'm
talking about her *friends*, abolitionists. My parents'
thing, namesaking us after black heroes. My little

brother was George Washington Carver, that's why we called him "Carve." So his whole name was George Washington Carver Carter.

ABEBE: I too am a namesake! Abebe Bikila was told to keep an eye out for the Moroccan frontrunner, number twenty-six and Here are your Adidas who have sponsored these 1960 Olympics. But the Moroccan's number was switched to one eighty-five and the Adidas did not fit. So shoeless Abebe runs, neck and neck with one eighty-five while searching frantically for nonexistent twenty-six. Abebe wins, the first African to take Olympic gold, Olympic gold for a marathon he ran barefoot! Went to Tokyo in '64 to provide moral support, in the end he competes, this time in Asics sneakers. He wins! four minutes ahead of second place. He wins! the first Olympic athlete to take the marathon twice. I too have a quote! When asked in 1960 about the barefoot race, Abebe replies: "I wanted the world to know that my country, Ethiopia, has always won with determination and heroism."

H.J.: Wow. 'S he still alive?

ABEBE: Twice Olympic gold, twice he comes home to a hero's welcome! The second time the emperor presents him with the gift of a Volkswagen. In a country of few cars, it is a Rolls Royce. In 1969 he is in a car accident. It leaves him a quadriplegic. Surgeons work tirelessly and miraculously, and he recovers! Now only a *para*plegic! He begins to compete in paraplegic archery and jokes that he would win his next Olympic gold from his wheelchair! *(Laughs heartily.)*

H.J.: Wow. 'S he still alive?

ABEBE: In 1973 at age forty-one he is dead, having succumbed to a cerebral hemorrhage related to the car accident of four years before.

H.J.: Wow.

(Silence.)

ABEBE: Someday *I* will drive a Volkswagen! I have God's work to do, God will provide!

H.J.: How *are* the driving lessons going?

ABEBE: Much improvement! The car slipped onto the sidewalk only twice yesterday! *(Baptism.)* In the nineteenth chapter of Acts, Paul comes upon disciples in Ephesus –

> *(Suddenly the muffled sound of the John Lee Hooker album playing downstairs.)*

H.J.: Guess she's home. MOM! STOP PLAYING THAT, WE'RE HAVING OUR SACRED MOMENT!

> *(The music stops. Sound of footsteps. ABEBE's left hand on H.J.'s back, right hand holding up the Bible.)*

ABEBE: In the nineteenth chapter of Acts, Paul comes upon disciples in Ephesus –

(A knock at the bathroom door.)

PICKLE: *(Off.)* This the baptism? Can I watch? *(H.J. sighs.)*

ABEBE: Please join us, Pickle!

> *(PICKLE enters in a nurse's uniform and carrying a letter.)*

PICKLE: House all quiet, thought yaw finished already, went out.

ABEBE: You were only hearing the tranquility of holiness!

PICKLE: Seein' that girl get a little a the devil knocked outa her's worth it, even if she just actin' the part. Letter for you! From Ethiopia!

ABEBE: Thank you!

PICKLE: I'll set it here 'til you're dry.

> *(PICKLE sets the letter on the back of the toilet, then sits on the closed seat. ABEBE's left hand on H.J.'s back, right hand holding up the Bible.)*

ABEBE: In the nineteenth chapter of Acts, Paul comes upon disciples in Ephesus –

> *(A hip hop ring tone offstage.)*

H.J.: That's me!

> *(H.J. gets out of the tub, snatching HER towel to cover HERself.)*

PICKLE: Don't be on that cell phone all day! *(H.J. exits. Waving the letter, to ABEBE.)* Stamp's pretty! *(ABEBE takes the letter, opens it.)* How'd you get her in the baptismal tub? *Her* Bibles geometry and physics.

ABEBE: An even trade. It was her turn to do the vacuuming this afternoon but I assumed the task.

PICKLE: Sound like she made out on that deal. Wonder what's goin' on in East Africa?

> *(ABEBE looking at the letter. HIS face is serious.)*

PICKLE: Bad news?

ABEBE: Good news! We must always see the good!

PICKLE: That sounds bad.

ABEBE: No! My brother Seyoum has reported –

PICKLE: "Brother"?

ABEBE: My adopted brother Seyoum has reported that there is talk of a World Bank funded megadam coming to our village.

PICKLE: Oh! That sounds good.

ABEBE: No! However! It takes just such a crisis to galvanize a community, my friends will stand strong and prevent this catastrophe, they will prevail, *God* will prevail and our community will be made even stronger!

PICKLE: That *is* good news! *I* have good news!

ABEBE: What!

PICKLE: Look like the water bottling plant's finally gonna go through! Jobs!

ABEBE: *Terrible* news!

PICKLE: That's right, you got a thing against bottled water. What's your thing against bottled water?

ABEBE: Tons of plastic waste! Tons of fuel to deliver! Minimal health testing!

PICKLE: Oh. Guess you gonna write about it in your school paper.

ABEBE: Indubitably!

PICKLE: How's school goin'? Classes?

ABEBE: I am excelling in every subject! Including driver's education!

PICKLE: Knew you could do it! Studyin' the book?

ABEBE: I have memorized the Safe Drivers Manual! Stop for the school bus! Sixty-five on the freeway!

PICKLE: *(Horror.)* You goin' on the *freeway?!*

ABEBE: Hypothetically!

PICKLE: Oh. *(To H.J.)* H.J., YOU KNOW YOUR CELL MINUTES'RE NUMBERED!

ABEBE: I also have had a plethora of phone calls today! Two! First, Tay's schoolteacher called to ask if I would be interested in supplementing my Lunch Buddy status by becoming a Big Brother to Tay outside of school. Yes! I replied. Next, Mrs. Cindy Lambert, Tay's temporary guardian called to second the notion, and said she would like to drop Tay off here before her morning Wal-Mart shift Saturday, her husband Pete will pick him up. Okay?

PICKLE: Okay! How's he doin'? Better?

ABEBE: Better! He has family things he holds tight to, and I think this is very good. Mrs. Lambert is concerned about only one of these family things. This would be Tay's pajamas. When the murdering was finished, he came to his mother, held his blood-soaked mother. The police wanted the pajamas for evidence but Tay refused. The police shrugged: The case was shut-and-open after all. It took three days to get Tay to take off the pajamas, covered in dried blood. Mrs. Lambert would like to burn them but Tay has expressed his discomfort with this notion in no uncertain terms. However, aside from this attachment to the butchery and his commitment to being a mute, Tay is doing quite well!

> (PICKLE turns HER head as if SHE has heard something. SHE listens a few moments: the sound makes HER happy.)

PICKLE: Hear that?

ABEBE: No.

(*Beat.*)

PICKLE: You ever hear the dead?

ABEBE: Always! Although I am usually asleep. Do you?

PICKLE: No!

(*Pause.*)

PICKLE: She tests me.

(*ABEBE confused.*)

ABEBE: H.J.?

PICKLE: Put me on a trial. You think 'at's right? Somebody do that to their own mother?

ABEBE: No! Accuse you?

PICKLE: Yes!

ABEBE: Of what?

PICKLE: Everyone got their own way a grievin'! right? Can't nobody tell nobody else how they s'posed to mourn. Right?

ABEBE: *Very* right! It is written in Ecclesiastes, "To everything there is a season, and a time to every – "

PICKLE: Hey! Lemme tell ya a funny story 'bout the dead! Hal's story. Miss Ivy taught eleventh grade English he tole me, (*indicates.*) lived crost the crick. When my husband was little his mother cleaned for her awhile. One day, no one to babysit, Hal's stuck there with his mama. Miss Ivy the kind got all sorta magnets on her fridge, more 'n *me*. "Bahamas" with a palm tree and "Alaska" with a polar bear and "I'm not cheap but I'm on special this week" and amid the hordes near the back wall little Hal spies a plastic cartoon magnet a this little black boy, wide surprised Sambo eyes, his bare behind just off the toilet with this caption above:

Nigger nigger

All refine-y

Still your ass is

Black and shiny

So! A warm evenin' later in the week, Hal decides to hide in the bushes under Miss Ivy's kitchen window. He try to make up his own poym but, like I say, he's little so all he come up with:

Whitey whitey

Shiny shiny

Whitey whitey

Shiny shiny

But apparently his voice don't come through the window like a little boy: squeaky eerie Miss Ivy don't know what! Worshin' the dishes think she hear some mouse speakin' English. Or ghost! Somebody dead come back to greet her, Miss Ivy searchin' everywhere, don't know where the words emanatin' from, spooked!

ABEBE: Very amusing! You tell very funny stories about the dead, Pickle!

PICKLE: Hal tol' me that story after we's first married, moved here. That thing tickle us so bad, ever after we be sittin' up in bed, all one a us gotta say is "Shiny shiny" and we both crackin' up! And next thing we know slippin' under the blankets. Together.

> *(PICKLE and ABEBE smile. H.J. enters.)*

PICKLE: H.J.! I was just tellin' Abebe 'bout Miss Ivy, remember your daddy's eleventh grade – ?

H.J.: Whitey whitey shiny shiny. That was Alene Douglas. *(Ay-leen.)* She said you were bothering her little brother. *Marky* Douglas.

PICKLE: *(Beat: stares at H.J.)* I don't know what you talkin' about.

H.J.: She said you guilted him into coming into the office. He told the principal you saw him in the market perusing the toys while his mother in frozen foods, you come to him and talked and you and he agreed Carve oughta get the fourth grade math prize from last year, he earned it. So Marky offered to give it back. To which the Principal said No.

PICKLE: Carve *would*a earned it!

H.J.: Carve didn't make it to fourth grade! And they *gave* him an award –

PICKLE: Bullcrap award! *(To ABEBE.)* Spaghetti for dinner?

(ABEBE, confused, nods.)

PICKLE: You'll like mine. Gobs a garlic!

(PICKLE exits.)

H.J.: He wouldn't have earned the fourth grade math prize anyway. In third grade he was number three in math.

ABEBE: What did he earn?

H.J.: The Posthumous Math Prize. Certificate just said something about "commemoration for excellence" but no live kids ever got it. *(Steps into tub.)* Whoo! better get goin', water already plunged well below lukewarm.

(ABEBE holds the Bible out to H.J.)

ABEBE: Read please?

H.J.: *(Reads.)* "Then cometh Jesus from Galilee to Jordan unto John, to be baptized of him.... and, lo, the heavens were opened unto him, and he saw the Spirit of God descending like a dove... saying, This is my beloved Son, in whom I am well pleased."

*(ABEBE very gently takes H.J.
backwards under the water, H.J.
pinching HER nose closed with HER*

fingers. When SHE emerges, SHE
seems changed.)

ABEBE: You felt something?

H.J.: Yeah. I mean . . . Yeah.

ABEBE: What?

(Pause.)

H.J.: They drowned.

(Pause.)

ABEBE: Your father, brother. Your grandfather.

H.J.: Katrina.

(ABEBE nods.)

H.J.: Two-thirds of our bodies water, two-thirds'
the earth water. We start in water, fetus in the sac.
So why in the end put down in the dirt? Water is
home, sailors got it right. Burial at sea.

Scene Five

(ABEBE and TAY in the kitchen.
Against the wall are professionally
printed signs as would be carried by
protestors in a demonstration:

"Stop the Glendale Springs Plant: Tap
Water Is Safe Water"

"Keep Glendale Springs Flowing"

"30 Million Plastic Bottles = 1 Day's Litter"

On the fridge are plastic letters, numbers and shapes that have been arranged in an equation:

2 *THANKS* : 1

On the kitchen counter are many paper cups. ABEBE pours water into each, filling them halfway. TAY, sitting on a stool, looks on. HE wears the cartoon backpack from scene three. A paper cup set apart from the others holds the two Confederate flags. Also on the counter are TAY's shoebox, a magnifying glass and a copy of Masaru Emoto's The Hidden Messages in Water.*)*

ABEBE: "In the beginning God created the heaven and the earth…. And the Spirit of God moved upon the face of the waters." Do you know these Bible verses, Tay? *(TAY nods.)* Sunday School? *(TAY nods.)* Very good! The other verse that begins "In the beginning" begins "In the beginning was the Word, and the Word was with God, and the word was God." So we have learned God's creation began with water, and with the word.

(ABEBE has finished filling the cups and now leans over one of them, speaks into it.)

ABEBE: The Word.

(HE takes the cup and puts it into the freezer. Now HE leans over another.)

ABEBE: Heaven.

(As ABEBE puts it into the freezer, the distant rumble of thunder.)

ABEBE: God willing, it may finally rain today. Cindy told me she asked you to pack your raincoat into your backpack. Did you do this? *(TAY nods. ABEBE smiles.)* We await the miracle of rain, but hurricanes are the *catastrophe* of rain, the climate-changing wages of the sins of the wealthy of America downpoured upon the destitute. But today! Today we shall rejoice! As we do in my village after a drought. We would collect the rainwater via the little dams, I showed my people how to build the little dams and we were saved! A little dam is a blessing, a gift from God. A *mega*dam is a curse, a gift from the World Bank, but I have written to my brother Seyoum, we will prevent this, I will stand strong with my village! *(Beat.)* From here.

H.J.: *(Entering, wiping HER sweaty brow.)* Humid!

ABEBE: God willing, it may finally rain today!

H.J.: *(To TAY.)* Hello.

ABEBE: H.J., this is Tay. Tay, this is H.J.

H.J.: Hey Tay.

*(TAY stares at HER. THEY stare at
TAY. Then ABEBE turns back to H.J.)*

ABEBE: That means "Hello, H.J.!"

*(H.J. takes a can of soda out of the
fridge, snaps it open and drinks.)*

H.J.: Used to get like this in Mississippi. We went
every summer to my grandfather's, two weeks. 'Til
last summer. *They* went. I stayed with Mom, her
gall bladder operation. *(Now seeming to notice chaos
in the room for the first time.)* What's going on?

*(ABEBE hands H.J. the book. SHE leafs
through it as ABEBE speaks.)*

ABEBE: Perhaps you are not familiar with the work
of Masaru Emoto. Dr. Emoto has studied ice that
has crystallized. Ice that in its liquid state had been
exposed to positive language produced intricate,
exquisite designs. Ice that in its liquid state had
been exposed to negative language formed
hideous, incoherent muddles.

H.J.: You don't think Dr. Emoto's a heathen?

ABEBE: *(Pleased that SHE has recognized this.)*
Indubitably! However, he insists upon the
existence of God, and this alleviates some of his
paganism. There are many heathens who, despite
their deception regarding the Truth, do appreciate
the holiness of water. The Koran states, "We have
created every living thing from water." Hindu
temples are always located near water. The Shinto
of Dr. Emoto's Japan believe waterfalls to be

sacred, and in the Tao Te Ching it is written: "Water gives life to the ten thousand things and does not strive." Unfortunately these people are all in for a surprise because I hear there is not much water in hell! *(Laughs heartily. Then a new thought.)* Ah!

(Speaks into a cup.)

ABEBE: Hell.

(Puts it into the freezer.)

H.J.: *(Book.)* Abebe. This looks like the containers have to be kept at the perfect temperature of minus four Fahrenheit, which I'm pretty sure our freezer isn't. And they have to be in the freezer exactly three hours, are you timing them? And Emoto used Petri dishes, not paper cups. And they still have to be minus four while you look at them under a *high-powered microscope.*

ABEBE: Check!

(ABEBE picks up the magnifying glass.)

H.J.: I don't think that's gonna work.

ABEBE: Well, *(winking at TAY)* it is our experiment, we shall see! We set the bad cups on the bottom, the good tops on the top.

(ABEBE thinks, then speaks into a cup.)

ABEBE: Love.

*(TAY suddenly runs out of the room.
H.J. looks after HIM, then at ABEBE.)*

ABEBE: Tay is a frequent urinator! *(Confidentially.)*
Cindy tells me he always naps from three o' clock
until four, and he knows for this he must wear his
rubber underpants. *(Puts cup into the freezer.)*

H.J.: You sure play some funny games with Tay.
Next guess you be taking him to the
demonstration. *(Glancing at the signs.)*

ABEBE: You know about my protest! I just initiated
it and it is already causing a groundswell!

H.J.: I know about it now. Don't be surprised to see
protestors protesting the protest. *Their* signs'll read
"The Glendale Springs Plant Will Provide Jobs."

ABEBE: There are better jobs! The government can
create jobs meant to *preserve* the environment.

H.J.: So what about your major? Theology or
ecology?

ABEBE: My plan is twofold: Save the planet! Save
its souls!

H.J.: Good, you shouldn't drop the other. You
could make a good preacher, Mom thinks you
could make a good preacher. *(Beat.)* I think you
could help her.

> *(Pause: TAY returns, takes HIS seat,
> holds a cup out to ABEBE.)*

ABEBE: Thank you! *(ABEBE thinks, then speaks into the cup.)* Gratitude. Dr. Emoto tells us that love and gratitude have the most striking and far-reaching effects inside and outside of us. We must engage in both sentiments, though gratitude is the more potent, and more rare. The formula Dr. Emoto suggests is two parts gratitude to one part love. *(Puts cup into the freezer.)*

H.J.: Even if it could crystallize, how could it distinguish when you say every word exactly the same?

ABEBE: Tone is irrelevant. Most pertinent is the word itself. Dr. Emoto typically used written words, no tone.

H.J.: Tone is everything. We don't even need words.

> *(Leans over a cup. As if something (or someone) is delicious:)*

H.J.: Mmmmmmmmm.

> *(Puts it in the freezer.)*

H.J.: *(Another.)* AAAAAAAAAAAAAAAAH!

> *(HER sudden scream startles ABEBE and TAY. This was H.J.'s intention, and SHE is laughing as SHE looks up at THEM. At this point SHE notices for the first time the Confederate flags.)*

H.J.: AAAAAAAAAAAAAAAAAAAAAAAAAH!

(TAY quickly runs off.)

H.J.: What's *that?*

(ABEBE at first confused.)

ABEBE: This is the flag of Tay's father. And forefathers. In a note Tay wrote the word: "Heritage."

H.J.: His father was a cracker! *(ABEBE confused.)* Racist! These are Confederate flags. Rebel banners. Slaveholders!

ABEBE: In America there are *still* slaveholders?

H.J.: *No!* Hope not. But that's where those things originated, pennant of the Defeated. You know what it's like growing up here, hicksville, ninety-five percent the students white? Act like you're an outsider in your own hometown! And when white people say the flag's not about racism, it's about Southern heritage, well what the hell else *was* Southern heritage?

> *(TAY returns. There seems to be no outward indication that HE has heard the conversation until HE sits down and takes the flags, possessively clutching them to HIS chest and staring at H.J.)*

H.J.: Guess blood's thicker 'n water.

ABEBE: Correct! *(Reconsiders.)* But there is water *in* our blood.

H.J.: An expression. I mean Like father, like son.

(ABEBE ponders.)

ABEBE: Your Saltine crackers are white! This is what you and Pickle mean by "cracker"!

H.J.: I think it came from someone cracking the whip.

ABEBE: This discussion is quite enlightening! When Tay and I were at the jungle gym, I pointed to the swing. Tay did not respond. I pointed to the monkey bars. Tay did not respond. I pointed to the slide. Tay did not respond. I pulled out my flag, which Tay gave me. Tay responded. Tay pulled out his flag. Tay and I made a parade, marching around the blacktop. Now everyone else responded. The parents and the children instantly ceased their activities to stare at us, but said nothing. I did not understand, I thought there must be a rule against playground parades! *(Laughs heartily.)*

H.J.: That's so funny. Believe me when those white people got home to anecdote the afternoon to their spouses, didn't you give *them* a hoot: The crazy African come to town.

ABEBE: *(Embarrassed, trying to laugh.)* Well, I doubt-

H.J.: What do *you* care? Entertain the fools and leave, you can go back overseas anytime you want. But by school tomorrow your parade be the joke of the town, white boys asking me, "How's your houseguest? George of the Jungle."

ABEBE: I don't think –

H.J.: You *ought*a come to my school, guest speaker. Betcha those white boys get a big kick outa you: the grinning African. *(TAY runs off with the flags.)*

ABEBE: *No!* It is not –

H.J.: And STOP WASTING OUR WATER! Experiment, you sure find some funny uses for water in a drought! Talk about two parts gratitude, you come from Africa, think you'd *show* a little gratitude for us, gratitude for the ever-convenient American guarantee of H_2O!

ABEBE: AFRICA HAS WATER! The Blue Nile Ethiopia, the *Nile!* You think *I* don't appreciate water? I *respect* water, I do not take water for granted, how many gallons does one person in Ethiopia use per day? Three! One person in the United Kingdom? Thirty-one! One person in the United States? One hundred fifty-one! *(TAY appears in the doorway but, aware of the tension, stays there, unnoticed.)* Americans talk about conservation but you do not *really* think it will run out, only *one percent* of all the world's water is usable, when it is gone, *gone, look at this drought! And last year Katrina, too little water or too much –*

> *(H.J. has reacted to the reference to Katrina, and ABEBE sees that HE has upset HER, though SHE tries to cover. HE is ashamed and embarrassed by HIS outburst and tries to regain HIS cheer, to calm things.)*

ABEBE: So much water God has provided in Africa. Did you know Ethiopia's River Gihon is one of four that nourished the Garden of Eden – ?

H.J.: *(Glaring and guttural.)* Don't you goddamn try to save *me*, preacher.

> *(PICKLE enters from the outside with grocery bags.)*

PICKLE: *(Wiping HER sweaty brow.)* Humid!

ABEBE: I believe God may bring rain today. Seventy-one without rain! *(From HER angle PICKLE sees TAY, though HE tries to conceal HIMself.)*

PICKLE: *(Smiles.)* Hello.

ABEBE: *(Startled to realize TAY has been standing there.)* This is Tay. This is Mrs. Carter.

H.J.: You just went to the market yesterday.

PICKLE: *(Plops HER bags on the counter.)* Well guess I forgot a few things. *(Looking from the paper cups to the signs.)* Someone's been busy in here! *(H.J. unpacking bags.)*

ABEBE: *(Embarrassed.)* I shall clean up my mess!

PICKLE: Wa'n't a accusation.

H.J.: Oreos!

PICKLE: Got everyone's favorite! *(To ABEBE.)* Red hots, right? *(ABEBE smiles. PICKLE takes out colored liquid in plastic strips.)* You like ice pops, Tay?

*(TAY stares. Then comes to HER,
points to a pop.)*

PICKLE: Chocolate? Lemme freeze it for ya.

*(PICKLE smiles, opens the freezer
door to put the ice pops in. Stares.)*

PICKLE: Yaw already makin' snow cones?

ABEBE: Are you familiar with the work of Dr.
Masaru Emoto, Pickle? Speak a good word into a
cup and it will freeze into a spectacular, glorious –

*(But PICKLE isn't listening to ABEBE.
SHE has thrown the ice pops into the
freezer and continues to unpack
groceries, speaking to TAY. H.J. will
stop unpacking to listen to PICKLE.)*

PICKLE: I knew a little boy once, 'bout your age.
See that tree out back? He climb it, almost to the
top, don't *you* try it! Useta scare me to death! "You
come down from there!" I'd call, and always he
did, but next day soon's my back turned he fly back
up it. Set him in the time-out, deny him the peach
cobbler, smack his behind: nothin' stop it. So I just
keep offerin' up the punishments and pray he grow
out of it, pray he don't hurt hisself be*fore* he grow
out of it, then one day wipin' the kitchen table I spy
him. Slam open that slidin' door, "WHY YOU
GOTTA *BE* UP THERE, CARVE?" He say, "Come
up, Mommy! You come up, you'll see why!" I say
"Then *both* us break our neck!" He say, "Close
your eyes! Close your eyes you'll see it!" We argue

awhile, then finally he win. *(Stops unpacking and closes HER eyes. Gradually smiles.)* I *do* see it. Snuggled in the branches, nobody on the ground notice me. Quiet. Only the blue jays here, I get it! I get it! *(Beat.)* But when I open 'em *(does)* I'm all shaky. Cuz what I seen eyes-closed is why my boy liketa fly away, soar away from down here. Never come back. *(Goes back to unpacking groceries.)*

ABEBE: Pickle. You know that God is always with us in our adversity –

PICKLE: Yep. Cabbage was on sale.

> *(PICKLE continues taking out groceries. TAY takes a toothbrush from HIS backpack and shows ABEBE.)*

ABEBE: *(Glancing at HIS watch.)* Very good! Tay has remembered he must brush his teeth before his nap. *(TAY exits.)*

PICKLE: Ain't he big for a nap?

ABEBE: Cindy says it is his idea and he wakes on his own.

> *(PICKLE pulls out a package of red shoestring licorice.)*

H.J.: *(Alarmed.)* Mom . . .

PICKLE: *(Chuckles.)* Punchin' in the candy and the cake and the ice treats, girl at the register goes "Yaw havin' a party?"

H.J.: *Who's left in this house likes shoestring licorice?*

(PICKLE stares at HER.)

PICKLE: NO TRIAL!

> (PICKLE, very upset, rushes out of the
> room. H.J. starts to follow. ABEBE
> blocks HER.)

ABEBE: I think she would rather be alone.

H.J.: MOVE!

ABEBE: She has told me she does not like your tests.

H.J.: (Trying to get past HIM.) That's too bad, they're for her own good –

ABEBE: She weeps.

> (H.J. stops, sighs. Then starts slamming
> the groceries away as SHE speaks.)

H.J.: It's not a trial. (Yelling offstage to PICKLE.) EXAGGERATOR!

> (ABEBE stares at H.J. During HER
> monologue, TAY will return and sit,
> moving two cups close to HIMself.)

H.J.: You think I like it? Sadist? She's my mother! Everything seemed okay, considering, all these months she's relatively normal, now the first anniversary come around and suddenly she . . . Little memory proof, big deal. What scares her is not ace-ing the test well what scares me is her showing up for my baby brother's soccer game, then go into a panic, wonder why he's not in the lineup. What scares me is her out driving alone, then turn around to chat with two or three backseat passengers who aren't there, slam into a guardrail, or tractor-trailer. Do I take the car keys from her? *no. Should,* her safety, but her dignity I protect instead, you think I want to humiliate her? Just trying to keep her in one piece before it's too late! Then I come up with an idea. Maybe an occasional reality check might prevent "too late." *(Pause.) You* supposed to be the man of God! She's my mother, *I* want to help her!

(*Pause.*)

ABEBE: *I* want to help her.

> (*A sudden redundant humming, akin to the purring of a cat. It is TAY. H.J. and ABEBE turn to HIM. TAY makes this sound of contentment over one of the two cups HE has pulled to HIMself. Moving to the other cup HE makes the cry/caw of a lonely bird. Now back to the first cup, HE creates the prior humming. Now back to the second cup, the crying again, but it continues, sounding increasingly more terrified and desperate, and seeming without end.*)

Scene Six

> (*Half-hour later. Kitchen/dining area with the sliding glass door to the*

*outside. Three chairs have been pulled
from the table and set in the middle of
the floor. H.J. sits next to an empty
chair, both these chairs face ABEBE in
HIS chair. ABEBE holds HIS Bible.)*

ABEBE: Perhaps we should let *Pickle* lead the
service! Pickle!

> *(PICKLE appears in the doorway,
> reluctant.)*

PICKLE: What.

ABEBE: I know these tests have frightened you in
the past, but I promise I am a kinder and gentler
H.J.! *(Laughs heartily.)*

PICKLE: Thought it *wa'n't* a test, thought it was
church.

ABEBE: It *is!* Please join us, sister!

PICKLE: How we have time for church? You said
Tay's naps only an hour.

ABEBE: Then we must begin immediately! Do you
have a favorite verse you have memorized?

> *(PICKLE, stubborn, hesitates.)*

PICKLE: I like the verse where Jesus calmed the
sea.

ABEBE: Then come! Recite!

(PICKLE saunters over to the empty chair, sits. Then.)

PICKLE: I like the verse where Jesus calmed the sea.

(ABEBE and H.J. wait for more. None comes.)

ABEBE: *(Finally.)* Very good!

H.J.: That's not memorization!

ABEBE: Well she at least has remembered the content, if not the exact words!

H.J.: That's like saying "I remember the ingredients, just can't recall if it was a *pinch* of salt or a pint."

ABEBE: *(Flipping through HIS Bible.)* I am betting Pickle's memory only needs a prompt. I know the verses she speaks of, Matthew 8. *(To PICKLE.)* Please, jump in! *(Reads.)* "And, behold, there arose a great tempest in the sea, insomuch that the ship was covered with the waves: but he was asleep."

PICKLE: *(Remembering.)* Yeah!

ABEBE: "And his disciples came to him, and awoke him, saying, Lord, save us: we perish."

PICKLE: Yeah!

ABEBE: "And (Jesus) saith unto them, Why are you fearful, O ye of little faith?"

PICKLE: That part's red.

ABEBE: "Then he arose, and rebuked the winds and the sea, and there was a great calm."

PICKLE: Yeah!

ABEBE: Excellent!

H.J.: Excellent *what?* she didn't recite anything! Anyway, I want some real answers.

PICKLE: No trial!

H.J.: When were you born?

PICKLE: Year before my first birthday.

ABEBE: Pickle! Can you name the Ten Commandments?

H.J.: We finished the Bible. *Now* –

PICKLE: You promised church! I thought this was church!

H.J.: Yeah, we're moving on to a subcategory: "Our Family and Church."

PICKLE: Who are *you*, Alex Trebek?

H.J.: Faster we get through this, faster it's over with.

PICKLE: *(Turns to imaginary person next to HER.)* What you thinka that, Alex? *(Becoming Alex Trebek.)* "Pickle, I think H.J.'s appointed herself dictator of the room which definitely puts you in Double

Jeopardy" how's that? 'M I crazy enough for you now?

H.J.: Too bad sarcasm isn't a symptom of lucidity.

ABEBE: Perhaps Pickle would like to select her *own* memory to share!

H.J.: That won't –

PICKLE: *Yeah!*

> (*H.J. sullen. PICKLE thinks. Now the sound of a middle-aged man's chuckling. Then: a Head appears. The face needn't be distinctive, nor colorful – perhaps, on the contrary, white like a ghost or a tombstone bust. Its voice should not sound like a call from The Beyond, but rather as if it is here, now, alive. PICKLE, H.J. and ABEBE do not seem to notice "the Head, which was the chuckler.")*

HEAD 1 (Hal): Alex Trebek! You better watch it, Pick, she *really* gonna think you lost it!

PICKLE: I loved Miss Ruby. Taught all the Sunday School grades, black Baptists. For awhile went with those kids to the white church but that didn't stick.

H.J.: Why'd you switch?

PICKLE: Huh?

H.J.: Why'd you start going to the white Baptists?

PICKLE: *I* don't know –

H.J.: You told us a million times.

(PICKLE confused.)

HEAD 1 (Hal): 'Leven o' clock. Noon. One.

PICKLE: White Baptists got outa church on time!

H.J.: Right! But you had to go back. Black church.

PICKLE: 'Course!

H.J.: Why?

(PICKLE puzzled.)

HEAD 1 (Hal): Come on, Pick. Easy.

PICKLE: *(Remembers.)* The music. Never liked the music.

H.J.: Yes!

PICKLE: Never sang "This Little Light of Mine." Did sing "Amazing Grace" but never sounded right.

H.J.: Remember Dad's favorite?

PICKLE: How I forget that? Hal wake us up with it every Sunday.

PICKLE and HEAD 1 (Hal): *(Singing.) There is a balm in Gilead to make the wounded whole*

HEAD 1 (Hal): Remember my favorite poym? *(Little voice.)* "Shiny shiny."

(Now PICKLE turns to HEAD 1, an affectionate, sly smile on HER face. Meanwhile another HEAD appears, identical to HEAD 1. An older man's voice.)

HEAD 2 (Pappy): Not too many Jesus songs I was partial to, I was partial to John Lee Hooker.

H.J.: Remember that Fourth of July picnic in Mississippi, when Daddy and Pappy got in that big fight over whether we bring Pappy's silverware or pick up plastic forks? *(PICKLE grins.)*

HEAD 1 (Hal): Buy utensils just to throw in the garbage later, now ain't *that* real environmentally conscious in the 21st Century.

HEAD 2 (Pappy): Didn't notice *you* volunteerin' to worsh no dishes.

H.J.: So why didn't we go South last year?

(Now PICKLE glares, turns to ABEBE.)

PICKLE: *(To ABEBE.)* You said "kinder and gentler H.J."!

H.J.: It's not a hard question, Mom.

PICKLE: It ain't *church!* Funny thing *you* testin' since you ain't seen the inside a no house a worship since God created Adam.

ABEBE: *(Grins.)* That goes for the *both* of you!

HEAD 1 (Hal) and HEAD 2 (Pappy): *(Beat.)* Uh oh.

PICKLE: *Huh?*

ABEBE: Sometimes you sleep in on Sunday and you are not sick! *(PICKLE stares at HIM. Laughing.)* I am merely stating a fact!

H.J.: I bet. Look, Mom –

PICKLE: This just what I mean: *Mean!* Gall bladder surgery, I couldn't go!

H.J.: Great! Now why – ?

PICKLE: You gonna push it, ain'tcha? You always gotta push it!

ABEBE: *(Joy.)* Jesus is in this room! I feel the spirit, I feel the holy! Let us pray!

H.J.: Abebe –

PICKLE: This is church! Pray!

> *(PICKLE bows HER head, followed by a contented ABEBE and a disgruntled H.J. Now a third HEAD appears. It is identical to the other two but smaller.)*

HEAD 3 (Carve): I tried not to climb it, Mommy! Every day I looked up from the ground, Mommy said not to climb the tree! But 'fore I know it, I'm clear to the top.

> *(PICKLE has looked up at HEAD 3 affectionately. ABEBE and H.J. don't notice that SHE has lifted HER head out of prayer.)*

ABEBE: God. *(PICKLE quickly goes back to prayer.)* We pray for peace and prosperity. We pray for harmony in this household. *(Beat.)* Pickle?

PICKLE: We pray to always have enough to eat. Our house and our neighbors. Even if the water-bottlin' plant don't go through. Which it prolly will. *(ABEBE glances up at PICKLE, then back to prayer.)* H.J.?

H.J.: We pray that someone will eat all that damn red string licorice. *(ALL eyes fly open.)*

HEAD 3 (Carve): I will!

H.J.: Cuz the one loves red string licorice,

HEAD 3 (Carve): ME!

H.J.: *I* don't see him.

PICKLE: *(To ABEBE.)* Ain't it time to wake up that little boy?

ABEBE: Cindy has told me he wakes on his own.

PICKLE: I have an idea! I'll write down the books a the New Testament! In order! *(Snatches a pen and pad and starts writing.)*

H.J.: That doesn't help –

ABEBE: An excellent suggestion! *(PICKLE writes.)*

H.J.: *What?*

ABEBE: Church! Church!

*(H.J. and ABEBE exchange glances,
H.J. glaring. ABEBE looks at what
PICKLE has written.)*

ABEBE: Very good! And with no prompting from
me this time! *(PICKLE smiles at HER work, then
continues.)*

HEAD 1 (Hal): Hey, Pick, you still sing Beethoven
in the shower? *(Laughs.)*

HEAD 2 (Pappy): *(To HEAD 1.)* You *know*
Beethoven was black.

HEAD 1 (Hal): False! Heard that theory before:
disproved!

HEAD 2 (Pappy): Mother was a Moor! This from
one of his contemporaries, quote: "Negroid traits,
dark skin, flat, thick nose."

PICKLE: *(Reads from what SHE's written.)* "Matthew,
Mark, LukeJohnActs, Romans – "

H.J.: You know what, Mom? I'm gonna ask you just
one more question. Answer it and we're done.
(PICKLE stares at HER.)

HEAD 1 (Hal): You think everyone was black.

HEAD 2 (Pappy): You obviously ain't seen the
sketches!

PICKLE: *(Suspicion.)* It better be a fair question.

H.J.: It is.

HEAD 2 (Pappy): Lemme show you a couple Nineteenth Century engravings of Ludwig van Darkie!

H.J.: What they find in Pappy's attic?

> (Silence. PICKLE and the HEADS staring at H.J.: shock, fear. ABEBE, sensing the stress, also nervous. Finally:)

HEAD 3 (Carve): You don't have to answer, Mom!

HEAD 1 (Hal): Why not? It's a good question.

HEAD 3 (Carve): It's mean!

ABEBE: Pickle, you and H.J. have been through a lot this year. God will see you through it.

PICKLE: *I* know!

ABEBE: *(Preacher.)* We must pass through it to get past it. Let go and let God! *(Memorized.)* "And Moses stretched out his hand over the sea;"

H.J.: Shut up, Abebe! let her think.

ABEBE: "and the Lord caused the sea to go back by a strong cast wind all that night, and made the sea dry land, and the waters were divided."

HEAD 1 (Hal): Took Moses all night. Took Charlton Heston two minutes. *(Chuckles.)*

ABEBE: "And the children of Israel went into the midst of the sea upon the dry ground: and the waters were a wall unto them on their right hand, and on their left."

HEAD 2 (Pappy): You know, Bible sound better with a African lilt.

ABEBE: "And Moses stretched forth his hand over the sea, and the sea returned to its strength… and covered the chariots, and the horsemen,"

HEAD 3 (Carve): If Abebe were in my class, he'd be the boy we'd give wedgies to. *(Giggles.)*

PICKLE: Like the monster come outa the ocean and into the Gulf. *(Important: while PICKLE may be "seeing" the storm, SHE never goes into any trance-like state; SHE is always in control and aware.)*

HEAD 3 (Carve): NO!

PICKLE: Gulf water lifted high: spinnin', spinnin'.

H.J.: Good, Mom.

HEAD 3 (Carve): Mommy!

HEAD 1 (Hal): She gotta live it, son.

HEAD 3 (Carve): I don't wanna go, Daddy! I don't wanna go there again!

PICKLE: That gall bladder surgery. I couldn't go last summer.

H.J.: *Yes.*

PICKLE: And H.J. stay with me. My recuperation.

H.J.: *(Startled and confused.)* Cuz you needed somebody. *(To ABEBE.)* She needed somebody. Cook for her, walk her to the bathroom –

PICKLE: First we think, everybody skip Mississipp' this year. But Carve wanna go bad, see his pappy, and laid up *I* couldn't do for him. So Hal and him go down.

H.J.: *I* wanted to see Pappy too! I just . . . somebody had to care for you!

ABEBE: Pickle! Do you accept Jesus Christ as your Lord and Savior?

> *(ALL, including the HEADS, turn to HIM.)*

PICKLE, H.J., HEAD 1, HEAD 2 and HEAD 3: *Huh?*

ABEBE: Our Lord Jesus Christ died for your sins, his blood shed –

PICKLE: You don't gotta tell *me.*

HEAD 2 (Pappy): Pickle been a Jesus freak ever since she a little thing!

ABEBE: We must all be humble before God!

H.J.: What are you *talking* about?

ABEBE: I am just –

H.J.: *I* know what you're talking about. *(To PICKLE.)* You been paying attention? He thinks he's here to save us, the heathens. After all our generosity to take him in.

ABEBE: *No!*

HEAD 1 (Hal): This is off the subject.

H.J.: I thought you could help me help her. But just an opportunist, just an opening to help yourself.

ABEBE: That is *not* –

H.J.: Think you can save America, well all you're saving's the rent.

ABEBE: No! Pickle!

HEAD 1 (Hal): Stay with it, Pick. *(PICKLE turns to HEAD 1.)*

ABEBE: You took me in, treat me like family!

HEAD 1 (Hal): Mississippi! Humid. Mosquitoes. Catfish.

ABEBE: There is more gratitude in my heart to you and H.J. than my words could ever express!

PICKLE: Then the rains came.

> *(ABEBE quickly flips through HIS Bible.)*

HEAD 2 (Pappy): We didn't get it like N'orleans.

HEAD 1 (Hal): Was the broke levees brought them the grief.

HEAD 2 (Pappy): But Katrina slammed into Mississipp' too!

ABEBE: *(Reads.)* "In the six hundredth year of Noah's life, the same day were all the fountains of the great deep broken up,"

HEAD 2 (Pappy): Mississipp' the *direct* hit!

ABEBE: "and the windows of heaven were opened."

PICKLE: All our men in Mississippi.

ABEBE: And the rain was upon the earth forty days and forty nights."

PICKLE: One day they here, next: gone.

HEAD 1 (Hal): Gone.

PICKLE: *Vanished!* My daddy! Husband! Son!

H.J.: Okay!

PICKLE: Three generations!

H.J.: That's it, Mom, you got it!

PICKLE: *Gone!*

H.J.: We're done, Mom, finished!

PICKLE and ABEBE: *(Confused.) Finished?*

H.J.: You remembered! You remembered, your memory's intact. Trial's over, you passed!

(Pause.)

ABEBE: But what about the question? *(H.J. confused.)* The question you asked was "What did they find in Pappy's attic?"

H.J.: It's okay! we don't have to . . . It was just a test question, we don't need it. I know you remember now, Mom, you're aware. For now. You know they're gone, you said "Gone."

PICKLE: *(Going back to HER vision.)* Corpses.

H.J.: Mom . . .

PICKLE: Up to the attic they went, tryin' to get safe.

H.J.: Mom!

ABEBE: You must walk to the other side too, H.J. "Yea, though I walk through the valley of the shadow of death, I will fear no evil."

H.J.: SHUT UP, ABEBE!

PICKLE: Why he gotta shut up?

H.J.: None of his business!

PICKLE: Who dragged him into it?

H.J.: We gotta end this, Tay's gonna wake up –

PICKLE: The waters rose, and they climbed to the attic.

H.J.: *(Tears.)* MOM!

PICKLE: They climbed to the attic and the waters rose still.

HEAD 1 (Hal): *(Encouraging HER to go on.)* That's it, Pick.

PICKLE: Got the call from Mr. Winston, Daddy's neighbor. He smelt it, investigated. Three bodies.

H.J.: I COULDA GONE! I *WOULDA* GONE but *you!* Operation, somebody had to care for *you.*

PICKLE: Here's what he found in Pappy's attic. Three bodies.

H.J.: NOW ALL I GOT LEFT IS YOU! And the hole left from Carve! Daddy!

PICKLE: *(Points (not at the Heads) as if SHE sees the corpses.)* Man. Man. Boy.

H.J.: *YOU AND THE HOLE! EMPTY! EMPTY!*

> *(For the first time since "Who dragged him into it?" PICKLE turns to H.J., concern. The military march* section of the Ninth Symphony begins, the Heads speaking over it.)*

HEAD 1 (Hal): Movin' on down the road, Pick. Later, alligator.

---

* A little more than a third of the way through the fourth movement of Beethoven's Ninth is a pause, followed immediately by drums, followed immediately by what is commonly referred to as a "military march."

HEAD 3 (Carve): I know this song! You sang this song to me, Mommy!

HEAD 2 (Pappy): I prefer the blues! But this tune's nice too.

HEAD 1 (Hal): Pick! You still sing it in the shower?

> (Cut music immediately to the choral verse after the military march. PICKLE's eyes still on H.J. Though the HEADS appear to be singing, and PICKLE with them, only the recording can be heard, PICKLE's voice drowned out by the volume.)

HEAD 1, HEAD 2, HEAD 3 and PICKLE: *Freude, schöner Götterfunken, Tochter aus Elysium, Wir betreten feuertrunken, Himmlische, dein Heiligtum!, Deine Zauber binden wieder, Was die Mode streng geteilt;*

> (Recorded music and HEADS disappear.)

PICKLE: *(Continuing a cappella.) Alle Menschen werden Brüder –*

> (Enormous clap of thunder. ALL silenced. ABEBE, PICKLE and H.J. turn to the sliding glass door as the rain starts to fall. ABEBE slowly walks to the door. The rain is sudden and monsoon-heavy. Now the sound of TAY giggling uncontrollably from off. As HE enters ALL turn to HIM. HE

*is cracking up, sometimes covering HIS
mouth as if HE is trying to suppress a
private joke but it keeps coming back.
HE wears HIS blood-dried pajamas and
HIS backpack, now unzipped and
empty. Finally TAY stops giggling long
enough to speak.)*

TAY: Blood's thicker 'n water.

*(This sends HIM guffawing again. HE
walks to the glass doors. Once more HE
stops laughing briefly.)*

TAY: Blood's thicker 'n water.

(TAY is in stitches! The rain pours.)

End of Act One.

Act Two

Scene One

*(Seven years later. Enormous roar of
water. ABEBE stands on the edge of a
megadam, solemnly staring down into
the falls below HIM. Suddenly, like a
dolphin popping its face out of the
water, SEYOUM's head surfaces. HE
stares at ABEBE. ABEBE smiles.)*

SEYOUM: Abebe! Have you prepared my funeral?

ABEBE: Of course.

SEYOUM: *(Smiles.)* One moment.

> *(SEYOUM disappears again. The sound
> of the water suddenly stops.
> SEYOUM's head reappears.)*

SEYOUM: Had to turn off the damn dam. Now I can hear. Please.

ABEBE: Seyoum was my brother. His family took me in after my family died, he was the oldest child and wherever he walked with his birth brothers he brought me. Seyoum wept when I left for America, and when I returned four years later we had a joyful tearful reunion. And yet: the heartbreak, the sadness he always carried with him since the change. I have been in the capital these three years hence, teaching at Addis Ababa University. Finally I have come back to my people only to find out just one day before Seyoum had died, and now *I* weep for *my* brother. *(Beat.)* Did you know I was coming today?

SEYOUM: I had heard. I did not believe it.

ABEBE: But couldn't you have waited just one more day to see?

SEYOUM: I am only a man, Abebe. Death can come at any time, we know not when, we are merely mortals. This is why we must always be prepared in our faith, for God may take us at any moment –

ABEBE: Seyoum, death came when you walked up here yesterday and flung yourself into the dam!

SEYOUM: *(Shrugs.)* Still.

ABEBE: *(Sighs.)* Seyoum was a wonderful farmer, a wonderful father, providing for his wife Meseret and five children. He had much grief in his last years: the loss of Meseret and three of his progeny. But we may rejoice that in God's kingdom, they are all together now. Seyoum had walked on this earth thirty-three years –

SEYOUM: Thirty-four! Don't cheat me!

ABEBE: My dear brother Seyoum shall be greatly missed, and always and forever loved.

(Pause.)

SEYOUM: That's it?

ABEBE: I have been in Addis Ababa three years, Seyoum, you may have to catch me up.

SEYOUM: You referred to "the change," now I suggest you expound upon it. *(ABEBE unsure.) Where are we standing?*

ABEBE: Three years ago I returned from America with a degree majoring in water and minoring in God, and a license to drive which I earned after only the sixth attempt with the road test. I flew into Addis Ababa, rented a car, and immediately drove to my village. But my village had vanished. *(Points to the dam.)* Underwater.

(Pause. Then SEYOUM sighs.)

SEYOUM: Help me out, Abebe.

*(SEYOUM offers HIS arm, and ABEBE
helps pull HIM up and out.)*

SEYOUM: Okay, try this. *(As if making a speech to a
large audience.)* MEGADAM! FIVE THOUSAND
DISPLACED! I had eight productive hectares,
twenty-three cattle, then they move us to infertile
land, give us all the same two point five hectares,
three cattle! Oh yes we got the tin roofs they
promised, but leave the dirt floors, rainy season our
floors are mud! And other people already lived
here, put us on *their* grazing lands! And latrine
poorly constructed! And polluted streams! And
malarial mosquitoes, my wife and three youngests
die! All this on a loan of three hundred million
dollars from an Italian corporation, right after the
Italian *government forgave* our debt of three hundred
million dollars, now ninety-four percent Ethiopia
dependent on hydro power, what happens the next
drought? *Fools!* I would like to take my overfull
latrine and drop it on their heads! Shit on the
president! Shit on the Ministry of Water Resources!
Shit on the Italian Development Corporation!
(Turns to ABEBE, now calm, smiling.) Like that.

ABEBE: "Shit on" would be unconventional in a
eulogy.

SEYOUM: Well it's my-logy, not *you*-logy.
(Chuckles, back into the water.)

ABEBE: SEYOUM!

> (*SEYOUM, now only HIS head visible as at the top of the scene, turns back to ABEBE.*)

ABEBE: *I tried!* I built the little dam, it was a glorious remedy! For awhile. Do you remember the joy then? For awhile? I am sorry the little dam could not prevent the big dam but it *almost* worked! E̲ for effort!

> (*ABEBE laughs nervously. SEYOUM continues staring at ABEBE. ABEBE stops laughing. Silence.*)

ABEBE: How about this? When Seyoum dove into the waters that had flooded his village, that had buried his village, he was really only trying to find his way back home.

> (*SEYOUM considers this.*)

SEYOUM: Sure, Abebe. It's your dream.

> (*SEYOUM disappears back under the water. ABEBE staring into the water, as before. The roar of the water's rush returns.*)

Scene Two

> (*One year later. The dining area of PICKLE's kitchen. The stereo console is no longer here. Many balloons, PICKLE*

90

*blowing up another. ABEBE appears,
grinning in at PICKLE from the other
side of the sliding glass door. PICKLE
doesn't see HIM. Then SHE does.)*

PICKLE: AAAAAAAAAAAAAAAH!

*(The balloon flies across the room.
ABEBE is as terrified by HER scream as
PICKLE was in seeing someone staring
in at HER. Then SHE recognizes HIM:
delight.)*

PICKLE: Get in here!

*(SHE slams the door open, and ABEBE
enters. Hugs.)*

PICKLE: Whatchu doin', sneakin' 'round the back!
Siddown! Said you be here for my birthday but I
couldn't believe it.

ABEBE: There was the research I needed to do in
America, very easy to schedule it for now.

PICKLE: Take you out to dinner! Celebrate!
Tomorra! Tonight's *my* party.

ABEBE: And tonight I shall take *you* out to dinner!
H.J. emailed me about a new restaurant-

PICKLE: Save it. H.J. talkin' 'bout that Italian place,
well noodles I'm all for but no damn tiramisu,
gelato. This number fifty, I wannit done right. Got
my favorite on the stove, my own roast beef and
buttered potatas, and later some friends over, I

plan to celebrate my first half-century home with the bakery-bought, frosted inch thick, covered in the yellow roses and blue. Already got it.

ABEBE: You picked it up? (*PICKLE grins.*) You should not pay for your own cake!

PICKLE: (*Goes to fridge.*) Then I'll bill you and H.J. Like a slice?

ABEBE: *Before the party?*

PICKLE: Watch!

> (*PICKLE takes out a large bakery box. Lifts the lid for ABEBE to see. HE smiles but is worried SHE may cut it.*)

PICKLE: And!

> (*PICKLE puts the cake back in the fridge, now takes out a small bakery box. Lifts the lid. ABEBE looks, is confused. PICKLE cracks up.*)

PICKLE: Cain't never wait to bite once I bought it! So after years a makin' my party guests sick cuz obvious I took my finger all 'round the edge for a test taste, I started whenever I got the big one to pick up an accompanyin' baby, hold me over. (*Sets the cake on the table.*) Gotta finish the blowin' first though, here.

> (*PICKLE hands ABEBE a balloon. THEY both blow. Sound of a large truck*)

roaring by. PICKLE runs to the glass
door, slides it open, screams.)

PICKLE: SHUT UP!

(Slides the door closed.)

PICKLE: Sometime that just make ya feel good. Ooooo, bet they be fifty people here today! At least five! All my nurse friends, told 'em you was comin'. You know they all had a crush on you. "That boy's only twenty!" I used to say. Not no more! Twenty-eight? *(ABEBE nods.)* Now tell me whatcha know new! Any girls?

ABEBE: *(Embarrassed.)* No.

PICKLE: Almost a wife though. Right? You emailed. *(SHE listens while quietly blowing up a balloon.)*

ABEBE: There was much pressure from my village, very old to be a bachelor. But I was not in my village very often, I stayed in the city, I wanted to focus on my studies, I thought marriage and children would be a distraction. People found this odd, especially as I have lost my entire birth family. My brother Seyoum wrote to me –

PICKLE: Aw, Abebe, all caught up in my five-oh, hadn't even reiterated my condolences. Broke my heart to hear 'bout your friend.

ABEBE: Thank you.

PICKLE: Shame. Last year?

ABEBE: Last year about this time.

PICKLE: Shame.

ABEBE: Thank you. So my brother Seyoum wrote to me about Antu, from my village and now living in the city. Antu and I would have dinner and laugh, and I felt I was finally ready to tie the knot, although I still worried that our hours together were a great sacrifice of my work time. These dinners were quite frequent, sometimes occurring as often as once every six weeks. Then an idea came to me: after our wedding I would reduce my time with my wife by half. Now I was ready for God to join us together! and happily shared my notion with Antu. But it was she who ended the courtship. She performed the math, and came to the conclusion that seeing her husband four times a year, *my* idea of marriage, varied notably from hers. *(Blows into a balloon.)*

PICKLE: *(Snatches balloon out of ABEBE's mouth.)* Okay enough blowin', you want some coffee with your cake? Cuz you gonna have some cake with me.

ABEBE: *(Smiles.)* Yes.

PICKLE: *(Pouring and cutting.)* Now tell me 'bout your studies.

ABEBE: My dissertation –

PICKLE: *Dr.* Abebe! *(Giggles.)*

ABEBE: *(Smiles.)* My monograph will explore the matter of public versus private water.

PICKLE: *(Frowns, confused.)* You mean my private faucet versus a public fountain?

ABEBE: I mean privatization. Water as a commons versus water as a commodity.

PICKLE: *(Chuckles.)* You come to the right place for the latter. Go on.

> *(Another truck. PICKLE goes to the door again.)*

PICKLE: GO ON! AND TAKE YOUR STINKY DIESEL WITH YA! *(The truck now gone, SHE chuckles.)* Wound up today, ain't I? Just tired a the noisy filthy things.

ABEBE: I don't remember so many trucks.

PICKLE: You wouldn't. They came with the plant. Two years ago. Don't worry, you'll be able to sleep. They stop runnin' after six.

ABEBE: Plant?

PICKLE: Water bottlers.

ABEBE: *(Nods, grave.)* Yes.

PICKLE: I wrote you about it, right?

ABEBE: I do not believe you did. However I heard from my comrades who protested with me, our struggle against it.

PICKLE: Guess that was a disappointment, huh.

ABEBE: Yes. *(Beat.)* But we must take this as a temporary setback, not a defeat. We must be vigilant, documenting the trucks and the depletion of the spring as a warning to other towns trading life for jobs. Water is life!

PICKLE: You'd be happy! No more the worst waste around here, car worshin', lawn sprayin'. I got a dusty sedan, beige yard so what? Rain'll come sometime. Taste that! Enough sucrose make your head explode!

> *(ABEBE tastes the cake. PICKLE waits eagerly.)*

ABEBE: I can feel the landmines maiming my brain cells.

PICKLE: Whoo-ee! *(Laughs heartily.)* 'Course you tasted my birthday icin' before, 'cept that one summer you went missionaryin' 'round the country. And skippin' 'round the world come fall!

ABEBE: Yes!

PICKLE: Cameroon!

ABEBE: No! Cambodia!

PICKLE: Cambodia!

ABEBE: In a few days I should get my confirmation for the travel fellowship. Every year at the start of the rainy season, the Tonle Sap overflows, causing the direction of this tributary of the mighty

Mekong to reverse. In America floods are bad, but in Cambodia it is the good flood! A thousand fish species call the Mekong their home, and its accessibility to all makes the country money-poor but food-rich: Cambodians of the most meager means all well fed! A million people gather for the annual celebration of the reversal and thanks to the funding I generously will be awarded, this fall I shall make it a million and one!

PICKLE: *(Lifting HER coffee cup.)* Cheers! *(THEY clink.)*

ABEBE: The people are prepared! Waiting for the rush, the crashing waves the villages are on stilts! The homes. Schools. Shops. Post offices. I hope to learn something from a very poor community that nonetheless has had the good fortune to be able to take abundance for granted. Something to bring home to my village. I am not sure what that lesson could be. When I get there, I shall find out.

PICKLE: *(Lifting HER coffee cup.)* Holla! *(THEY clink.)* Hey I wrote you about H.J. goin' all Christian, right?

ABEBE: No!

PICKLE: 'Bout three years ago. H.J. not baptized yet though, you been writin' about comin' back for years now, she decided you started it, the bathtub, you're the one oughta finish it. Christen her.

ABEBE: I am touched.

PICKLE: Wanted it to be the same water hole I was baptized in, but now that's Nestlé's water hole.

ABEBE: Glendale Springs.

PICKLE: You heard of 'em? Chocolate?

ABEBE: I know Nestlé.

PICKLE: Don't know if you remember when you were livin' here was a coupla bottlers vyin' for the water. Nestlé came out on top.

ABEBE: *(Pause.)* Perhaps I should have stayed. I started the demonstration against the plant, it went on for years and we staved them off! But as soon as I left . . . And when I abandoned Ethiopia to come here, I built the little dams and we staved off the megadam! But as soon as I left –

PICKLE: You wanna wallow in guilt, stave *that* off another day. This *my* day!

ABEBE: *(Smiles sadly.)* Okay.

PICKLE: I'm pleased as punch 'bout H.J. goin' to God, but if she gimme another dang Bible for my birthday I'ma smack her with it!

ABEBE: I am so happy to know that H.J. has heard the Gospel!

PICKLE: Yeah. All seemed to come together 'bout the time she got knocked up in college. I wrote you about that, right?

ABEBE: No!

PICKLE: Well she was almost finished, graduated on time. Baby born two years ago, gave her up for adoption. Same age as the plant. Well, you knew.

ABEBE: No!

PICKLE: Well I'm sure I wrote about H.J. annullin' her marriage.

ABEBE: Pickle, every time I wrote you with my news, you wrote back "Everybody fine, same old same old"!

PICKLE: Well maybe we *were*, day I wrote you. Anyways that's how she become a Christian. Baby's father landed a good job at the water bottlers. Help me.

>*(PICKLE pulls out a greeting card store banner: letters spelling out "HAPPY BIRTHDAY PICKLE." Indicates for ABEBE to help HER hang it.)*

PICKLE: Hey. I ever ask how come you demoted God to minor?

ABEBE: Many times.

PICKLE: Remind me. This time fifty, I'm old, not crazy!

>*(PICKLE cracks up. Then notices ABEBE glancing at HER seriously.)*

PICKLE: I ain't embarrassed! You exorcised them heads away.

ABEBE: It was not an exorcism.

PICKLE: Still. Never saw 'em again.

ABEBE: *(Beat.)* Do you miss them?

> *(Pause. PICKLE does not reply. THEY complete the task.)*

PICKLE: You ain't answered what I asked ya.

ABEBE: You want to know why I settled on Environmental Studies with a focus on water.

PICKLE: Yep.

ABEBE: My missionary expedition, the summer after my junior year?

PICKLE: Trip when you totaled your old VW in Arkansas?

ABEBE: The same! I had been splitting the ecology classes and Bible studies since my sophomore. After my Christian road trip, which was quite successful, saving the souls of many Americans!, I realized I would soon return to Ethiopia, where Christians are abundant but safe drinking water scarce. Thus I dedicated my senior year fully to the environment, rendering Religion and Spirituality my minor.

PICKLE: *Converts?* I don't remember you tellin' us converts! How many you make your twelve-week tour? I mean seven cuz runnin' over that black lawn jockey in Little Rock cut your expedition a mite short, right?

ABEBE: Two converts!

PICKLE: *(Lifting HER coffee cup.)* Nazel tov! *(THEY clink. Then ABEBE confused.)*

ABEBE: "Nazel tov"?

PICKLE: I seen it on a movie.

ABEBE: Navel tov! Two more who have seen the glory of Christ!

PICKLE: What was they like?

ABEBE: The man was very ill. These new believers were in Tennessee, and they asked for immediate baptism. "Can we go to the crick?" he said. They called the creek "the crick," like you, and they took me: sparkling, clear, pure.

PICKLE: You took him under?

ABEBE: I took him under. Them. Saved.

PICKLE: Aw! Hey you want some ice cream? Plenty fresh in the basement freezer for tonight, but we still got that gallon up here leftover from Monday. H.J. plunged right down through the middle leavin' this big hole where the chocolate was, but plenty a vanilla and a little strawberry left.

ABEBE: I can wait until tonight.

PICKLE: Tay used to love chocolate too! didn't he? *(ABEBE smiles, nods.)* I wrote to you 'bout him gettin' locked up in the California state pen, right?

ABEBE: *(Sighs.)* No.

PICKLE: Remember after that first year some aunt in California laid claim to him? He'd just turned ten. So Social Services come with those dang relatives outa nowhere, already had three kids don't know why they took on a fourth if they couldn't handle it cuz little more than a year later he's back in fosters out there. Shuffled around, this place then that, all the while him gettin' angrier, angrier. So last year, sixteen and by this time apparently been through the gamut of abuse, latest foster dad snaps nasty, callin' him "stupid" on the wrong day and Tay's steak knife through the man's heart. Tay be middle-age before up for parole.

ABEBE: Who told you?

PICKLE: Cindy Lambert. His first foster mom? Here?

ABEBE: Of course.

PICKLE: Somehow kept up with him over the years, too bad he couldn't'a stayed with her. Cindy showed me the picture in the paper, him arrested. The tattoos, cheek scar. *(Shrugs.)* People grow up. But the look in his eyes: that's what shook me. Dead. After the tragedy his little boy's eyes had the terror, sad. But those is livin' things. His sixteen-year-old eyes looked more frozen than those ice crystals yaw tried to make.

(*Sound of a speeding truck, its roar louder and more sudden than the previous ones.*)

PICKLE: (*Near tears.*) The damn diesel trucks gimme the migraine!

(*PICKLE goes to a cupboard, snatches a prescription bottle of aspirin, swallows a couple.*)

ABEBE: *Are you alright?*

PICKLE: Yeah, for now. Wrote you about that, right? My head pains from the exhaust?

ABEBE: No, you didn't.

PICKLE: Abebe. I gotta go lie down a minute, honey.

ABEBE: I'm sorry you feel bad, Pickle.

PICKLE: It'll pass half-hour, plenty a time for the shindig. Why don't you go settle in your ol' room?

ABEBE: May I bring you something? Water?

PICKLE: No, you go get some rest. Aintcha jet-lagged? (*HE smiles.*) Just my headache pills. Wouldn't think that cause no hallucination, huh? But sometimes, when the bright lights calm down and the ache's gone, I think hey – this must be what morphine's like: morphing. Cuz suddenly here I am, some peaceful desert island, or swimmin' in calm seas with H.J.'s daddy and Carve. Toldja I ain't crazy no more! don't worry. But the truth? I sure recall some fun hours bein' cuckoo! *(Giggles, then sighs.)* Always happens, though. Just when you're havin' the time a your life, one day, out the blue, you go sane.

Scene Three

> *(Car: ABEBE driving, PICKLE shotgun, H.J. backseat.*
>
> *The following indented speeches are spoken [sung] simultaneously:)*

PICKLE AND HJ: *(Sing.) Shall we gather at the river*

ABEBE: *(Sings.) Aaaaaaaaaaaah*

PICKLE AND HJ: *Where bright angel feet have trod*

ABEBE: *Aaaaaaaaaaaaaah*

PICKLE AND HJ: *With its crystal tide forever*

ABEBE: *Aaaaaaaaaaaaaah*

PICKLE AND HJ: *Flowing by the throne of God?*

ABEBE: *Aaaaaaaaaaaaaah*

> *(PICKLE suddenly cracking up.)*

PICKLE: *(To ABEBE.)* Eight years later, you still don't know that hymn?

ABEBE: *(Grinning.)* The chorus I am letter perfect! *(Sings:)* Yes, we'll

ABEBE (Cont'd), PICKLE and H.J.:
(Sing.) gather at the river,
The beautiful, beautiful river,
Gather with the saints at the river
Flowing by the throne of –

PICKLE and H.J.: AAAAAAAAAH!

> *(ABEBE has violently swerved the car and braked. A dog is heard squealing away. ABEBE's, PICKLE's and H.J.'s eyes follow its path.)*

H.J.: It's not hobbling, must've missed it.

PICKLE: *(Good-natured nervous.)* Abebe, don't hog the wheel! Almost there, if I don't drive now I won't get my turn!

ABEBE: *(Also good natured.)* True, but H.J. was hogging the wheel first: four hours! I have been driving only forty minutes! You both may relax, I had better take these last few curves as I am familiar. They can be a bit treacherous. You are all in your safety belts?

PICKLE and H.J.: YES!

> *(ABEBE drives contentedly a few moments.)*

ABEBE: This must be a very big adventure for you, H.J.

H.J.: It *is*. What a blessed event for our reunion!

PICKLE: You already re-uned. My birthday.

H.J.: Abebe and I barely talked then. Too many people.

PICKLE: National holiday! *(Giggles.)*

H.J.: When Mom told me about the creek which you baptized those born-agains in that summer, I thought *this* is why I have postponed my baptism! God has provided this splendid, pristine place for Abebe to come back and lay his hands on me. So road trip: Tennessee!

ABEBE and PICKLE: A-men! *(ALL laugh.)*

ABEBE: H.J.! I have loved the fellowship of the drive, the singing and chatting of small things, but we really must catch up! Pickle tells me you have been having sex and babies without a husband!

(Silence.)

H.J.: Only one baby so far.

PICKLE: Abebe, maybe H.J. doe'n't want to talk about that.

H.J.: *I'll* talk about it. None of your business, Abebe, but sure, I'm not ashamed. We met when I was in college, summer after my junior. Saw him shooting hoops all alone at the playground one night, never seen him around town before. Said his name was Tich, here visiting his cousins. He found our town exciting, the mall, softball leagues. Things to do because apparently there are places even

hickier than this. Then I said, "Twenty-one?" –
testing his chauvinist quotient, if he'd be up to play
a girl. "Okay," he said. He didn't know I was on
the school team. He tried to play gentlemanly, not
putting in his best effort, but in the end he was
panting and sweating and barely got me, twenty-
one nineteen, and immediately followed it up with
our first pizza date which I'm certain was really
about preventing the next words out of my mouth:
"Two out of three?"

ABEBE: A baby did not come from basketball and
pizza.

H.J.: True: This isn't Bethlehem and no angel ever
visited me. The finer points I'm not revealing but
suffice it to say year later a beautiful little girl came
out of the deal, and I'm not sorry for that.

ABEBE: Then you married.

H.J.: Mistake!

ABEBE: But she was his daughter –

H.J.: Chances are.

ABEBE: What!

> (ABEBE had turned to look at H.J., the
> car going wild. H.J. and PICKLE
> scream. ABEBE quickly adjusts.)

PICKLE: Abebe! I *really* think it's my turn –

ABEBE: (*Pointing.*) Almost there almost there! Just
turn onto this dirt road, see?

(ABEBE makes a safe left.)

ABEBE: Mistake?

H.J.: *(Sighs.)* He had this thing about giving the baby a name. I'm like, What century *you* live in? *I* have a name so the baby'll have a name. But he pestered me crazy, finally I said okay, so there was the wedding which was a total of him, Mom, me, my six-months belly and a preacher which Mom insisted on, kiss me "I do" – and I'm trembling. Resta my *life?* Who makes a decision like that? twenty-two. I stare at stained-glass Jesus praying at Gethsemane and something clicks. That night told my husband I want the couch, and the happiest dream of the nicest people taking care of my baby, this woman with warm in her voice and a cross 'round her neck. I still see that cross after I wake up next day. And a sudden deep yearning for two things: annulment and a church. Tich didn't know about me and God but the annulment I did tell him, which he found strange coming out of a happy dream and not a nightmare and argued but not very convincingly, I think he had a few second thoughts himself, he married me to prove something which suddenly felt ridiculous so annulment was easy, we hadn't consummated the marriage anyway, all the consummating we did while we were dating.

(Pause.)

PICKLE: He's at the bottlin' plant now.

(Pause.)

PICKLE: Nice to see a black man in management.

H.J.: Nice? They confiscated the spring!

PICKLE: *Gotta* be makin' decent money.

H.J.: Good for him.

PICKLE: You musta heard he recently broke up with his girlfriend.

H.J.: Now how would you know that?

PICKLE: Common knowledge. But I'll keep my mouth shut.

> *(PICKLE makes a motion of locking HER lips and throwing away the key.)*

H.J.: Any music here, dead of nowhere?

ABEBE: I seem to recall a very exciting gospel station!

> *(ABEBE fiddles with the radio, settling on very white traditional Christian music, à la Mormon Tabernacle Choir. ABEBE is pleased, bouncing as if to an African beat. Finally H.J. reaches over the seat to click the radio off.)*

H.J.: That's not gospel.

PICKLE: Pass the salt and vinegar.

> *(As H.J. hands a big bag of potato chips to PICKLE.)*

ABEBE: What is the job of your water bottling plant friend? Tich?

H.J.: Who knows.

PICKLE: You.

H.J.: Inventory. *(Shrugs.)* Office work.

PICKLE: Day job, no graveyard shift for him! Some kind of exect.

ABEBE: It sounds like a very powerful position!

PICKLE: *(Glance at H.J.)* Gotta be.

ABEBE: Then I shall light a match that the two of you will marry!

PICKLE: *(Beat.)* You mean light a candle?

H.J.: I think he means *make* a match, he wants to play matchmaker.

ABEBE: Indubitably!

H.J.: *No.*

ABEBE: But if you are lonely and desperate perhaps he is too.

H.J.: Who said I'm lonely and desperate?

ABEBE: In this way I will clarify your availability to him!

H.J.: Don't do it, Abebe, I mean it.

PICKLE: I think she still likes him.

(H.J. bangs the back of PICKLE's seat.)

PICKLE: None of my business! *(Another motion of locking HER lips and throwing away the key.)*

H.J.: How many spare keys you got for those?

ABEBE: It is my humble opinion that once you have carried a man's child to term you need to consider taking the relationship to the next step!

H.J.: That subject's closed, Abebe.

ABEBE: In the eyes of God you are still husband and wife –

H.J.: CLOSED!

(Silence.)

PICKLE: You tell H.J. 'bout your trip to Calcutta in the fall?

ABEBE: Cambodia.

PICKLE: Cambodia!

ABEBE: I was not awarded the fellowship.

PICKLE: Awww . . .

ABEBE: No worries! I also completed the application process for study in Bolivia, and this will surely come through!

H.J.: Pass the Oreos. *(PICKLE passes the package as ABEBE speaks.)*

ABEBE: Officials in Cochabamba, Bolivia, hand over control of the public's water to Bechtel, a U.S. corporation. Bechtel quickly raises the price of the water. The cost now well out of reach of the poor, Bechtel begins to charge the people for the water they pull from their own wells, for the rainwater they collect. A few hundred thousand people gather together, screaming the city to a screeching halt, and the government asks Bechtel to please hit the road Jack. Now the people own their water again, I would like to go and see how I might learn from this triumph of the human spirit and bring such knowledge back to Ethiopia!

PICKLE: You know what I wonder? I wonder how come he gotta drive forty-five minutes every Friday after work to shoot hoops *our* playground –

H.J.: Back on *that.*

PICKLE: (*uninterrupted*) – right down the street, right where you first found him.

H.J.: Who said he does?

PICKLE: Hah! *You!* Forgot, didn't ya? One afternoon you ponderin' aloud, "Wonder how come he gotta drive forty-five minutes every Friday after work to shoot hoops – ?"

H.J.: Who cares! (*Takes a swig out of a tap water canister.*)

PICKLE: Seem like you support him.

H.J. This look like Poland Spring to you?

PICKLE: Pretty responsible job. He gotta be pullin' in some good benefits.

H.J.: Maybe *you* oughta marry him.

PICKLE: Cold feet! *That*'s the problem, I think you both need to learn to act adult.

H.J.: *You*'re the one called him "T for Trouble" whole time I dated him! *You*'re the one said he's after only one thing!

PICKLE: Well he got that on about Date Number Two so there's really nothin' left for me to suspect him of, is there.

> *(The car stops. As H.J. and PICKLE had continued arguing, ABEBE had become increasingly confused by HIS surroundings. Only now do the WOMEN take note.)*

PICKLE: Why we stopped?

ABEBE: We are here.

> *(Silence. Then ABEBE gets out of the car, the WOMEN following, H.J. still holding HER canister. THEY stand just outside the vehicle.)*

H.J.: I don't see any water.

> *(ABEBE walks a few steps, H.J. and PICKLE behind. ABEBE stops, THEY stop.)*

ABEBE: Here. We stood here, waist deep. They called the creek "the crick," like you. The man was very ill.

(Pause.)

PICKLE: I see the bed.

H.J.: Barren as the Saharan.

(Pause.)

PICKLE: Corporate farm, they waste the most, right? *(Looking around.)* Maybe a nearby farm?

H.J.: Or a recent drought.

ABEBE: Or a megadam.

(Pause.)

ABEBE: Waist deep. The crystal water, we could see perfectly our feet, toes, this creek pristine, blessed, then two received God *this water was holy!*

(Silence.)

H.J.: Who needs a river. Catholics baptize their babies with a few drops.

> *(H.J. holds out HER canister to ABEBE. A few moments for HIM to understand. Then HE takes the canister. H.J. kneels.)*

PICKLE: I remember my baptism! Glendale Springs. Preacher say, "Do you accept the Lord, Patricia?" I look at him all confused, so nervous for a second forgot my own name!

H.J.: What'd the congregation sing?

PICKLE: "Gather at the River." We already done that.

(H.J. thinks.)

H.J.: *(Sings.) I looked over Jordan, and what did I see*

H.J. and PICKLE: *(Sing.) Comin' for to carry me home,*

ABEBE: But the Jordan River has been polluted and depleted. Job wrote of the great river's "rage." Now it is barely a stream.

H.J.: Then I picked the right song. *(Sings.) I saw a*

H.J. (Cont'd) and PICKLE: *(Sing.) band of angels comin' after me*

> *(ABEBE pours a little water into HIS cupped hand, then holds HIS hand over H.J.'s scalp.)*

H.J. and PICKLE: *(Sing.) Comin' for to carry me home.*

> *(The water gently trickles down to H.J. through ABEBE's fingers.)*

Scene Four

> *(Playground, around dusk. TICH shoots hoops. ABEBE enters smiling.)*

ABEBE: Hello!

> *(TICH startled, confused.)*

115

TICH: Hey.

> (*TICH continues shooting, ABEBE watching. Eventually:*)

TICH: Twenty-one?

ABEBE: (*Laughs.*) I am not very good.

> (*TICH shrugs, shoots.*)

ABEBE: Years ago I had a little friend Tay, sometimes we would play, this basket. (*TICH shoots.*) Okay!

> (*TICH passes the ball to ABEBE.*)

TICH: Take it out.

> (*ABEBE immediately shoots, the ball sailing high over the backboard and disappearing. The sound of a car screeching, a loud puncture of the ball. TICH and ABEBE stare in silence. Finally:*)

ABEBE: (Cheerful.) You win!

TICH: I'ma charge you for that ball.

ABEBE: May I pay you back in dinner?

> (*TICH startled.*)

TICH: Hey I'm not gay.

ABEBE: I am! I am very gay to invite you to dinner with my friends Pickle and H.J.!

(TICH frozen.)

TICH: H.J. Carter?

ABEBE: Correct!

TICH: How you know H.J. Carter?

ABEBE: I was her and Pickle's houseguest, four years.

(Pause.)

TICH: By "gay" you mean happy, not homo.

ABEBE: True!

TICH: Me and H.J. broke up.

ABEBE: But I hear that you have recently been dumped rendering you available, and she too is available, and you both have already had sex, including with each other, there is an excellent chance you are the father of the child she adopted away, so a dinner may lead to a date may lead to marriage and the both of you sinners finally reconciling yourselves with God!

TICH: *(Delighted.)* H.J. told me about you! You're the e-God-ogist!

ABEBE: The same!

TICH: *(Frowns.)* "There's an excellent *chance* I'm the father – "?

ABEBE: Do not think H.J. has sent me! Yes, she has feelings for you but keeps them hidden! Pride.

TICH: She keeps 'em hidden, how you know?

ABEBE: A woman always carries a torch for her first intimacy.

TICH: Sure but what about me?

ABEBE: You were the first to fertilize her!

TICH: Hey we did nothin' with fertilizer! Look . . . What's your name?

ABEBE: Abebe.

TICH: Abebe –

ABEBE: And you are Tich, Harry Tichnell, and H.J. a Harriet. Only God could bring about such a cute factor, God has a great sense of humor!

TICH: Abebe. It's really none of your business.

ABEBE: And yet, hearing that you were on the rebound, I could not help but seize the opportunity!

> (*TICH stares at HIM, then chuckles vaguely.*)

TICH: I don't know . . .

ABEBE: If it ended without bad feelings, what is the harm in one dinner? If there is a spark, you and H.J. may plan another dinner alone. If no spark, you will have enjoyed a delicious Ethiopian meal. I can cook! And found ways to improvise the ingredients here.

TICH: Ethiopian?

ABEBE: H.J. and Pickle were initially reluctant, but I won them over! Their only complaint now is no matter how much I have made, I have not made enough.

TICH: That i'n't the stuff you eat with your hands, is it?

ABEBE: The same! You tear off the bread, "injera," then snatch up the food.

TICH: Americans don't generally like to eat with their hands. Whadju call it again?

ABEBE: If you are afraid, I am sure I can manage some familiar dish. You would prefer hot dogs and macaroni and cheese?

TICH: I would, but who said I'm afraid?

ABEBE: Then you'll come!

(Pause.)

TICH: We were dumb. I was all for marriage though. At first . . . I stuck by her, pregnanter and pregnanter. I was hopin' it was the hormones, that soon's it all be over, soon's the two of her was back to one *we*'d be back. Maybe not husband and wife, but *some*thin'. I offered her this. Said I'd hold her hand when the time came but when the time came she never even called. Week later I'd heard through the grapevine all went well, the grapevine bein' all

I had cuz her number never popped up on my cell phone again.

(*Beat.*)

ABEBE: You worry about awkwardness.

TICH: I worry we ended on good terms, warm . . . I like to keep that. I know it ain't a tall house a cards, but if it's all I can hope for –

ABEBE: I shall assess the situation and report back to you!

TICH: Yeah, but –

ABEBE: And you may be pleasantly surprised! You only fail if you do not try!

(*ABEBE grinning. TICH thinks.*)

TICH : When?

ABEBE: Tomorrow!

TICH: *Tomorrow?* I work tomorrow!

ABEBE: Sunday!

TICH: Well –

ABEBE: Monday!

TICH: Wait! I gotta check my schedule at the plant! Get back to ya.

ABEBE: Tuesday!

TICH: Wednesday! I'm pretty sure I got Wednesday off –

ABEBE: Done!

> (TICH stares at ABEBE, then laughs to HIMself. Goes to HIS backpack, pulls out a bottled water, takes a big swig.)

ABEBE: I have heard about your work at the plant. Very powerful position!

TICH: Inventory. *(Shrugs.)* Office work. Sometime assist in the PR office, arrangin' the pamphlets.

> (TICH is absentmindedly playing with the charm of a chain around HIS neck, formerly hidden under HIS shirt. It is a tiny plastic pig.)

ABEBE: *(Delighted.)* Piggy! Very charming you wear a pig around your neck! Is this some primitive paganism or are you a huge fan of pork?

> (TICH, embarrassed, quickly hides the pig back in HIS shirt.)

TICH: I'll be by Wednesday! *(Gets ready to leave.)* Hope you use bottled water in your cookin'. Safer.

> (ABEBE holds HIS grin, struggling against a temptation to jump on TICH's comment. Finally:)

ABEBE: Your question about our exotic practice of eating with our hands, food stuffed between the bread? We call it a "sandwich." *(Still grinning.)*

Scene Five

> *(Dining area of the kitchen. ABEBE*
> *setting the table: plates, glasses, a glass*
> *pitcher of ice water. PICKLE looking on.*
> *THEY are dressed nicely for a special*
> *dinner. A large round tray of hot*
> *covered food on the kitchen counter.)*

PICKLE: Red stuff!

ABEBE: Lentils!

PICKLE: Green stuff!

ABEBE: Collards!

PICKLE: And spiced up *so* good! You won't lemme
help?

> *(ABEBE shakes HIS head no as H.J.*
> *enters.)*

PICKLE: *(To H.J.)* Go down to the basement freezer
and bring up that gallon a vanilla, put it in *this*
freezer. *(H.J. exits through the door to the basement.)*
Now I been theorizin' on the mystery guest. I put
forty cent on a girlfriend, I remember there was
that one you flung with your junior-senior.
Tameka?

ABEBE: Tamara.

PICKLE: That's right! rhyme with "marinara"! You
two tryin' a restart?

ABEBE: Tamara I hear married and moved to North Carolina.

PICKLE: Oh.

ABEBE: My guest is male.

PICKLE: Oh. *(New thought.)* Oh!

ABEBE: Yes, I *am* happy, but as in gay, not homo!

>   *(ABEBE laughs heartily. Doorbell.)*

ABEBE: Ah!

>   *(ABEBE exits to answer the door. H.J. enters with a gallon of ice cream.)*

H.J.: Rock hard. I'll leave it out on the counter.

>   *(ABEBE enters with TICH.)*

ABEBE: This is Tich,. but then again, I believe Tich requires no introduction!

>   *(ABEBE laughs. TICH smiles at H.J. H.J. stares, stunned. PICKLE is stunned. TICH stops smiling. H.J. runs out of the room.)*

TICH: *(To ABEBE.)* She didn't know? *(Looks from ABEBE to PICKLE.)* You didn't know?

>   *(PICKLE shakes HER head no.)*

TICH: You said you told 'em!

ABEBE: When you asked if I had mentioned it to H.J., my reply was, "Everything is all set!"

PICKLE: Lemme talk to her. H.J.! C'mon, no rudeness! *(Exits.)*

TICH: I better go.

ABEBE: Please! I cooked for four!

TICH: Toldja, she and me weren't enemies before, I don't want that now.

ABEBE: I assure you her anger is directed at *me*.

TICH: Yeah well the two of us got that in common at the moment.

H.J.: *(Entering with PICKLE, to TICH.)* Look, I'm not mad at you, I'm mad at *him*.

ABEBE: *(Delighted.)* You see!

TICH: He told me he told you!

H.J.: No doubt. Abebe's nose got a habit of getting stuck *where it doesn't belong*.

ABEBE: And now we shall all stick our noses into this beautiful aroma!

> *(ABEBE lifts the cover off the tray.)*

PICKLE: Ah!

> *(TICH unsure. ABEBE moves the tray from the counter to the table.)*

ABEBE: On this plate we have the injera. And on this plate some hot cloths for hand washing. Please do not confuse and wash your hands with the injera!

> *(ABEBE laughs, demonstrates with the cloth. ALL sit, H.J. dragging.)*

ABEBE: So! Here we have the lamb, here we have the chicken, here we have the yemisir kik wat the lentils, here we have the shiro the split peas, here we have the gomen the collard green, here we have the carrots and string beans –

H.J.: We know our colors.

TICH: *(Panicked about the food.)* NO! this helps! Go on.

ABEBE: Here we have the key sir alicha the beets, and in the middle is the cold salad. Now! *(Demonstrating.)* Tear off a piece of the injera, snatch some food. *(Pops it into HIS mouth.)* Chew!

PICKLE: *(Tearing off injera, to TICH.)* Go on! Dig in!

> *(TICH looks at H.J.)*

TICH: H.J.'s not eating.

H.J.: *(Dry.)* You're the guest.

PICKLE: Go on!

> *(TICH reluctantly tries: ALL eyes on HIM.)*

TICH: *(Pleasant surprise.)* Yeah!

> *(ABEBE and PICKLE cheer.)*

ABEBE: Nazel tov!

> *(Now EVERYONE digging in, H.J.
> least enthusiastic.)*

PICKLE: I was scared too first time he brung it out, but after you had it, you wannit every day!

H.J.: *(To TICH.)* I think I said the same thing to you once.

TICH: *(Embarrassed, trying to change.)* Beets?

ABEBE: Yes!

TICH: *(Tastes.)* Mmmmm.

PICKLE: I love that we all eat from the same tray. I'n't that community?

ABEBE: As in communion. Taking the bread and the wine from the same plate.

TICH: My family was Baptists.

PICKLE: Us too!

TICH: We drank grape juice 'steada wine.

PICKLE: Us too!

ABEBE: Taking the Wonder Bread and the grape juice from the tray, I never cease to be moved by this great show of sharing! H.J. is saved!

(*Pause.*)

TICH: (*Eyes on H.J.*) Like Christian saved?

ABEBE: Indubitably! H.J. has accepted Jesus Christ as her Lord and Savior, and as a show of commitment, she was recently baptized –

H.J.: (*Eating.*) I can speak for myself.

ABEBE: Please!

(*Silence. H.J. continues eating.*)

TICH: Well that's great.

H.J.: Is it.

TICH: Yeah! (*Beat.*) What?

H.J.: Why would you think it's great? You're not a Christian.

TICH: Who says I'm not a Christian?

H.J.: You go to church?

TICH: Who says you have to go to church to – ? (*H.J. snickers.*) What?

H.J.: I don't believe you have to go to church to be a Christian. However, if the only time you ever think about Christianity is when you say "I don't believe you have to go to church to be a Christian" I believe your Christianity is suspect.

ABEBE: This is quite a change. I remember when H.J. never went to church! When you first walked through the door, God must have said, *"H.J.? H.J. who?"* *(Laughs heartily. H.J. glares at HIM.)*

TICH: What about good works? What if you love one another like Jesus said to?

H.J.: Where's it say that?

TICH: Somewhere!

ABEBE: Jesus spoke in red: "This is my commandment, That ye love one another, as I have loved you." John 15:12.

TICH: I thought you said you weren't mad at me?

H.J.: I'm not mad at you! I just get sick of hearing "You don't have to go to church to be a Christian" easy! Lets 'em off the hook.

TICH: Lets *who* off the hook? *(No answer.)* Sinners? Callin' me a sinner?

ABEBE: "For *all* have sinned, and come short of the glory of God." Romans 3:23.

TICH: You know what? Sometimes it takes two to sin.

ABEBE: Very true! On the other hand, H.J. has been saved. H.J. has denounced her past sinful life and has been reborn –

H.J.: Shut up, Abebe. Okay, Christian, where are your great good works? Long weeks at the bottling plant, then what? You a Big Brother to some kid? Volunteer at the old folks' home, what? Cuz shooting hoops alone every Friday night, don't think that counts in anybody's book as "good works."

TICH: How *you* know I shoot hoops every Friday night?

(*H.J. caught: a nervous pause.*)

H.J.: Abebe told me.

TICH: That's funny. Cuz when Abebe found me at the playground he already knew who I was in relation to you. Which would imply somebody who knew me told him where to find me.

H.J.: I didn't tell him to find you!

TICH: But you knew where I was. (*H.J.'s face fire-hot. TICH enjoys.*) 'S okay to look. Our bodies *are* the temples of God.

ABEBE: That is a common and grave misinterpretation of the scripture! The actual text from First Corinthians begins "Flee fornication. . . . What? know ye not that your body is the temple of the Holy Ghost which is in you – "

TICH: Aw I'm teasin', H.J., don't be mad! We weren't mad before, why now?

(*Silence.*)

TICH: We *were*n't mad before. Right?

(*Pause. Then H.J. looks directly at TICH.*)

H.J.: We weren't mad. But over is over. You can't go back.

> (*TICH stares at HER, a little surprised and hurt, then nods. The eating resumes, a cloud of melancholy. Eventually:*)

PICKLE: Abebe's going to Belize!

ABEBE: Bolivia.

PICKLE: Bolivia!

ABEBE: No.

PICKLE: No?

ABEBE: I was not awarded the grant.

PICKLE: No!

ABEBE: But there are many other opportunities to learn! Before I leave America I would like to visit the Hoover, its megadam legacy bequeathed to and imposed upon the Third World via World Bank loans. Though it will heartbreak me I must behold the Aral Sea in Russia, which has lost *ninety percent* of its volume since the 1960 obsessive drive to produce cotton! I must travel to the West Bank, where Palestinians spend a third of their income on water for drinking and bathing while their Israeli settler neighbors fill swimming pools. And next year I will try again for the Bolivia grant, for the Cambodia –

TICH: *(To H.J.)* Remember I took you to that place in Harper's Addition for your birthday? I ate like a hog, pork chops and corn on the cob, butter rollin' off the biscuits. You thought your appetite held the title, the undefeated champ, but *you* stopped after thirds, *I* took the cake. Then walkin' Main Street, you see this teeny tiny plastic pig, you say "Wait a minute," go in the store, you buy that wee sow for me.

H.J.: That's a weird thing for you to remember.

TICH: *(Careful.)* I thought . . . You know every May that restaurant has a Can't Wait 'Til Thanksgiving special, turkey and stuffin', I was thinkin' . . . It's next Saturday, I was thinkin' . . .

> *(H.J. sadly shaking HER head no. A pause. Then TICH reaches into HIS shirt, pulls out the pig. H.J. is stunned.)*

PICKLE: Piggy!

ABEBE: I remember! You were wearing it the night of our exciting 21 match! *(TICH has not taken HIS eyes off H.J.)*

TICH: I wear it every day. Inside my shirt, I didn't . . . I didn't know what you'd think.

> *(A long pause.)*

H.J.: Okay.

TICH: *(Beat: confused.)* Okay? You mean . . . Saturday? *(H.J. smiles shyly. Now TICH smiles shyly. After a few moments:)*

ABEBE: Well I think there should be acknowledgement that someone here has lit a match! *(H.J. mortified.)*

TICH: Huh?

PICKLE: Eat all you want! But better be savin' room for my cherry pie, ice cream toppin'!

TICH: I'll be ready! *(Pats HIS stomach happily. ALL eat.)*

H.J.: I took five of Mom's cherry pies to the church bake sale last week. They were sold out ten minutes after I got there, everyone wild about her flaky crust.

PICKLE: Crust's the best part!

ABEBE: Pickle's cherry pie is truly a work of art! Just as her double chocolate cake was once equally a masterpiece, but since coming back to Maryland I have developed less of a taste for chocolate as it reminds me too much of the despicable Nestlé bottling plant!

(Silence.)

TICH: *(Laughs, trying to lighten.)* "Despicable"? That plant pays my rent, Abebe.

ABEBE: And that is certainly reason enough for the area to have lost her beautiful public spring, so that a chain link fence could be built to keep all the local people out of what is now the property of Nestlé!

(Pause.)

TICH: Well . . . yeah. *(Laughs.)* Sure, shame about losin' the swimhole but I think healthy drinkin' water's a pretty good trade –

ABEBE: Five hundred gallons of water pumped every minute, two hundred sixty three million gallons a year and Nestlé paid a total of one hundred dollars for permits and receives sizable tax breaks. Sweet deal!

TICH: Like I *said* –

ABEBE: Americans are very fortunate to have clean clear water straight from the tap. And yet they prefer to pay for it. The joys of consumerism! Westerners pay three times as much for one gallon of bottled water than for one gallon of gasoline!

H.J.: *(To ABEBE.)* What are you doing.

TICH: Tap water's not all clean and clear.

>*(ABEBE snatches up the glass pitcher, puts it to HIS face, looking through it as if it's a fishbowl.)*

ABEBE: *(Grinning.)* I see you, Pickle!

TICH: Not *all* tap! Sometime I assist in the PR office, I seen the articles. Kid in West Virginia, his teeth all rotten from the spigot water. Which come out cloudy, oily. And scabs on his skin, what fool wanna touch *that?*

ABEBE: Do you bathe in bottled water?

TICH: *No* I don't bathe in –

ABEBE: Ah! you bathe in tap water! But I see no scabs on *your* skin. And you have the teeth of a fine horse!

PICKLE: Hey! this discussion is tomato-tomahto, Abebe stick with tap, Tich drink the bottled. Now. Who want whip cream top a their à la mode?

TICH: Tap water's different everywhere, turn that spigot, you don't know what you're gettin'. Least with bottled, you know what it is.

ABEBE: Yes! it is tap! Pepsi's Aquafina is tap water! Coke's Desani is tap water!

H.J.: It is *not*, Abebe –

TICH: Treated!

> (H.J. looks at TICH, startled. TICH turns to H.J., a bit embarrassed.)

TICH: It *was* tap. But it got treated.

PICKLE: Well Tich don't work for Pepsi or Coke no way, Tich works for Nestlé.

TICH: Pure spring water, we know that!

PICKLE: Nice to see a black man in management.

ABEBE: Nestlé, manufacturer of Poland Spring.

TICH: Yeah!

ABEBE: Nestlé, manufacturer of Deer Park.

TICH: Yeah . . .

ABEBE: Nestlé, manufacturer of Ice Mountain, Zephyrhills, Arrowhead, Calistoga, Vittel, Pellegrino, Perrier, so many products! No wonder Nestlé has dried up so many springs, turning them into mudholes! *(Laughs.)*

H.J.: If you got a point to make, Abebe, go ahead and make it.

PICKLE: *(To ABEBE.)* Jobs! This place depressed decades, people needed work! Half the people I know was on welfare, Abebe, think they liked it?

ABEBE: Very few workers full-time.

TICH: *I* am!

PICKLE: Why you pickin' on Tich anyway? He ain't the president a Nestlé, how he know what the water made of.

TICH: I *do!*

ABEBE: The government can create jobs to *preserve* the environment –

PICKLE: *But they didn't!* So here come the water bottlers, a plan. No ugly strip minin', no smokestack blackenin' the sky, ear-crashin' machinery –

ABEBE: *(The first sentence pointedly to PICKLE.)* Four hundred diesel trucks a day to blacken the air! Thirty million bottles sold a day, ninety percent of those *not* recycled: landfill or litter!

TICH: Look! when it's said and done, bottled's healthier, o*kay?* Even if it's treated tap, it's better 'n-

ABEBE: The EPA mandates that *no* E. Coli bacteria be allowed in tap water. The FDA consents to a *minimum* of E. Coli bacteria in bottled water!

TICH: The EPA *"mandates"?* The Clean Water Act been violated half a million times last five years –

ABEBE: Municipal water is tested frequently by certified laboratories, in New York City tap water is tested five hundred thousand times a year!

TICH: Yeah but –

ABEBE: Water bottlers on the other hand may use *any* lab, no need for certification, and test only *once* a year.

TICH: *And what happens when the gas drillin' go through?* Huh? Frackin', New York City's tap water all clear and enviable now, how about that gas frackin' they proposin' in New York State, *spoil* the city's tap –

ABEBE: Then STOP IT!

TICH, H.J. and PICKLE: *(Beat.) What?*

ABEBE: *Demand* the purity of tap.

(THEY stare at HIM.)

ABEBE: *(Laughs ironically.)* No, you would rather throw up your hands in despair, accept the theory of pure bottled water *a lie*, and not fight to keep spigot water clean and available to all. How spoiled are Americans to just let it slip through your fingers!

TICH: *(Standing.)* Okay I better go.

H.J. and PICKLE: NO!

ABEBE: I know Nestlé! Ethiopia struggling during a devastating famine offers to repay a one and a half million dollar debt, which Nestlé recalculates to *six* million dollars!

TICH: THEY FIXED THAT! They got flack for that, now *all* the money they gave back –

ABEBE: I know Nestlé! Advising starving African mothers to choose formula over breast milk, claiming the mothers will pass on their disease to their babies while *exponentially* more infants die from drinking formula mixed with bad water *killed my sisters!* My mother in mourning her entire life, her entire short life mourning blame herself *killed her* KILLED MY FAMILY!

H.J.: THAT'S NOT TICH'S FAULT!

ABEBE: Powerful man! Powerful man at the plant *he can do something!*

TICH: I'm no powerful –

ABEBE: I speak truth to power HE CAN DO SOMETHING!

TICH: *WHAT?*

PICKLE: It ain't your fault, Abebe. Those grants is competitive, you'll get another, help your people. You don't gotta feel your hands is useless.

> (*ABEBE snatches the glass pitcher, holding it in the air, HIS fist on the handle tight and trembling with emotion.*)

ABEBE: It is a RIGHT! Water is *not* a commodity Water is a RIGHT!

TICH: (*Walking toward ABEBE.*) Okay, now put that down –

ABEBE: A *RIGHT!*

> (*In THEIR brief, tense struggle over the pitcher, the icy water is all suddenly poured over ABEBE. Though it happens lightning fast, and is in no way premeditated, it is clear the incident was not wholly accidental on TICH's part. HE is immediately startled and ashamed.*)

TICH: Oh God. Oh God, Abebe, I'm sorry –

PICKLE: Abebe, lemme get you a towel –

TICH: God, Abebe –

> (*ABEBE violently shakes HIS head no,*
> *HIS entire body shivering and adamant.*
> *Silence.*)

ABEBE: I understand now, Pickle. What you said:
You cannot cross the same river twice. The first
time I crossed, there *was* the wide crick, waist deep.
And I baptized them, two new converts receiving
Christ, a *miracle!* But when I returned to the crick to
baptize H.J., when I returned to the miracle . . .

H.J.: (*Beat.*) Gone.

> (*Pause.*)

ABEBE: Gone.

Scene Six

> (*Bedroom. The stereo console has been*
> *moved into here. A shopping bag has*
> *been placed on top of it. PICKLE lying*
> *on HER bed, HER arm covering HER*
> *eyes. SHE calls weakly.*)

PICKLE: Abebe.

ABEBE: (*Comes to the door, quiet.*) Yes, Pickle.

PICKLE: Thought I heard the back door. Where
you been all day?

ABEBE: The library. I saw your door closed, I did
not want to disturb you. Get you anything? Glass
of water?

PICKLE: No, medicine kick in, few minutes. Listen. Cindy Lambert dropped that bag off this mornin'. She called first, I said Well you better bring it by today, he be home, Ethiopia tomorra. *(Beat.)* When you think you be back this way? 'Nother eight years?

ABEBE: Sooner! if I can.

PICKLE: Later if you can't.

ABEBE: I will come, Pickle! half of my heart I leave here. As soon as I can set aside enough money for the trip after helping the neediest of my village, as soon as I am granted leave from the university, as soon as I feel secure that I am not abandoning my village –

PICKLE: I'll miss you too. *(Quiet.)* Gotcher farewell dinner all ready. H.J. be by, little while.

ABEBE: A marvel she does not hate me.

PICKLE: Aw fights happen, Abebe, that was days ago. They still set on the Thanksgivin' restaurant, see what's what. Water under the bridge.

ABEBE: I was rude! I wanted . . . I thought Tich had power, that he . . . God *gave* water to us, not to buy and sell! Do they charge us for the air we breathe?

PICKLE: Would if they could.

ABEBE: *I was wrong* but I thought . . . I thought I could try –

PICKLE: You tried.

ABEBE: I tried. I tried.

(Pause.)

ABEBE: I am an average student, Pickle, *(laughs sadly)* whatever convinced me I would receive a grant for study? *(Beat.)* I can be inspired! When I introduced that little dam to my village, it was as if we saw God! God working through me, I felt I could do great things! But take only one megadam to wash out all the little dams *everything, I just wanted to . . . help I wanted to –*

PICKLE: You tried.

ABEBE: *I tried!*

(Pause.)

ABEBE: *(Brighter.)* However, I believe I have made amends with Tich! I drove all the way to his house with the new basketball I had bought for him. At first he was still angry, then took me to his backyard and we shot the hoops. *(Laughs.)* I may be the namesake of Abebe Bikila but I have never been mistaken for a sportsman! The first game Tich won twenty-one zero. The second game Tich won twenty-one zero. I begged him for a third. He said firmly, *"Last time."* When the score was four zero I shot: Swish! We both stopped, stunned. Then I said, "Okay! I shall quit while I am ahead!"

> *(ABEBE starts laughing heartily, covering HIS face with HIS hands. Gradually HIS laughter transforms into*

*silent weeping. PICKLE's arm still over
HER eyes.)*

PICKLE: *(Eventually.)* Not s'posed to say, but H.J.
tell me she makin' you a from-scratch cake, now
that *gotta* be love! Don't worry though. I also got
you a baby bakery-bought, I'm a do ya right,
Abebe. *(ABEBE wipes HIS face, smiles sadly.)* What's
in the bag?

> *(ABEBE reaches into the shopping bag,
> pulls out a small package and an
> envelope.)*

ABEBE: A letter. From inmate six four three three
dash one five four.

PICKLE: Tay.

ABEBE: Tay.

PICKLE: Well. What he know new?

> *(ABEBE unfolds the letter. Reads.)*

ABEBE: "Dear Abebe. I hope you are well. I heard
from Cindy you were in town. I know what you
must think, Thou shalt not kill but Thou shalt not a
lot of what was done to me so that's that. I lost my
father's flags so I took the credit card of the foster
bitch starving me and ordered another flag off the
computer. When I was on trial Cindy came to see
me I asked her to hold some stuff it's here. Through
the bars I watched a knife fight and wondered was
there anything I ever had to smile at. You and
Pickle and H.J., Cindy and Pete, he died last spring

when a diesel truck slammed his car. All these people for me never last long, but they was real. Two parts gratitude, right?"

(Pause.)

PICKLE: What'd he send?

> *(ABEBE reaches into the package. Pulls out the shoehorn. PICKLE lowers HER arm to see.)*

PICKLE: That it?

> *(ABEBE reaches into the bag again, pulls out a rubber-banded flag, the size of the little Confederate flags. Takes off the band and unfurls it.)*

PICKLE: What flag is that?

ABEBE: Ethiopia.

PICKLE: *(A sudden relief.)* Oooooooh!

ABEBE: Pickle?

PICKLE: *(Sits up.)* Just hit it. Headache gone. I'm morphing. Hey, switch up the volume, wontcha?

> *(ABEBE turns up the console turntable, the record in the middle of a song. It is the same John Lee Hooker selection that PICKLE originally played in Act I but now the record is very much used and scratched. ABEBE keeps the volume very low.)*

ABEBE: No longer "almost mint."

PICKLE: Maybe I'll try to replace it again. *(Beat.)* And maybe not. Every bump a badge, these are the battle scars me and John Lee been through together. *(Beat – now something new.)* Hey Abebe. Guess where I am?

ABEBE: Where, Pickle?

> *(Lights: The room changes so it appears the bed is an island, water all around. The record fades out, replaced by the sound of the tropics.)*

PICKLE: Floatin'. Tunnel . . . Tunnel sap?

ABEBE: Tonle sap.

PICKLE: The good flood! I'm in my house on stilts. Better jump up before you drown!

> *(PICKLE reaches out HER hand, ABEBE takes it. Pulls HIM onto the bed - Should not in any way seem sexual.)*

PICKLE: The fish rich and abundant. See 'em fly?

ABEBE: *(Smiles.)* I do.

> *(Nine-year-old TAY stands at the doorway, holding HIS roller skate. PICKLE doesn't see HIM.)*

TAY: Abebe. You never saw my other skate?

(From under a pillow, ABEBE pulls out the other skate, showing it to TAY and smiling. TAY, beaming, dives onto the bed. Putting on HIS skates.)

TAY: I wanna skate on the ice!

ABEBE: Frozen over now, Pickle.

PICKLE: Frozen?

ABEBE: We are on the pond. Ice. *(PICKLE smiles.)*

TAY: Skate!

ABEBE: Did you know water is the only substance heavier in liquid form than in solid?

PICKLE: Is?

ABEBE: This is why ice floats. Otherwise the sea would freeze from the bottom up. And all life on earth would be extinguished.

PICKLE: I remember us on the bank. You, me and Tay.

TAY: Abebe's first snow!

ABEBE: So soft! We stand on the edge, a tree limb overhead. Temperature rise, and now the miracle: three states of matter! Solid ice, and its gas mist hovering above it, and liquid: a sparkling icicle from the tree branch melts.

(ABEBE, TAY and PICKLE are looking up at the imaginary icicle.)

ABEBE: Drip. Drip. Drip. Drip.

>   *(Immediately followed by the sound of a faucet in identical rhythm: Drip. Drip. Drip. Drip.*
>
>   *Blackout.)*
>
>   **End of play**

LIGHT RAISE THE ROOF

Script History: *Light Raise the Roof* was originally commissioned by Manhattan Theatre Club in New York City as part of Ms. Corthron's 1997 NEA/TCG residency. In 1998 it was read as part of the first Women Playwrights Festival in Seattle sponsored by A Contemporary Theatre and Hedgebrook. In 2002 it was workshopped at the Long Wharf Theatre in Connecticut, and that fall was read at New York Theatre Workshop, which commissioned a rewrite.

Light Raise the Roof received its world premiere at New York Theatre Workshop in 2004, produced in association with AT&T:OnStage®, administered by Theatre Communications Group, under the direction of Michael John Garcés with set design by Narelle Sissons, costume design by Gabriel Berry, light design by Allen Lee Hughes, sound design by Robert Kaplowitz, & production stage management by Shelli Aderman. The cast was (in alphabetical order):

Em..................…..…..Moe Moe Alston
Zekie………....…………….Rob Beitzel
Arnell, et al.........Caroline Stefanie Clay
Toddo's Wife, et al…...……..Romi Dias
Toddo, et al……...…..........Royce Johnson
Mai…………......…………Mia Katigbak
Free, et al……….……...J. Kyle Manzay
Cole………….....……...Chris McKinney
Boy 2, et al……..…….…..Andres Munar
Bebbie, et al…...April Yvette Thompson
Marmalade, et al……...Colleen Werthman

CHARACTERS

(in order of appearance)

FREE - a black man, around 30

COLE - a black man, 40s

TODDO (Todd with an O) - a man, 36

Toddo's WIFE - a Latina woman, 37

ENVIRONMENT WOMAN - white, mid-40s

ZEKIE - a white boy-man, 26

BEBBIE (rhymes with Debbie) - Free's sister, a black woman, mid-30s

MAI - a Vietnamese woman, 40s

MARMALADE - a white woman

BAY - a man

MAN in the shelter

EM - a 7-year-old black girl

ARNELL - a black woman, Em's mother

2 COPS

PARKS DEPARTMENT WORKER

1ST WOMAN in the Congregation

2ND WOMAN in the Congregation

WOMAN WITH INFANT

DEPRESSED WOMAN

BOY 1 - a teenager

BOY 2 - a teenager

A possible actor-doubling scheme:

1) a black man, 40s: Cole

2) a white man, 20s: Zekie

3) a black woman, 30s: Bebbie

4) a black woman, 30s : Arnell

5) an Asian woman, 40s: Mai

6) a black girl, 7: Em

7) a black man: 20s-30: Free

8) a Latina woman, 30s: Toddo's Wife / 1st Woman / Woman with Infant

9) a black man, 30s: Toddo / Bay / Cop 1 / Boy 1

10) a white woman, 40s: Environment Woman / Marmalade / 2nd Woman / Depressed Woman

11) a white man, 20s-30s: Man / Cop 2 / Parks Department Worker / Boy 2 .

(10 actors if Bebbie and Arnell double.)

Act One

Scene One

> *(FREE stands in a downstage corner.)*

FREE: *(To audience)* He ast for one. I give him three.

> *(The scene behind FREE: COLE builds a house – two-room, single-story. On the ground beside HIM is HIS duffel bag. TODDO is standing, observing COLE. Toddo's WIFE sits on curb, arms nervously hugging legs. Two shopping carts full of stuff. FREE is outside of the action.)*

COLE: Diversity. Color, texture. Shape. That a good architect considers off the bat, aesthetics, what creative touch be a asset, what mix a visual metaphors likely clash. Next: balance. Whether it be symmetric whether it be asymmetric but also moves us into the science, mechanics. Why a structure don't fall down: beams and whether they better served in tension or compression. But maybe we ain't yet addressed the issue first and foremost: function.

TODDO: Don't be gettin' fancy! Deal's a deal. Five bucks.

COLE: Mr. Wright.

TODDO: Twenty-four hours. Ain't it already comin' up on twenty-two? *(Eyes on HIS wristwatch.)*

COLE: "Usonian" was Mr. Frank Lloyd's word for United States of North America, and for these houses he had a plan. One: avoidin' the same ol', two: takin' into account the dwellers – people, three: respectin' the outside surroundin's, makin' sure it all compatible.

WIFE: *(Stares into space – the street)* "5 o'clock," he say, "5 PM have the back rent or the street!" Five oh one we homeless.

COLE: Think I ever prop some International glass shoebox in a 'hood a Eastlake Victorians?

WIFE: *(Glances at shopping carts.)* Grab what we could. Fast.

COLE: *(More to HIMself, touching the parts of building)* Livin' room slash kitchen. Bedroom. Two rooms, that give yaw the possibility a privacy. Space. *(Adjusts door lock.)*

WIFE: "Go to Cole," everybody say.

FREE: *(Indignant)* I said it first.

WIFE: "Cole build you a place twenty-four." "How much you got?" Cole say. "Five dollars. Five dollars in the world, Toddo 36, I 37, five dollars we got to show for it, here."

COLE: *(Opens the door.)* Home.

> *(TODDO, still staring at HIS watch, now looks up at COLE, then at his WIFE. SHE looks at COLE, stands,*

looks at TODDO. It is only now apparent that SHE is quite pregnant. SHE grabs from a shopping cart a wedding photograph, frame glass cracked, and SHE and TODDO pause at the door looking in before entering: wonder.)

FREE: *(Raising two fingers)* Two.

(A small house, the back half buried in dirt. COLE cleans a large sheet of glass. ENVIRONMENT WOMAN enters with a large paper cup, hands it to COLE.)

ENVIRONMENT WOMAN: "Keep the coffee comin' Keep the coffee comin'," you don't know what I gotta go through to arrange it. Hey! Where's my glass roof?!

COLE: *(Sips.)* No glass roof.

(HE leans the glass at an angle against the house.)

COLE: Envelope-passive solar energy. Warm air sucked in between glass and house. It'll rise, go behind, under, rise, behind, under. Circle a warm.

ENVIRONMENT WOMAN: Hey! How come half my house in dirt! Who asked for a bunker!

COLE: Insulation. When the shivers hit the air, temp in the earth remain a mild 57.

ENVIRONMENT WOMAN: Hey! Not facing right! I ordered the morning sun East!

COLE: Low sun in winter, you want the most solar heat this sucker kiss south.

ENVIRONMENT WOMAN: That's the bran name glass cleaner! That ain't my budget eight dollars sixty-seven cents all I have! Ain't I toldju?

COLE: 'Bout eight hundred sixty-seven times. Don't accuse me a jackin' up, I don't go back on deals. *(Back to work.)*

ENVIRONMENT WOMAN: *(Beat.)* My choice. I had it. Silver spoon. Don't believe me? Three weeks before I graduate Swarthmore I say fuck it. Fuck *them*, my mother and him. Don't believe me?

COLE: What your major?

ENVIRONMENT WOMAN: Math. Gonna be a teacher. High school.

COLE: Who's him?

ENVIRONMENT WOMAN: Stepfather. My home's been the street since. Twenty-three years. Problem: last couple I get a winter cold I can't shake. I wanna live. *(Fingers near glass.)* I was told you made to order but I didn't believe it. Environmental house. *(Beat.)* Where you find your stuff? Sheet a glass?

COLE: Resourceful parta the job. And discretion regardin' revealin' sources. You travel?

ENVIRONMENT WOMAN: Did my rich white girl thing, college. Europe.

COLE: When ya go back to bein' rich and white, get your train ticket: Arizona. Paoli Soleri. Know him? *(SHE shakes HER head no.)* He got the conscience, and the action. Not just talk, not just on-paper architect, he buildin' it, him and some friends and some grants: Arcosanti, self-contained city. Challengin' the environmental shame of the sprawlin' metropolis, Arcosanti built up 'steada out. It got its employment its entertainment. Guess what it obsoletes? Cars. *[Sudden rays of sun.]* Your thermostat. *(THEY smile.)*

> *(FREE holds up three fingers.*
>
> *Now: a still smaller house, just tall enough to sit up in, made of old rotting boards. COLE is leaning on it, face buried in HIS arms, asleep. ZEKIE stoops, bouncing, constantly scratching HIS arm. HE wears a white paper cap, written on it: "Jackson County Fair" or something similar. Periodically HE will stand and pace rapidly, then just as suddenly drop back to HIS stooped bouncing. HE never looks at COLE. HIS mumblings are nonstop. If HIS overlapping text finishes before COLE's, ZEKIE should add more movies (never the same two in a row) so that HE never pauses.*

*The indented speeches are spoken
simultaneously:)*

ZEKIE: *(Mumbles)* Streetcar Name Desire On the
Waterfront 'Pocalypse Now Godfather

> ZEKIE *(Cont'd)*: Sayonara Streetcar Name
> Desire On the Waterfront 'Pocalypse Now
> Godfather Streetcar Name Desire On the
> Waterfront 'Pocalypse Now Godfather Streetcar
> Name Desire On the

> COLE *(Lifts head, back to work)*: This do ya for
> the temporary, these boards not too winter
> resistant but winter ain't hit yet, still got a few
> days. Under the steel bridge, that give ya some
> overhead protection. Holdja. 'While.

ZEKIE *(Cont'd)*: Waterfront 'Pocalypse Now
Godfather Streetcar Name

> ZEKIE *(Cont'd)*: Desire On the Waterfront
> 'Pocalypse Now Godfather Streetcar Name
> Desire On the Waterfront 'Pocalypse

> COLE: Function, you spend a lotta time in the
> stoop, ain't much belongin's, this playhouse do
> ya. Time bein'. Rope from the inside provide a
> lock.

ZEKIE *(Cont'd)*: Now Godfather Streetcar Name
Desire

ZEKIE *(Cont'd)*: On the Waterfront 'Pocalypse Now Godfather Streetcar Name

COLE: Winda out the back. See? C'mere.

> *(COLE brings ZEKIE to the window. ZEKIE stands long enough to walk to the window, then back to stooping, never pausing in the mumbling. COLE reaches through the window.)*

ZEKIE: Desire On the Waterfront 'Pocalypse Now Godfather *(Repeat list under COLE.)*

COLE: Ya pull this rope ya got yourself a security system. It ain't the greatest thing but not like you harborin' some cd stereo component, right? *(ZEKIE continues mumbling.)* Know not much space move around but . . . Sleeper. Like a train, it got one function, rest shelter. When ya need to do other stuff, walk, stand, got plenty a outdoors. *(ZEKIE continues mumbling.)* You be okay. Grown man, how old?

> *(ZEKIE continues mumbling while rapidly flashing two fingers, then six fingers, two   six two six. COLE, tired and poor eyesight, peers close to count.)*

COLE: Twenty-six? *(ZEKIE continues mumbling.)* Twenty-six grown man, you be alright. *(ZEKIE continues mumbling, pulls out a twenty-dollar bill from HIS pocket.)* Keep it! ain't takin' money for this job, half-ass. *(Beat.)* I make you a sleeper, for me: no sleep. Fifty-four hours. When I get sleep I'll come back, revise. Then we talk business.

> *(COLE leads ZEKIE into the house and helps HIM lock it, ZEKIE mumbling the whole time. ZEKIE comes to the window, still mumbling. COLE looks at HIM, then walks away. ZEKIE still mumbling.)*

Scene Two

> *(Now COLE moves to a bench, sits. The Park. COLE sitting up, dozes and jerks HIS head awake, dozes and jerks awake. FREE stands in front of COLE.)*

FREE: Hey.

> *(COLE is asleep.)*

FREE: *Hey!*

> *(COLE is awake.)*

FREE: Where my cut? *(COLE confused.)* My twenty-five percent, that's one twenty-five outa five dollars, that's two seventeen outa eight sixty-seven, one twenty-five and two seventeen make three forty-two, and that boy show me a twenty-dollar bill, *five* my commission that's three forty-two plus five if you wanna make it easy on yourself you can round my pay off to a even nine bucks.

COLE: Who said twenty-five percent? You ain't lifted a hammer the first nail nobody said nothin' 'bout no twenty-five percent.

FREE: *I* said it! *I* brung in the consumers, you ast for one, I give ya three! Not for my sharp management you be on the subway minstrel-showin'.

COLE: Like you.

FREE: Twenty-five! That's one twenty-five outa five dollars, that's two seventeen outa eight sixty-seven, one twenty-five and two seventeen –

COLE: Okay! But forget the last one, took nothin' from that boy.

FREE: Fibber! You think I'm a *idiot?* I saw you gatherin' the boards don't tell me you made no house!

COLE: I made a shack. I got pride I take no pay for poor work.

FREE: *You* take no pay? What about me? I done my job!

COLE: What happens you overwork your client.

FREE: What?!

COLE: How I'm s'posed to give him a house, sturdy hang-your-hat I ain't slept two days? Any builder worth a dime know what I done lackin' kosher.

FREE: He wanted a roof a dang four walls you made it. Dag! He was the gold, just released from the looney place he had his live-on money, he was the prize you blew it!

COLE: *(Closes HIS eyes.)* Says you.

FREE: *(Pause.)* Hey!

COLE: *(Awake.)* What!

FREE: You still owe me three forty-two.

BEBBIE: *(Enters.)* For what?

> *(SHE sits on the curb, eating from HER bag: burger, fries and a drink.)*

FREE: I'm his agent. *(BEBBIE snorts.)* Mind your business!

BEBBIE: I'm the one he owes the cut, I ain't askin', Cole, I got my own job you keep the reimburse. *(Directed at FREE:)* But if I *was* askin' I'd be gettin' the big money, I'm the one told you about Zekie, don't let Free horse-swindle ya, Cole! Keep two eyes open! Cuz when it comes to cash, Free got three!

FREE: "Don't let Free horse-swindle ya, Cole," don't play like you Cole-protectin' it's Bebbie, Bebbie don't trust her own brother ain't that a crime, and by the way Zekie be only one a three customers, I dug up the rest. And by the way Zekie turn out to be the dud. Cole's work for him on a strickly volunteer basis.

BEBBIE: He had money.

FREE: He didn't pay! (*This line loud and into COLE's ear, waking COLE.*)

BEBBIE: I'm the one gotchu Zekie, Cole, he showed me money, I never woulda sent him to ya I thought he was gonna hold out –

COLE: He ain't hold out. Wa'n't prouda myself, sorry job I done for him. He offered I didn't take.

BEBBIE: (*To FREE*) You ha' me believe he was holdin' back. You ha' me thinkin' lessa my friend Zekie.

FREE: He coulda insisted! I say. Cole go, "Weeeell . . . uh, maybe not so gooda job – " "Okay!" Zekie quick stash the cash back his pocket.

BEBBIE: Sure that's the videographic veritae truth a the event.

COLE: Soon's I get fifteen winks I'm back! Give him all he ordered, before hundred percent satisfied customers, now my record tainted. Him not complainin' but I recognize shabbiness, I ain't lettin' it stand!

FREE: And when you *do* build the house and *do* collect the money, don't forget who you owe, I be around collect mine.

COLE: Lick 'n' a promise. (*FREE and BEBBIE exchange glances.*) Roof for tonight but I ain't leavin' it, advertise my bad work. I be back, tomorra. Make good on that promise.

FREE and BEBBIE: (*Giggling, little kids*) Lick 'n' a promise Lick 'n' a promise!

COLE: I ain't translatin'! I was born below the Mason-Dixon tireda playin' U.N. interpreter to your Bronx asses! Ignorant.

> (*FREE watching BEBBIE eat. Until HE speaks again, COLE will drift in and out of sleep.*)

FREE: My sister won't even offer us lick a the bone.

BEBBIE: Hamburger bone.

FREE: Bun then! Starvin' and she gonna semantics me.

BEBBIE: Not too starvin' or ya woulda complained when I first come in I know why. Had your smörgåsbord. Indian and Thai and smack a burrito, little a this, little a that ain't the garbages filled with delight.

FREE: Guess it ha' to be like that, risk the stomach cramps the pukin' bad meat like last week, guess that be my fate, my very own big sister gettin' a paycheck not loan me a penny.

BEBBIE: Work!

FREE: I work! You got one job I got a hundred and one. (*BEBBIE rolls HER eyes.*) But better 'n us I guess, she got a *taxable* income. Ask where she live.

BEBBIE: I got a job jus' cuz it don't pay enough pay rent don't make it less a dignity.

FREE: Better 'n us I guess, she got a roof well ain't nothin' to brag about. Piled on our cousin's floor, Nadine got a two-room apartment, five kids a man and you know when things get tight who you think gonna be tossed to the street? again?

BEBBIE: Yeah you know it all –

FREE: And don't go knockin' on Mommy's door!

BEBBIE: I never!

FREE: Stress her bad heart worry 'bout homeless grown kids.

BEBBIE: I ain't worry Mommy I ain't you! Homeless with a habit like that ain't her heartache enough.

FREE: She think she way above us, how long before you back in the shelter? Again.

BEBBIE: You say somethin'? My ears plug up when people talk stupid you didn't speak, didja?

FREE: Snob. We grow up same house we see you tonight when be next time? Spring?

BEBBIE: I make it a solemn point visit my blood relative every other week but maybe you ain't always so conscious of it. Crackhead.

FREE: (Soft, to the tune of "Where Is Thumbkin?")
Where is Mesha?

BEBBIE: *(A deep-throated warning)* Stop it.

COLE: *(Suddenly awake)* Where Arnell go? Matthew. And Lindsay. How come everybody we know suddenly gone? This Argentina?

BEBBIE: Cleanin' up the streets.

COLE: And the Speechtalker! 'Member? She had all the words, in English in Vietnamese. Soapboxin' to effect.

> *(MAI appears in a special light. No one sees HER.)*

MAI: *(Speech)* Family of three, how much welfare allot housing? Two hundred eighty-six dollars a month! You ever see New York apartment two hundred eighty-six dollars a month? Guess how much taxpayers pay, house one family in one-room slum welfare hotel? Three thousand dollars a month! Biêť cho cap cho bao nhiêu dê~môt gia-dińh ba ngu'o'i sông không? Hai trăm tám mu'o'i sáu mot tháng!

> *(The indented speeches are spoken simultaneously:)*

> MAI *(Cont'd)*: Máy có bao gio thay nhà o New York mà hai trăm tám không? Do biêť lá nguoì chã thuêť phãi trã bao nhiêu dê gia-dińh dó o môt căn buo'n cuã nhà khách-san bo-thí? Ba ngàn dôńg môt tháng!

COLE: Lotta people get up that grandstand stage, talkin', talkin' say nothin'! But then the

164

Speechtalker take off, some remote corner the audience, *everybody* turn around! Listen!

MAI: Since 1998 number of New York City homeless families in shelters doubled!

BEBBIE: Don't forget the Park. Hundreds residin' happy 'til the city blew the whistle, clear 'em out.

MAI: Sixteen thousand children in the shelters!

BEBBIE: I saw 'em tear down the tents the babies cryin', three years old, four "Out!"

MAI: Number of households on New York City public housing waiting list: one hundred thousand!

BEBBIE: Make the park a safe place for all children got the luck, their parents brag a five-figure paycheck.

MAI: Compassion fatigue! *(Exits.)*

COLE: And Arnell! 'Member her? Arnell had the artistic eye. Sewin', needlepoint she could smell out the right feel: pastel or primary. Soft texture or rough.

FREE: Ain't you Mr. Sentimental soft-shoein' down Memory Lane.

COLE: I was thinkin' . . . I could use me a partner.

FREE: Got one!

COLE: You're a agent, middle man. I spend a lotta time thinkin' how the place be functional, how many rooms, do they like sunlight. These specs all crucial and personalized but. What say I start a business with a decorator. Somebody got the interior eye. Cuz what I sense when I make a client happy is they walk in, think "Hmmm . . . I can make this into home." But what say I make it so they walk in think right away "Hey. This *is* home." *(Pulls a big book out of a hole in a tree.)*

BEBBIE: Hard wood floor? Crystal chandelier?

COLE: *(Flipping through book.)* Gimme a vague idea but buildin' from scrap a more inventive mentality. I need a resident artist, and did I mention the superior homemakin' talents a my ol' friend Arnell? *Where they go?*

BEBBIE: The vans.

FREE: Dog catchers. *(Begins barking, a mad dog. BEBBIE talks over it.)*

BEBBIE: Pick 'em up. Dump 'em in the Bronx I heard. Beyond the sensitive sight sensitive smell a the Manhattaneers.

COLE: *(Hoping not)* They don't.

BEBBIE: Compassion fatigue. Was a time the homeful had empathy for the homeless. Then it got old.

FREE: Fat fib.

COLE: They don't pick up people, urban remove 'em out their homeplace.

FREE: She tellin' a ghost story. Then what? Take 'em to the butcher, sell 'em and . . . Hey. What kinda meat that burger – ?

BEBBIE: *(Mouth full of burger.)* Liketa hear *your* facts! Where else they be.

> *(COLE has been squinting to read, book very close to HIS eyes.)*

COLE: Never touch me. Defyin' the dog catcher, I develop the catnap. My deepest sleep still got one eye open.

FREE: I know where some of 'em be. *(Beat.)* I know where Arnell be.

COLE: Where?

FREE: Maybe she don't want her whereabouts be made public. *(Beat.)* Maybe her whereabouts made public cost a little bit.

BEBBIE: Keep it. How come you don't live in a house?

FREE: Too nomadic. Too free spirit I can play the agent but settlin' myself –

BEBBIE: I was talkin' to Cole. Builder. *(FREE sulks.)* You got the skills. How come you choose to boy scout, make camp some not-too-damage park bench every dusk?

COLE: I dunno. Too picky? Maybe I'm waitin' 'til the idea a the perfect abode come to me. *(Beat.)* That place. Broke glass, walls crashin'.

Condemned school, I wannit. Renovate I could turn it to apartments.

BEBBIE: Apartments? *(COLE smiles.)* Renovatin' – ain't that a departure? Thought you like creatin' from the seed. Renovation you just the maintenance gardener.

COLE: Apartments, lotta people under a roof quick. Sure, ultimate pleasure is my present line a work, few people left in the world feel the frontier sensual, fingers touchin' blank plank, orphan nails and suddenly: walls, roof. But renovation there's a timeline practicality. And no dismissin' renovation, art to itself, I ain't opposed to the investigation. I'll clean, do the electricianry. Figure I bring in tenants 'fore first frost. Tenant number one: Zekie.

FREE: *(Still sulking.)* Zekie Zekie Zekie, what, you give birth to him? Make a mistake, *you* think, now ack like you owe him the world.

COLE: Owe him what I promised! Pride *my* work but why waste my breath. "Integrity" a word you smoked outcher brain long ago.

FREE: Guiltface.

BEBBIE: People *did* live that place, six years? seven back. Didn't they get the boot, the place fortressed by a wall a wood and "No Trespassin'," "Violators Will Be Prosecuted." The signs *and* the fence gradually torn, rotted away. Now you gonna reclaim it for the homesteaders.

COLE: Zackly.

BEBBIE: Pipedreamer.

FREE: "Homesteaders" "Homesteaders" dontcha dare say "squatters"!

BEBBIE: And how the hell you think you gonna get in? Ain't this neighborhood a circus, fulla baton-twirlin' pigs?

COLE: They ain't come around yet.

BEBBIE: *(Looks at HIM.)* You started?

FREE: You don't think I work hard? "I was talkin' to Cole, builder." I work hard, it ain't convention but still a job, lotsa jobs, Cole's agent be jus' one. I got plenty a skills, I spread 'em around. I work harder 'n convention.

BEBBIE: Yeah, I seen you workin' the uptown D recently.

FREE: It's work. *(BEBBIE smirks.)* You couldn't do it. You'd starve.

BEBBIE: Yeah, I'd rather –

FREE: NO! wouldn't *rather* you'd try but no one give you a dang penny *then* you'd starve. You ain't got it. I got it.

> *(BEBBIE studies HIM a second, then holds up a few fries – an offer:)*

BEBBIE: What?

(FREE stands.)

FREE: Ladies and gentlemen. I don't mean to bother you but I'm hungry, I'm homeless. I don't mean to bother you but I use to be like you, I had a job, garbage collector, then the city cuts cut me now I garbage collectin' my dinner If I don't get just a quarter from you, I get the half a Big Mac the rat nibbled on first. Ladies and gentlemen, I use to be like you. My Wall Street high pressure then I get this eye disease can't read the stock market displays no more See me? If I don't get just a nickel from you, couldja just look up from your book please? See me? I was never like you. Ignore somebody like me if I don't get just a red cent I may just haveta put on my display pull down my pants and pee pee your paperback.

> *(FREE snatches fries, sits, eats.*
> *BEBBIE and COLE had been glancing*
> *at each other, perhaps an occasional*
> *giggle.)*

BEBBIE: No. Really.

> *(FREE stands.)*

FREE: Gentlemen and ladies. I don't mean to bother you but I noticed you're new to this 'hood, ten years ago wouldn'ta been caught dead this place after dark or otherwise but ain't it changed, ain't it changed. Here, I got a welcome mat for ya. *(Perhaps does a little jig as HE recites:)*

Ten little pickaninnies

Lyin' in the bed,
One rolled off
And another one said,
"I see your heiny!
It's black and shiny!"

> *(FREE sits. BEBBIE and COLE
> giggling.)*

BEBBIE: No. *Really.*

> *(FREE stands. HE is serious now but
> COLE and BEBBIE, at first, still
> giggle.)*

FREE: It wa'n't a good job but it was okay.
Cleanin' the offices overnight. Come home, hey.
When they paint the halls? Through my own door,
Hey. When they throw out that ol' round thing?
when we get this modern 'frigerator? Hey, when
they finally replace that chipped tub? where come
this new showerhead? Firsta the month: *Hey!*
Twice the rent? Seven years ago I'm out: the street.
Last week I walk by my ol' stompin' grounds, hey!
Who threw out my black neighborhood, replace it
with white?

> *(FREE pauses. COLE and BEBBIE no
> longer laughing.)*

FREE: Then I sing "This Little Light a Mine."
(Pause.) Wamme sing "This Little Light a Mine"?

BEBBIE: If ya want to.

(*FREE considers this for several seconds.*)

FREE: I don't want to.

(*FREE sits. Quiet awhile.*)

COLE: I guess Arnell move out the neighborhood. Uptown.

(*FREE shakes HIS head slowly but doesn't speak. Finally:*)

BEBBIE: We ain't payin' ya, Free! If you waitin' for a business proposition –

FREE: *Down.* (*THEY look at HIM.*) Under.

(*FREE looks at the ground. COLE and BEBBIE look at the ground. Next: a sudden cold wind. ALL shudder, panic. THEY rub THEIR arms, look up to the sky, the elements: fear.*)

BEBBIE: Weather's turnin'.

(*THEY continue staring.*)

Scene Three

(*ZEKIE's house destroyed. ZEKIE, stooped, shivers. HE has scissors, is cutting playing cards into strips. A cardboard box nearby, maybe two feet square, upside down. COLE enters. ZEKIE does not look up. COLE stares at the debris, stares at ZEKIE, what to*)

*do? Takes off HIS parka, puts it around
ZEKIE.)*

COLE: *(Nervous laughter.)* Ain't I unusual. Most
people I know pretty possessive a they coat, slash
anyone come try take it. Well, ain't that cold
nohow. Nip come, fall definitely here but can't say
we tasted no winter yet, no real...

*(COLE stares at ZEKIE, whose
shivering hasn't subsided. ZEKIE
continues cutting.)*

COLE: Under the bridge, I know ain't weather took
it down. Police? Parks people? *(ZEKIE doesn't
answer, continues cutting, shivering.)* Stop the
shivers. (COLE waits. Shivers don't stop.) Stop
the shivers!

ZEKIE: Streetcar! Sayonara! Superman!

COLE: *(Sits on the ground.)* Cranky, pay no 'tention
to me. Bad enough all night bein' kicked awake by
cops, parks workers, but not a wink the forty-eight
before.

*(Stillness awhile. Then ZEKIE tosses
the coat off, goes to the box, lifts it. An
intricately designed apartment building
made of playing card strips. ZEKIE
carefully, expertly, adds HIS freshly cut
pieces.)*

COLE: Ah!

(COLE slowly walks to the complex structure. Touches it gingerly.)

COLE: Beauty!

ZEKIE: Twenty-two 'partments. You want studio? two-bedroom?

COLE: I see it! I picked up that blueprint. And bathroom. Patio. Ground-floor lobby. Closets!

ZEKIE: Basement: Olympic pool, workout room.

(ZEKIE pulls out a tiny barbell to show COLE. COLE laughs, delighted.)

ZEKIE: My house.

COLE: Your house! Take a math instinct, artist mind. Creator! you got the callin'. Skill and the eye, sensa purpose. Ain't you a genius. Aintchu the visionary. *(COLE gently turns ZEKIE's face, forcing HIM for the first time to look at COLE.)* My dream! We nigh onto clashin' pretty in our sights, livin' compartments, units. You liketa come 'round with me? helper? apprentice You like that? *(No answer.)* Don't judge me on this! this my *worse* work no sleep. *(Beat.)* I don't mean to claim there's a reason for a bad job ain't! No excuse. Jus' askin' you trust my word. I got the skills. And need a colleague. You like that? *(ZEKIE nods: COLE pleased.)* I like that! I got a ambitious target in my eyeview. Apartments. Ain't you the perfect thing walk with me. We got a bridge, Zekie, inside. Meetin' a minds. We touch. You understand? *(ZEKIE nods.)* Look.

*(COLE starts to sketch in the dirt.
After a few seconds ZEKIE suddenly
knocks the building apart.)*

COLE: NO! *(Too late. COLE picking up some of the
pieces.)*

ZEKIE: Sunday! Mommy come. Mommy come
Good boy.

COLE: Why you do that?

ZEKIE: *(Ashamed.)* Toy.

COLE: No. Why you say that? Cuz it small? real
person couldn't fit? [ZEKIE nods.] It's real. It's
real.

*(COLE regretfully looking at the pieces
in HIS hand. ZEKIE walks over to
COLE's sketch and rapidly, expertly
finishes it. COLE stares, stunned.)*

ZEKIE: School.

COLE: School! How you know?

ZEKIE: *(Last touches.)* 'Merican flag. Hmmmm . . .
Playground the roof –

COLE: Zekie.

*(COLE gently turns ZEKIE to face
HIM again. Then touches ZEKIE's
head a few seconds, then with the same
hand touches HIS own head. Nods.)*

175

COLE: School. But soon to be homes. Twelve to a floor, four floors and down the road I figure basement studios. You ain't jus' be the builder under my instructions, your input gonna matter. Leave some spaces to your creativity, right? *(ZEKIE nods.)* Partner? *(ZEKIE nods.)* You know Arnell? *(ZEKIE shakes HIS head no.)* You will. Here's how it's gonna be: You and me design the outer structure, split the specialty tasks – like I get a light switch intact while you prepare the exercise room. Then Arnell come, final touch make our house a home: curtain. Couch cover. Interior decorator: that make our team complete. Okay?

> *(ZEKIE goes back to add to the building sketch. COLE sees.)*

COLE: *Air conditioner?* Whew! better leave the project budget to me. *(Beat.)* I got the plans hid. I be back half-hour with 'em.

ZEKIE: Partner.

COLE: *(Grins.)* Wait here.

ZEKIE: Good boy.

COLE: Good boy. Good boy. *(Exits quickly.)*

> *(ZEKIE goes back to the strips and begins starting over, rebuilding the structure. After a bit HE laughs out loud.)*

ZEKIE: Good boy the volts, good boy, volts fix ya, volts run through little boy burn, it alright it

alright. Tom Edison jolt me legs. Chest Mommy
see you Sunday, little boy, Mommy come Sunday
Good boy Blow out the candles. Visitin' Day Hi
Mommy! Blow out the candles little boy Get my
wish! You good boy first year here, Mommy see
you next week you good boy. Mommy see you
next year How many years I been here, Mommy?
26 I'm 26 I remember my birthday here Mommy! I
remember I was a good boy! Good little boy They
gimme the volts I don't cry! Electric volts my head
I don't cry I wake up blow out all the candles my
cake. All nine.

Scene Four

> (*ZEKIE is gone. MARMALADE waits.
> A shopping cart nearby, its contents
> concealed by a garbage bag. COLE
> enters.*)

MARMALADE: You the House Man? You the one
made his house a straw? they huff puff it away?

> (*COLE looks around.*)

COLE: Where – ?

MARMALADE: I'm Marmalade. I'm a singer. I
had another name but I changed it, who's gonna
gig Brenda Aberdeen? Marmalade, just
Marmalade, the cover of my most famous album
Marmalade Jam had me naked in the centerfold and
all these men spreadin' raspberry marmalade and
grape marmalade and what's the yella kind?

Spreadin' it over me with the butter knife. No. Their hands. You know how many bubble baths I had to take, get that stuff offa me? Eight!

COLE: You seen him? Boy in the house where he go?

MARMALADE: You don't have to pronoun him I know his name. Zekie. We serve time together. Hospital 'til our butts chucked to the pavement. All the men marmalade-spreaders was black black and I was white white, whiter than now, producers had me soak in milk days. 1971 we woulda been regarded wholly controversial but it was '91. Wholly pretentious.

COLE: Which die-rection Zekie walk?

MARMALADE: Make me a house! You got the scrap crap right here I want my walls. I need a place to hang my platinum LPs you don't know how many times I woke up the shelter havin' to smack somebody's tricky fingers tryin' to lift 'em.

COLE: Where Zekie gone?

MARMALADE: Tell ya where he's at. When my house built. I know the system, he been dogcatched I can deduce the pound. (MARMALADE shows money.) That just parta the deal.

COLE: (Stunned.) Twenty-two?

MARMALADE: *(Snatches back half.)* Eleven upfront. Eleven when I walk through my front door.

(Beat.)

COLE: How I know you got the knowledge?

MARMALADE: Badgerin' me since howdy-do for the facts, finally I offer, suddenly you the skeptic?

COLE: Cuz suddenly I gotta build a house in exchange for the facts think I like to be sure.

MARMALADE: Buildin' a house in exchange for proper payment and then some! *(Beat.)* Maybe you don't really want the info. Maybe now I'm willin' to give it up you comin' too close to facin' your guilt object.

> *(COLE stares at HER. Then starts looking over the boards left from ZEKIE's house, separating the good from the bad.)*

COLE: Salvage bitta this. But closer to the river I know some cement cubes which I ain't breakin' my back transportin'. You willin' pack up start a new life? Five blocks east?

MARMALADE: Neighborhood good?

COLE: Homesteaders the vicinity, look out for ya.

MARMALADE: I seen it all. 'Boveground and under, I know: location's everything.

COLE: Under? You lived below? *(SHE stares at HIM.)* What it like?

MARMALADE: You holdin' it 'gainst me?

COLE: No, just wonder –

MARMALADE: Don't call me "mole"!

COLE: I jus' –

MARMALADE: Ain't for everybody. Nobody wants tourists down there so we keep our basement adventures to ourself. Thinkin' a movin' south?

COLE: No! *(Shudders. Beat.)* You know Arnell? Ever see her? the Subterrane?

MARMALADE: Know no Arnell. Like sayin' "You know Bob? He lives in Manhattan." *Cities* below the surface! can't know everybody.

COLE: Hard to believe.

MARMALADE: Well if Arno –

COLE: Arnell.

MARMALADE: If he –

COLE: She.

MARMALADE: Whatever! If they new to the down under, I wouldn't know 'em. Topside three years now.

(COLE is staring at a board.)

MARMALADE: What? Termites?! Leave it My abode ain't inheritin' Zekie's trouble!

> (COLE turns the board around so SHE can see. A detailed blueprint sketch plan for the apartment building.)

COLE: Zekie's designs. We had a plan. Apartments.

MARMALADE: If that board's good keep it. I'll paint over the scribblin'.

> (COLE obviously separates this board from the others but MARMALADE doesn't notice. Back to going through the boards.)

COLE: (Not looking up from work) Zekie say anything 'bout me?

MARMALADE: Like what?

COLE: (Shrugs.) I just wonder he say anything. My work.

MARMALADE: Why, you afraid his crazy talk? I known him a long time and lemme tell ya, he was a good little boy. Normal little boy bit hyper, bit gabby, temper tantrum once or twice that ain't normal? *Healthy* boy ain't a thing wrong with him but get on the adults' nerves sometimes so they "treat" him. Here's the treatment: drugs, electrashock. Well. Guess what make him crazy.

COLE: So . . . he didn't say –

MARMALADE: Said nothin'! Superiority complex! what make you think you the lively topic a other people's chitchat?

COLE: Well how else my reputation precede me? Architect.

MARMALADE: He ain't enlightened me to that beat for that I thank the grapevine. For your whereabout specifics I know who hold the information: Anchor.

COLE: Anchor?

MARMALADE: I call him Anchorman cuz he got all the news and happy to spread it. For a price. Twenty-nine and change I start with, and Anchor say I'm willin' to let loose of it I can get me a house built. But first *he* gotta tell me where to find the Builder, so first seven and a quarter go to him: twenty-five percent.

COLE: Free.

MARMALADE: Need a kingsize bed. Believe the rumors: Weak mattress ain't enough hold all the lovemakin' a superstar produce.

COLE: How you know Free?

MARMALADE: Three years ago, Bebbie and me on the same gig, onct or twict Free visit. Parcheesi, our matches was struggle to the death. We got a rapport by then but first time I seen her, thought she was a cat.

COLE: Cat?

MARMALADE: Me and Zekie roamin' the corridor, he talkin' 'bout all his relatives. How Vivian lost the land, she come on a streetcar to visit sister Kim but Kim's husband Marlon so mean to Vivian. Move by the day room, that place full of cats, still as stone, they fade to the furniture.

COLE: Cata*tonics.*

MARMALADE: This new statue, drool her chin, out the blue slowly turn her face I feel I'm lookin' at some shop window movin' dummy. Here's Bebbie, Bebbie the cat: *(Moves HER head like BEBBIE.)* "Desiiiire," she say. "Desiiiiiire." Then dead asleep.

Scene Five

> *(Shelter. Dark. COLE on a cot, sitting up, blanket over HIMself, shivering. Periodic moaning in the background throughout the scene. Eventually COLE notices a tattered duffel bag under the next cot, where BAY lies. Part of ZEKIE's cap is visible sticking out of it. COLE moves toward the cap. When COLE is close, a switchblade in BAY's uncovered hand snaps open.)*

COLE: Come in peace! Come in peace!

> *(BAY sits up, stares at COLE.)*

COLE: Lookin' for somebody.

183

(Silence: BAY stares at COLE.)

COLE: Zekie. White boy. Skinny. Brando.

(Silence: BAY stares at COLE.)

COLE: *(Moving around like ZEKIE)* Streetcar. Waterfront. 'Pocalpyse –

> *(BAY chuckles to HIMself, lies down. After a few moments:)*

BAY: Don't know him.

COLE: I think ya do. I think that's Zekie's cap ya got. Askin' no questions jus' where he be now.

BAY: What he do?

COLE: *(Taken aback.)* Nothin'.

BAY: Then why ya lookin' for him?

COLE: *(Shame)* Done him wrong. Need to make good on a promise.

BAY: *(Chuckles.)* You lookin' for him cuz you done *him* wrong?

COLE: That. And protégé. I was gonna train him, raise him up, he had the potential. *(BAY chuckles.)* And learn from him! 'Case I sound like I know it all I don't. Parta me. He a piece I didn't know I had missin', now it gone again.

BAY: Here. Disappear. Who knows.

COLE: I ain't gettin' mad cuz you stole from some defenseless crazy boy, jus' thought maybe he mention where he might be headed.

> *(Brief scream in the distance. COLE jumps. BAY laughs.)*

BAY: You ain't a shelter frequenter.

COLE: Hate 'em.

BAY: Sleep under the stars. Jus' the steam from the subway grate keepin' ya warm ain't you the Outdoor Woodsman.

COLE: I'm all in favor a housin'. Shelter. This ain't shelter. This is . . . I don't know. Punishment.

BAY: Whatchu got better?

COLE: I'm a builder.

BAY: *(Uninterested.)* So I heard.

COLE: Who toldja? Zekie? *(No response.)* Work I need to do, 'complish 'fore I settle myself. *(BAY's eyes closed.)* I got a ambition. Apartments. Promised I do it with him and promises I keep. But lookin' for him holdin' up the work. But doin' the work less efficient minus his input plus I be distracted worried where is he –

BAY: Maybe he mention somethin'.

> *(COLE looks at BAY. BAY looks at COLE, then BAY holds up three fingers.)*

COLE: *(Searching HIS pockets)* I got it! Three bucks I definitely . . . *(Turns HIS pockets inside out: empty.)*

BAY: You got it.

COLE: I *had* it! I had it WHO STOLE IT? Fucker mother FUCKER WHO STOLE MY MONEY? I'LL FIND OUT! SOMEBODY BE SORRY I'LL FIND OUT! *(HIS yells, all directed to the others, are answered by "Shut the fuck up," etc.)*

BAY: Tryin' to getcher ass kicked *hard* outa here.

COLE: I had your price –

BAY: Yeah.

COLE: I had it I'LL FIND IT! *(Yell to the others.)* I just done a job, put up a house I had your cash 'til – *(Beat.)* Listen. I could owe it to ya. *(BAY snickers.)* I could pay ya, bigger 'n money. House I build worth lot more 'n goddamn three dollars –

BAY: Want no house.

COLE: Twenty-four hours! You wanna shower? Hook your place to the underground pipes. Space heater? TV?

BAY: Want no house!

MAN: Bay!

> *(A MAN has entered, stays in a corner. BAY gets out of bed, walks over to the MAN. BAY walks with an exaggerated limp. An exchange: money passes from*

*BAY to the MAN, the MAN passes
something to BAY which BAY quickly
pockets. The MAN exits, BAY limps
back to HIS cot, sits on it. Eyes COLE
suspiciously.)*

COLE: Don't worry 'bout me I ain't interested in
whatever you got. Crack, smack, forget it I'm
clean, no thievery nor freeloadin' here.

*(BAY takes the object from HIS pocket.
It is a bottle of lotion. BAY lifts a pant
leg. HIS leg is hideously diseased and
dry. BAY begins sparingly applying
lotion.)*

COLE: Well. I don't know how to pay ya and I
need that information. Fifteen dollars and sixty-
three cents I walk in here with now empty pockets.

(Pause.)

BAY: Fifteen eighty-one.

(COLE looks at BAY.)

BAY: Feel cheated. Heard you pulled ten and a
quarter yesterday plus the more recently acquired
eleven down payment I shoulda pulled twenty
plus.

*(BAY starts chuckling. COLE, furious,
starts toward BAY. BAY grabs the
knife, which HE'd lain on the cot.
COLE backs off.)*

BAY: Least accordin' to that crackpot, come take white boy away. "Man gonna walk in here, got twenty-one and change on him," he says. "Easy pick." I give him the interested look. "But settin' this up," he goes on, "I need a itty bitty advance. Five thirty-one," he says, "my usual cut.

> *(The following indented speeches are spoken simultaneously:)*

BAY *(Cont'd)*: Twenty-five percent."

COLE *(Seething:)* Twenty-five percent.

Scene Six

> *(FREE smokes from a crack pipe.)*

FREE: *(Sings)*
Where is Mesha? Where is Mesha?
Here I am. Here I am.
How are you today, sir?
Very well I thank you.
Run away. Run away.
Where's Ricardo? Where's Ricardo?

> *(Now notices COLE, who has entered.)*

COLE: Where's Zekie?

> *(FREE holds up fingers.)*

FREE: Five bucks.

> *(COLE jumps FREE. THEY are tumbling. THEY finish, panting.)*

COLE: Five bucks? How the hell I'm s'posed to have five bucks that shelter punk stole every cent I had! Backstabber! Everything you got go into your goddamn pipe Everything your friends got into your goddamn pipe! If I wanna call myself your friend *no more!* This friendship costin' me my livelihood my life!

FREE: Who said "friend"? I don't recall "friend" all I ever said was "business partner" I don't cost your livelihood I *make* your livelihood! How many customers you bring in yourself? Spent the night in a homeless shelter least two hundred potential clients there how many hits ya make? None! Don't even haveta answer so committed to your fierce manhunt for a boy you don't see the forest!

COLE: I remember a time I raise a house, eat awhile, raise a house, eat. Little money in my pocket. Then you decide you gonna represent, suddenly I kill myself, house after house no sleep. And no money! Ain't that a fun pun on me!

FREE: Any fool know to keep his hand clutched to his cash the shelters.

> (COLE jumps FREE again, a brief
> tussle.)

COLE: How he know I *had* the money! Stake me!
(Beat.) Why I even try reason with you. Junk brain.

> (COLE starts to leave. Just before HE is
> gone:)

FREE: Took him down. Arnell's. *(COLE stops, looks at FREE.)* Protect him from the shelters.

COLE: You mean strategize him for your profit.

FREE: *(Flat)* Yeah I ain't got a decent bone my body. *(Puffs on pipe, COLE stares. Suddenly:)* Don't it suppress the stomach pangs?! Better high than hungry. *(Puffs more, then looks at COLE.)* Scared to go down, aintcha? *(No answer.)* You askin' eager 'bout Arnell but make no move toward her once you apprised to the information you freaked to go down!

COLE: No! *(FREE chuckles. Quiet awhile.)*

FREE: Someday I be holdin' down the job. Six figures. Not you. You the freelance prince 'til the day you die go ahead! Scrape 'til you kick in not me. Call me Mr. Corporate I can pass the proper yessirs skip the brown-nose jig. *[Stares at pipe.]* Authority I understand.

Scene Seven

> *(ARNELL's place: tunnels beneath Manhattan. Very comfortable: tables, chairs, grill, pots. Along the walls, several elaborately embroidered tapestries. Lit by a single ceiling bulb.*
>
> *ARNELL on the couch embroidering. MAI seated on the floor wearing cassette player headphones. SHE conducts music. EM wandering around inside and outside the place, searching:)*

EM: Meow meow meow meow meow meow meow meow meow meow meow meow meow

ARNELL: Homework.

EM: I done most of it I gotta find my cat meow meow meow meow meow meow meow meow

ARNELL: That filthy ugly thing be back. Feed a cat your place suddenly a revolvin' door.

> (COLE enters. ARNELL, MAI and EM look up, startled. COLE is startled to see MAI.)

COLE: Free point me the general direction off 14th Street platform. Darkness, I touch 'n' go resta the way. Hi Arnell.

ARNELL: Hi Cole. This my roommate Mai. *(MAI, who has removed headphones, nods.)* You know Em.

COLE: Em! I remember a little baby girl, this look like a growed woman.

EM: Girl!

COLE: Thought she with her daddy, what his name? Lare. Ain't Lare got the roof 'n' walls?

ARNELL: Was with him, didn't work. How you find us? Stranger our darkness.

COLE: Pick up my clues.

ARNELL: Lucky you ain't kilt, you know nothin' 'bout the ins 'n' outs a down under.

(COLE nods, HIS fear at having made the trek now apparent.)

COLE: Tiptoe. Why I startle you sorry. Didn't know who . . .

(Pause.)

ARNELL: What compel you journey beneath, Cole?

COLE: Free know where you been, me not a postcard. Wa'n't we friends?

ARNELL: Think that trickster be down here on the invite? Found his own way, who knows his reasons but you can bet they got a dollar sign in front. How much he charge *you?* Plenty, knowin' Free.

COLE: Free.

ARNELL: *(Surprised.)* Tea? Got the herbal, or caf.

COLE: Caf.

ARNELL: Dark eye circles. Look like caffeine a drug you better be checkin' your abuse on. *(To EM:)* Homework.

(EM sits at a child's table, works with HER pencil and crayons. ARNELL goes to get tea. MAI puts HER headphones back on, resumes conducting.)

COLE: Grown girl. We was at Riverside Park that night admirin' the sundown. Here come Lare, and her, new girlfriend, and Em, hardly high as their knees. She jumpin' happy, sight a you.

ARNELL: Most times I come see Em, she stuck in her room watchin' TV cuz Lare and company gettin' romantic all over the house. Once I drop by the school. Twenty degrees, Em on the playground shiverin' her pink spring sweater. "Where your coat?" "Daddy couldn't find it," she say, told her she oughta keep up with her stuff and sent her dressed for summer in the freezin'. Guess she try be a stepmother, just too young and dumb. But him. No excuse neglectful bum, only cuz his mother make him do he go for full custody. And once they cut my welfare, evict me and Emmy to the street, he get full custody. *(Has brought two cups of tea.)*

COLE: Sorry.

ARNELL: Hated welfare! But least I home to care for her, least enough put food on the table. Next, welfare reform, I forced to get a job, but job I can get don't make the rent let alone the babysittin' fees. Here costa livin' completely covered, this I call my welfare reform home. *(Shrugs.)* Her nothin' daddy outa our life anyway.

COLE: Outa your life legal?

> *(ARNELL sips HER tea, no answer.*
> *COLE looks around.)*

COLE: Some place. The electricity ... ol' Exit signs. Lively subway once. Ancient history.

ARNELL: Showers. Water pipes, the city provide all the raw materials. Can make a decent life here don't take but a hair's width a ingenuity.

COLE: This where everybody disappear? Underground? *(No answer.)* I remember Mai. Speaker. She useta stir homeless up. She useta be the moutha the park, "budget cuts" and "filthy hotels" and "murderous shelters," she raise a uproar in English then raise a uproar Vietnamese. *(Beat.)* Rumors FBI snuffed her out. Rumors she snuck a boat back to 'Nam meanwhile she right under our nose. How you rate? shackin' with the famous.

ARNELL: She's a welcomer. How long ago now? year? Me and Em wanderin', stumble on the place. She jus' claim it day before. I say, "This a nice parta the tunnel?" She say, "I dunno, jus' moved in. Guess we both find out." Her invitation for a roommate. Build it together. I ain't got your memory though, I ain't recognized I'm livin' with celebrity 'til I hear her preach. Church.

COLE: Church?

ARNELL: Our church. Buddha her father, Jesus from mother. Catholic. She get her inspiration from the classical music station.

COLE: You get radio here?

> *(ARNELL points to wires from the radio leading through a hole in the ceiling.)*

COLE: Genius.

ARNELL: *(Indicates MAI)* Her genius.

COLE: Warm, your home. *(ARNELL smiles.)* Why?

ARNELL: Why what?

COLE: Why she invisible? Why you invisible?

ARNELL: To you. *(Beat.)* Overlookin' the obvious. Ain't I my daughter's kidnapper?

EM: *(To COLE)* Wanna see my rabbit?

> *(EM has a piece of chalk and sketches on the wall.)*

COLE: Very good. I can draw too.

> *(COLE sketches.)*

COLE: Know it? *(EM shakes HER head no.)* Parthenon, Greece. 432 B.C.

> *(COLE sketches. Points to it. EM shakes HER head no.)*

COLE: Temple of the Sun, Mayan. Chiapas, Mexico, 642 A.D.

> *(COLE sketches this. Points to it. EM stares.)*

COLE: TWA Terminal, Kennedy International. New York City, 1962. A.D.

> *(EM snatches the chalk from HIM.)*

EM: Wanna see my rabbit?

*(Before COLE can answer, EM pulls
back a curtain to reveal HER bedroom,
mattress flat on the floor and blankets.
A brand new big needlepoint bunny on
the wall.)*

COLE: Your mama's an artiste. *(Gently touches a
tapestry, looks at ARNELL:)* Truly.

ARNELL: Thank you. Whatchu want, Cole?

COLE: Two things. One: white boy. Seen him?
(ARNELL stares.) Free tol' me he sent him to you.
(ARNELL stares.) Why I b'lieve 'at liar.

ARNELL: Zekie. *(COLE, surprised, nods.)* Here.
Gone. Local rule: women and children only.
There's a men's neighborhood, I offered to show
him but he had the scare in his eyes. Found his
own way out.

> *(COLE slumps in a chair, exhausted.)*

COLE: How long I gotta do this? Wild goose.

ARNELL: Said two things.

> *(COLE forces a temporary recovery
> from HIS frustration.)*

COLE: I got a proposition. Sizin' up the client
needs, build four walls up from the ground to meet
'em, I got the skill. Now: bigger plans. Got my eye
on reclaimin' what we had once, convertin' that
P.S. 'round the corner: apartments.

> *(Beat.)*

ARNELL: That ain't no proposition but nice information. Luck to ya.

COLE: Inside: fancy touch. Curtain, doily. Tapestry. Somethin' make 'em walk in, feel at home. *(Beat.)* Look at this place! You got the arteye! The Midas magic, could make a lotta people happy plus nickels in your pocket. Ain't that the ultimate? Work give ya pleasure, others pleasure, *and* meat to eat.

ARNELL: What're you talkin' about?

COLE: I need a partner.

(ARNELL *stares at* HIM.)

ARNELL: Forget it.

COLE: *Why?*

ARNELL: Deaf? Toldja I stay below.

(COLE *stares at* HER.)

COLE: *Forever?*

ARNELL: Your words. Warm. Home.

MAI: *(Removes headphones.)* Don't let her bulldoze! Sure utopia now but *on our toes!* Seen what happen to other 'hoods, two miles uptown, south by the bridge, three months ago they come close! Down the track, remember? Find your house, destroy! They say protect us, police say get us to fresh air, safe from moving trains bullshit! *(Beat.)* We a happy family. Now. *(Beat.)* No guarantees. *(Starts to put headphones back on.)*

COLE: Thought you couldn't hear under them 'phones.

MAI: *(To COLE)* Presumer.

COLE: I remember you! You had the passion the dramatic rise. You could whip 'em up, united front!

> *(MAI stares at HIM another moment, then returns to HER place, increases the volume so it now can be heard outside of the headphones, puts headphones back on, resumes conducting.)*

COLE: You like bein' invisible, Mai? That help the situation a whole lot, while the city play the fascist. We poor so they got the right to pick us up 'gainst our will, whisk us away to shelters, wherever, 'boveground half the people I know jus' vanished don't tell me it's cuz Mr. Mayor come down offer 'em all jobs. What you used to say? your math: Democracy plus capitalism equals free the rich, smash the poor.

MAI: I ain't thirty-five no more.

COLE: Now you old enough disappear yourself save them the effort. I got eyes to the yet to come! And down here to share 'em, ask solidarity, I get the fast no.

MAI: "Solidarity." You got a rich-quick scheme, hope for accomplice.

COLE: I wanna get us up and out. *(Beat.)* What *you* suggest? Let the buildin' rot? Cuz the less improvements they make, the less taxes legal owners have to pay weren't them your words?

ARNELL: Don't come down here pickin' a fight, Cole.

COLE: Tax system awards negligence while how many New York homeless? Skin exposed to the perils a the freeze and the thieves.

ARNELL: Quiet!

(Silence.)

MAI: 70,000. New York homeless.

EM: *(Suddenly calls into the distance)* Meow meow meow meow. *(OTHERS, startled, turn to HER. EM puzzled.)* I thought I heard my kitty. Thought I heard a rustlin' the distance.

ARNELL: *I* got a proposition.

> *(ARNELL pulls out a big sheet of dirty plastic, not quite clear. A huge tear in it.)*

ARNELL: Need a replacement. Our church window, kept out the cold the weather 'til who-knows-who vandalized it see? We think it a miracle, Jupiter Effect. Our temple levels beneath the street but perfect alignment so a little topside light come down reach us. We find it a holy thing, we call our church Ánh sáng.

MAI: *(Correct pronunciation)* Ánh sáng.

ARNELL: The Light.

> *(Beat.)*

COLE: You askin' me to replace it? *(ARNELL nods.)* You namin' me Errand Boy?

ARNELL: Favor.

COLE: You ask me to favor you after you just refuse me ain't that clever.

ARNELL: My appeal to you's a one-time requisition! You askin' me to give up my house and home my *child*, move up there to the blindin' bright, the rain and snow, take up a new occupation cuz it be convenient for you!

> *(COLE looks at ARNELL. Then takes the plastic.)*

COLE: Filthy.

ARNELL: Dulls the glare. Now we got no barrier, all wearin' sunglasses to Sunday services. If sheet you find too transparent don't worry 'bout it. We muss it.

COLE: *(Beat: decides.)* I'll get it. I'll get it and bring it back to your church.

MAI: No.

COLE: No?

MAI: Church is women only. We never make that rule it just work that way now we all come comfortable.

COLE: I wanna see your church I like churches. Gargoyles. Stained glass. I wanna see how your scrap worship place measure up When I bring back your plastic window I'll meetcha there.

ARNELL: Never find it. And we ain't tellin'.

COLE: I'll find it. Found *this* place I'll get my feelers, gather the evidence I'll grope my way to the holy house.

ARNELL: Good luck.

COLE: See ya Sunday.

EM: A black cat cross my path.

> *(EM shows HER homework. On the*
> *lower half of the page are lines for a*
> *child to write text. The upper half has*
> *no lines and here EM has colored a huge*
> *black cat and a little human mother and*
> *child.)*

COLE: That your pet? One you tryin' to meow out?

EM: No that guy's tan. *(Reads:)* Black cat cross my path. Bad luck Mommy say. Cat disappear everything dark. Everything black but cat's eyes yellow low glow.

(EM shows another colored drawing: yellow cat eyes in the black. MAI looks it over.)

MAI: Good. Not <u>A</u> plus. *(EM looks at HER.)* How many <u>S</u>s, "disappear"?

(EM looks at HER paper, confused, then back up at MAI who holds up one finger. EM smiles, corrects.)

COLE: *(Chuckles.)* <u>A</u> plus. Must be bored down here, Mai, now spend your time Play School?

MAI: Think we got no school? Other kids here. (COLE is surprised.)

EM: *(Reads)* One night I dreamed everybody had cat heads. I brought them milk but they said We can't have milk it makes us pee.

(Shows HER drawing: girl offering milk and cat with "Pee!" in a cartoon balloon.)

COLE: That ain't the enda the story. What happen next?

EM: *(No longer reading.)* In the dark I spy the cat again. For sure it was a cat, yellow eyes in the dark. But then the cat went Quack Quack.

ARNELL: Ain't no cat go "Quack Quack."

EM: Quack Quack.

ARNELL: Tellin' a tale want the teacher to <u>F</u> you?

EM: *(Jumping.)* Quack Quack Quack Quack

> *(EM is jumping and "quack"ing around
> the room. SHE and the ADULTS
> laughing.)*

MAI: *(Suddenly:)* Sh!

> *(Silence. MAI listening, ARNELL and
> EM tense, COLE confused. Several
> moments, then suddenly again:)*

MAI: *(Whisper)* Go!

> *(ARNELL quickly picks up EM, runs.
> MAI grabs COLE by the arm, turning
> the overhead light bulb to extinguish all
> light before THEY rapidly exit. In the
> black: rustling, flashlight beams. At
> first the lights wildly roam the area.
> Then settle directly on the home,
> examining all of it. Obviously the
> inhabitants were missed by moments:)*

COP: Dammit!

> *(The two COPS enter the space from the
> direction EM had entered after SHE'd
> heard the rustling. Kicking, tearing,
> grunting. In the darkness, little of the
> action is visible to the audience.
> Occasionally a flash of light on THEIR
> badges identifies THEM as COPS but
> THEIR faces remain unseen. THEY
> exit.*

*Dim lights up. The place is in a
shambles. Furniture busted. EM's
story, the plastic window, the curtain to
EM's room, and all embroidery pieces,
including the one ARNELL was
working on, in shreds.)*

End of Act One.

Act Two

Scene One

*(Darkness except for a flashlight:
BEBBIE holds it for COLE who is
fiddling with open wires in a fusebox.
COLE gives wires a few twists:)*

COLE: One. Two. *Three.*

*(Sudden bright light everywhere. Now
audience sees THEY are in a basement
and that FREE is there too. BEBBIE
cheers.)*

BEBBIE: Move the people in!

COLE: Gotta check upstairs. Jus' cuz electricity in
the basement don't necessarily mean it everywhere.
But looks good.

BEBBIE: And your wirin' a course. Quality-control
your wirin'.

COLE: Take a look at the boiler: heat.

BEBBIE: Faulty wirin' no joke.

COLE: And once I get a little advance rent, maybe pool the money for paint. Wouldn't it be nice cover up 'em ol' fingerprints?

FREE: Wouldn't it be nice provide some shelter 'fore the subzero hit? nobody waitin' around for the Hilton!

COLE: Sure. Boiler the priority, wall paint the B list.

BEBBIE: Thought you want Zekie's input?

COLE: (Sad.) Couldn't wait forever.

BEBBIE: You still lookin' for him?

COLE: Feel like I been lookin' for him years. Chill's set in, I can't leave potential tenants to freeze while I ... (Pause.) This place fill quick. I wanted a nice live-place for anybody move in, functional, but no Zekie I ain't got the time. So they half-baked? Least save some lives.

BEBBIE: Toldja I know where he is, where they –

COLE: Need a brain break. Extracurricular.

> (COLE goes to a plastic garbage bag filled with glass – bottles, etc. – and begins slamming it, smashing it into small pieces. Spills out the bits, then puts on protective rubber gloves.)

COLE: (To FREE) Any empty caps?

FREE: Quarter apiece.

*(BEBBIE snatches FREE's tattered
backpack and pours out the contents,
grabbing the emptied crack vials.)*

FREE: Hey! *(Grabbing stuff back.)*

BEBBIE: You ever hearda givin' without gettin'
back? Think your karma could use the bonus
points and how many you got in here anyway?
Whatchu need with empty caps? *(Gives to COLE.)*

FREE: *(To COLE)* Whatchu need with empty caps?

*(COLE doesn't answer. HE has rubber
cement and is working on a mosaic with
the glass and plastic.)*

BEBBIE: Whatchu doin', Cole?

COLE: 'Nother contract no worry. Ten minutes
here then over to the boiler. What time – 7:20?

BEBBIE: *(Looks at HER watch.)* 7:18.

COLE: Pretty good with the guessin' after sold my
wristwatch few winters back. 7:18. Fourteen,
fifteen hours' work easy 'fore bedtime.

FREE: Joke! Apartments, how long you think
Powers That Be let you stay?

COLE: Got the right. Sweat equity, 'member it?
'80s, you could trade renovation labor for a land
title. Or the other school a thought: nobody made
the land, land oughta belong to nobody.
Everybody. Henry George, 1871.

FREE: If Henry George ain't got the deed to hand over, his share-the-land philosophy don't mean too dang much.

COLE: How your butt get gentrified to the street? So landlord finally fix up the buildin' it ain't just that. Cleanin' the streets, the schools, bringin' the infrastructure, thousand things upgrade your block, who done 'em? Taxpayers. Taxpayers done the big investment, taxpayers of which you were one but who got the profit? Taxpayer I'm lookin' at got nothin' but the boot.

FREE: Talk talk.

COLE: I ain't takin' it. Changes.

FREE: Always been poor people, always be poor people. American way.

COLE: Lettin' the cold and hunger drop ya deep pit a despair, I seen it too many times. 'Case I ain't mentioned before, I'm a fair-weather friend. Blues too contagious, you drownin'? Call me once you found your life preserver.

FREE: Who's blue? I ain't blue, you the one blue cuz you know what I am: realistic.

COLE: Kiss my ass.

FREE: Kiss *my* behind.

BEBBIE: Cole. When you project it be ready? And who – How you decide who get in first?

FREE: Busted! Nadine putcha out, huh?

BEBBIE: No! *(Pause.)* Enda the month.

FREE: *(Guffaws.)* Knew it! Whatchu do now? Ain't
never been a happy subway-grate camper.
Shelters! Your friends the shelter cops sure be
happy see ya.

BEBBIE: Shut up!

FREE: One chance I have be a uncle again but
Bebbie learn this trick with a hanger.

BEBBIE: NO CRACK BABIES!

FREE: Coulda been the cause of a blessed event but
dontchu put a stop to that.

BEBBIE: He talkin' 'bout rape! He talkin' 'bout
shelter cops rapin' me so I get my stuff history! A
former self, why you got nothin' better to do than
bring it up?

FREE: Don't rape imply force? I don't remember
nothin' 'bout no force you needed the high as I
recall it was pretty much a free trade agreement.

BEBBIE: Don't know why I even answer back when
I oughta learn to *ignore!* Ignore the crack, what
make you evil.

FREE: You mean lacka crack.

BEBBIE: What's the difference? Crack problem
always immediately followed by lacka crack
problem.

FREE: I still ain't heard how you plan to solve the homeless problem.

BEBBIE: Cole! *(Beat.)* How you – ? Who you got in mind – ?

> *(COLE pulls from HIS pocket a wrinkled piece of paper and pen. SHE is confused.)*

COLE: The wait list.

BEBBIE: Oh.

COLE: Save a few rooms for special needs. Special needs is women with children. *(Not unkind:)* That ain't you.

BEBBIE: Oh. *(Pause.)* No exceptions to the rule huh. Friends?

COLE: Situation change, some people get a check out the blue, or go home to their family, Arizona, wait list'll let up. Eventually.

> *(BEBBIE sadly sighs as COLE goes back to work.)*

BEBBIE: What about – ? What if somebody find ya Zekie. They get bumped up the list?

FREE: Zekie?

BEBBIE: Ain't askin' for special favors! Even the basement. Even a ol' office.

COLE: If I had it to give to ya –

BEBBIE: But what if I did? Find your right-hand man.

COLE: I scour the city north to south, topside and under, no sign a that boy but you just up unearth him.

BEBBIE: You ain't looked everywhere. How many times I gotta repeat it? Dumped. Bronx.

COLE: Not that again. (*Teethes a glove off to work more closely.*)

FREE: Zekie and the dogcatchers! (*Starts barking.*)

BEBBIE: So find him? bring him back? I get walls?

COLE: Ain't goin' to so no point –

BEBBIE: But what if I did?

COLE: Dumb talk –

BEBBIE: But what if I did?

FREE: "But what if I did?" "But what if I did?"

COLE: How I get the job done you two gnats buzzin'!

FREE: You the one ask me be the lookout while you slip in, I'm doin' you the favor.

COLE: I paid you that ain't a favor.

BEBBIE: Cole lost Zekie in the parlor but look in the den cuz light better there. *Safer.*

COLE: Why you still – ?

> *(COLE suddenly makes a sharp sound, having accidentally cut HIMself. Sucks HIS wounded finger. FREE laughs.)*

FREE: Look! kiss his finger better! This our fearless savior, the architect!

COLE: *(Back to work, not looking up at THEM.)* Where you meet Zekie?

FREE: I remember the day I first see him, all alone he is, I stroll by –

COLE: Not you.

BEBBIE: *(Shrugs.)* I dunno. Wanderin' the street, talkin' to hisself. He was lost –

COLE: I think you meet him same place you meet Marmalade.

FREE: Hah! Onta ya!

BEBBIE: Why you wanna know? *(COLE shrugs.)* Sound like you already do. Sound like I bringin' up a truth you don't wanna hear, yeah, any a us be picked up anytime taken away Zekie case in point! So guess you figure be mean to me, hope it shut me up well might shut me up but don't change the facts.

COLE: Facts!

BEBBIE: Ain't my fault your sloppiness screw that boy over now he who-knows-where with who-knows-who doin' who-knows-what to him.

COLE: If you a looney fine jus' wisht ya told me!

BEBBIE: What's it to ya?

COLE: Useful info. Know how much to take your talk serious.

FREE: (To COLE) Like anybody take you serious, "I build the 'partments, I build 'em 'fore winter" shoot. Anybody be silly trust your word your word mean doo doo.

COLE: You ain't comin'! Don't ask for tenancy you ain't invited!

FREE: Boody hoo hoo! I can't be parta your fiction high-rise dream it ain't gonna happen! Shoot, you act higher 'n I ever got.

BEBBIE: Even ol' closet just a bit Cole! Please! Find Zekie don't I deserve six feet a floor space?

COLE: Okay! I ain't kind to get your hopes up you ain't findin' him but promise you leeme 'lone sure!

BEBBIE: I be back! Me and Zekie! I find him by supper back tonight!

FREE: You ain't findin' him.

BEBBIE: Will, and me and Zekie be wavin' at you down on the street from our fourth-floor window.

FREE: You and Zekie ooh maybe then I get a little halfie, half-color halfwit nephew. *(To COLE)* No hangers in the rooms is they?

BEBBIE: NOTHIN'! You was always nothin' you amounted to nothin', Ghost! Ain't worth the ashes pipe turned you into, your senior year they wrote it right: "Most Likely Be Forgot"!

FREE: *(Softly sings)* Where is Mesha?

> *(BEBBIE slams both palms on the pieces of glass. Silence. Eventually FREE walks over, takes one of BEBBIE's hands. Blood. FREE gently starts to pick out tiny glass pieces, one by one.)*

Scene Two

> *(Park. FREE with blanket, shivering. An ash can nearby. COLE enters.)*

COLE: Get to the shelter. Ten below count the wind chill. *(No answer.)* Free –

FREE: NO SHELTERS! Freakin' shelters they ain't stealin' *me* rapin' *me!*

COLE: Alternative tonight: death.

FREE: Fine! You wanna give yourself up to the wolves your perogative not me! *(Beat.)* Look like col' weather caught up to us but I ain't sayin' nothin'. *(Making a fire in the ash can.)*

COLE: Boiler got a quirk, Free, gotta fix it! I was there earlier, coulda kept meat froze the livin' rooms, You wanna kill the idea 'fore it starts? Let some cop wander in find a froze corpse?

FREE: Witches! I'm doin' my thing, express A to 125th, they sittin' they behinds, maybe 17, maybe 22 tellin' me "Get off the car! We effin' don't wanna hear the tune Go work" I work! Whatchu think I'm doin'? And whatchu think that projects trash does? *nothin'!*

COLE: Drunk? Didn't know you drink but how else you chitchat casual through the treachery.

FREE: I tell 'em "I work!" They say "You 'on't do nothin' but stink, mothereffer" I say "Now ain't that a sweet way for young ladies to talk." They say "Yeah, n-word, like you don't use it" I say "Don't be callin' my mouth my life X-rated cuz yours is I'm better!" *(Tends to the fire)*

COLE: Ain't gonna do it, Free. *(No answer)* That little fire ain't be enough –

FREE: I AIN'T MOVIN'! *(Silence)* Your electrician work done?

COLE: Sure! *So?* You think hands under the desk lamp keep ya 'live?

FREE: You right. Not cut corners, cut corners you lower your standard. Lower yourself to the level a the city. Where I grew up, the elevator inspection notice? Last signoff be decade before. And fires, one year three kids out my third grade burn dead, no arson. Faulty wirin'.

COLE: *(A gust)* Gusts!

FREE: 'Bout once a year Bebbie fall out with
Wendell, come home to me and Mommy. "His kids
too let him watch 'em once!" I'm 23, she 28.
Middle a the night phone ring. Bebbie screamin'.
Her whole buildin': burn to the skeleton. No life
insurance, they Potter's Field all three of 'em.
Wendell. Mesha seven. Ricardo three. Put her in
the crazy house awhile!

> *(Beat)*

COLE: Didn't think you cared.

FREE: MY SISTER! *(Silence)* Evil brother. Ain't I?
Didn't used to be, didn't used to . . . My sister.

COLE: I'm leavin'. *(No answer)* I'm leavin'! Now!
With you or without.

> *(FREE makes no move. COLE starts*
> *toward HIM, a plan to physically move*
> *HIM. When COLE is within inches,*
> *FREE, growling and aggressive, bites*
> *COLE's hand. COLE yell-moans, looks*
> *at FREE. FREE glares. COLE exits. A*
> *few moments' silence.)*

PARKS DEPARTMENT WORKER: *(Off)* You gotta
go to the shelter.

> *(FREE doesn't move.)*

PARKS DEPARTMENT WORKER: *(Off)* You wanna stay warm you wanna stay alive I gotta call a cop, cop come, take you to the shelter.

> *(FREE doesn't move. Eventually shakes HIS head no.)*

PARKS DEPARTMENT WORKER: *(Off)* I gotta call a cop.

> *(PARKS DEPARTMENT WORKER, identifying uniform insignia, enters. Insomuch as possible, HIS face will not be visible to the audience.)*

PARKS DEPARTMENT WORKER: No fires in the park.

> *(PARKS DEPARTMENT WORKER puts the fire out. Exits. FREE continues shivering. The shivering will gradually become more and more violent. After a peak, it will slow down. Slow down. Nothing. Still staring.)*

Scene Three

> *(Underground. Church. Shaft of light. Chaos. MAI preaches passionately. SHE sits on a raised platform cross-legged (lotus, if possible). HER legs will not budge throughout the scene though HER arms may move wildly. ARNELL, EM, and two other WOMEN are the CONGREGATION. EVERYONE, including MAI, wears sunglasses. 1ST*

WOMAN rocks back and forth, periodically "Hm mm"ing MAI's message. 2ND WOMAN sits on the floor playing the electric keyboard in front of HER. The tune is "This Little Light of Mine." SHE plays solemnly with one finger. ARNELL, EM and 1ST WOMAN sing. A button on the electric organ is stuck so the tune is accompanied by a ridiculous beat, disco or polka. EM shakes a bottle with a few pennies inside, accompanying the music. Throughout all this, the constant sound of rushing trains, sometimes under the CONGREGATION, sometimes so loud as to drown out the CONGREGATION.)

MAI: Khi chung minh tao ra cai nha tho nay, chung minh da noi "Nu khong thoi." Day la mot cong-dong co tinh-tuong! Day la mot cong-dong day tinh-thuong! Christ said, "The meek shall inherit the earth." *We've inherited everything below!*" Day la coi thien-lien. Day la dat cua Chua Je-su. Day la dat cua phat. Buddha said, 'Three things cannot be long hidden: the sun, the moon, and the truth." Dem la dep! Coi doi cua chung minh! Khi chung minh tao ra cai nha tho nay, chung minh da noi "Nu khong thoi." Day la mot cong-dong co tinh-tuong! Day la mot cong-dong day tinh-thuong! They say, "God helps those who help themselves." We have! Day la coi thien-lien. Day la dat cua Chua Je-su. Day la dat cua phat.

217

Buddha said, "She is able who thinks she is able."
Buddha said, "Peace comes from within." Dem la
dep! Coi doi cua chung minh! Coi doi cua chung
minh! Coi doi cua chung minh!

> (COLE enters carrying an item wrapped
> in a garbage bag. No one in the
> CONGREGATION expected HIM, and
> THEIR noise gradually ceases. COLE
> pulls out of the bag a stained glass
> window, a beautiful mosaic (the piece
> HE was working on in Two-one)
> intricately created of broken glass, vials,
> etc. Only the sound of the trains (loud)
> remains as HE carries the window
> toward the light source. HE holds up
> the window to the shaft, and the
> CONGREGATION removes THEIR
> sunglasses as the train sounds fade to
> silence. Multicolored light pours
> through, reflecting off the space, off
> EVERYONE. The CONGREGATION:
> joy.)

Scene Four

> (Day. Outside of The Building. COLE
> works on the outside door. Propped
> against the wall next to HIM is the
> board with ZEKIE's sketch blueprint.
>
> A WOMAN carrying an infant and a
> paper grocery bag full of belongings
> enters.)

218

WOMAN WITH INFANT: (Smiles.) I heard doors opened today. Vacancies? (COLE looks up at HER and the baby.) She no trouble! such a good baby make no noise.

COLE: 'S okay.

WOMAN WITH INFANT: (Uninterrupted) Had to leave the hotel, at hotel no 'frigerators so welfare formula go bad so no address and state steal her away they find out no address You won't hear a peep, useta be she scream when the hunger hit hard no more, now she quiet, she 'on't hardly even wake up much no more we be quiet! ideal tenants!

COLE: Welfare ain't gonna count this address so don't tell 'em.

WOMAN WITH INFANT: (Surprised.) Stay?

COLE: You one a the last, special needs rooms 'bout full. Communal fridge for the baby's milk. Three dollars.

> (WOMAN WITH INFANT, happy, eagerly begins pulling many coins from HER pocket. As SHE gets near the end, SHE begins reaching, reaching in HER pocket: not enough. Junk – paper clip, napkins. SHE is near tears.)

COLE: Give ya the credit. Eighty-six cent you owe. (Pulls a key from HIS pocket.) Unlocks this door, outside. No locks on room doors, figure we be a community a trust, anyone break the trust they out. Second floor. 211.

(*SHE looks at the key, then up at COLE.*)

WOMAN WITH INFANT: I'm good for the eighty-six promise.

COLE: I'm assumin'.

(*SHE takes the key, goes inside. COLE gets back to work. A WOMAN enters, HER head low, depressed. SHE stands nearby awhile before COLE notices HER. SHE will keep HER face down, never looking up.*)

COLE: Can't take everyone, not right away. Just a few rooms left, we start with greatest need, later expand. Kids?

(*DEPRESSED WOMAN shakes HER head no.*)

COLE: Where you sleep?

DEPRESSED WOMAN: 'Frigerator box. Six Street.

COLE: See there's somethin', you jus' ain't dependin' on a bench and newspaper.

(*COLE gets back to work. DEPRESSED WOMAN doesn't leave, HER face still down.*)

COLE: Don't look at me like the EAU! I ain't bureaucracy! Sorry, word got around fast, I already got requests –

DEPRESSED WOMAN: Before, here.

(COLE stares at HER, confused.)

DEPRESSED WOMAN: Before, (touches building without looking up) here.

COLE: You one a the ol' homesteaders?

(DEPRESSED WOMAN nods. COLE thinks.)

COLE: Dollar.

(DEPRESSED WOMAN pulls out the money, also much change, counts, gives to COLE. COLE shows HER a key.)

COLE: Outside door. (Hands HER the key.) One oh nine.

DEPRESSED WOMAN: (Still not looking up.) Dollar dollar dollar. Pretty rich. (Chuckles nervously. Doesn't move.)

COLE: Go on.

(DEPRESSED WOMAN hesitantly walks in. COLE continues work. BAY enters. COLE stares at HIM: suspicion. BAY pulls out a bottle of cheap champagne, two cups.)

BAY: Grand openin'.

(THEY smile, drink.)

BAY: You livin' here? *(COLE smiles)* The settler settlin' himself?

COLE: Eventually build me a house. But all these tenants need a super, I serve the purpose the interim. *(COLE holds up a key)* Seventeen. *(BAY stares at COLE, makes no move to take the key)* The basement. This place female heavy, all the sudden I realize could use some man muscle, help with the maintenance. Substitute for me when I out on a contract job. Free rent.

BAY: Me.

COLE: Other men come by, I don't know 'em.

BAY: Whatchu know a me don't exactly make you wanna turn your back, do it.

COLE: *(Shrugs.)* You here, that say somethin'. I'm a fool? I'll know soon enough.

BAY: And how long you think they letchu stay here? Day? Week?

(COLE sets the key down.)

COLE: Change your mind lemme know. I'll notify the wait list. *(Back to work)*

BAY: They gonna come. With their hostility, like it was okay apiece, they tolerate the eyesore, us, awhile, but outa hand now "Stop it!" And don't say "cops," cops ain't the problem, *main* problem, it's everyone else. The "*citizens*," gonna call and complain, think cops get a kick outa it? Waste their

222

time, move us around? Homelessness no crime!
Poverty no crime! Cops got better things to do but
citizens can't stand sighta us, smella us, half of 'em
think they so liberal, so progressive 'til we on *their*
sidewalk citizens can't stand *existence* a us so
citizens push the cops to push us. *(Beat)* Me
always ponderin' why everybody gotta hate poor
people, can't stand sighta people fell in a sorry spot
they can't get outa "Stop the poverty! tired of it!"
They think we ain't?

>	*(Pause. BAY studies The Building.)*

BAY: Where the builder's abode?

>	*(COLE points to a window.)*

COLE: Partitions, turn my big classroom space
from a open loft to a one-bedroom easy. Separate
office. Question I ask people 'fore I build 'em their
house, I ask the same a myself: What the single one
thing define "at home"? *(Pulls a book light from HIS
duffel bag)* Readin' in bed.

>	*(BAY picks up the key and enters The
>	Building. COLE finishes his job,
>	swings the door back and forth a couple
>	times to check the hinges, then picks up
>	ZEKIE's sketch and walks in, closing
>	the door behind HIMself. In HIS
>	apartment the little book light comes
>	on.)*

(Lights change: Day to Night. BEBBIE enters, opposite ZEKIE. SHE carries a filthy garbage bag.)

ZEKIE: Whatchu doin' here?

BEBBIE: Business. Whatchu doin' here?

ZEKIE: You tol' me come. You say Cole lookin' for me say Cole get me a 'partment. There.

BEBBIE: Then why you hidin'? ain't gettin' no apartment he don't know you here.

ZEKIE: Sh.

BEBBIE: How come you hidin'?

ZEKIE: Thinkin'. Thinkin'.

(Beat.)

BEBBIE: Tell him what happened last night.

ZEKIE: Streetcar Guys 'Pocalypse –

BEBBIE: Tell him what happen to me. Last night. *(SHE lies under the plastic bag – "blanket.")*

ZEKIE: No. Don't remember don't remember.

BEBBIE: Zekie, stop hoggin' the cover!

ZEKIE: Don't remember!

BEBBIE: Remember!

(Pause. ZEKIE remains stooped where HE is, now looking down.)

ZEKIE: Julius Caesar Whatchu doin' out here with me, Bebbie? Sayonara They kick you out? Tango.

> (BEBBIE, satisfied that ZEKIE is now reliving the event with HER, closes HER eyes.)

BEBBIE: I *told*ju Takin' you home tomorra. We got a home: Cole's buildin'.

ZEKIE: My buildin'. Cole's/my buildin'.

BEBBIE: Yeah yeah.

ZEKIE: Now.

BEBBIE: No! I don't know this neighborhood, walk to the subway. Rapists. We go in the light. *(Looks around)* Good eye. This place. Safe. We go in the light.

ZEKIE: Bebbie. Why you cry?

BEBBIE: *(Beat.)* Ain't that funny. Lookin' for you five days and you the one spy me all lost and weepy. Last week . . . bad. They cut twenty percent the employees and I among the last hired first . . . "reorganized." Left the apartment every day like work, scared to tell Nadine, puttin' in applications. No calls. Hand to mouth so when Friday come and I ain't got the weekly contribution to the household . . . Well been tight awhile anyway, hearin' the yellin', her and new man . . . I ain't worryin' my poor moms! *(Beat.)* Missed breakfast today. And lunch. You ain't got . . . little somethin'?

*(ZEKIE shakes HIS head no, ashamed.
Then pulls out change.)*

ZEKIE: Quarter. Penny. Penny.

*(HE holds it out to HER. SHE stares at
it momentarily, then lifts the "blanket.")*

BEBBIE: Come on.

*(HE happily jumps in beside HER.
SHE rolls over. Quiet awhile. Then
ZEKIE starts whispering:)*

ZEKIE: Fugitive Kind On the Waterfront Teahouse
August Moon The Godfather Mutiny-

BEBBIE: *(Snaps up.)* You gonna do that all night?!

ZEKIE: Bebbie. Can I have a pancake? Can I have
a pancake breakfast Cole's/my house? I wanna
pancake breakfast everyday. Cole's/my house.

BEBBIE: Tell ya tomorra, Sayonara. *(Lies down.)*

ZEKIE: *(Giggles.)* Tell ya tomorra, Sayonara.
(Giggles.) Tell ya tomorra, Sayonara. *(Giggles.)*

(Quiet awhile.)

ZEKIE: *(Loud whisper)* Bebbie. *(No answer.)* Bebbie,
I gotta tinkle. *(No answer.)* Bebbie, I gotta pee pee.

*(No answer: BEBBIE's asleep. ZEKIE
exits. Quiet awhile, then sound of an
offstage scuffle, laughter. More quiet.
Then:)*

BOY 1: *(Off)* I ain't never played a round without I get my 35 bonus for 63 plus at the top.

BOY 2: *(Off)* Liar.

BOY 1 *(Off)* Yeah you said that when I bragged Backgammon and I whip your ass every time.

BOY 2: *(Off)* Not every –

BOY 1: *(Off)* I'm not talkin' 'bout acey-deucy damn game a luck, I'm talkin' Backgammon, skill hey.

> *(BOY 1 has entered. Smiles at BOY 2, still off. Then BOY 1 kicks BEBBIE. SHE wakes, terrified.)*

BEBBIE: I'm leavin'! I'm leavin'!

BOY 1: Ooooh don't leave yet.

BOY 2: *(Off)* Whatcha got?

BOY 1: God it stinks!

BOY 2: *(Off)* What *is* it?

BOY 1: It's a thing, it's a dirty, smelly – What are you?

BEBBIE: Bebbie.

BOY 2: *(Off)* *What* is it?

BOY 1: It's a bubble. It's a blubber.

BOY 2: *(Appearing in a stage corner.)* It's a homeless!

BEBBIE: Wamme gone?

BOY 1: *(To BOY 2)* Wannit gone?

BEBBIE: I go! Wamme go? I go! Wamme gone?

BOY 2: *Yeah!*

> *(BEBBIE starts to get up. BOY 1*
> *quickly snaps HER back down, sits on*
> *HER.)*

BOY 1: Three ones, a two and a five. I had my three-of-a-kind open I had my full house open-

BOY 2: Who the hell gonna put ones in three-of-a-kind? What a dumb move what a low score.

BOY 1: I didn't say –

BOY 2: Any option beats ones in three-of-a-kind. Next time I pull out the cards and the high-stakes chips, remind me to deal you in, buddy. Patsy.

BEBBIE: Zekie!

BOY 1: *(To BEBBIE)* Shut up! *(Holds HER face in the dirt. To BOY 2) SO* since I KNOWED I didn't want ones for THREE-OF-A-KIND, I gathered up the two and five, try for my full house. Roll. Three and four.

BOY 2: Straight.

> *(BOY 1 has taken out matches, begun*
> *lighting them one at a time, blowing*
> *each out.)*

BOY 1: Thought about straight, but I got a feelin', snatched up them dice, tray and four, shoot 'em out. Ones! All five, second Yahtzee hundred bonus points!

BEBBIE: I can't breathe!

BOY 1: *(Bouncing HIS butt on HER.)* Can ya breathe now?

BOY 2: Beatcha. Once I had everything filled up but twos, toss 'em suckers. I get two sixes, one four, one five, one two. Bein' safe, most limpdicks go for the security a the twos. Not me, leave them sixes, roll: four, four, three.

BOY 1: Lost your twos!

BOY 2: Not even a pause in my action. Grab them babies, slam 'em the cup, roll, boom! Five sixes, double Yahtzee, bonus!

BOY 1: Bullshit!

BEBBIE: ZEKIE!

BOY 1: *(Snatches BEBBIE's torso up, points to the distance)* That what you callin' for? Thing tied to that fence? Snapped him up mid-piss stream, lucky bastard. We said the fifth homeless we find's gettin' it. He was number four.

BEBBIE: NO!

BOY 1: You did not get no goddamn double Yahtzee!

BOY 2: Ask my sister! Weren't she cryin' the loser blues?

> *(BOY 2 has moved forward. Now visible to the audience: BOY 2 holds a gas can behind HIS   back.)*

BEBBIE: Won't come back lemme- *(Beat. SHE stares at BOY 2.)* Whatchu got behind your back?

> *(BOYS start laughing. BEBBIE desperately tries to escape but both BOYS are now on top of HER, holding HER down. BOY 2 pouring the gas on BEBBIE. Freeze as chaos erupts: light beams on The Building, sirens, indecipherable bullhorned speech. COLE rushes out. At some point during HIS speech ZEKIE will go back to where HE previously stood observing COLE.)*

COLE: No gas! No tear gas we're here! Put the guns down *children!* Babies! you firin' into a buildin' you know gots *people?!* Buildin' a *children?!* We *improved* it! Owner sittin' on it, gettin' off scot-free tax-free for lettin' it rot we fixed it now *we* punished? *NO!* OURS! How we s'posed to get a good job? no house. How our kids s'posed to go to school filthy? We take care a ourselves! We here ain't leavin' *You* go! *You* go We ain't invisible *You* disappear! We're here!

> *(One by one the lights from the windows of The Building are turned on.*

*The chaotic noise dies to silence. The
door opens. The DEPRESSED
WOMAN comes out, stands with
COLE. Then WOMAN WITH
INFANT, any other available actors,
then BAY. Simultaneously the BOYS
get off BEBBIE, walk off. BEBBIE sits
up.)*

BEBBIE: *(To ZEKIE)* When ya gonna tell him? Last
night. I went down, ashes to ashes. When you
gonna say?

ZEKIE: Tomorra. *(Beat)* Tomorra Sayonara.
(Giggles sad)

BEBBIE: Tonight. *(Exits)*

*(A beat. Then ZEKIE slowly stands.
COLE sees HIM.)*

COLE: Zekie.

*(MAI is the last to come out of the
building.)*

MAI: *(To the police)* Our house.

Scene Five

*(A wooden fence built up in front of The
Building, blocking the lower level.
Numerous signs: "No Trespassing,"
"Keep Out," etc. COLE slumped,
staring into space. Another "stained*

*glass" window on the ground beside
HIM. ZEKIE pacing.)*

ZEKIE: We have us a house. 'Partments! We rent
'em. No, share 'em. Everybody do their part, I do
the paintin' Cole do the cookin'. I do the laundry
Cole do the electrician Hi Mai! Hi Mai! Hi Mai!

(MAI has entered.)

MAI: Hi Zekie.

ZEKIE: I do the dishwash Mai fix the TV. Color! no
black 'n' white. Mmmmmm . . . 'Cep' for On the
Waterfront. Mmmmmmm . . . 'cep' for Streetcar
Name Desire. Mmmmmmm . . . 'cep' for The Men
'cep' for The Wild One mmmmmmm 'cep' for
Julius Caesar.

MAI: *(To COLE)* You got the lows? *(No answer)*
Never expect it, you. Protesters, we outa jail
quicker 'n the law's plan. That not a hopeful? *(No
answer)* Got no project? Always you got a project.

*(Silence. MAI notices the window,
smaller than the one for the church. In
the pattern it says "BEBBIE" and
"FREE.")*

MAI: Pretty.

COLE: Zekie gonna take me. Their mama.

ZEKIE: Bebbie point it to me Bronx. When we get
there I show ya I show ya.

MAI: Where you stay now, Zekie?

ZEKIE: Sleep at the church but Cole gettin' me a 'partment. Cole and me make 'partments Bebbie said.

MAI: *(Eyes on COLE)* Yes, his promise.

> *(COLE irritated but doesn't look up. MAI takes out of HER bag two beautiful needlepoint doormats, one saying "Cole," the other "Zekie." ZEKIE comes, takes HIS and hugs it as if it were a stuffed animal.)*

ZEKIE: *(Giggling)* Arnell!

MAI: Her apologies. Meant for your grand opening but a little tardy. *(To ZEKIE)* Wipe your feet. Your door.

> *(ZEKIE serious now, possessively holding the mat: No way. MAI looks at The Building.)*

COLE: Ript it apart. Everything I worked, electrical, pipes.

MAI: All?

COLE: Most. Wild tearin'. Missed a few things. Little electricity left, coupla rooms.

MAI: How you know?

ZEKIE: Here ya go, Mai! Here ya go! *(HE touches a board in the "Keep out" structure.)*

MAI: You been inside? 'gainst the law?

ZEKIE: 'Gainst the law! *(Giggles)* 'Gainst the law! *(Giggles)*

MAI: How you get in?

COLE: Window. Then jiggled the lock. Don't take much mechanical brains.

MAI: Increase crack-the-whip signs but not crack the whip? Why cops not stop your loiter? Their protected fortress.

COLE: They come after me. Look at me, fear determination. At first. *(Shrugs)* Weeks go by, cops relax. I got the defeat-face now, cops look at me, no threat.

MAI: No suspicion a threat.

COLE: No threat.

MAI: Why you sneak back in then? *(COLE shakes HIS head)* Tell me I gotta come up and out, face the world now look at you. Surrender. Let the building rot, let the people freeze. 2004: Thirty-eight thousand homeless in the shelters every night, highest in New York City history. Sixty-one thousand vacant New York City apartments –

COLE: *(Trying not to)* I ain't gonna cry!

ZEKIE: Here ya go.

> *(The board ZEKIE has been touching is loose. It moves in. Creaks.)*

ZEKIE: Listen.

MAI: Came upstairs, topside. Try things out, test the water. *(Looks around)* Think I stay. Awhile. Time for a change.

ZEKIE: Throw us out back in we go. Cole. Ain't we a boomerang.

> *(ZEKIE, still holding HIS mat, pushes the board in and steps through the wooden fence. The audience hears HIM open and close the door to   The Building behind HIM. MAI looks at   COLE, then follows ZEKIE into the house,   opening the door to The Building, leaving it   open. COLE considers, then picks up HIS mat   and the window and follows MAI into The   Building, closing the door behind HIM. Visible   from COLE's apartment window: The book light   is turned on.)*

<u>End of play</u>

TAP THE LEOPARD

Script History: *Tap the Leopard* was originally commissioned by and workshopped at the Guthrie Theatre in Minneapolis under the auspices of a Bush Foundation grant. It was also workshopped at New York Theatre Workshop in New York City.

CHARACTERS

(in order of appearance)

LIKA – girl/woman, 12, 28, 29, 35: Acts I and II

NETTIE – woman, 60s: I-i

BUTCHIE – white man, 40s: I-i

WOODROW – man, 70s: I-i

GERTIE Rawlings – white woman, 30s: I-ii

WILLIS Rawlings – white man, 40s: I-ii

AUGUSTUS Freeman – man, 30s: I-ii thru II-iv

MOSES – man, 60s: I-ii

Dr. GEORGE Sherman – man, 30s or 40s: I-iii-a & -b, II-i

SARAH Sherman – woman, 20s or 30s: I-iii-a & -b

CHESTER Sherman – boy, 10: I-iii-a & -b, II-i

LOUIS Russell – man, 30s or 40s: I-iii-a & -b, II-iii

AMELIA Sawyer – woman, 20s or 30s: I-iii-a & -b

Rev. JOHN Gibson – man, 40s or 50s: I-iii-a & -b

MR. LEONARDS – white man, 40s: I-iii-a, -b

CAPTAIN – white man, 40s: I-iii-c

NATIVE AFRICANS – I-iii-c

Kpelle CHIEF – man, 50s: II-I

KPELLE MEN,
 including MUSICIANS – 4 who speak: II-i

QUITA – girl, 12, 18: Act II

ALICE – woman, 40s: II-ii thru II-iv

TOMMY – man, 25, 31: II-ii thru II-iv

BERTHA – woman, 50s: II-iii, II-iv

AUDIENCE MEMBERS – 3 who speak: II-iii

COMBATANT GIRL 1 – III-i

COMBATANT GIRL 2 – III-i

KOLU – woman, 24: Act III

DOUGBA – man, 40s: III-i, III-iii, III-v

TAPPER FATHER – III-i

TAPPER SON – III-i

MARDEA – woman, 25: III-i, III-ii, III-v

JOSEPH – man, 30s: III-i, III-iii

IDP CAMP DWELLER – woman: III-i

CONTRACTORS CAMP DWELLER – man: III-i

MALE VOTER – III-i

ZOE – woman, 70s: III-i, III-iv

FEMALE VOTER – III-i

CHARLES TAYLOR – man, 57: III-i

MR. KONNEH – 60s: III-iii

ESTHER – woman, early to mid-30s: III-iii, III-v

TOBIAS – man, mid- to late 30s: III-iii

BOY COMBATANT – 10: III-iii

SUAH – man, 20s or 30s: III-i

Rev. TAMBA – man, 30s or 40s: III-iv

MIRIAM – woman, 20s: III-iv

AMOS – man: III-iv

CONGREGATION MAN – III-iv

MARGARET – woman, 40s: III-iv

BAIMBA – man, 30s or 40s: III-iv

SMITH – white man, 30s or 40s: III-iv

TAPPERS

All characters are black unless otherwise noted.

A possible doubling scheme with 12 actors:

1. black woman: Lika/Mardea/Miriam

2. black woman: Nettie/Kpelle Man 2/Bertha/Combatant Girl 2/Zoe

3. white man: Butchie/Willis/Mr. Leonards/Captain/Smith

4. black man: Woodrow/Moses/John/Chief/Charles

Taylor/Mr. Konneh/Amos

5. white woman: Gertie

6. black man: Augustus/Tapper Father/Joseph

7. black man: George/Contractors' Camp
       Dweller/Suah/Baimba

8. black woman: Sarah/Kpelle Man
          3/Alice/Esther/Combatant Girl 1/IDP Camp
          Dweller/Female Voter/Margaret

9. black man: Louis/Kpelle Man 1/Dougba/Tamba

10. black boy: Chester/Tapper Son/Boy Combatant

11. black woman: Amelia/Quita/Kolu

12. black man: Kpelle Man 4/Male
          Voter/Tommy/Tobias/Congregation   Man

Act I takes place in the United States: in 1824 Atlanta, 1840 Washington, D.C., and on a ship setting sail from New York City across the Atlantic to Liberia, late 1840 to early 1841.

Act II is set in Liberia, 1841 and 1847.

Act III is Liberia, 2005. Liberians in the 21st Century, as I observed in 2004, were all dark-skinned.

Act One

Scene One

> *(December 24, 1824. From a distance,*
> *the sound of slaves singing in church:*
> *last lines of "Go Tell It on the*
> *Mountain." In a cabin, NETTIE stirs a*
> *stew. HER mouth is disfigured from a*
> *childhood incident. HER 12-year-old*
> *granddaughter LIKA looks on.)*

LIKA: Like a spring bud just 'fore the blossom. Like a shootin' star, sign a good fortune, promise.

NETTIE: Like a rainbow, that God gi' the world, his wrath over, peace. Peace.

LIKA: *Done yet?!*

NETTIE: When it done you glad you waited, meat for you, broff for me, and tomarr, Christmas Day no work! Like a fresh pail a water out the brook.

LIKA: Like a black rat, razor teef. Claws.

NETTIE: Where 'at ugly come from?

LIKA: Where *I* come from? The dirt, Ollie tell me I borned in a hole like a animal, like a bug.

NETTIE: What Ollie know? Ollie the dumbest pickaninny Ollie the laziest thing I ever heared tell of.

LIKA: Ollie say I firs' open my eyes, people say "Name her 'Lika,' she like a mole hatched in a hole, like a worm!"

NETTIE: Ollie work his mouf but never his brains. Get away wif it cuz he light. Cuz he got Massa Butchie's eyes, nose. *(Quiet.)* They whip your mama. Strap her down nine monfs' big, dig a hole, put the belly in the hole, proteck the belly.

LIKA: So it true.

NETTIE: Naw, you was comin' in the hole but they take her out, put her on the groun', cut you out the belly.

LIKA: How come she get it?

NETTIE: Didn't make her numbers. Cotton. They gib us numbers. As' lessa her on accounta big wif you, still she ain't make it. You comin', the pain slow her. She holdin' the tears while the overseer addin', I know she pray he slip, or have mercy, ain't she bringin' inta the world another two toilin' hands?

LIKA: That why they whup her to the grave?

NETTIE: Thirty-nine. 'At 'on't usually mean dead but nine monfs' big . . . Twenty-five she near gone, Massa coulda stop. *(Shrug.)* Guess that make him look soff.

LIKA: It gonna burn black!

NETTIE: Naw, gettin' tender. Juicy. Chicken for my Lika, broff for Grammy. *(A new spiritual from the distant congregation: "Children, Go Where I Send Thee." NETTIE joins in.)* "How shall I send thee? I'm gonna send thee one by one. One for the little bitty baby . . . " *(Continues.)*

LIKA: Chicken stew, and outa *our* garden: carrots, peas, onions. *Our* garden!

NETTIE: Tatas.

LIKA: Tatas! *(NETTIE resumes singing.)* Me and Grammy's garden. White tatas and sweet tatas. And . . .

> *(LIKA takes two biscuits from HER pockets.)*

NETTIE: *(Abruptly cuts off her song.)* Where you get that? *(LIKA, surprised that SHE is in trouble, opens HER mouth to speak but can't.)* You steal from missies' table? *(LIKA shakes HER head a vehement no.)* You steal from missies' table?! *(LIKA: a harder no.)* Gimme here!

> *(NETTIE snatches the biscuits, slapping LIKA's hands, and stomps on the food, smashing them into the dirt floor. LIKA stares in horror.)*

NETTIE: Teach you!

LIKA: She gimme!

> *(NETTIE stops. Beat.)*

NETTIE: Who?

LIKA: Missies. Christmas.

> (NETTIE stares at HER, then at the
> crumbs. Then goes back to the stew.
> Quiet awhile except for the background
> singing. Then the song ends.)

LIKA: *(Trying to make up.)* "Mary, Mary, great wif child."

NETTIE: "And it came to pass in those days, that there went out a decree from Caesar Augustus that all the world should be taxed" somethin' somethin' "And Joseph" somethin' somethin' "to be taxed with Mary his espoused wife, being great wif child."

LIKA: What I worry for? borned in a hole. The good Lord borned in a barn, he sleep where ol' Bessie cud-chew.

NETTIE: Like a beam a sun, after a monf a rain. Like a cool breeze in summer, like a shiny penny's why we name you "Lika": hope.

> *(Pause.)*

LIKA: Duskin' the parlor chess, Miss Hannah goin' through, "Niggas stealin'! Lazy thieves!" I don't know who stole what, she pretty general on the subject. Later not rantin' no more, sit on the loveseat. Start her knittin'. "I guess niggas figger it's Christmas, they jus' *take* they presents. My own niggas, robbin' me bline!" I jus' keep with the duskin'. Then she fly outa there to the kitchen, come back. Han' me them biscuits. "Merry Christmas. I don't mine gibbin' I jus' don't like bein' took from!" She say . . .

> *(LIKA stops, looking at NETTIE, unsure of whether to go on with the story.)*

NETTIE: Say what?

LIKA: She say, "Look at your grammammy, mouf all twisted like the devil. *My* grammammy learnt her not to steal when she jus' a pickaninny, she ain't stole since!

> *(Long silence. NETTIE stirring the stew. Then LIKA picks up a rock, and starts to scratch on a wooden beam.)*

LIKA: Look, Grammy, this the star a Beflehem, shape jus' like the crost!

NETTIE: You know that rocker? parlor? One nobody never sit on? *(LIKA nods.)* Eight years ole, I was hongry. Skin 'n' bones orphan, all I gots the scraps they toss from the kitchen every morn, starved! Miss Hannah's grammammy was Miss Liza. *Mean.* Know I near faint from the honger, Christmastime on purpose she lee a peppermint stick out on 'at rocker, full view a me, she 'on't say nuttin but all clear she darin' me to tech it. Sweep the floor, try not think on it, but Day Three it *still* sit there, cain't help myself. Quick in my pocket for later, then worry they find it 'fore later, I suck it down fass. In come Miss Liza, I barely tall as seat a the chair, she tower o'er me "Nettie! You eat that peppermint stick?" "No ma'am, maybe it fall behine the dresser, maybe another nigga take it." "Don't *lie*, Nettie!" "I *ain't* lyin', swear I seen no peppermint stick!" She rush out the room, I skeer but 'fore figger what to do feel the rawhide rip my back. *Screamin'!*, I try run but she grab me, then call her daughter Miss Irene to help, they push me under that rocker and ol' woman sit on it, rock that rocker on my face, all her weight crushin' my little cheek, I feel crackin' my head, pop. Miss Hannah little girl herself then, cryin', "Shut up!" they say. "You *better* learn ta make a nigga mine!" Her little brother, Massa Nate laughin' at my bones breakin', some people jus' born no heart. Later I wake up, doctor say nuffin to do for my mouf and from that day forward no more whuppin's for me and no more food scraps, cain't chew no food scraps. Jus' broff. *(Pause.)* Miss Hannah musta been dippin' in the Christmas punch, tell you that. On the regular she 'on't like to recall 'at day.

> *(The distant church singing resumes.*
> *NETTIE blows and tastes the stew.)*

NETTIE: Mmmmm.

LIKA: Ready?!

> *(NETTIE pours out stew into a wooden*
> *bowl for LIKA. The food is steaming.)*

246

NETTIE: Swallow this scald your insides to deaf. Count me five hunnert, by then it cool down, a safe boil.

LIKA: *Five hunnert?!*

NETTIE: Soonest you start, soonest we eat.

LIKA: Onetwothreefourfivesixseven –

NETTIE: Now do it right.

LIKA: One. Two. Three. Four.

BUTCHIE: *(Off.)* One.

> (*Distant sound of a whip lashing a back. The victim screams.*)

LIKA: Five.

BUTCHIE: *(Off.)* Two.

> (*Lash. Scream.*)

LIKA: Two – he mess up my numbers!

BUTCHIE: Sh!

NETTIE: *(Off.)* Three.

> (*Lash. Scream.*)

BUTCHIE: Four.

> (*The counts followed by the lash and victim's screams will continue for many counts, the victim's reaction gradually*

*dying out. The singing swells in the
background. Eventually.)*

LIKA: How come they singin' louder, Grammy?
They don't wanna hear the whuppin'?

NETTIE: They singin' for Jesus to stop it. *(The
whipping stops.)* He did!

> *(The door to the cabin suddenly swings
> open. A light from an outside lantern
> illuminates the intruder from behind,
> rendering HIM momentarily into an
> unidentifiable silhouette. With the door
> open, the music has angelically swelled.)*

LIKA: *(Awed and delighted.)* Jesus!

> *(The man steps in, slamming the door
> shut behind HIM. It is not Jesus but
> rather Master BUTCHIE, a middle-aged
> white man. LIKA and NETTIE terrified.
> In the distance, the song ends.)*

BUTCHIE: All year I take care a ya damn niggers,
whatcha do to me Christmas? Rob me while I sleep,
I jus' whupped hell outa Tiny, caught her red-
handed runnin' with a hen, and I got four other
cluckers missin'. *(Beat.)* What kinda stew's that,
Nettie?

NETTIE: *(Stammering.)* Massa Butchie –

BUTCHIE: Aunt Hannah cryin' her eyes out,
"Treacherous darkies! Don't turn your back on
'em!" Bet she never guess the stencha guilt lead

right to Nettie's cabin. Nettie the untouchable Nettie the loyal well my daddy Master Nate tol' me "You keep a eye on Nettie." Hannah always protectin' 'at ol' wench, she get away with murder 'roun' here!

NETTIE: No Massa –

BUTCHIE: Drink it.

(*Pause.*)

NETTIE: Massa?

BUTCHIE: To the last drop.

NETTIE: Massa I jus' took it off to boil, eat it I burn up my insides. (*The pot is still steaming. The distant singing begins again.*)

BUTCHIE: Shoulda thoughta that durin' your career as a chicken thief.

NETTIE: This the firs' time Massa I ain't never done it before.

BUTCHIE: An' won't again after this lesson. (*To LIKA.*) You know this song?

NETTIE: Please Massa it still boilin'.

BUTCHIE: (*To LIKA.*) Sing.

(*LIKA is confused, terrified.*)

NETTIE: Sing for the Massa! He tell you sing, Sing!

(LIKA begins singing the song with the congregation. It is something joyous and lively, such as "Ride On King Jesus!")

NETTIE: Awww . . . She sing so purty. She sing so purty for the massa.

BUTCHIE: EAT THAT GODDAMN STEW!

(This startles LIKA to silence. BUTCHIE glares at LIKA, and SHE resumes singing. NETTIE, trembling, slowly brings the steaming pot toward HER lips. When it is very close:)

NETTIE: Oh please don't make me, Massa –

BUTCHIE: *(A quiet threat.)* If you don't swallow-

NETTIE: It boil my insides, Massa! it kill me! kill me!

(BUTCHIE, lost patience, charges to NETTIE, upturning the pot so that the contents flow swiftly into HER, the scalding liquid on HER cheeks, down HER throat. HER eyes wild as HER organs begin exploding. HER convulsive body begins to horrifically flop across the stage, a fish out of water (or some physicality similarly ghastly). This goes on for a lengthy period – at some point the congregation's song ends but LIKA, tears, horror, continues singing. Suddenly NETTIE's body is still. BUTCHIE goes to HER, checks

HER while LIKA sings. HE speaks
loudly enough to be heard over LIKA.)

BUTCHIE: Well she's dead.

(This announcement stops LIKA's song.
BUTCHIE kicks what's left of the stew
onto the dirt floor, smashing the food
into the ground.)

BUTCHIE: Guess that make you a real orphan,
huh? Mammy dead, grammammy, brothers sisters
all sold.

(LIKA doesn't answer.)

BUTCHIE: You bleed yet?

(LIKA shakes HER head no.)

BUTCHIE: Don'tcha know how to talk!

LIKA: I don't bleed, Massa.

BUTCHIE: Liar.

LIKA: No Massa I swear!

BUTCHIE: *(Laughs.)* I know, Hannah keep tracka
all the women business. Lucky for you I nearly
killed that Pawnie with it. Ten years old, now
useless. Cain't bear nothin', lost my whole damn
investment! So if you ain't bleedin', we ain't
breedin'.

(LIKA continues staring. Then
BUTCHIE picks up the writing rock

and etches the word "MASTOR" on the
beam – the writing a struggle for HIM
as HE is apparently only semi-literate –
then drops the stone on the ground. HE
steps back from HIS work.)

BUTCHIE: Read it.

(LIKA stares at the word. Silence.)

BUTCHIE: Don't pretend, I know you can read.
Which is huge grounds for sellin' ya, and when I
do I'll make sure the new master not one wait for
'em rob *him*, he be the type jus' give mandatory
weekly whuppin's, keep the innocent in line too.

(BUTCHIE knocks on the door to the
outside: a summons. WOODROW, an
elderly man, enters.)

WOODROW: Yes, Massa?

BUTCHIE: Woodrow, can you tell me what that
scribblin' be?

WOODROW: Look like writin', Massa, but I don't
understand no writin'.

BUTCHIE: You know why Woodrow don't
understand no writin'? Cuz he a good nigger,
honest. Loyal. Not like these things comin' up all
cocky. And female to boot, ain't never trust no
wench –

(BUTCHIE is cut off by LIKA's sudden
cross to the writing. SHE picks up the

*rock and scratches an "E" over the "O"
in "MASTOR." BUTCHIE stares at it
for several moments before HE realizes
HE has been corrected.)*

BUTCHIE: *(Staring at HER in disbelief.)* Son of a . . .

(BUTCHIE grabs LIKA.)

BUTCHIE: Bring that corpse, Woodrow! And git a shovel.

*(BUTCHIE pulls LIKA through the
cabin door and offstage. LIKA
struggling and HER "NOOOO!"
before the sound of a whip against flesh,
followed by HER screams. Another lash,
another scream. Another. Another, the
screams weakening. While the torture is
inflicted, WOODROW drags the corpse
toward the door. Then stops. Goes to
"MASTER," picks up the rock and
etches "ON" over the "A":
"MONSTER." Resumes dragging the
corpse out.)*

Scene Two

*(February 1840. Washington, D.C. A
parlor. GERTIE is at the piano, singing
and playing (which may start in the
scene transition), periodically drinking
from a glass. SHE is dressed for a party
and wears a Mardi Gras mask. SHE*

neither sings nor plays well. LIKA is
polishing. LIKA ignores GERTIE.)

GERTIE: *(Tune: "The Star Spangled Banner".)*

"To Anacreon in Heav'n,
Where he sat in full glee,
A few Sons of Harmony
Sent a petition
That he their Inspirer
And Patron would be;
When this answer arrived
From the Jolly Old Grecian:
'Voice, Fiddle, and Flute,
No longer be mute,
I'll lend you my name
And inspire you to boot,
And besides I'll instruct you,
Like me, to entwine
The Myrtle of Venus
With Bacchus's Vine.'"

(WILLIS enters, grabbing HIS coat and
wraps in a rush)

GERTIE: *(To no one in particular.)* Ain't it purty, like
a poym? Sound a lot sweeter 'n "bombs burstin' in
air" but it dirty! it dirty! That so, Willis?

WILLIS: That's your last glass, Gertie.

GERTIE: I ain't Gertie! *(Regarding the mask.)* Do you
see me? Gertie is no longer here. *(Giggles; singing
and playing.)* "To Anacreon in Heav'n..." Who
Ancreon?

254

WILLIS: Greek poet sang about wine and love.

> *(GERTIE hums "Like me, to entwine,"
> then:)*

GERTIE: What Myrtle?

WILLIS: A Mediterranean shrub with dark berries.

GERTIE: Shrub? You mean a *bush*? *(No answer.)*
And we *know* what shape a vine be, long and
slender. *(Singing and playing.)* "Like me, to *entwine* /
The *Myrtle* of Venus" – *myrtle*'s the bush – "With
Bacchus' *Vine*" it dirty! *(Guffaws.)*

WILLIS: *(Exiting.)* When I walk back through this
door, be sober. *(Gone.)*

GERTIE: *(Calls out the doorway.)* It Fat Tuesday! *(No
answer.)* Who you pickin' up, train depot?

> *(Sound of the offstage outside door
> closing.)*

GERTIE: Well that won't be for hours, he get to the
train station so early, I tell him, "Willis, you ever
knowed the train to be early?" *(Beat.)* You think
that ol' drinkin' song dirty? How come they steal
'at tune for the Star-Spangle anthem? *(Glances at the
window.)* He gone?

> *(Until this moment LIKA had seemed to
> be paying GERTIE no attention. Now,
> working near the window, LIKA glances
> out.)*

LIKA: Gone.

(Both WOMEN start drawing the curtains so that no one from the outside can see in.)

GERTIE: I remember Fat Tuesdays when I was a gal, Nawlins, look forward to it better 'n Christmas. The parties, masqueradin'. Ain't nobody know nuffin 'bout no Mardi Gras here, the col' col' North! "Frighten she look away, dimurr and modiss"!

(GERTIE has snatched off HER mask and sat down, eager. LIKA has pulled from a hiding place a book, turning to the appropriate page.)

LIKA: *(Reads.)* "Frightened, she looked away, demur and modest. But a strange warmth filled her face, an unevenness in her breath. Her sight faltered, and she feared she may faint.

"'Have you fallen ill, sweet miss?'
"Assured that she was steady, he stepped back gently, his hand brushing against hers. His skin, dark as the sky carpet of night, hers golden as sun – "

GERTIE: That romance, that Dixie! I'm a Worshington wife but my real home *always* be the French Korter. You miss the South, Lika? The *real* South? I know pickin' the crop might not a been the most lookin'-forward-to-itest thing in your mind, but dontcha crave Febooaries in the great outdoors?

LIKA; No ma'am.

GERTIE: *I* miss the South, but guess it be differ'nt I was a nigger. When Master Rawlings go down to Georgia lookin' for a he'p to me, I say "She ain't gonna like it! She ain't useta no city slavin'!" But seem like you take to it fine. Well, here you ain't one slave in a hunnert on the place, we got just four blackies, guess it nice, the individual attention?

LIKA: Yes ma'am.

GERTIE: He don't like my Carnival celebratin'! He say "We don't do that Catholic stuff up here!" Well tamarr I be pious 'til the Resurrection, but tonight I get jes a little bit happy. *(Bottoms up, then refills HER glass.)* "Hers golden as sun."

LIKA: *(Continues reading.)* "Hers golden as sun. 'High yellow' the other plantation children had taunted, every feature on her urchin face a testament of the master's crime. Her hazel eyes, now a spring green in the meadow of April blossoms, searched his deep browns, his flesh flawless save a cut above the right brow, no doubt the lifelong emblem of a punishment, the wrath of that incubus who in blasphemous deference to Our Lord Savior dare go by the name 'Master.' For what Negro among us has not escaped the gash of the lash? Not even a free man of color can say he has not a relative- "

GERTIE: This the part goes on three pages?

LIKA: Yes ma'am.

GERTIE: Skip to the lips.

LIKA: *(Turns pages, picks up reading.)* "He stared into her shining eyes. 'Adelina, Adelina!' *(Add-a-LEE-na)* And in the proper way she nodded, and day drew on to the coolness of evening, and in the moonlit night they rowed a boat out onto the pond. Knowing they were alone she leaned into him, and his lips met hers, a tender passing of curved flesh against flesh – "

GERTIE: *(Giggling.)* Ooooooh, that a goodie! That negress writer sure do know how to hit it! Someday I take ya to Nawlins, Lika, setcha free! Master Willis always "You ain't from no Nawlins!" Three years I there with my auntie while my mama ailin', age six to nine, them's years what stays with ya. *(Sudden tears.)* Me an' Willis hap'ly married fourteen years, how come we ain't yet brought forth no bundle a joy? Back room upstairs perfeck for a nursery, Willis say nothin' but I see the way he look at me funny, well what about *his* equipment? *(Drinks.)* "Pat, pet, pit, pot, put." *(The last rhyming with "nut.")* Then you come "and sometimes 'y'," I haul off and smack ya one! Musta boiled your blood, as' ya teach me to read, then get all sore cuz I cain't catch on.

LIKA: No ma'am.

GERTIE: Make it square. *(Indicates HER cheek.)* Hit me back. *(LIKA surprised.)* Go on!

LIKA: No ma'am!

MOSES: *(Steps into the room.)* Miss Gertie, if you ain't needin' me for awhile, I be out feedin' the horses. *(Exits.)*

GERTIE: Well I don't know maybe I *will* be – Moses? MOSES! *(To LIKA.)* You see that? Hate me! Moses never show me no respeck oh I miss Ol' Elmer. You never knew Ol' Elmer, wanna know how he got set free? Master Willis and Elmer get to talkin', and *drinkin'*, Master Willis never could hold his liquor straight, he always ack like *I'm* the fool on liquor! well lemme tell ya. Some ways Elmer chats Master Willis into writin' up his freedom. Nex' day Master Willis cain't remember head nor tail, but Elmer tell him 'bout the document, "You lock it up there in your dess, Master Willis." Which he done, there it be, dated and signed and Master Willis ain't happy but a man a his written word, that day Elmer walk outa here, ever I get the hankerin' to free my husbin's property I know where his bourbon be! Then you an' me in Nawlins! me with Aunt Frenchie and you'll come on Sundays, read me. An' in the parlor'll sit your purty pickaninnies, and your handsome octoroon broom-jumper, get your daguerrotype done and people'll travel from miles around to look at Lika's lovelies and say, "What . . . *teeth!*"

> *(In the corridor beyond the doorway, the sound of the outside door and muffled voices of two MEN.)*

GERTIE: He's back!

(LIKA quickly hides the book, then helps GERTIE with opening the curtains. WILLIS enters with AUGUSTUS. HE is black, and this surprises GERTIE and LIKA.)

WILLIS: Mr. Freeman, this is my wife, Mrs. Rawlings.

AUGUSTUS: How do you do, Mrs. Rawlings.

(AUGUSTUS holds out HIS hand. GERTIE looks stupidly from AUGUSTUS to LIKA, then grins. WILLIS, concerned GERTIE may say something embarrassing, quickly resumes the introductions.)

WILLIS: And this is our Lika.

AUGUSTUS: *(HIS hand now out to LIKA.)* How do you do, Miss Lika.

(LIKA, still unsure and confused, nods.)

WILLIS: I do apologize again, Mr. Freeman.

AUGUSTUS: It's nothing.

WILLIS: I mistakenly thought Mr. Freeman was arriving on the 5:15 but it was the 3:15. He had been patiently waiting for nearly an hour.

GERTIE: That's because you weren't wearin' your spectacles again.

WILLIS: That has nothing to do with –

GERTIE: I know what "3" look like and it and "5" is two differ'nt things!

AUGUSTUS: It really was no trouble, Mr. Rawlings.

WILLIS: You are very gracious. Mr. Freeman is a free Negro living in New York City. He has been traveling since very early this morning to speak at our meeting this evening.

GERTIE: What meetin'?

WILLIS: Our Washington chapter of the American Colonization Society, I'm sure I told you, Mrs. Rawlings. Mr. Freeman has come here to support our efforts in relocating our free Negroes to Africa.

GERTIE: Oh, *that.*

WILLIS: Lika, fetch Mr. Freeman and myself some refreshments.

GERTIE: Yes, refreshments, Lika. (*Handing HER empty glass to LIKA.*)

WILLIS: Perhaps you could assist Lika, Mrs. Rawlings.

GERTIE: I never assisted her when we had twenty people on Christmas, think she know how to serve three.

LIKA: I'll be back directly, Master Willis. (*Exits to the kitchen.*)

GERTIE: So what is it you do, Mr. Free-Man Freeman?

AUGUSTUS: I am a merchant, Mrs. Rawlings. I also edit a newspaper for colored people.

GERTIE: An' who mindin' the store while you down here on this silly business?

AUGUSTUS: My brother. Do I sense a distaste for the American Colonization Society?

GERTIE: Them nekked Africans with they spears!

WILLIS: Mrs. Rawlings!

AUGUSTUS: Africa is the land of my ancestors. And apparently the only place a black man can truly be free.

GERTIE: You free! How you get that? *(Hopeful excitement.)* Escaped? Them Unnerground Rail Tracks?

AUGUSTUS: My master allowed us half of Sunday to rest or to rent ourselves out to other plantations. I chose the latter and after many years saved enough to purchase my freedom.

GERTIE: Then why you wanna leave? Free an' all?

WILLIS: You don't have to defend yourself, Mr. Freeman. Mrs. Rawlings, you are treating our guest as if he is on trial.

AUGUSTUS: Oh, this is nothing compared to the interrogations I undergo when I have spoken before the colored people, Mr. Rawlings! *(To GERTIE.)* "Freedom" only means I may no longer be compelled into forced labor. *(LIKA returns with a tray of drinks and sweets to offer.)* "Freedom" does not mean I can vote, I cannot. "Freedom" does not mean that if I and a white man were to do the same job we would be compensated the same, we would not. Freedom is not enough if it comes without justice. Thank you, Miss Lika. *(Regarding the treat from the tray.)*

GERTIE: But why you gotta go way crost the Atlantic?

AUGUSTUS: There were proposals for a colony in this hemisphere, in this country even, west of the Mississippi. But there were concerns.

GERTIE: Such as?

> *(AUGUSTUS and WILLIS exchange glances.)*

AUGUSTUS: That the colonists might harbor escaped slaves. That the colonists might join forces with Mexico, Canada or the Indians to make war on the United States of America.

WILLIS: *Thus* the Society has generously born the expense of providing for our beneficiaries' pilgrimage to faraway Africa.

GERTIE: *(Shrugs.)* Don't seem it be too catchy a enterprise.

WILLIS: We are not just some small, marginalized flank, Mrs. Rawlings. The third president of our great nation has been outspoken in support of our efforts, certainly conveying a moral consistency in Mr. Jefferson as the author of the Declaration of Independence.

GERTIE: Consistent how? Ain't he got slaves?

WILLIS: The Society was formed to relocate our *free* Negroes. Mr. Jefferson is consistent in wanting to form a nation wherein men who are *free* are independent, have broken the chains of tyranny. We also boast among our distinguished associates Mr. Daniel Webster, Mr. Francis Scott Key, author of our national anthem –

GERTIE: *(Sings.)* "To Anacreon in Heav'n, / Where he sat in full glee . . . " *(Giggles.)*

WILLIS: *(Trying to ignore HER.)* The first president of our organization was Mr. Bushrod Washington, nephew of the first president of our republic. And of course Mr. Robert E. Lee –

GERTIE: *Who?*

WILLIS: A rising military man.

AUGUSTUS: We would be drastically misrepresenting the American Colonization Society, an assemblage of white men, if we were not to mention its composition of hostilely oppositional entities drawn together by a common goal. Quakers and other abolitionists envision a safe haven where colored people may govern

264

themselves, far from the authority of law subjugating black to white. Southern landowners, and let me stress that they comprise the vast majority of the membership, have on the other hand a two-pronged design for the Negroes of this country. They are satisfied with those of us who remain in bondage. It is only we who are free that are being enticed to emigrate and I consider that to be a major *in*consistency in the treatment of colored people, slaveholder Mr. Jefferson among these contradictions and for this reason my conscience was painfully ambivalent regarding the invitation to speak before your Washington chapter, Mr. Rawlings.

> *(WILLIS suddenly tosses a book onto the table. ALL stare at it.)*

WILLIS: I wonder whether you feel any ambivalence regarding *that*, Mr. Freeman. *(AUGUSTUS picks up the book.)* Lika, you may be excused.

GERTIE: Lika, stay! What if somebody need more to drink? I ain't servin' 'em, Fat Tuesday, my day off!

AUGUSTUS: Mr. David Walker's *Appeal to the Coloured Citizens of the World,* –

WILLIS: Mr. Freeman –

AUGUSTUS: *(Uninterrupted.)* – *but in particular, and very expressly, to those of the United States of America.* Have you heard of it, Miss Lika?

WILLIS: Mr. Freeman! I think you can understand that these are issues I'd rather not discuss in front of my servant.

GERTIE: Why? It *dirty?* It a dirty book?!

WILLIS: No! Besides one of its four articles written expressly in antithesis to our colonization efforts, the book urges slaves to rise up against their masters. And originally published one year before that brutal episode in Virginia.

> *(GERTIE screams in horror. THEY stare at HER. SHE stares back. Then.)*

GERTIE: Nattie Turner!

WILLIS: Not woman nor child spared – How many whites did he and his monsters-in-arms kill? Fifty?

GERTIE: Vicious!

AUGUSTUS: Certainly not the first slave uprising, not the first threat to the established order. The Haitian revolt of 1791 ultimately resulted in the abolishment of slavery there –

GERTIE: You like it? Blood?

AUGUSTUS: The blood of whites shed in revolution is just as red as that shed by blacks in whippings, in amputations, how many slaves had a foot severed for running off?

LIKA: For getting caught. *(ALL turn to HER, startled.)* Ones that got away kept their feet.

AUGUSTUS: *(A smile.)* I stand corrected.

WILLIS: *(Hard look to LIKA.)* What we of the Society are offering is a compromise to make both races happy. Peacefully! What Mr. Walker is calling for is blind revenge. *(Opens to a marked page and hands the book to AUGUSTUS.)*

AUGUSTUS: *(Reading.)* "It is just the way with black men – eight white men can frighten fifty of them, whereas, if you can only get courage into the blacks . . . one good black man can put to death six white men . . . the black, once you get them started, they glory in death." *(AUGUSTUS flips pages.)*

WILLIS: You see!

AUGUSTUS: *(Reads.)* "America is more our country than it is the whites . . . (W)e have enriched it with our blood and tears. (W)ill they drive us from our property and homes, which we have earned with our blood?"

(Pause.)

WILLIS: You persist in presenting arguments for staying put, Mr. Freeman. As the sponsored guest of the American Colonization Society, may I ask whether you subscribe to any comparable defense for emigration?

(Pause.)

AUGUSTUS: When I toil the land, I want to know that now and forever it will be *my* land. And I would like the choice *not* to toil the land, if I would prefer to perform the duties of merchant, or constable, or newspaper editor. If I were to take a wife I would want to know that our children will be educated, and that they may grow up to be doctors, or lawyers, or president of my nation. I would like to live in a country where not only am I respected as a citizen with full rights, but that every other human being regardless of color enjoys those same rights. I do not believe such progressive ideals will come about in this country in my lifetime. I regret to say I have no great confidence such a utopia will *ever* come about in the United States and for this reason I respectfully accept the offer of the American Colonization Society to cover the financial burden of my emigration to Africa.

WILLIS: *(Clapping.)* Brilliant! Oh, there will be a few grumblings, "Why cannot our generosity gracefully be received without criticizing the land of your benefactor?," but I suspect your conclusions will be met with unanimous thunderous applause.

AUGUSTUS: Yes. And Mr. Rawlings, I would presume it has occurred to you and your colleagues that a *true* symbol of your commitment would be to mimic the actions already taken by several Southern gentlemen in favor of colonization, Mr. Robert E. Lee quite notably, and to free some, or all, of your slaves under the condition that the newly emancipated immediately emigrate to our American African colony.

(Silence.)

GERTIE: Send Moses!

WILLIS: Gertie!

GERTIE: Moses our butler, he ol', Willis! How many years he got leff in him? We could buy a new young'un to replace him –

WILLIS: Moses has been in the Rawlings family for over sixty years!

GERTIE: He sneaky. *(WILLIS raises a dismissive hand.)* He likes *you*, Willis, I'm jes the wife what come after!

WILLIS: Gertie, we'll discuss this later –

GERTIE: Wouldn't it be breath a fresh air? Get a cute little baby nigger. An' Moses could git one a them free coloreds what reads to write letters home to us 'bout his adventures in the jungle, wouldn't that be fun?

WILLIS: The men Mr. Freeman has spoken of have large plantations! In a population of one hundred slaves, what matter if two or three are released? We have four servants in our modest home. I am not a wealthy Southern planter, Mr. Freeman, I do not have the means to just buy another slave at will *(hard look to GERTIE)*, my beggary exasperated by having lost the potential income of selling my investment by instead setting it free –

GERTIE: Moses never did think I was good enough for you!

WILLIS: *Quiet!*

(*Quiet.*)

AUGUSTUS: What of Miss Lika?

GERTIE: NO! Willis, no, Lika he'p me, we cain't be partin' with her! Valu'ble!

WILLIS: You took no issue with the prospect of my Moses's departure.

GERTIE: He di'posable, Willis! If Lika go, who he'p me with the cookin'?

WILLIS: We're not letting Lika go.

GERTIE: Mr. Freeman, I got nuttin 'gainst what you say, but I need my Lika.

WILLIS: *(To GERTIE.)* We are *not* –

GERTIEL: Not *now!* But later you go out with your Society people, come back drunk an' he as' you agin, you sign our Lika away "*Sure* Mr. Freeman." Willis, you know you cain't hold your liquor!

WILLIS: Mrs. Rawlings! may I please speak to you in the kitchen?

> (*WILLIS has stormed offstage into the kitchen. GERTIE glances at AUGUSTUS and LIKA, embarrassed.*)

WILLIS: *(Off.)* NOW!

GERTIE: Scuze me.

(GERTIE exits to the kitchen.)

GERTIE: *(Off.)* What?

WILLIS: *(Off, trying to keep HIS volume low.)* What are you doing?

GERTIE: *(Off.)* You talkin' 'bout givin' Lika away –

WILLIS: *(Off.)* So? I paid for her she's my property!

GERTIE: *(Off.)* NO! SHE A PRESENT!

WILLIS: *(Off.)* Would you please keep your voice down!

GERTIE: *(Off.)* YOU GI' HER TO ME!

WILLIS: *(Off.)* Into the back room, Gertie!

> *(A door can be heard opening and closing off.)*

AUGUSTUS: Do you have an opinion, Miss Lika?

LIKA: I was not treated well in Atlanta, Mr. Freeman. I am treated respectably here. I have served Master and Mistress Rawlings sixteen winters, since I was twelve, and I have never been beaten.

AUGUSTUS: Is that all you ask of life? Not to be beaten?

LIKA: I am not a fool, Mr. Freeman. Bondage is an evil. But if it is a given, then I prefer a bondage without complications. And I favor it as a known entity over a so-called freedom in a mysterious jungle, a universe away from the world and culture with which I am familiar.

AUGUSTUS: You speak as though you spend an inordinate amount of time dusting in the library.

LIKA: And unlike my mistress who finds my master's meetings a bore and rapidly excuses herself to tasks elsewhere, I am left to serve tea to the gentlemen and so have heard of troubling letters home: of disease, of poverty, of hostility from the natives. Many settlers have returned.

AUGUSTUS: Many more have stayed.

LIKA: Perhaps their poverty has prevented their return.

AUGUSTUS: Or the thought of coming back to a nation in which thousands of human beings are measured as three-fifths of a person, their life and death at the whim of a white man.

LIKA: Are you practicing your speech on me, Mr. Freeman? *Your* appeal to the colored citizens of the United States to leave the land of their birth and blood behind?

AUGUSTUS: No, Miss Lika, because my appeal, if you recall, may only be to *free* blacks. That does not apply to you.

> (*The offstage door can be heard opening and closing again. WILLIS and GERTIE re-enter.*)

WILLIS: I apologize for our brief hiatus, Mr. Freeman.

AUGUSTUS: No apologies necessary, Mr. Rawlings. *(Confidentially lowering HIS voice.)* May I request a moment? *(Pause.)* Of privacy?

(ALL stare at HIM, confused.)

GERTIE: *Oh*, the chamber pot! I hope you ain't been holdin' it too long, Mr. Freeman, I hear that's very bad for your constitution. MOSES! I'll git Moses to show ya. MOSES! Oh, he must be out back, I'll take ya to the pot, then show ya to your room.

(GERTIE starts to exit, then realizes SHE isn't being followed.)

GERTIE: You don't gotta go no more?

AUGUSTUS: I'm sorry, Mrs. Rawlings, I was just confused. My room?

GERTIE: You goin' back to New York to*night?*

WILLIS: There *is* no train back to New York tonight.

AUGUSTUS: Mr. Rawlings thoroughly investigated the matter. It was assumed I would feel more comfortable in the home of a local free colored family.

GERTIE: But we got plenty –

WILLIS: The Society believes Mr. Freeman would be more at ease –

GERTIE: Why? He free. Don't that make him kinda white?

WILLIS: Mrs. Rawlings –

GERTIE: Aw let him sleep here Willis, I like the way he talk –

WILLIS: *It has been decided!*

　　　　(Silence.)

GERTIE: *(Sighs.)* Let me lease have Moses assist ya with that other. *(As AUGUSTUS follows HER off.)* I cain't believe you ain't found you a wife yet, Mr. Freeman. You speak s' nice, and you one purty . . .

　　　　(GERTIE and AUGUSTUS are gone.
　　　　Quiet a few moments.)

WILLIS: If you were given the choice, Lika. If I offered you freedom in exchange for your emigration. Or you could stay here.

　　　　(Pause.)

LIKA: You treat me well, Master. No complaints. *(WILLIS nods, satisfied.)* But an adventure would be nice.

　　　　(WILLIS, surprised, gazes at LIKA a
　　　　few moments, then takes a key from a
　　　　pocket and opens HIS desk drawer.

Takes out a piece of paper and writes.
When HE is finished:)

WILLIS: Does this meet with your approval?

LIKA: Master…?

WILLIS: I know you can read, Lika, I would like you to take a look at this document authorizing your freedom under the stipulation of your emigration to Africa and tell me if you find it satisfactory.

> *(LIKA slowly walks to WILLIS and stares at the paper.)*

WILLIS: I am not a hypocrite. Yes, there are men of our cause who find no discord between their provision for a colony of liberation, a *Liberia*, on the one hand, and on the other their devotion to, and determination to maintain, our way of life: the institution of slavery. Our work has always been concerned with the relocation of *free* colored, *only*. However. I understand the conflicts Mr. Freeman is struggling with, and with respect to that I am willing to offer this compromise, "a symbol of my commitment" as our guest would put it.

> *(LIKA stares at the paper without touching it.)*

WILLIS: Perhaps you would like some time to think about it. Freedom can be an overwhelming responsibility. You may be opening yourself up to hunger, fear, loneliness-

LIKA: You did not sign it.

(Pause.)

WILLIS: Perhaps *I* would like to think about it. I will allow it a few hours' penitence and this evening shall return with a decision.

(WILLIS locks the paper into HIS desk, puts the key back into HIS pocket.)

WILLIS: Would you be considering this had I not called you when you were sixteen? *(No reply.)* I waited until that age of womanliness, I would never take a child, and I only called you thrice. I do *not* believe in miscegenation. I *do* believe in three meals daily, and in hard times the production of salable merchandise may be necessary to provide for such amenities. In those days we were experiencing some financial difficulties . . . At any rate you obviously were not built for manufacture. It became speedily apparent you are barren, I seem to have an uncanny talent to select women . . . I bought you for pennies thinking I'd cheated the poor man but, as it turned out, *I* was the duped.

(GERTIE and AUGUSTUS return. MOSES steps into the room.)

GERTIE: Mr. Freeman has successfully completed his private affair and is ready for your little men's klatch.

MOSES: I git the buggy, Massa?

276

WILLIS: (*Checking HIS pocket watch.*) Yes or we'll likely be late. Moses, will you take Mr. Freeman to the coach? I'll be there directly.

AUGUSTUS: Thank you for your hospitality, Mrs. Rawlings.

GERTIE: Thank *you*, Mr. Freeman.

AUGUSTUS: And for yours, Miss Lika.

LIKA: Good evening.

>(*AUGUSTUS exits on the heels of MOSES. WILLIS gets HIS coat and wraps.*)

WILLIS: I don't know that you would be happy in Africa, Lika. (*GERTIE bewildered.*) You covet freedom now. If you were free, how would you feed yourself? And if you think life may be harsh here in America –

GERTIE: You wanna go, Lika?

WILLIS: The irony of our experiment is that occasionally our success is at once our downfall. It will be unfortunate for our cause to lose such an articulate and eloquent speaker as Mr. Freeman to Africa. I almost lament that he is not in bondage so that we may demand he stay and continue to urge others to enlist in our venture. Perhaps that's an idea. Our replacement orator, to address the free blacks, could be an impressively articulate slave who only *wishes* she could be free to emigrate. (*Eyes on LIKA.*) I'll meditate on that prospect.

(WILLIS exits.)

GERTIE: You ain't really goin', is ya, Lika? *(No answer. Suddenly glowering.)* You an' him: same! Go away *lee* me! Wonder where Willis end up after he drop Mr. Freeman off at the coloreds? *He have all the little fillies he want!* Willis think I don't know the trash he up under I do. If it was a nigger I'da understood, but no. No, he got his little blond birdie in town, little dirty-headed thing well she better not be layin' no litters! Willis ain't made me no mother, her neither! *(Pause, then GERTIE starts drawing the curtains.)* Aw, this foolishness blow over quick enough. Let's jes read. Mr. Freeman, dontcha think he were one handsome – ?

LIKA: Master Willis knows I can read. *(GERTIE continues with the curtains.)* No need to draw –

GERTIE: *(Turns on HER.)* ALWAYS THE SAME! Don't like no changes, read me in the private.

> *(GERTIE finishes with the curtains,*
> *then sits comfortably, hands the novel to*
> *LIKA.)*

GERTIE: "His lips met hers, flesh 'gainst flesh." *(LIKA doesn't open the book.)* Whatta matter? *(No answer.)* How you gonna make it inna wild? Tigers an' snakes, they *eatcha!* Cannibals, them Africans you 'on't know which way they turn.

LIKA: His will in that desk. And my freedom agreement. I need to see them both. His signature on the will. To copy on to the freedom paper. You know where the extra desk key is.

(*GERTIE stares at HER. Then looks away.*)

LIKA: He wrote up a promise. My freedom, in Africa.

GERTIE: No –

LIKA: You said he gave another slave his freedom when he saw he had signed the document. You said he'll come home drunk, won't remember –

GERTIE: Elmer was ol', served his whole life. An' Master Willis *did* sign *that* paper, jes didn't recall it. He never signed yours, you talkin' 'bout deceit. Pull a trick on him.

LIKA: He *gave* me the choice, then took it back. He pulled a trick on *me*.

GERTIE: NO! You wouldn't like it there, Lika –

LIKA: Won't know until I find out.

GERTIE: No! Stay with ME!

LIKA: Replace me.

GERTIE: He ain't gonna replace you! Cheap! An' how you be replaced? You my frien'. Who gonna read me? You my frien'.

(*THEY stare at each other.*)

GERTIE: READ ME! *(Pause. Then LIKA slowly opens the book.)*

LIKA: "His lips met hers, a tender passing of curved flesh against flesh. He had never imagined skin so soft, breath so sweet." *(A pause.)* Weeks turned into months, months into years. *(GERTIE looks confused.)* She understood his commitments, his marriage to *her.*

GERTIE: I don't remember this part.

LIKA: Then came the influenza epidemic. His wife stood near, sleepless for nights. He lay there, feverish, thin. Her eyes filled, for they were childless, and she already felt the crush, the overwhelming years of loneliness she would endure subsequent to his rapidly approaching death. Finally his lips parted. "Adelina! Adelina! Adelina!"

On the road her carriage raced to the cottage. She sprang through the door, throwing the wife aside: "Edward!"

GERTIE: This ain't –

LIKA: "The children, Adelina," he whispered. And her reply: "They are well, my Edward."

"Adelina" was the last word to pass through his lips. And, surprising to all, but especially to his faithful wife, the only woman's name in his will.

> *(A pause. Then GERTIE goes to a bookshelf. Now LIKA looks up. Tucked inside a particular book is an extra key*

to the desk. GERTIE unlocks the
drawer. LIKA quickly pulls out the
freedom paper and the will. SHE puts
them on the desk, and carefully forges
WILLIS' signature from the will onto
HER freedom document. GERTIE
pointedly indicates the will. LIKA picks
it up.)

LIKA: *(Reading.)* "I, Willis Rawlings, being of sound mind and body . . . "

Scene Three

a.

(December 1840. Many black people
standing on a docked ship, talking in
small groups, LIKA among THEM.
AUGUSTUS emerges from below deck.
GEORGE and SARAH, with 10-year-
old CHESTER in tow, rush to HIM.)

GEORGE: Mr. Freeman! Mr. Freeman, I must make your acquaintance! *(Shakes AUGUSTUS' hand heartily.)* I am Dr. George Sherman, and this is my wife Sarah and my son Chester.

SARAH: How do you do, Mr. Freeman.

GEORGE: Mrs. Sherman and I heard you address an audience in Hartford, and we would just like to thank you for your rousing words.

SARAH: We had discussed emigrating to Africa many a time but could never summons up the courage to undertake such a journey. That is, before we heard you speak.

AUGUSTUS: I am very flattered that you found my lecture so inspiring, but I do hope you listened closely enough to ascertain my opinions were all formed on this side of the Atlantic. I would be mortified to think my words could have been misunderstood, interpreting my praise of Africa as a sentiment of firsthand experience.

SARAH: Oh no, Mr. Freeman, you were by no means misleading!

AUGUSTUS: Two months from now I will stand on African soil for the first time, just like you.

LOUIS: (*Enters the conversation.*) You were quite clear, Mr. Freeman. I was fortunate to have been part of an audience you addressed at a church in Richmond. My name is Louis Russell, and I am a cobbler by trade.

SARAH: Mr. Freeman, we are all so rude in not even acknowledging what this day means for you. Congratulations, sir!

GEORGE: Yes, congratulations!

LOUIS: Much luck, sir!

AMELIA: (*Entering the conversation, holding a baby.*) Mr. Freeman! My name is Amelia Sawyer, an' my massa set me free after hearin' you speak! This my daughter Cinda, eight babies 'fore her all sons an'

the massa sol' all my boys but set me free wif my
baby you the one! You the thanks, me an' my chile
together forever!

JOHN: *(Standing near LIKA and OTHERS, calls.)* Mr.
Freeman! Don't we have some business to attend?

> *(AUGUSTUS, smiling, walks to stand
> next to LIKA, before JOHN.
> EVERYONE ELSE gathers around,
> attentive.)*

JOHN: For those of you whom I haven't yet met, I
am Reverend John Gibson, and I would like to
introduce to you Mr. Augustus Freeman and Miss
Lika Rawlings. I believe they have some things to
say to each other.

> *(LIKA smiles at AUGUSTUS, faces the
> crowd, then reads from a small book. At
> first ALL smile but, as the text
> continues, the smiles of the OTHERS'
> fade into expressions of confusion.)*

LIKA: "And there were lights in the sky…stretched
forth from east to west… (A)nd shortly afterwards,
while laboring in the field, I discovered drops of
blood on the corn…and I then found on the leaves
in the woods hieroglyphic characters…with the
forms of men in different attitudes, portrayed in
blood… For as the blood of Christ had been shed
on this earth…the Saviour was about to lay down
the yoke he had borne for the sins of men, and the
great day of judgment was at hand…. I told these
things to a white man, on whom it had a wonderful

effect – and he ceased from his wickedness, and was attacked immediately with a cutaneous eruption, and blood oozed from the pores of his skin, and after praying and fasting nine days, he was healed… After this I rejoiced greatly, and gave thanks to God." *(Looks up to OTHERS.)* These are *The Confessions of Nat Turner*, and as we embark on our great adventure, (smiling *eyes to AUGUSTUS)* and as *we* embark on *our* great adventure, I know that we too will go under the direction and with the blessing of God.

> *(LIKA still smiling. An awkward pause from the OTHERS. Then:)*

JOHN: Augustus?

> *(AUGUSTUS, also confused, pulls out a piece of paper from inside HIS vest.)*

AUGUSTUS: *(Reads.)* "Before these kind witnesses, I vow my lifelong dedication and loyalty to Lika Rawlings."

> *(ALL wait for more. There isn't.)*

JOHN: Then let them jump.

> *(The crowd backs up to reveal for the audience a broom on the floor in front of the couple. THEY jump over it. ALL cheer but the applause only lasts a few seconds before a bell is heard. ALL fall to silence. A sudden great jerk of the ship, then MR. LEONARDS, a white man, appears.)*

MR. LEONARDS: Welcome, passengers! My name is Mr. Leonards, and I am the agent representing the American Colonization Society for this voyage. You may want to take your last glance at America.

> *(ALL rush to stare at the shore, except LIKA, HER back to it, and AMELIA who comes to stand next to LIKA.)*

AMELIA: All my boys Massa sell, worry what he do with this'n: gal. Then he hear your husband speak. An' here we be. *(Turns to the shore.)* But my other eight still there. America.

> *(AMELIA goes to stand with the OTHERS. AUGUSTUS, near LIKA, turns to HER.)*

AUGUSTUS: Last chance, Mrs. Freeman. America about to become history.

LIKA: It already is.

> *(LIKA keeps HER back to the shore, refusing to look at it. AUGUSTUS smiles and turns back to gaze at the shore for the last time.)*

b.

> *(January 1841. In the darkness, the sound of vomiting. Lights up: Several PASSENGERS puking over the side of the ship, including SARAH, JOHN and MR. LEONARDS. Among those not regurgitating are LOUIS, GEORGE,*

CHESTER, AUGUSTUS and LIKA.
The noisy illness will continue
throughout the conversation.)

LOUIS: These waves. Storm again.

GEORGE: Nothing compared to what awaits us in Africa. Eighty-eight Negroes and three ACS agents set sail from New York City on the *Elizabeth*, virgin voyage of the colonists. All survived the journey but three weeks on Sherbro Island just off the Dark Continent, twenty-two black and all three white were dead. Yellow Fever. The survivors turned tail back to Freetown, where they had initially anchored.

CHESTER: Where's Freetown?

AUGUSTUS: Sierra Leone, our soon-to-be neighbor to the north. Britain began to colonize an African haven for its Negroes in 1787 –

LIKA: Thirty-three years before the United States.

CHESTER: There's colored people in Britain?

AUGUSTUS: American slaves who were granted freedom in England in exchange for fighting for the British during the Revolutionary War. England has also populated the African settlement with former slaves from its Caribbean colony, Jamaica –

(AMELIA enters from the lower deck,
walking and humming to HER baby.)

LIKA: *Former* slaves, there is no slavery under British rule, England set its slaves free through the Emancipation Act of 1833. America could learn by example.

GEORGE: Miss Sawyer. Has the nausea passed?

AMELIA: Oh she's much better, thank you, Dr. Sherman.

> (*AMELIA disappears humming around the bend of the boat. SHE will periodically appear, circling the deck with HER child.*)

LOUIS: We shall reach the equator in two days' time. Then, at least, we should be past the worst of the weather.

CHESTER: How much longer until Africa?

AUGUSTUS: We have been at sea four weeks. We are about halfway through our journey.

CHESTER: *(Dismay.)* Halfway?

> (*A sudden violent roll of the ship, followed by a new dramatic outburst from the VOMITERS.*)

GEORGE: When we arrive we must be prepared to adjust to a new diet. No apple pie, there are no apples and there is no wheat. There will be plenty of rice, and yams, and a native staple, often referred to as cassada, *(pronounces it KASS-i-da)* while the correct pronunciation is actually "cassava." *(KASS-i-va)*

LOUIS: *(Corrects pronunciation.)* Cas<u>sa</u>va. *(Ka-SAH-va)*

GEORGE: I have read several letters from colonists, I think I know –

LOUIS: Unless the colonist posted himself with the letter you've only *read* the word, not heard it.

LIKA: There are only two seasons in Liberia, rainy and dry. Will that not affect our farming?

GEORGE: Our time-tested routine of farmers planting in the spring and harvesting in the fall shall be rendered a comedy in the land of all-summer. Further, we must maintain our vigilance in protecting our property, as I have read of hostile actions perpetrated by the natives against the colonists. A militia has been established at the ready.

LOUIS: Please, Dr. Sherman, if you provide us with any more of your good tidings I suppose we will all just have to leap overboard.

GEORGE: I'm sorry if I am not pretending Africa is the land of milk and honey, as we near our destination it occurs to me that it is high time we consider the reality that will be ours in a few short weeks.

CHESTER: "Liberia" came from liberty. Where "Monrovia" came from?

AUGUSTUS: The capital of our colony was named for our fifth president, James Monroe, a staunch supporter of colonization.

LIKA: I have been troubled that the principal municipality of a Negro land should bear the name of a white man. What about "Turner Town" for Mr. Nat? Or Mr. Paul Cuffe? Does everyone know of him?

AUGUSTUS: I think we would be better concentrating on establishing ourselves as good neighbors and citizens to our fellow Liberians before we commence changing the names of their cities.

JOHN: *(Cleaning HIS mouth, momentarily recovered.)* In addition to the Yellow Fever I have been told of African fever, a wholly separate illness –

LOUIS: Why we have set sail in December to arrive in February, to establish some immunity before the return of the epidemic, more active during the rainy season months of June, July and August.

GEORGE: How knowledgeable. I hadn't realized you were also a doctor, *Mister* Russell.

LOUIS: After I provide shoes, people no longer walk around barefoot to catch fevers in the winter or cut their feet in the summer, I'm *better* than a doctor: I preclude the need for one.

JOHN: There are those who believe the ailments are the result of unclean living. Drunkenness, infidelity –

LOUIS: *(Smirk.)* God's punishment?

JOHN: You question an active God who makes known His displeasure in His people? Mr. Russell, how may we offer the cup of Christ to our new countrymen if there are those in our own midst who refuse to drink of it? *(Suddenly sick again, rushes to the ship's side.)*

GEORGE: He questions you as a man of faith and me as a man of science. What *do* you believe in, Mr. Russell?

LOUIS: I believe our current locale in the middle of the Atlantic is a peculiar place for you to start orating on all the hardships we are about to endure. If you were having second thoughts perhaps it would have been more kind to have shared those concerns while we were still standing on American soil.

GEORGE: I am *not* having second thoughts! I am only asking that we face the truth! I would *not* have mentioned these issues then, in our early days of excited anticipation, I had no intention of frightening would-be pioneers into remaining in the land of White Rule. What of those still in bondage who were granted their manumission in exchange for emigration? Why would I encourage them to re-think the worth of their new freedom?

LOUIS: No, wait and let them re-think it *now*.

GEORGE: Would it be better if I were to suppress my knowledge? I suppose that would be *your* strategy, Mr. Russell. That would be *if* you had any knowledge to impart.

LOUIS: *(Indicating the vomiters.)* Yes, I can see how our fellow passengers have so greatly benefited from the privilege of *your* honorable knowledge. *Doctor.*

> *(GEORGE slugs LOUIS, LOUIS jumps GEORGE: a knockdown dragout. OTHERS trying to pull THEM apart. AMELIA comes around the bend again. SHE kneels beside GEORGE on the floor.)*

AMELIA: Dr. Sherman. Dr. Sherman. Dr. Sherman. Dr. Sherman.

> *(AMELIA's voice is soft, not trying to speak over the brawl; SHE doesn't seem to take notice of it. Eventually SHE is heard, which halts the blows. All falls to silence, even the upchucking now mute.)*

AMELIA: Her fever all broke, she ain't hot no more. She ain't sweats no more she col'! Skin like ice. Hard like ice. See?

> *(Now ALL stare at the bundle, only AMELIA unaware that the infant is dead.)*

c.

(February 1841. About 4 AM. LIKA and AUGUSTUS on the bow of the ship, looking out.)

LIKA: Almost there?

AUGUSTUS: *(Nods.)* Captain says a few short hours.

LIKA: I was speaking to him earlier. He had not heard of Mr. Paul Cuffe.

AUGUSTUS: Really? *(LIKA shakes HER head no.)* A true Christian. Visionary –

LIKA: A wealthy Quaker, the owner of a fleet of whaling ships this free Negro Massachusetts philanthropist, builder of a children's school, arranged for a ship to transport thirty-eight free blacks to Africa, paying out of his own pocket for the thirty who couldn't afford the fare. The captain was clearly stunned to hear of such an affluent colored man, to imagine that such a successful man would be so generously giving to his people. The captain was clearly determined *not* to imagine such a prospect, staring at me as if I were the teller of tall tales, and my blood began to boil and I had to suppress hard my tongue, it wanted to lash out sharply oh Augustus! Tolerating such small-mindedness will soon be in the past. God has given us this gift: *our* country! Yes, we have had to endure sickness and wickedness on our journey but it will be alright! We'll marry Amelia off and she'll have another baby, one to keep forever! And Dr. Sherman will heal us, and Mr. Russell will *(touches*

HER shoe) heel us *(chuckles)*, and we'll be Africans, Augustus, Africans!

AUGUSTUS: When this orator asked a freed slave girl to marry him he had no idea her chatter knew no bounds. *(Pause. LIKA turns to HIM.)*

LIKA: Listen. You might learn something.

CAPTAIN: *(Enters.)* That light in the distance? *(LIKA and AUGUSTUS look.)* Monrovia.

> *(THEY stare, in awe.)*

LIKA: Liberia. Just waiting for us.

> *(Lights will come up in the audience revealing many NATIVE AFRICANS, standing, staring at the ship in the distance. Waiting.)*

> **End of Act One.**

Act Two

Scene One

> *(March 1841. In the darkness, Kpelle music. Lights up. A Kpelle village. A meeting of KPELLE MEN, some or all playing instruments. The music continues, then suddenly stops.*
>
> *English translations will be {italicized and bracketed} following the Kpelle text. When the Kpelle speak to each other in English, they are really*

speaking in Kpelle: no accents. When the Kpelle speak English to the Americans later in the scene, there should be accents.)

CHIEF: Kátua. Kwá guyEn ni kEi à gEE gbàlôi melaai kuâi, kukú kùla perê korí zù. *{Greetings. We are gathered to avert a crisis.}* They are coming. *(The MEN look at each other, nervous.)* They do not understand Kpelle. We spoke in pictures. *(With a stick HE draws a line in the dirt to demonstrate.)* They do not understand Poro. Our way of life. Our guide empirically, spiritually, permanent and perpetual. They do not understand *pele.* Our music, our dance, our speech, temporary and fluid. Twenty-one years ago they began to arrive. They purchased land but reimbursed the people only half what they had promised. The people told the intruders to take back their paltry remuneration and return the land. When one of their whites came to speak on behalf of their blacks, the people seized the white man and again demanded he reclaim what his people had given and return the land to Africa. The white man was told his people could stay until they found another place to live. The white man did take back the items and appealed to Botswain, an African chief *they* had selected, who ruled in *their* favor, and pledged to behead any African who attempted to undermine his ruling.

MAN 1: Why are we gathered? What did you say to the intruders?

CHIEF: I negotiated so that we may co-exist peacefully. To prove our commitment we will offer a gift of hospitality and accept one in-kind.

MAN 1: I don't want them here!

MAN 2: Land thieves!

MAN 3: Who can trust them?

MAN 2: We know how to share the land! They don't!

CHIEF: They have agreed to distance, not to encroach upon our area of hunting, of dwelling.

MAN 1: Oh they'll be here. Trying to convert us to their religion. Demanding we cover our bodies with their ridiculous garments.

CHIEF: They have promised to be respectful of our beliefs.

MAN 1: *(Running HIS fingers in the dirt.)* Is that what they said in the ground?

MAN 3: *(Stern, to MAN 1.)* Respect!

MAN 2: One of their spirit men traveled through years ago, remember? He had learned Kpelle and spoke of incomprehensible tortures across the ocean, of men and women toiling dawn to dusk 'til they dropped dead. Of whippings, amputations. And of one man who was nailed to wood, and this is the one who will save us all?

MAN 1: How can we trust they won't try to force their fairy tales on us?

> *(The following indented speeches are spoken simultaneously:)*

MAN 1: Brainwashing our children!

MAN 2: It happened just two villages away!

MAN 3: I would refuse to listen!

CHIEF: They have promised to leave us alone! We must believe them.

MAN 1, MAN 2, MAN 3 and MAN 4: *Why?*

CHIEF: Because the alternative is war.

> *(Silence.)*

CHIEF: We outnumber them many, many, many times. But we have spears, we have guns a man can hold. Their guns are giants, it takes several of their warriors to move even one. The bullets big as a man's head.

MAN 3: What is the gift of hospitality you have offered?

CHIEF: I pointed to one of their children, and I drew this. *(HE sketches in the ground.)* One of theirs for one of ours. Our peoples will be eternally linked.

> *(The MEN look down: Not mine. Finally.)*

CHIEF: We have done it with other tribes, a symbol of good will.

MAN 1: The other tribes were African!

CHIEF: So were the fathers of the fathers of these people.

MAN 1: They have forgotten that!

MAN 2: Who would give them their child? They will erase everything we have taught!

MAN 1: Then turn the child against us!

MAN 2: Fight with them to ruin us!

CHIEF: No! this will prevent that! This gift will guarantee peace!

MAN 4: *(Eyes low.)* My daughter.

(Silence: ALL stare at MAN 4.)

CHIEF: Get her. *(MAN 4 stands.)* Make sure her breasts are covered. *(MAN 4 exits.)*

MAN 1: We are Mandingo.

CHIEF: We are *not* Mandingo! We are Kpelle, we will *never* facilitate the whites' slave trade! You compare this to the Mandingo, selling Africans to who knows what across the sea? Collaborators! Traitors!

MAN 3: But when we offer such a trade to other Africans, when we offer a *slave* to other Africans, that servant has a place in the new community. The right to start a family. The right to purchase land. The culture that reared *these* black men equates a slave with an animal.

MAN 2: From what I have heard I would not treat an animal so savagely.

CHIEF: I know the stories from across the sea. The men that have settled here are black.

MAN 2: Their leader is white.

MAN 1: Everything these men know they learned from the white tyrants!

CHIEF: They will be giving one of their own in return. They would not treat one of ours differently than they would want us to treat one of theirs. Slavery, in its most primitive form, these black men are all too familiar with. I trust they of all people will rise above it.

> (*MAN 4 returns with HIS 12-year-old daughter QUITA.*)

MAN 4: I have spoken with her.

> (*A rustling in the distance. ALL turn to it. AUGUSTUS enters from the forest with GEORGE and CHESTER. AUGUSTUS and GEORGE lug a wooden crate, setting it down at the clearing.*)

CHIEF: Peace.

AUGUSTUS and GEORGE: Peace.

CHIEF: *(Sketches as HE speaks.)* Kwà faá ma à gEE ká nEnívelei síve, *{According to our agreement, you will take the girl,}* *(Indicates QUITA)* kúan ku zúronvelei síve *{and we will take the boy}*. *(Looks at CHESTER.)*

AUGUSTUS: He's talking about a trade. *(Beat.)* Our gift. That girl.

(GEORGE stunned, confused.)

GEORGE: He wants us to take her?

AUGUSTUS: He explained it to me. In the ground. A gesture of peace, as I understand it.

GEORGE: They just give their children away –

AUGUSTUS: I wouldn't –

GEORGE: And that's why you asked me to accompany you? You expect me – ? Food scarce as it is and Sarah to deliver any day, how do you propose we feed an adopted third child?

AUGUSTUS: It's an offering of *peace*, Brother George, of *good will*.

GEORGE: And why did I have to bring Chester?

AUGUSTUS: He was playing nearby when the chief and I communicated. I think he appreciated that Chester was well taken care of, he wanted the others to see how well a child is raised in the settlements.

LIKA: *(Enters.)* Augustus.

AUGUSTUS: Lika! What are you doing here? *(The KPELLE confused by LIKA's presence.)*

LIKA: I followed you. It wasn't a far journey.

AUGUSTUS: I told you –

LIKA: Not to come. Why? These people are our neighbors and it took us five weeks to visit, it is high time we started acting more cordial. *(Smiles at the KPELLE.)*

CHIEF: Sinaa kuyEn kaa! *{This is a meeting of men!}*

AUGUSTUS: Lika, these men are indecent!

GEORGE: *My* wife would not be here!

LIKA: We live in Africa now, *your* wife and I had better get used to seeing men and women clad more . . . sparingly.

AUGUSTUS: Lika! I asked you not to come for your safety –

LIKA: I worked the plantation as a child, I've seen whippings and been whipped, I watched my grandmother's insides fry her to death, protect someone else from life's adversities, Augustus, it's too late for me.

CHIEF: Nányã fekE bE! *{No women!}*

GEORGE: I believe the chief is also distracted by the presence of a woman.

LIKA: But there's that girl.

(QUITA goes to LIKA as AUGUSTUS
grabs LIKA's pointing hand.)

AUGUSTUS: Don't point! You don't know how the gesture will be interpreted.

QUITA: napâi kEi iyêi? *{Will I live with you?}*

(LIKA stares at HER, confused, then
touches QUITA's head gently.)

AUGUSTUS: Lika!

CHIEF: Kà nEnívelêi sive, ká zuronvelêi lEE. *{Take her and leave the boy.}*

GEORGE: He wants to give us that girl. For what? We left slavery behind us.

AUGUSTUS: This is not slavery, no one is abducting the child, she's coming of her own free will.

GEORGE: I don't want her!

MAN 1: Lebe kEi bE? *{What's going on?}*

CHIEF: (To MAN 1:) ImEi saa. *{Be quiet.}*

LIKA: They're giving the child away?

AUGUSTUS: An offering of hospitality. It seems to be their custom.

GEORGE: Give them *our* gift and let us leave!

AUGUSTUS: Insult him? Insist they take our offering then refuse his?

LIKA: What *is* our offering?

AUGUSTUS: Mirrors, wine glasses, rum –

LIKA: Doesn't seem to be an equivalent trade –

AUGUSTUS: Lika!

GEORGE: Reverend Gibson will commence service
soon, do you want to be late? You said this
wouldn't take long.

AUGUSTUS: I never –

GEORGE: "How long?" I asked and you replied
"As long as it takes to offer our gift"!

AUGUSTUS: I replied "As long as it takes."

> (*AUGUSTUS walks to the CHIEF,
> offering the wooden box. The CHIEF
> opens it. HE is confused. AUGUSTUS
> bows and turns to exit, accompanied by
> LIKA, GEORGE and CHESTER.*)

CHIEF: Ka maakpon kE! *{Wait!}*

> (*The AMERICOS turn around. The
> CHIEF runs to QUITA, holds HER arm
> out to THEM.*)

CHIEF: Ka líla! Ka líla! *{Take her! Take her!}* Peace!

AUGUSTUS: No you don't need to –

CHIEF: MEni fa kpElE fEE mEni namelaai woo e
kEzu to noo. Ka líla! *{An agreement is not sealed until
both sides have committed. Take her!}* Peace! Peace!

LIKA: Augustus. *(Takes HIM aside. Confidential.)* I am twenty-nine years old. No longer young.

AUGUSTUS: Lika –

LIKA: The master was certain . . . I told you –

AUGUSTUS: Not here.

LIKA: She could help me. Around the house. And I could teach her English, teach her how to read. *(Beat.)* We may not have a child any other way.

> *(AUGUSTUS considers. Then nods. LIKA is delighted.)*

LIKA: *(Goes to QUITA, palm on HER own chest.)* Lika.

QUITA: *(Palm on HER own chest.)* Quita.

LIKA: Well Quita, we had better find a dress for you fast or we'll miss church.

> *(LIKA takes QUITA by the hand and exits into the forest from where SHE had entered. AUGUSTUS once again bows to the KPELLE and turns to leave with CHESTER and GEORGE.)*

CHIEF: Kpera ma! Iwoo samasEn koo? *{Stop! What about your gift?}*

GEORGE: *Now* what?

CHIEF: Kanaa kulon síve. Kakawoi lEE bE! *{You've taken our child, now leave yours!}*

AUGUSTUS: *(Points to the box of trinkets.)* This is our gift to you. Please accept it with our humblest –

CHIEF: *(Points to CHESTER.)* Kateé zur noi tí ma! *{Leave the boy!}*

GEORGE: *(Dawns on HIM.)* It's a trade! Now that we took that girl he expects us to leave Chester!

CHIEF: Kateé zùr noi tí ma! *{Leave the boy!}*

GEORGE: I'm going to get that girl back. (Calls:) Sister Lika!

AUGUSTUS: They'll only demand we take her again!

GEORGE: I'm not leaving Chester!

AUGUSTUS: I'm not asking you –

GEORGE: Look around you, Augustus! These huts, *hundreds!* We have to abort the transaction before they summons reinforcements. SISTER LIKA!

AUGUSTUS: They're too far away to hear! Please calm yourself, George! *(Indicating the box, to the CHIEF.)* Our gift.

MAN 4: Kateé zùrônoi tí ma! Káfa p rî liî a nanEnoi ká n n lí a ká sur noi! *{Leave that boy! You can't keep my girl and keep your boy too!}*

CHIEF: *(To MAN 4.)* ImEi saa! *{Be quiet!}*

MAN 4: Kwa kukpaan mEni kE! Kakaw i kE! *{We sacrificed, now you sacrifice!}*

AUGUSTUS: We don't give away our children! We are from America! We are from America where they take our children away and sell them, we cannot *give* away our children! We are free now, our children stay with us forever!

> (MAN 4 *furiously grabs the trinket box and throws it on the ground, smashing it. The KPELLE MEN stand, alarmed.*)

AUGUSTUS: Please believe us, we want only the best for us all! We want to co-exist we want to be ideal neighbors! We want no trouble from you, we'll *cause* no trouble for you! We only want to live in harmony PEACE! PEACE!

> (*A long silence.*)

CHIEF: Peace.

> (*It takes a few moments for AUGUSTUS to recognize that there is relative calm – that HE, GEORGE and CHESTER are in no immediate danger. AUGUSTUS then leads the AMERICOS' exit. A few moments' silence.*)

MAN 4: (*Bitter.*) They take from us. And pay us with garbage. (*Kicks the trinkets.*) It's a crime for them to steal. It's a catastrophe for us to give so they don't have to.

CHIEF: We have made the greatest sacrifice to maintain peace. The conference was successful. (*Silence.*) In every war both sides sustain casualties.

Yes, they have the big guns, they would ultimately win, but they would suffer greatly in the battles, they want war no more than we. And as they saw. We are many. They are few.

> *(The MUSICIANS begin playing again, marking the end of the meeting. But as the music continues, ALL become confused by a strange sound discordant to THEIRS. It is coming from the distance, but swells and overwhelms the Kpelle music, finally causing the KPELLE MUSICIANS to stop playing, drowned out by the power of its volume. It is a Christian hymn rising from the colonists' church.)*

Scene Two

> *(November 1841. The kitchen area of a settler's house, two opposite doors to the outside. ALICE frantically searches for something. QUITA wears an American dress and reads from the Bible as LIKA listens. QUITA's American English is excellent, though HER Kpelle accent is still quite pronounced. SHE is not distracted by ALICE's frenzy. LIKA is.)*

QUITA: *(Reading.)* "And Jesus went forth, and saw a great multitude, and was moved with compassion toward them, and he healed their sick."

*(ALICE has found what SHE was
searching for: a burlap bag, and exits
out the back door with it.)*

QUITA: *(Uninterrupted.)* "And when it was
evening, his disciples came to him, saying, This is a
desert place, and the time is now past;"

*(An uproar of chickens squawking from
outside where ALICE had exited.)*

QUITA: *(Uninterrupted.)* "(S)end the multitude
away, that they may go into the villages, and buy
themselves victuals. But Jesus said unto them, They
need not depart; give ye them to eat."

*(ALICE enters holding the bag,
obviously now filled with a live chicken
squawking and struggling to be free.
With determination SHE charges
through the room and exits out the front
door.)*

QUITA: *(Uninterrupted.)* "And they say unto him,
We have here but five loaves, and two fishes."

*(The sound from outside of a single axe
blow, silencing the squawking.)*

QUITA: *(Uninterrupted.)* "He said, Bring them
hither to me."

*(ALICE enters, blood on HER dress and
face, holding the headless chicken.
Sloppily wipes HER face on a dry part
of HER dress, fills a pot with water.)*

QUITA: *(Uninterrupted.)* "And he commanded the multitude to sit down on the grass, and took the five loaves, and the two fishes, and looking up to heaven, he blessed, and brake, and gave the loaves to his disciples, and the disciples to the multitude."

(ALICE slams the pot on the stove and drops the chicken into it.)

ALICE: Stew!

LIKA: How? All meat and no vegetables.

ALICE: *I* supply the chicken, somebody else supply the cassada. Rice.

LIKA: *Who?* Nobody around here wants to farm!

ALICE: Farmin' since I was six, slave field work, tarred a farmin'!

LIKA: So we starve.

QUITA: *(Reading.)* "And they did all eat, and were filled:"

ALICE: You were a house nigger, you wouldn't know about it.

LIKA: I've been in the field, I know the fields!

ALICE: No matter. *(Pulls a couple of yams out of a wooden box.)* Somebody took to it here. I traded for a hen this mornin'.

QUITA: "And they that had eaten were about five thousand men, beside women and children."

LIKA: Very good, Quita. *(To ALICE.)* This was *supposed* to be your reading lesson too.

ALICE: I ain't readin' that.

LIKA: Do you know why the Liberia Ladies Literary Institute was founded?

ALICE: *(Pouring coffee for HERself.)* You want some coffee? Gone cold but you wanna sip, I'll make it fresh.

LIKA: Limb cut off! Or lashing at the least, been here so long you don't remember? How we were treated in America for the great crime of learning to read. The Liberia Ladies Literary Institute was established to correct that great injustice.

ALICE: *(Making coffee.)* I *said* I ain't readin' *that*. I heard enough a *that* in North Carolina, white preacher the master brung in and he ack like only one verse in the book: "Servants, be obedient to them that are your massa's accordin' to the flesh with fear and tremblin'." Then he open to another page, and start on this: "The Lord Almighty say, 'Niggers dontcha steal Massa's chickens!'" – like he readin' it, like he speck we b'lieve it's right there in red-letter print. "And as Jesus descended into heaven, he look down on the people and saith, 'Niggers dontcha steal Massa's pigs!'" *(Beat.)* Warner boy died yesterday.

LIKA: *(Nods.)* Ten years old. Not enough food! And the sewage problem. And the rainy season, seems to multiply the victims.

ALICE: Skeetas.

LIKA: *(Confused.)* Mosquitoes? *(Amused.)* You think African Fever comes from mosquitoes?

ALICE: They sure a-plenty durin' the rainy season. *(LIKA laughs.)* Ain't nunna the educated come up with a better idea HEY!

> *(HER interjection in response to the sudden squawking of chickens outside. ALICE grabs a shotgun and goes to the door, aims.)*

ALICE: DONTCHA TOUCH MY CHICKENS I'LL BLOW YOUR HEAD OFF!

> *(LIKA has rushed to grab the rifle barrel and force its aim toward the floor.)*

LIKA: Alice!

ALICE: Don't "Alice" me! And don'tcha dare say "hypocrite," we toiled dawn to dusk no pay the massa owed *us* the occasional hen! *These* savages ain't done a speck a work, then slip in – *(Yells out the door.)* TOMMY!

LIKA: Did you *see* a thief?

ALICE: No, but –

LIKA: Then it could've been anything got those chickens squawking. A wild animal –

ALICE: I know what it was! TOMMY!

(TOMMY enters. HE is dressed in work clothes, a bandana tied around HIS neck.)

ALICE: You see somebody try steal my chickens? *(TOMMY shakes HIS head no.)* Got a nice pile a wood chopped? *(TOMMY nods.)* Bring some logs in here, fire gettin' low. *(TOMMY exits.)* Probably wouldn't tell me he *did* see the thief. Stick together. Savages.

LIKA: I wish you'd stop using that word.

ALICE: And I wish *you* stop tryin' tell me how to talk, my house!

LIKA: I came to teach you to *read*. At *your* request.

QUITA: Wash your cups for you, Miss Alice?

ALICE: Well thank you, now ain'*tchu* a polite one. *(Out the door.)* TOMMY! Slow as molasses. They's some hot dishwater over there, Cheetah. *(QUITA goes to the task.)*

LIKA: Quita.

ALICE: Quita. When you changin' her name to somethin' normal?

LIKA: I'm not.

(TOMMY enters with HIS arms full of logs, proceeds to start the fire. After a few moments.)

ALICE: That word what bothers you. I don't use it *that* often. And know it ain't right, sayin' it 'round Tommy, he a good boy. Gimme some trouble while back but . . . *Watch.*

> (*Suddenly the stove fire blazes. ALICE whoops in delight.*)

ALICE: How he *do* that? Like he got a magic flint in his finger!

> (*TOMMY exits. ALICE gets out coffee beans to prepare a fresh pot. Hands LIKA a knife, and LIKA starts dicing the yams, ALICE to join HER while the coffee is on. When QUITA is finished the dishes, SHE will read the Bible to HERself silently.*)

ALICE: How long you been here now? Year?

LIKA: Nine months.

ALICE: Then you been around long enough to know what he owe me.

LIKA: (*Confused.*) Tommy?

ALICE: Congo.

LIKA: (*Nods.*) Seven years.

ALICE: Already served six. I didn't make up that number it's the law. And ain't slavery. Some new settlers actin' all shocked, you ever hearda Massa back home free every slave after seven years? Innergrate 'em inta society? And don't he set at the table with me, eat with me, some people think it strange but some people need to mind their own businesses. They servants sure but more 'n' at. Apprentices. Learn 'em to be civilized, Christian, just cuz I don't read the Bible don't mean I don't know God. Give 'em proper clothes. The women is worse! Breasts hangin' out all free, now they know they gets fined for indecent exposure, but go traipsin' through the bush, don't you see 'em all sneaky, back to their old ways, floppin' around *animals!*

QUITA: To Americans breasts are carnal, to Africans they're functional. Nourish their children.

(LIKA and ALICE stare at QUITA:
LIKA startled, ALICE suspicious.)

QUITA: *(Embarrassed.)* That's how *they* feel.

LIKA: I obey the law. It doesn't mean I have to agree with all of it. Spreading the word of the Lord to the Africans, teaching them to *read (look toward ALICE) –* These are positive actions that benefit all. On the other hand, Tommy was kidnapped from Africa by illegal slave traders and brought to America. In America, the ship was seized because the slave trade has been outlawed, while slavery itself of course still legally alive and well, so the pirate ship was seized and Tommy put on another ship to Liberia. *Not* his home, we'll never know where in Africa he came from, he's now labeled "Congo" and required by law to undergo seven years' indentured servitude, that to me is a crime.

ALICE: I *said* it ain't the same as slavery.

LIKA: I heard what you said, Alice.

QUITA: If you were running a race and passed the person in second, what place would you be in?

(*ALICE confused. LIKA chuckles.*)

LIKA: Riddles. We're always telling them to each other at home, I *never* get them. (*Thinks.*) I guess first is too obvious –

ALICE: Second! To be first you'd have to pass the person in *first* place.

QUITA: Correct! What falls but never breaks? What breaks but never falls?

(*ALICE and LIKA ponder.*)

ALICE: Night falls and never breaks! Day breaks and never falls!

QUITA: Yes!

LIKA: You're good!

ALICE: I am. Name three days come one after the other, but there's seven words you can't say: "Sunday," "Monday," "Tuesday," "Wednesday," "Thursday," "Friday," "Saturday."

(*QUITA and LIKA think.*)

QUITA: Yesterday, today and tomorrow!

*(ALICE nods, ALL laugh. A sudden
squawking from outside. ALICE grabs
the rifle again, rushes to the door.)*

ALICE: Toldju to GIT!

LIKA: *(Snatches the shotgun.)* Are you crazy?! You
don't even see what you're shooting, Tommy's out
there in the bush somewhere could've killed him!

ALICE: If you were here durin' the skirmishes
you'd have a little more tolerance a the rapid
trigger finger! *(Furiously getting two cups to serve
coffee.)* Charge in with they spears and muskets,
shoulder to shoulder, wall a Africans, eight
hundred of 'em! Our army numbered thirty-five.
Sometimes we fired the first shot know why?
Preventin' their slave traffickin'! *(TOMMY enters.)*
You finished mendin' that fence? *(TOMMY shakes
HIS head no.)* GIT! And when you done fix that
chair! *(TOMMY exits.)*

*(ALICE momentarily confused by the
look LIKA is giving HER.)*

ALICE: AIN'T SLAVERY! *(Beat. Indicates QUITA.)*
And if it was, what do you call that?

LIKA: I raise Quita as a daughter, not a servant!
And we were given her, her tribe, gift of peace!

ALICE: And I saved Tommy! But you don't know
that story, do ya.

QUITA: The Vai and the Mandingo.

315

(ALICE and LIKA turn to HER, confused.)

QUITA: They engaged in the slave trade.

ALICE: Zackly!

QUITA: But not the Kru. Not the Mende. Not the Kissi not the Belle not the Mano not the Bassa not the Krahn not the Gio not the Dei not the Gola not the Loma not the Sapo not the Grebo not the Gbandi not the Kpelle.

ALICE: *(Confused again.)* Yeah. But them other ones.

(Quiet a moment: ALICE pouring the hot coffee for LIKA and HERself.)

LIKA: At least coffee is plentiful here, wild. *(Beat. Suddenly.)* Where's the food shipments?! Didn't the Colonization Society pledge to support the settlers our first six months here? *(ALICE snickers.)* Augustus and I and our shipmates been here nine months, nothing!

ALICE: Welcome to Liberia.

LIKA: The governor keeps making promises –

ALICE: Damn the governor! White governors, ever hear tell a Pinney, few years back?

LIKA: I know –

ALICE: Governor Pinney inflate the price a corned beef and pork, then sell us spoiled cornmeal, blame it on a black shopkeeper. Mechlin? Governor

Joseph Mechlin accused a rapin' a married settler woman and never charged, meanwhile nine months later out pop this miracle baby, Mr. and Mrs. Coal Black and the baby like buttermilk.

LIKA: You can't blame Governor Buchanan for the sins of his predecessors. Besides, the poor man isn't long for this world.

ALICE: Ain't?

LIKA: You didn't know the governor was ailing?

ALICE: *(Shrugs.)* Your husband's the big wig.

LIKA: My husband's a county representative and as he *constantly* states he is the employee of the people, not the other way around. *(ALICE sucks HER teeth.)* Rumors are the governor may not live to see another day. The last white man here. *(Pause.)* Lonely in this colony, Alice. You have no husband, children. Isn't that the real reason you asked for the reading lesson. Company?

> *(ALICE stares hard at HER. Then goes to a drawer, pulls out a letter.)*

ALICE: Massa taken me when I was fourteen. I was teeny. He broke somethin' inside, birthin' almost kill me, and it be my first and last. Plenty before me Massa take to the barn, but somehow I make him feel bad. Twenty he free me, on the agreement I come here. And when my boy turn twenty-five, he commit to free *him*.

(ALICE stares at the letter, then hands it to LIKA.)

LIKA: *(Reads.)* "Dear Mother. I hope you are well. I am twenty-five, and I am free! Master made good on his promise. I have a wife now, Lavinia, and a daughter I named after your ship to Africa: Elizabeth. People in the Congress at odds. *(TOMMY enters and starts to fix a broken chair.)* Every time the West admit a free state they must admit a slave state appease the South. This country is evil. I want to come to Africa and be with you, my family in beautiful Africa where every black man is free. Respectfully, your son, Clancey."

(LIKA hands the letter back to ALICE. ALICE stares at it, all the information brand new to HER. Then shows LIKA again, points to the words.)

ALICE: "Dear Mother"?

(LIKA nods. LIKA is about to teach ALICE the next word but there is a knock at the front door. ALICE goes to the window, glances out cautiously. Then opens the door.)

ALICE: Mr. Freeman.

(AUGUSTUS enters.)

LIKA: Augustus! What are you doing here?

AUGUSTUS: *(Grave.)* I have some news to report, and I'm afraid it is not good. *(THEY stare at HIM: concern.)* Governor Buchanan has just died.

> *(A silence. Then, suddenly and simultaneously, LIKA, ALICE and AUGUSTUS begin jumping and cheering. QUITA smiles.)*

ALICE: She tol' me 'bout his sickness, but last white man, figured he hold on forever!

LIKA: Free at last! Bless his soul.

AUGUSTUS: We'd heard he'd taken a turn for the worst, we were just waiting for the messenger from Monrovia. I kept checking my watch, *(demonstrates with HIS pocket watch) please* die soon so the messenger may return before I miss my lunch!

LIKA: Who will be the next governor?

ALICE: *(Good humor.)* Some Christian! Body not even col'.

LIKA: Governor Buchanan would have wanted us to go on taking care of ourselves. Bless his soul. *(Giggles.)*

AUGUSTUS: The lieutenant-governor, Roberts.

LIKA: A black man?

AUGUSTUS: Have to be. In Liberia, white just went extinct.

> *(THEY cheer again.)*

ALICE: Taste a coffee, Mr. Freeman?

AUGUSTUS: *(Shakes HIS head no.)* I have to knock on more doors, spread the news. *(To LIKA.)* I may have to travel to Monrovia for the party. I mean, funeral. *(Exits.)*

LIKA: Changes around here! Finally the grand experiment begins, a country of black people *governed* by black people.

ALICE: *(Putting yam pieces into the pot.)* Now this stew be a celebration! Go feed the chicks, Tommy.

QUITA: May I? *(ALICE surprised.)*

LIKA: She loves doing it.

ALICE: Go to it.

> *(QUITA takes the sack of crumbs indicated by ALICE and exits.)*

ALICE: *(To TOMMY.)* Finish resta your mornin' chores? *(TOMMY nods.)* Then sit down and have a cup. *(HE pours a cup of coffee and sits on the floor away from THEM.)* He a good boy. Couldn'ta been more 'n' fifteen when they first brung him here, put him to work on the roads. He run off, they found him. Give him what he deserved. I told 'em I needed help, take him in, I *saved* him. Ain't forgot though, Tommy, never forget. Way you paid me back three years ago. *(Bitter.)* That I did *not* deserve.

> *(ALICE exits.)*

LIKA: What did you give Alice that she didn't deserve?

> (TOMMY *removes the bandana. There are scars on HIS neck, as if HE had tried to hang HIMself.*)

LIKA: Rope? (*No answer.*) What did they give you that you *did* deserve?

> (TOMMY *stands and removes HIS shirt, exposing numerous whip lashes. LIKA stares, considers. Then unbuttons the back of HER dress, revealing HER own whip-scarred back. TOMMY stares without obvious reaction. LIKA closes HER dress.*)

LIKA: Tommy. What is your name?

TOMMY: I pitch a noose 'round the low branch of a teak tree, I swing: dark, dark. But Alice walk out of her house, cut me down, anger. Before: They make us build the roads, I want home, look for home. But they find me, whip me. Before: America. White skin. They count us and herd us *animals*. Before: Chains, dark bottom, ship bottom, starve, seasick, my vomit I lie in, my waste I lie in. Before: My name – Kwame. I track an antelope step quiet, quiet. I aim for the antelope then the net. Net over the world, the ropes, tight, tight, my skin. I track the antelope a white man track me SCREAM! But mother too far, mother don't hear. Sometime I dream my mother cry for me. The dream is real, the dream tell the truth but not tell how to find her. My people have said, "Beware of the white man," we live our lives, this fear. But since I come to Liberia I see how tricky the white man is. In Liberia the white man wears a mask, a black face. But behind it he is white, white. Just the same.

Scene Three

> *(July 26, 1847. An outdoor event. Festive atmosphere.*
> *TOMMY is insane. HE moves from person to person – "Dance for you, boss?" Some ignore HIM, some give him a coin, "buying" a few seconds of HIS rendition of a traditional Ashanti dance. HE will then giggle and move on.*
> *LIKA and QUITA sitting, LIKA holding HER newborn baby. 18-year-old QUITA wears a pretty white dressy dress. There is a barrel near THEM, and THEY are drinking juice THEY had poured from it. LIKA pulls out a box tied with twine.)*

LIKA: Happy Independence Day.

QUITA: *(Unsuspecting and delighted.)* Miss Lika! *(No longer any trace of HER Kpelle accent. SHE stares at the package.)*

LIKA: Open!

> *(QUITA unties the string and looks into the open box. SHE is puzzled. Pulls out an old rusted iron mechanism.)*

LIKA: From the first plantation I worked as a child. Leg iron – locked around the ankle of a slave. The master kept them in a shed. He went in there one day, took down an iron and saw it was bent. Ruined. Some strong man, or men, just pulled the two ends apart. Master comes screaming at us, threatening, but no one owns up, nor indicts another. So he picks poor Aaron as an example, and while poor Aaron is lashed mercilessly I sneak into the shed and steal it. And even after I am sold, and even with the voyage here, I hold on to that broken chain, symbol of our freedom. Forever. You cannot own it yourself, no one of us is free until we are all free. *(Beat)* You've been with us six years now, all grown up. You will be the caretaker for awhile, and when he is old enough, you will pass it on to my son.

QUITA: I'll take good care of it, Miss Lika. *(Carefully puts it back in the box.)*

LIKA: *(Warm eyes on the baby.)* Six years married – we'd given up hope. Then this surprise. *(Looking up at QUITA.)* But even had God not seen fit to provide this miracle, we would have felt fulfilled. I couldn't have hoped for a better daughter. *(THEY smile at each other. Distant thunder.)*

QUITA: *(Looks into the sky.)* Rains coming.

LIKA: Yes, Augustus better get here soon or we'll all be soaked to the bone. *(Pause.)* Do you miss your village? Sometimes?

QUITA: *(Frowns.)* Why do you ask? *(LIKA shakes HER head: no answer.)* No. Perhaps had my mother not already been dead when I left . . . Remember two autumns ago? I went there, teach them to read? I saw my father. First time in all these years. He was angry because they were forced to move further upriver –

LIKA: We just didn't anticipate the town would grow like this –

QUITA: He looked at me with such . . . *loathing*, he did *not* want me to bring my reading, my American ways to his village. I thought he saw me as a traitor. But his sister said, "Tokpa, it's Quita." And now I see that he did not recognize me before. And he looks so . . . confused. How could he not know me? And I see in his eyes disappointment. Hurt. *(Pause.)* I really hadn't an interest in going back since.

ALICE: *(Enters. To QUITA.)* Thief! You stolen from me and you gonna die, but since I'm such a nice king I'll let you choose the method. Still, you're a wily one. Cheat me again! How?

> *(QUITA and LIKA at first startled, then realize it's a riddle. QUITA thinks.)*

QUITA: I choose to die of old age. *(ALICE grins.)*

LIKA: Any news from America, Alice?

ALICE: *(Takes out a letter.)* That dang Lavinia still refusin' to accompany my Clancey crost the ocean! And guess what? Bill in Congress to allow slave

324

catchers go to free states, bring back an escaped slave.

LIKA: No!

ALICE: Yep. An' whether the accused be escaped or whether his whole life he been free be his word 'gainst the slave catcher, now wonder how *that* rulin' turn out.

LIKA: Despicable.

ALICE: Suddenly some free peoples never no intention a emigratin' here before givin' the matter a serious reconsideration.

TOMMY: *(Enters THEIR circle.)* Dance for you, boss?

ALICE: You go on, Tommy, I'll be talkin' with ya later. *(TOMMY moves away from THEM, soliciting OTHERS.)* Never shoulda let him go. Don't know what happen to that boy, breaks my heart. Oh Lord! *(The last regarding BERTHA, who enters THEIR circle.)*

BERTHA: Hello, Sister Lika. Quita. *(Less friendly.)* Sister Alice.

LIKA: It's good to see you again, Sister Bertha. How are you finding our community?

BERTHA: Well it's definitely not the city.

ALICE: I ain't seen Monrovia since the *Elizabeth* docked me twenty-seven years ago and I ain't *inclined* to seein' no Monrovia. *(Pointedly to BERTHA.)* The <u>Elizabeth</u>.

BERTHA: *(Rolls eyes.)* Yes, Sister Alice, we all know you were among the Mayflowers. *(Turns to LIKA.)* Actually my resettlement has been respectably comfortable. I must say, I expected much more interaction with the natives.

LIKA: We do trade supplies frequently. And some of our men spend time in their villages –

BERTHA: So I've *heard*.

LIKA: I beg your pardon?

BERTHA: I know all about that. American descendant wife in the town and native "wife" in the village.

ALICE: Bet your *husband* know all about that too. *(Exits.)*

BERTHA: *(Confused.)* What? *(Calling after ALICE.)* What? *(To LIKA.)* She made that up!

LIKA: Of course.

BERTHA: Why she so rude to me? I didn't do anything to her!

QUITA: Would you like some mango juice, Mrs. Green?

BERTHA: Thank you, dear.

(QUITA *struggles to open the stuck lid*
of the barrel: no luck.)

BERTHA: She resents I'm from the city, as if we
Monrovians have our noses in the air when it's
obviously the other way round! She thinks I would
look down on her, country, not true! Monrovians
have consideration for our fellow citizens,
neighbors – *(To QUITA.)* Are you having trouble
there?

QUITA: It was fine before. Now . . . *stuck!*

TOMMY: *(Suddenly coming up to THEM.)* You fix it!
You fix it!

(QUITA *steps back as TOMMY opens*
the lid of the barrel.)

QUITA: He likes to fix things. *(Pours juice for*
BERTHA.)

BERTHA: *(To TOMMY.)* Thank you. But you say, "I
fixed it."

TOMMY: *(Confused.)* You fix it?

BERTHA: No, *you* fixed it but –

TOMMY: You fix it! You fix it!

LIKA: *(Sadness.)* He doesn't say "I" anymore.

TOMMY: Dance for you? African dance?

BERTHA: I think I'd like that.

(BERTHA *gives HIM a coin and HE*
does a brief dance. BERTHA laughs.)

TOMMY: *(To QUITA and LIKA.)* Dance for you!
African dance?

LIKA: Thank you, Kwame, maybe later.

TOMMY: *(Frowns.) Tommy!*

(TOMMY *moves away from THEM,*
soliciting OTHERS.)

BERTHA: What'd you call him?

QUITA: *(Looking into the distance.)* They're starting
the three-legged race. I'd like to try but they forbid
girls.

BERTHA: Naw, you'd get that pretty dress all
dirty. *(Looking at TOMMY in the distance.)* What
happened to him?

LIKA: Congo. Seven years he was a servant, then
he became a free man in our community. But he
never felt a part of our community. Then sent to a
Congo town but he never felt a part of that, then he
disappeared into the bush looking for his
birthplace, the second time he tried. Three years he
was missing. Then he returned: his mind gone. He
seemed to have finally found the state wherein he
fit.

AUGUSTUS: *(Enters.)* Lika! Quita! Hello Mrs.
Green.

LIKA: At last!

AUGUSTUS: *(To QUITA.)* I can sizzle like bacon / I am made with an egg / I have plenty of backbone / But lack a good leg.

QUITA: Snake! *(SHE and AUGUSTUS laughing.)*

LIKA: Augustus! You are the honored speaker and if we don't start soon we'll all be drenched!

AUGUSTUS: Yes, Mrs. Freeman, but I must share the good news first. Word just came from Monrovia. A new ship of Congos arriving from America within days!

LIKA: Wonderful!

BERTHA: *(To LIKA.)* Is it?

AUGUSTUS: Certainly! The greater our numbers, men to train, to civilize – We need them if this infant state is ever to gain an equal footing with the powerful nations of the world.

LIKA: It also means one more slave smuggler was apprehended and the Africans freed before ever seeing some ghastly American plantation.

BERTHA: But what about – ? *(Indicating TOMMY.)*

LIKA: *(Firm.)* Most Congos are living well in the Congo towns. And many have integrated into general Liberian society.

AUGUSTUS: And the new arrivals will be our neighbors! We will found a new Congo town. *(Points at an area in the distance.*

QUITA: *(Alarmed.)* Where?

AUGUSTUS: *(Understanding.)* These new arrivals don't know where they are from, Quita, they don't even speak the same languages. We have to help them find their way. Your father's people know this land, they can adapt easier a little further upriver than can these latest immigrants.

QUITA: But they've finally adapted to where they are! They're not going to want to move again!

AUGUSTUS: I'll talk to them.

QUITA: What can you tell them? Why would they want to start their lives over? Again?

AUGUSTUS: I'll *talk* to them –

QUITA: You'll *threaten* them.

LIKA: Quita!

QUITA: You won't say the words, Mr. Freeman, but they know American firepower is behind all you utter. They have no cannons!

AUGUSTUS: Quita, I assure you *you* are more upset than *they* will be. They understand progress, change. And with *your* education *you* should too. And I am *not* an American! I'm a Liberian!

QUITA: Their elderly won't survive a move! Their crops –

AUGUSTUS: Quita, the natives are a strong people! A rugged people!

QUITA: Mr. Freeman! We have just declared our independence as a sovereign nation. When we hold elections in October what do you think will happen with the native vote? They *are* the vast majority, and they'll remember how they were treated –

AUGUSTUS: Quita. The natives won't be voting.

> *(QUITA looks from AUGUSTUS to LIKA.)*

QUITA: What?

AUGUSTUS: In our new republic the Americo-Liberians will be citizens. The natives will be subjects.

> *(QUITA stunned.)*

QUITA: *I* can't vote?

LIKA: *(Eyes on AUGUSTUS.)* I can't vote.

AUGUSTUS: Someday it will change but for now, only Americo-Liberian *men*.

QUITA: But they pay taxes, Mr. Freeman, the government makes them pay taxes, how can taxes be levied then the people refused the right – ?

LOUIS: *(Enters.)* Brother Augustus, we have to begin.

AUGUSTUS: Yes of course. Quita, we'll discuss this later at home. *(Exits with LOUIS.)*

QUITA: I didn't mean to get upset.

LIKA: I know.

QUITA: Mr. Freeman and I never argue!

LIKA: We raised a daughter to speak her own mind. Now I guess we'll have to suffer the consequences.

BERTHA: You want a handkerchief, honey?

LIKA: You're an adult now. You're starting to think about things. Where you belong.

QUITA: Where I belong is *here!* My father gave me away. My father sent me away, if he wanted me he could have refused. He could have fought. Why didn't he fight? I belong *here, you*'re my family. You and Mr. Freeman and little Jeremiah, you took me in, taught me, you raised me like your own. *(Beat.)* When women get the vote, if I change my name to Constance may I vote too?

LIKA: Quita –

QUITA: I belong here! I just don't want to see my father's eyes like that again.

LIKA: You won't have to –

QUITA: I just don't want to see my father's eyes like that again! Not even in my dreams.

LOUIS: *(At the podium.)* Ladies and gentlemen. I am very excited to welcome you to our gathering in celebration of our recent independence from the United States of North America!

(Enthusiastic applause. ALICE gets the wandering TOMMY to sit still with HER, touching HIM gently and maternally. LOUIS' and AUGUSTUS' speeches are frequently punctuated by audience reactions.)

LOUIS: For those of you who don't know me, and you would have to be walking around barefoot not to, I am Louis Russell, cobbler and secretary to our county representative. I have known Mr. Freeman since we sailed together from the land of whips and chains six years ago. How far we have come in that time, and how far our colony has come since the original settlers – A few are present. *(ALICE and a few OTHERS cheer.)* Since those pilgrims sailed twenty-seven years ago. *So* far that henceforward "colony" is a bygone word. Without further adieu, I'd like to introduce our delegate in Monrovia, Senator Augustus Freeman.

(AUGUSTUS takes the podium.)

AUGUSTUS: Ten days ago, July 16th, 1847, Liberia declared its independence. Today we unfurl our flag for the first time.

(LOUIS and another MAN are doing this, and the AUDIENCE cheers as THEY glimpse the banner.)

AUGUSTUS: No longer a colony, a mere ward of a nation on the other side of the world. It is my great privilege and pleasure to present to you the *Republic* of Liberia!

*(AUGUSTUS begins to read from a
document. In the latter part of the
speech TOMMY will become restless:
first fidgeting, then an occasional clap.)*

AUGUSTUS: "We, the representatives of the
people of the commonwealth of Liberia… do
hereby in the name and on behalf of the
people…publish and declare the said
commonwealth a free, sovereign, and independent
state, by the name and title of the Republic of
Liberia….

"We recognize in all men certain inalienable rights;
among these are life, liberty, and the right to
acquire, possess, enjoy and defend property.

"We…were originally inhabitants of the United
States of North America.

"In some parts of that country we were debarred
by law from all rights and privileges of man – in
other parts, public sentiment, more powerful than
law, frowned us down….

"We were made a separate and distinct class, and
against us every avenue of improvement was
effectively closed….

"All hope of a favorable change in our country
was… wholly extinguished in our bosoms, and we
looked with anxiety for some asylum from the deep
degradation….

"Under the auspices of the American Colonization Society, we established ourselves here, on land, acquired by purchase from the lords of the soil....

"From time to time our number has been increased by immigration from America, and by accession from native tribes, and from time to time, as circumstances required it, we have extended our borders by the acquisition of land by honorable purchase from the natives of this country....

"The native African bowing down with us before the altar of the living God, declares that from us, feeble as we are, the light of Christianity has gone forth, while upon that curse of curses, the slave trade, a deadly blight has fallen, as far as our influence extends."

> *(There is more but by now TOMMY has burst into uncontrollable laughter and can no longer be ignored by AUGUSTUS.)*

AUGUSTUS: Tommy.

> *(TOMMY continues to laugh.)*

AUGUSTUS: Tommy.

> *(TOMMY, suddenly realizing AUGUSTUS is addressing HIM, stops laughing abruptly.)*

AUGUSTUS: You have a story to tell, don't you.

> *(TOMMY is nervous.)*

AUGUSTUS: I talk to Tommy sometimes. He may see the world differently from the rest of us, but he still can articulate in a way we all understand the ravages of slavery. While he never toiled a day under that vile institution, he has undergone an ordeal we have been spared since the time of our grandfathers: abduction from Africa in chains. Come, Tommy.

> (TOMMY, nervous, walks up to the
> podium. HE faces the AUDIENCE,
> confused.)

AUGUSTUS: Tell them about the chains.

> (TOMMY begins muttering.)

AUGUSTUS: Loud, Tommy, so all can hear.

TOMMY: *(Loud.)* I was in the bush and the net come over me, then they beat me, chain me. On the big ship... *(Suddenly confused again.)*

AUGUSTUS: And where did the ship take you? *(TOMMY searching frantically for the answer.)* To America, right?

TOMMY: America! All white people hate me, black skin, black skin, send me back to Africa! Liberia!

> (The AUDIENCE reaction is
> sympathetic toward TOMMY, irritation
> with AUGUSTUS.)

AUDIENCE MEMBER 1: Oh get that boy off the stage!

(The following indented speeches are spoken simultaneously:)

AUDIENCE MEMBER 2: He doesn't know what he's saying!

AUDIENCE MEMMBER 3: We need to finish before the rains!

AUGUSTUS: This is testimony, this is important! *(Complaints die out.)* Come on, Tommy, finish what you were saying. You were sent to Liberia?

TOMMY: Liberia!

AUGUSTUS: You were sent home, Africa! To an African country, where black people govern themselves! How do you feel now? *(Again TOMMY confused. Distant thunder.)* Hurry now. *(Looks up.)* Storm's coming.

> *(TOMMY suddenly takes out of HIS clothing the leg iron. QUITA, startled, looks in HER box and sees it is empty. Displaying enormous physical strength, TOMMY molds the iron so that the broken ends of the iron are rejoined. Looks at AUGUSTUS.)*

TOMMY: You fixed it.

> *(Blackout. In the darkness – the sounds of war: muskets, cannon, screams, cries. When it is over, BERTHA wails.)*

Scene Four

> (BERTHA wails. Lights up. The lifeless
> bodies of Americo-Liberians strewn
> everywhere: battle casualties. After
> several moments, LIKA enters carrying
> HER baby. SHE is in a panic, searching
> the dead.)

LIKA: (A steady stream.) Augustus? Augustus?
Augustus? Augustus?

> (LIKA turns over the prone corpse of a
> WOMAN to see HER face. It is ALICE,
> covered in blood as if shot in the torso.
> ALICE's hands clutch HER shotgun.)

LIKA: Ahhhhh . . .

> (LIKA continues searching, scared.
> Then SHE finds HIM.)

LIKA: AUGUSTUS!

> (SHE slumps over HIM. TOMMY
> enters.)

TOMMY: You fix it! You fix it. Dr. Sherman show
you how. Here's Dr. Sherman.

> (TOMMY sits next to GEORGE's
> corpse and starts sewing HIS severed
> arm back on. QUITA appears. SHE still
> wears the white dress from the previous
> scene, but now filthy, torn. HER face is
> expressionless. LIKA runs to HER.)

LIKA: Oh Quita thank God you're safe! Here. *(Puts the baby in QUITA's arms.)* Take the baby and go home. You don't need to see this.

> *(LIKA goes back to AUGUSTUS. QUITA doesn't move.)*

LIKA: Why'd they do it? Unprovoked. Just sneak up on us, unsuspecting –

QUITA: They didn't want to move.

LIKA: *(Confusion.)* What?

QUITA: They were *about* to be provoked. They were going to be moved. They didn't want to move again. If they had been provoked they would have lost. So they provoked first.

LIKA: What are you talking about? They didn't know . . .

> *(It slowly dawns on LIKA. Stares at QUITA in disbelief.)*

LIKA: You . . .

> *(Silence.)*

LIKA: He took you in. Like his own child! *(No answer.)* He treated you as if you were his blood. Alice was your friend!

QUITA: I just passed on the information. I didn't know what would happen.

LIKA: What did you *think* would happen?

TOMMY: You fix it, boss! *(HE moves over to sit by ALICE, sewing HER torso.)*

LIKA: *(Who hasn't taken HER eyes off QUITA.)* Liar.

> *(Silence. LIKA snatches the baby back.)*

LIKA: MONSTER!

> *(The baby begins to cry. LIKA walks with him, "Sh, sh.")*

QUITA: I'm going home.

LIKA: Not *my* home! Don't you *dare* set foot in my house again! Go back where you came from, *back to the bush!* Animal! *AFRICAN!*

> *(QUITA lifts HER dress over HER head. Now SHE is barefoot in a traditional skirt. SHE wears nothing above HER waist.)*

QUITA: *Yes.*

> *(QUITA turns and runs, disappears into the bush.)*

End of Act Two.

Act Three

Scene One

> *(2005. Day. Three young women – halter top, jeans, bright lipstick – are laughing and chatting in fast Liberian English, as if THEY had just come out*

*of a nightclub. THEY hear a bang and
drop to a stoop, suddenly silent,
cautious. COMBATANT GIRLS 1 and
2 quickly and subtly slip on Halloween
masks. Many bangs. Until now THEIR
weaponry would not have been obvious
to the audience but, at this point,
COMBATANT GIRL 1 pulls out an
assault rifle and starts shooting, and
COMBATANT GIRL 2 stands behind
1, a scythe at the ready. The third young
woman, KOLU, in casual pants and
halter, stares, not firing, and finally
makes a decision: walks away from
THEM and into the forest, carrying a
duffel bag from which SHE pulls out a
loose boyish work shirt and slips it on.*

  *Lights change: The
COMBATANT GIRLS are gone, and
now KOLU stands in a rubber tree
forest facing DOUGBA.)*

DOUGBA: No.

KOLU: I'm a hard worker! I'm fast!

DOUGBA: Everybody want a job now war is over,
every IDP want to tap rubber.

KOLU: I've *been* tapping rubber, I *told* you! I've
been working in the contractors' camp five weeks
now, I'm trained! *(A TAPPER FATHER and SON
enter, working on trees in the general area.)* All I'm
looking for now is full-time employment!

(DOUGBA *shakes HIS head no.*) A ton of sap a month we were expected to tap, I made my quota, ask my overseer! I made my quota *plus!*

DOUGBA: *I*'m the overseer here and a little concerned, somebody walk away from another good tapper job, try ask me for this one.

KOLU: Not steady there, *told* you! (*MARDEA enters working, hears KOLU's voice, looks up to see HER, is startled, keeps working.*) The contractors put in the old forests, trees no longer so productive. I want to be a *regular* worker, *young* trees, I want job security!

DOUGBA: Look! (*Indicates the TAPPER FATHER and SON.*) Father and son, mother surely nearby, whole family it take make the quotas, now you claim you do it, woman alone.

> (*KOLU looks around, spies MARDEA.*)

KOLU: What about *her?* (*MARDEA nervous, seeing SHE's being singled out.*)

DOUGBA: Mardea!

> (*MARDEA comes to THEM. SHE has a pronounced limp.*)

DOUGBA: Why you walk like that?

MARDEA: (*Eyes fixed on KOLU.*) The weight. Now we turn on the taps, *hundreds* of taps, when we return to collect the sap end of day we carry two buckets, seventy pounds each men, fifty pounds each women. One hundred pounds every trip to the storage tanks, many many many many trips to the storage tanks, broke my body. *(Suddenly to DOUGBA.)* Still make my quotas!

DOUGBA: How old?

MARDEA: Twenty-five.

DOUGBA: *(To KOLU.)* You?

KOLU: Twenty-four. *(By now the TAPPER FATHER and SON have exited. MARDEA limps back to HER work.)*

DOUGBA: *(Indicating MARDEA, to KOLU.)* You want to be that, year from now?

KOLU: I want a job. I want to *earn* the job, prove to you, I got strength, stamina, I do good for you, overseer, you look good for *your* overseer.

> *(DOUGBA stares at HER.)*

DOUGBA: Couldn't hire if I wanted. Huts all filled.

MARDEA: She can sleep with me.

> *(DOUGBA and KOLU turn to MARDEA, surprised.)*

MARDEA: *(Self-conscious.)* Whole hut to myself. I have room.

> *(DOUGBA considers.)*

DOUGBA: *(To KOLU.)* Only four days off per month.

KOLU: That's four more days than I got at the contractors'.

DOUGBA: Five hundred trees a day.

KOLU: Easy.

DOUGBA: On paper, that is what is expected. In truth, tap less than six hundred fifty you out.

KOLU: Okay.

DOUGBA: Six hundred fifty turn on the taps in the morning, six hundred fifty you return to collect the sap afternoon, so altogether thirteen hundred trees you attend a day, *every* day.

KOLU: I *know* how to tap, how many times I got to say?

DOUGBA: Follow Mardea. Learn the technique.

KOLU: I *know* the tech–

DOUGBA: Follow Mardea! I don't want to see the sloppy work of a contractor, someone hired on the spot, make it up as he go along!

KOLU: *Okay.*

DOUGBA: First month on trial. That's if you make it past first *week*.

(DOUGBA *exits.*)

KOLU: I know the technique. I don't have to follow you.

(MARDEA works.)

KOLU: Well guess I *have* to follow. Today. Otherwise how I find our hut among the hundreds? this camp.

(MARDEA works. KOLU starts working.)

KOLU: Probably best anyway, make sure our techniques are the same.

MARDEA: Yes. I work most efficiently in the silence. I don't think, I don't talk.

KOLU: Me too!

> *(The following, indicated by lights, are KOLU's thoughts. SHE and MARDEA continue working throughout. The PEOPLE in KOLU's thoughts don't necessarily look directly at HER. JOSEPH is dressed in a woman's wig, lipstick and painted nails: a combatant. This sequence will require quick changes – such as the IDP CAMP DWELLER who will likely double as the FEMALE VOTER – and these may be indicated simply, as with the placement and then removal of a scarf.)*

JOSEPH: Liar. You "don't think," your mind flooded with the thoughts!

> *(KOLU claps HER hands and JOSEPH "disappears": lights out on*

*HIM and up on the IDP (Internally
Displaced Person) CAMP DWELLER.)*

IDP CAMP DWELLER *(a woman)*: Kolu! You get
my husband a tapper job yet? Don't forget your
friends from the IDP camp!

CONTRACTORS' CAMP DWELLER *(a man)*: Don't
forget your friends from the contractors' camp!
Easy for *you*. DDRR – Bet they just *hand* you the
tapper position, no questions asked!

MALE VOTER: Vote for George Weah, president of
Liberia! From the bush to international football
stardom, man of the people!

CONTRACTORS' CAMP DWELLER:
Disarmament, Demobilization, Rehabilitation,
Reintegration. Forgiveness! or no peace. Assimilate
all the ex-combatants into society, if I'd known
that's the way to get a job, *I*'d have killed
somebody!

> *(ZOE uses a scythe, cutting HER sugar
> cane. KOLU sees HER.)*

KOLU: Mamada! *{Grandmother.}* War is over,
they're electing a new president!

ZOE: That's good, Kolu. When you come home?

IDP CAMP DWELLER: A regular tapper has a job
for life, childhood to old age. Don't forget us, Kolu!

CONTRACTORS' CAMP DWELLER: I hear the
drinking water's good there, Kolu! The UN put in a

346

new pump there. Not at the contractors'! remember? Our water: rotten.

KOLU: Sulfuric acid. The rubber processing.

FEMALE VOTER: Ellen Johnson-Sirleaf was our former Secretary of Finance, a Senior Loan Officer of the World Bank, experience! Ellen, Ellen, *She's* our man!

CHARLES TAYLOR: I was born Charles MacArthur Taylor. Sound like American descendant? My mother was a Gola, African! Call me Charles *Ghankay* Taylor!

IDP CAMP DWELLER: When the war start I young, no kids, run thirty miles through the woods to Guinea, refugee camp. Peace! I come back. War again! Now peace, I'm an IDP, Internally Displaced Person, refugee in my own country! *(Hopeful, to heaven.)* Maybe this peace will stick?

CHARLES TAYLOR: I will return to Liberia! Remember '97, the people chanting, "He killed my ma / He killed my pa / And I will vote for him!" And they did: landslide!

KOLU: Because the people were terrified! Butcher! They thought giving you what you wanted, you'd stop the massacre! All it did was give you power to trade guns for diamonds Sierra Leone, start *their* massacre, greedy bastard!

> *(Now a light indicates the square,*
> *cramped walls of a metal hut, wherein*

the CONTRACTORS' CAMP
DWELLER sits.)

CONTRACTORS' CAMP DWELLER: The huts at
the regular workers camp: new! Ours old, slats of
the roofs missing. It's the rainy season! *(Sound of
rain. HE looks up, many drops falling on HIM to drench
HIM in HIS hut.)*

ZOE: Kpelle don't usually keep track, but in our
family it passed down. You my grandchild, you out
of Margaret and Margaret out of me. My father
Emmanuel, son of Naomi. Naomi from Abraham
and Abraham bring Jesus to our village. This not
please his mother Kortolo, first child of Quita.
Quita! seven generations before you, Kolu. Quita
your great-great-great-great-great-grandmother,
Quita brought to the settlers, then Quita come
home. *(Turns to KOLU.)* When *you* come home?

> *(Around now, KOLU will take
> MARDEA's lead, each picking up and
> carrying on HER shoulders a pole with
> a two-foot deep bucket hanging from
> each end and filled with sap. A challenge
> for both but much more backbreaking for
> MARDEA.)*

IDP CAMP DWELLER: Kolu, the TV came to our
refugee camp! The NGOs, me on TV! But I worry.
America, Europe see, think "Ah Africa! Whole
continent poor, always poor." They put the
microphone in my face, I say, "I want my old life!
My television and *my* indoor shower, I want to go
to the theatre like before the war, I want to put a

Nigerian sitcom on the VCR, middle class! Like you." But the camera man cuts me off: "This is confusing." Then a little girl comes crying, stomach puffed out, hunger, he snatches his camera, *she*'s his star. No context to muddle things.

> *(MARDEA and KOLU put THEIR buckets down.)*

JOSEPH: Who's your friend, Kolu? Me, Joseph. *(KOLU claps HER hands.)* You can clap your hands to make me disappear *(KOLU claps HER hands)* but I won't go away. *(HE vanishes. Lights change back to natural.)*

MARDEA: *(Panting heavily.)* Finished. Twelve hours.

KOLU: See? Easy.

MARDEA: *(Stares at KOLU.)* I've heard that before. Day One.

Scene Two

> *(MARDEA in the tiny metal hut, lit by a flashlight standing upright from the floor as if it is a lamp. KOLU's duffel bag is open. MARDEA casually looks through a scrapbook. On its cover is written "HISTORY." KOLU enters, gasps as MARDEA turns a page. KOLU snatches the book.)*

KOLU: Use the toilet, come back and you going through my things!

MARDEA: *(Unfazed.)* Didn't seem so private.

KOLU: Out of *my bag!*

> *(MARDEA shrugs, lies down and turns away from KOLU to sleep. There is barely room enough for THEM both to lie down. No blankets. KOLU stays sitting up, quietly looking through the scrapbook. Eventually.)*

MARDEA: Don't waste the batteries.

KOLU: Where'd you get the flashlight? Saw no one else here with one.

MARDEA: My friend Esther, hut next to this. When her brother Tobias visit, he bring things. I give him money.

KOLU: *(Flipping pages.)* Not many pictures. Words mostly. Why you interested?

> *(MARDEA turns to HER.)*

MARDEA: Think I'm illiterate? Rubber tapper?

KOLU: *(Shrugs.)* Few *are* literate. Most from the bush, who needs to read? And war, no school.

MARDEA: No school don't mean no teacher. My mother taught me. *(Beat.)* Combatants no need to read either, combatants have a great use for books: toilet paper. But I wouldn't know about that. *(KOLU tries to ignore the implied question.)* You?

KOLU: No!

(MARDEA stares at HER, unbelieving. Then produces a ragged photograph. KOLU snatches it.)

MARDEA: *Rude.* I could have kept it, you wouldn't have known.

KOLU: I *would* have known. *(Pause.)* My grandmother. Only picture of her. Only family. *(Beat.)* Why'd you take it?

MARDEA: *Borrrowed* it. *(Shrugs.)* Made me think of *my* family. All dead.

(Pause.)

MARDEA: *(Indicating scrapbook.)* Why "History"? Why not now?

KOLU: History made now.

MARDEA: So?

KOLU: Understand history, we understand now. Understand now, –

MARDEA: *(Bored.)* We understand the future.

KOLU: We *make* the future.

(MARDEA snickers, rolls back over.)

KOLU: What was interesting?

(MARDEA turns back over to look at HER. Considers.)

MARDEA: Taylor. Embezzlement.

(KOLU finds the page. Reads.)

KOLU: "In 1983 when he was a senior official, Charles Taylor steals nine hundred thousand government dollars and escapes to America. He is arrested and imprisoned, and while awaiting extradition back to Africa he breaks out of the Massachusetts penitentiary, saws and knotted sheets, soon landing him back in Africa, and on his way to implementing a regional catastrophe."

(KOLU holds the book up for MARDEA to see KOLU's funny colored illustration of the event.)

MARDEA: American jails not strong enough to hold him?

KOLU: Maybe they didn't want to hold him.

(Beat.)

MARDEA: Firestone.

KOLU: *(Finds the page, reads.)* "Among the highlights of President King's administration was the 1927 granting of one million acres of Liberian land at six cents an acre for ninety-nine years to the American Firestone Rubber Company in exchange for Firestone's assistance in securing a U.S. loan of five million dollars." *(Looks up.)* The lease was extended and never amended. Firestone *still* pays sixty thousand a year for their million-acre plantation. *Their* plantation, nothing here ours! We could spend our whole lives this hut, it still belong to Firestone. *(Eyes narrow on MARDEA.)* And did you know "plantation" was a slave term back in America? And did you know "overseer" was a slave term back in America?

MARDEA: I want to go to America! I have family there I *will* go! Every house a cold freezer, flush toilet, every house rich!

KOLU: We had it. The cities. We too young to remember, war all our lives. Before the war indoor plumbing, refrigeration. Why you think all the modern fixtures? Now people go to the pump for water to drink, pump for water to bathe, pour it in the tub and use the dirty water to flush the toilet.

MARDEA: I want to go to America where the fixtures work!

KOLU: Before the war students from across the continent coming to Liberia, best universities in Africa! And Tolbert. President Tolbert the pan-Africanist, speaking before the U.S. Congress '76: "It is time…to usher in a new age of the American Revolution wherein this great Nation of nations will demonstrate its appropriate responsibility to the posterity of the whole of mankind. It is time for the U.S. Congress… to create and promote a universal conscience for international dignity and development…. (N)o extent of tyranny will prevent the courageous people of Africa from achieving their God-given rights"!

(The flashlight flickers.)

MARDEA: The light!

*(KOLU quickly turns the flashlight off.
Blackness for several seconds (an
indication of time passing), then the
light is clicked back on: it is in KOLU's
hand, and illuminates MARDEA
kneeling over KOLU with a knife.
Instantly KOLU snatches MARDEA's
threatening arm, rolls HER over,
overpowers HER, takes the knife.
Throws MARDEA to the side.
MARDEA shrieks in pain.)*

KOLU: For future reference: I sleep only one eye at
a time.

*(MARDEA catching HER breath. After
a moment.)*

KOLU: *Why?*

MARDEA: YOU KILLED MY BROTHER!

(KOLU stares at HER, stunned.)

KOLU: I – *What?*

MARDEA: Deaf?

KOLU: I didn't kill anybody!

MARDEA: And you weren't a combatant.

(Beat.)

KOLU: I was. Early in the war . . . I was small. My
father put me in a hole in the ground, I hid there
while Taylor's boys shot him, riddle his body . . .

My mother . . . They make her sick. Then I'm
fifteen, Taylor's boys return, won't touch my
mother, dying, but take me, keep me with them.
My mother dying, dead by now . . . I killed no one.
But saw a lot.

MARDEA: You killed no one.

KOLU: They gave me drugs. I was their hostage
but they acted as if I'd volunteered, their ally. If I
laughed hard enough when they did their evil they
let me eat the food I prepared.

MARDEA: And you learn to kill for Papay Taylor.

KOLU: No!

MARDEA: You and your girls.

KOLU: Taylor's boys took me! Then rebels killed
Taylor's boys, I was a rebel captive. Then the girl
army takes me . . . X-10! I don't remember your
brother but could have happened. X-10 carried the
scythe, X-10 did the slicing! rip a man to shreds.
And AK-47, she blow somebody away, I couldn't
stop them! Then one day: I walk away. On to an
IDP camp. Then a contractors' job, then regular
employee, here. In the war I went along for the
ride, no choice. Hate me for that you want, that I
did. Don't hate me for killing: that I didn't.

MARDEA: I had my chance to kill you and
couldn't. Don't care what you say one eye open, if I
really wanted . . . I will not try to kill you in your
sleep again. I will not kill you while we work, I will

not poison the food we share. I would just like you to admit what you did.

KOLU: I didn't.

MARDEA: Liar! *(KOLU shakes HER head no.)* Krahn dog!

KOLU: Kpelle.

MARDEA: *Kpelle? (Confused.)* Kpelle not combatants.

KOLU: The Krahn who raped my mother, which killed my mother, the Krahn that kidnapped me did not ask my tribe.

MARDEA: *I* am Gio.

KOLU: Think I like you better, enemy of Krahn?

MARDEA: Don't care what you think. *(Beat.)* My father Gio. My mother: Congo.

> *(KOLU's eyes flash.)*

KOLU: You don't even know what the word means.

> *(MARDEA stares at HER. KOLU grabs HER scrapbook, finds a page.)*

KOLU: *(Reads.)* "Congos: the abducted Africans brought to Liberia after their pirate ship seized." Now, anyone with American blood call themselves "Congo." Proud of it?

MARDEA: No pride, no shame. You talk like there aren't native families with money, who cares?

KOLU: How many native families with money, two? Three – ?

MARDEA: And what my great American blood get me?: Firestone! Broke body, twenty-five and I can't go to the toilet without the torture.

KOLU: History matters! Native Africans not permitted to vote 'til 1946!

MARDEA: If the candidates bad as now, the natives were lucky.

KOLU: Name one candidate.

> *(MARDEA opens HER mouth to answer, then closes it. SHE can't.)*

KOLU: What I thought.

MARDEA: I'm not ignorant! No radio here! And barely broadcasting since the war, how I find out – ?

KOLU: *(Softer.)* I know.

> *(Pause.)*

MARDEA: My brother was all I had left. After my mother and father died, the refugee camp. I pick up my brother's corpse, heavy, I carry him to the U.S. Embassy, I see all the bodies, the wailing, wailing, I drop my brother's body into the pile we *scream* to the U.S. Embassy *"Hear us!"*

KOLU: *(Beat.)* For future reference: I don't sleep. If I don't sleep, I don't dream. Your dreams tell the future?

MARDEA: Whose doesn't?

KOLU: My dreams do not tell the future, my dreams only re-live the past, and that I prefer not.

> *(MARDEA stares at KOLU, then goes to a pail in the corner, dips out a little water to drink. After the fight, HER awkward movements are even more severe than usual.)*

KOLU: Pain all the time?

MARDEA: Every night I weep myself to sleep, the agony. Don't worry, I'll learn to do it silent.

KOLU: Work here easy for me. If it's so bad for you, why don't you do something about it? Talk to the others, demand it: less weight, lower quotas.

MARDEA: Why don't *you* do something about it?

KOLU: Work easy for me. Compared to the Firestone contractors' camp? At least clean drinking water here! Firestone regular workers' camp a paradise! Relatively.

MARDEA: I'm *tired* of relatively! For once I'd like to be the people in the world *don't* got to say "My life not a misery, *relatively.*" I want to go to America!

(KOLU lies back down, turns away from MARDEA.)

MARDEA: I've seen an American. A white man. You ever see a white man? *(Beat.)* I don't mean *light*, I mean *white*, *American* white, ivory-pink skin, hair yellow like straw. *(KOLU glances at HER.)* Eight years ago I come to this plantation. I take work to stay alive, Taylor never let the war touch Firestone. Following the overseer down the main road, overseer look up. There he is, Mr. Smith, big white American boss driving his big grey American truck but he never see us, his eyes front. To him: we're the trees.

KOLU: Invisible. Thousands toil twelve killing hours a day to put tires under his damn truck, he don't see us!

MARDEA: Tires? *(Pause. KOLU looks at HER. MARDEA smiles.)* That's not the half of it.

KOLU: *(Confused.)* Rubber. Tires.

MARDEA: Rubber *sap*. Latex. Condoms. *(KOLU stares.)* I get letters from my cousin. My cousin Lika in America, named after our settler ancestor, Lika writes "Dear Mardea. People here are very aware of AIDS in Africa. The solution, they say, is simple: Stop having so much sex." But she finds this suggestion confusing because, as she continues, "I've never *seen* people as oversexed as Americans! They meet in bars they have sex, they meet in bookstores they have sex, they meet on the *internet* they have sex! Cheap: condoms in the grocery store, condoms in the drug store, condoms in the corner candy store, Americans have ten times the sex and Africans ten times the AIDS. But," she goes on, "there *are* sympathetic Americans, there are those who believe we can heal. If only Africans could exercise just a little restraint!"

Scene Three

> (*Near dusk. Outside ESTHER's and KOLU/MARDEA's huts.*
>
> *MR. KONNEH, a blind man, sits. DOUGBA writes figures into a ledger. KOLU enters carrying a pole with hanging pails on HER shoulders, looking dead exhausted. Drags HERself past DOUGBA without seeing HIM.*)

DOUGBA: Latex for your evening meal?

> (*KOLU looks at HIM confused, then suddenly becomes aware of the buckets.*)

KOLU: Aaaaaaaaaaah! (*Puts down HER load.*)

DOUGBA: Long walk back to the storage tanks.

KOLU: Crazy! Turn on the taps, clean the cups, spray the fungicide, collect the sap, carry the buckets to the storage tanks *heavy!* Feel like I'm sleepwalking, my brain stopped hours ago so legs point me home. A little early. This was my last load.

DOUGBA: "I can do it, hee hee, I'm fast, I never tire." Miss a day and you're out.

KOLU: "You're out," "You're out," I *won't* miss a day I *have*n't missed a day *four months!*

DOUGBA: Just reiterating.

KOLU: It's a lot! Six hundred fifty trees every day. Not human.

DOUGBA: Six fifty's the past. Take a good rest tomorrow, Monday the new quota's eight hundred. *(KOLU stares at HIM incredulously.)* As I understand it the superintendent whose section brings in the most latex gets a cash prize. Our superintendent apparently plans to win. *(Exits.)*

MR. KONNEH: Twice I did it. So tired I bring the buckets home with me. Twice in twenty-seven years.

KOLU: That how long it took to go blind?

MR. KONNEH: Slow process. Chemicals we use. The tree bark.

KOLU: We should have goggles! We should have gloves! Why's no one demand it? Everyone asleep?

MR. KONNEH: Why don't *you* demand it?

(No answer.)

MR. KONNEH: They say, "A starving leopard may *seem* asleep, but dare to tap him."

KOLU: How I demand it? What you think Dougba say? Big boss snap his fingers Dougba jump, think he ever suggest protection for tappers might cost the bosses pocket change?

MR. KONNEH: You the one asked why's no one demand it.

KOLU: I mean somebody *been* here longer, I mean somebody know Dougba, get around him.
MR. KONNEH: *You* know Dougba –

KOLU: I mean somebody else!

(*Pause.*)

MR. KONNEH: Dougba not a mean man. Born on the plantation, when I first come he a boy with his father, tapping with his father sometime wave to me through the trees "Hello Mr. Konneh! How's Esther?" Liked to play with Esther, her crawling then. He try do his best by everyone. But his numbers the superintendent watch close, hour he be back, make sure those pails transported. Don't wait.

> (*KOLU starts to pick up the buckets but is surprised by the sound of unfamiliar male laughter coming from inside ESTHER's hut.*
>
> *MR. KONNEH smiles.*)

MR. KONNEH: My son. He visit time to time, tell Esther, "Come inside, something for you."

KOLU: Tobias?

MR. KONNEH: You've met?

KOLU: I've heard.

> (*ESTHER and TOBIAS come out of the
> hut. ESTHER holds a large bag.*)

ESTHER: Pa, look what Tobias – Kolu! Tobias, this
my friend, stay with Mardea. Sometime we share
the rice. Kolu, this my brother Tobias.

KOLU: (*A Liberian handshake with TOBIAS.*) From
Monrovia?

MR. KONNEH: Tobias eleventh child, Tobias
raised by people in Monrovia. Give him clothes,
teach him book.

ESTHER: Look what Tobias brought me!

> (*ESTHER shows KOLU. The bag is full
> of fabric, sewing stuff.*)

ESTHER: See, Pa?

> (*SHE takes the bag to HIM, guiding
> HIS hand in. HE feels, smiles.*)

ESTHER: (*To KOLU.*) Sewing's my joy but who can
afford material? My rich city brother provide me!

TOBIAS: (*Rolled eyes.*) "Rich."

ESTHER: Pa! Why you not wear the new outfit
Tobias bring you?

MR. KONNEH: Wear my old outfit out first.

ESTHER: I sew something for you you'll not wait for the coffin to wear it! You too, Kolu. Make you a dress. Wouldn't Kolu look nice in a dress, Tobias?

TOBIAS: *(Considers.)* Wouldn't suit her.

ESTHER: You met her two minutes ago what *you* know? You need to accent your roundness, Kolu. You got some roundness, somewhere under those pants.

TOBIAS: Getting late. Early departure.

ESTHER: Tobias driving to Lofa tomorrow. Family there.

KOLU: *(To TOBIAS.)* Through Bong County?

ESTHER: Kolu's from Dbarnga.

TOBIAS: *(Irony.)* Ah, the stronghold of our fearless leader Mr. Taylor.

KOLU: *Not just him!*

> *(A momentary conversation stopper.)*

TOBIAS: No, not just him. Villagers. And rebels, all sorts of dogs trained in the bush.

> *(KOLU trapped. TOBIAS nods.)*

TOBIAS: Ex-combatant.

KOLU: Long ago! Forced! No choice!

TOBIAS: No doubt. Only Liberia has a war of all women. The boy *and* girl combatants, nail polish, wigs. You don't dress fashionable enough to be a soldier.

KOLU: I dress like a tapper. I'd like to ride with you. I grew up in Dbarnga but I'd like to see my grandmother's village, up from there.

> *(ESTHER and TOBIAS surprised by the request.)*

TOBIAS: Those villages are hours off the paved road. And the paved roads shot to bits, swerve to the right shoulder to avoid a pothole, then two seconds later fly into the left lane to avoid another.

KOLU: Just leave me in Dbarnga, I'll find someone take me rest of the way.

TOBIAS: Young woman traveling alone spells "refugee" or "ex-combatant," who's going to take a chance it's the latter?

KOLU: Pay them enough.

ESTHER: With what? All your Firestone disposable income?

> *(KOLU glances around to make sure no one else is looking, then pulls out an impressive wad of cash from a pocket sewn into the inside of HER clothes, surprising ESTHER and TOBIAS.)*

365

TOBIAS: I see helpless victim not prevented you from enjoying the spoils of war.

ESTHER: Why you want to go all that way?

KOLU: My grandmother, haven't seen her since before the war, fifteen years. Or heard from her. *(ESTHER and TOBIAS exchange glances.)* I know, maybe she dead by now. This journey I'll find out. Pay you half the gas to Dbarnga.

TOBIAS: Fifteen years ago you were . . . ten?

KOLU: Nine.

TOBIAS: And now, adult, you remember the way.

> *(KOLU goes into HER hut, retrieves HER scrapbook, turns to a page with a sketched map. As SHE speaks TOBIAS, fascinated, takes the book.)*

KOLU: Here's Dbarnga. Here's the road to my grandmother's village. These are the villages we will pass along the way. *(Beat.)* I was there. Not long ago. War time. I said I hadn't seen my grandmother fifteen years, I didn't say I hadn't seen her village.

TOBIAS: *(Beat.)* You know the flag? Entrance to this camp? *(KOLU nods.)* Meet me there. Dawn.

ESTHER: You're not serious? *(Sees THEY are. To KOLU.)* Lose your job! Never get where you're going before late afternoon, think you be back before Monday daybreak?

KOLU: Tuesday, latest.

ESTHER: Tuesday *too* late.

KOLU: If I sleep less next week, I can make it up, make the quota. New quota.

ESTHER: *New* quota?

> (*KOLU nods gravely. ESTHER is dejected.*)

ESTHER: Come on, Pa, let's fix your bed.

> (*ESTHER helps her FATHER into the hut as TOBIAS continues flipping through the scrapbook. HE pulls out a paper cutout of a traditional Kpelle mask, puts it over HIS face.*)

TOBIAS: Do you see me? I am no longer here. A spirit has entered me.

> (*KOLU startled. TOBIAS laughs, gives the mask back to HER.*)

TOBIAS: I understand the mask. I grew up Monrovia but spent plenty time with relatives, the bush. (*Shrugs.*) Monrovia may as well be the bush. No electricity. And if there was, no matter for the streets, lights shot right off the lampposts. People sitting behind the tables along the road, candlelight, thousands of burning candles. Magic, romance. Except for the nagging reality that our capital city been pushed back to the pre-industrial age.

(KOLU gazes at HIM. Then opens the scrapbook to a multicolored page: design for a flag.)

KOLU: The Liberian flag was something created by the Americos, resembling the American flag. We need an African flag. African colors. Black background, red sun in the center of sixteen green circles representing the sixteen tribes of Liberia. *(Points to a word in the corner.)* And "Ducor." Monrovia had a name before the Americans came.

TOBIAS: You made this up? *(KOLU nods.)* The stars?

KOLU: For the Americos, they're also Liberians. But only two, and they're in the periphery.

(KOLU closes HER scrapbook, starts to take it back to HER hut.)

TOBIAS: Doe ignited the tribal rivalries, *(KOLU stops)* but something much bigger on the way, out of the bush, a monstrosity that if unleashed would render unspeakable ravage. So in 1989 I walk down to the pier, and there they are. The ships: America! Of *course* they would come, we were there for them when they needed an African base during the Cold War, we were there for them when they needed a spy to gather data on our fellow African Libya, America our friend! But no one comes off the ships. Even a token show of U.S. military force would have been enough to stave off coward Charles Taylor but the American ships anchor just long enough to evacuate American citizens and foreign nationals and leave. Still I wait. Surely America will send more ships! save us! I wait. I wait. While I wait Iraq invades Kuwait and if there ever had been any reason to dream America would care about us, the dream is now dashed: fifteen bloody, brutal years.

(Silence.)

TOBIAS: Take you to the bush with me tomorrow. Kill me? Rob me? Rebel?

KOLU: How many times I need to say it? *Forced* to follow, I killed no one!

(TOBIAS smiles.)

TOBIAS: *I* was a rebel. Remove the bastard from office, that good idea went a bad way, oh? On the handle of my assault rifle were tic marks, one for every person I slew, and there were quite a number of them. Our favorite game was "Beg." We'd pick somebody, or some family, one of us would point and say "Beg." Then we would explain: "We will kill you unless you beg us to kill you." Confused at first, then we aim and they, on their knees, "Please kill me, please kill me," the tears streaming, "Please kill me" 'til finally we got bored and did. Sometimes we would first call them "dissident collaborator," we didn't know what it meant but we felt important spatting the accusation, it gave our murders political dignity. In Monrovia yesterday, the market, someone calls out to me. He was one of my former gang, and he invites me to his house, dinner. He's married now, three little ones. The oldest's name is "Christian," *they* are Christians, he embraces Christianity, I say the colonists brought Christianity to us so aren't *you* a dissident collaborator now? He says the colonists Christianized us for good reasons, what he loves is that one is born again in Christ, *he* is born again in Christ, the past was another life, not *his* life. "But we can't forget," I say, "It was our doing, lose history and it repeats." "But that wasn't *me*," he insists. "That was another life, an old life, a dead life." Then he takes me into a room, the furniture soft and comfortable, but it has a chilly feel as if the family never enters it. Hung on the wall is his AK-47 with its dozens of tic marks. And carved into the tiny vertical lines are now tinier horizontals. Crosses.

> *(TOBIAS exits. KOLU stares at nothing. Then sleepy, sleepy, asleep. Lights change. Dream: JOSEPH enters with a BOY COMBATANT of about ten. JOSEPH carries a pan of food and sets it in front of HIMself. Then sits, painting HIS fingernails bright red. Beside HIM the BOY COMBATANT sits staring into space. Around one arm the BOY COMBATANT clutches a teddy bear, thumb in HIS mouth. In the other hand HE holds an AK-47.)*

JOSEPH: Who's your friend?

> *(The sleeping KOLU immediately stands, awake, stares at HIM.)*

370

KOLU: You, Brother Joseph.

> *(KOLU goes to HIM, starts feeding*
> *HIM from HIS plate.)*

JOSEPH: Right. I'm the one rescued you from *them*.
Taylor's thugs. Have we ever touched you? no!
Forced drugs on you? No. If we'd left you Taylor's
boys would've just come again, we're your saviors.
What we did to those women yesterday – they
were enemy. Their husbands collaborators of
Taylor, I sense these things. We ever do that to
you? No. And everything you've learned –
anything ever happen to us you'll be ready. But
don't worry. We're protected.

> *(JOSEPH pours water on the ground,*
> *making mud.)*

JOSEPH: I was a kid '79, the rice riots, my mother
took me to church. My little sisters and brother
starving, sick, prayed to God my little sister
wouldn't die. She did. Prayed to Jesus my little
brother wouldn't die. He did. Father, mother,
prayed they'd live, they died. *(Glances at KOLU.)*
You don't remember the coup. *(KOLU shakes HER*
head no.) Nineteen consecutive presidents, all
Americans and their descendants, finally Samuel
Doe, *African* takes the presidency: dancing in the
streets! Even I dry my orphan tears to step. But Doe
was a military man, not a diplomat. The dancing:
short-lived.

> *(JOSEPH rubs the mud onto HIS face.)*

JOSEPH: This is good juju. Keep their bullets from harming us. So far *this* juju *much* better than prayer, that *Jesus* juju *never* worked. But *this?* How many battles?, I'm still standing.

> (*HE has completed HIS mud face, shows KOLU.*)

JOSEPH: Safe. (*Looks around, makes sure no one is listening.*) But in the unlikelihood we come across enemy whose juju's a drop stronger, you'll know what to do with an AK-47, this is your apprenticeship.

> (*SUAH enters wearing a woman's wig, painted nails. HE appears exponentially more threatening than JOSEPH: his walk, his eyes. HE hands a paper bag to JOSEPH.*)

SUAH: (*To JOSEPH.*) Time. (*To KOLU.*) My rice was cold.

KOLU: Sorry, Mr. Suah!

> (*SUAH exits. JOSEPH takes a huge inhalation from the paper bag, passes it to the BOY COMBATANT. The BOY COMBATANT inhales from the bag. JOSEPH puts on a women's wig, long hair and curled effeminately. Pulls a scythe out of HIS clothing. The BOY COMBATANT puts on a Donald Duck mask.*)

BOY COMBATANT: Do you see me? I am no longer here. A spirit has entered me.

JOSEPH: *(Looks at KOLU.)* Battle stations.

> *(JOSEPH exits, the BOY following closely. KOLU following more slowly.)*

Scene Four

> *(Inside ZOE's home, a dried mud hut (modest but considerably larger than the Firestone metal variety) in a traditional Kpelle village. A curtain hanging in the back divides this space from a tiny adjoining room. Several people sitting in a circle of chairs, singing a hymn, a fusion of Kpelle musical rhythms and instruments with African-American gospel. On a table before THEM is a pitcher and glasses. On the floor next to MIRIAM is a basket wherein a year-old infant sleeps in blankets. The song finishes.)*

TAMBA: I believe Brother Amos has something to share.

KOLU: *(Off.)* Mamada! Mamada!

> *(KOLU rushes into the room from the outside. SHE stops, surprised by the roomful of people.)*

ZOE: *Kolu?*

(KOLU, self-conscious, goes to kneel next to the seated ZOE.)

KOLU: Yes, Mamada, it's me.

ZOE: Kolu! *(Moved, HER hands on KOLU, to the OTHERS.)* This is my granddaughter, Kolu!

OTHERS: Hello, Kolu. / Welcome. / Good evening.

ZOE: I haven't seen her since before the war!

OTHERS: Praise God. / Praise Jesus.

ZOE: We've been waiting for you, Kolu. *(KOLU looks at the OTHERS, confused.)* But we'll talk later. I'm hosting evening devotion. *(Concern.)* Everyone brought their chair, I don't have more!

KOLU: It's okay, Mamada, I'll wait outside 'til you're through.

ZOE: No!

MIRIAM: How about this bucket?

(MIRIAM takes a bucket from the corner, turns it upside down in the circle. KOLU, embarrassed and uncomfortable, nods HER gratitude, sits. MIRIAM re-takes HER seat, by TAMBA. Responses to the following devotions ("Amen!" etc.) may be spontaneous, and occurring within devotions.)

TAMBA: Brother Amos was about to speak?

AMOS: Yes! I just wanted to say, as you all know, my nephew had been quite ill. My sister moved to Monrovia last year, and little Elwood just turned two, and we thought we might lose him, but the medicines came through and he has recovered *completely!* And I wanted to thank all of you for your prayers, and for the wonderful gift of the mosquito net! and I wanted to thank God for looking after my nephew and bringing him back to us.

OTHERS: Amen. / Praise God. / Praise the Lord.

(*A pause.*)

ZOE: You all know the personal pain I have been suffering these many years. And then after my sickness before the rains, I am thankful that God has seen fit to let my eyes witness another year, and to behold my grandchild come home!

OTHERS: Praise Jesus. / Amen. / Thank you, Jesus.

(*A pause.*)

CONGREGATION MAN: I am *so* grateful that you found us, Reverend Tamba, that you've been with us these last four months. I am thankful you have brought with you your kind fiancée, who has been a wonderful comfort to the sick. I praise God that people like Sister Zoe's granddaughter are no longer afraid, are returning, a certain sign that this peace will be the lasting one!

OTHERS: *Amen!* / *Yes*, Lord! / Praise God!

(A pause.)

MIRIAM: As a Loma girl, I am *very* thankful to have learned Kpelle so that I may be conversing with you all right now. *(OTHERS laugh.)* I am so grateful that my very active daughter is taking such a long nap. *(OTHERS laugh.)* I thank you sweet Jesus for bringing Reverend Tamba into my life. It was very hard, my parents slaughtered, and then the men . . . And the Reverend could have said he would not want his wife to have brought forth another man's child, whatever the circumstances. But the Reverend is a good man, and a loving man, and a generous man.

TAMBA: *(Smiles.)* I praise God to have found a wife-to-be so equally good, and loving, and generous. And in that spirit of generosity, we will all be tested in our hearts as we undergo the DDRR. The Disarmament-

TAMBA (Cont'd) and OTHERS: Demobilization, Rehabilitation, Reintegration

TAMBA (Cont'd): – process. We may not be able to forget. But we can forgive.

> *(Silence. TAMBA stares at the OTHERS, awaiting a response. None comes.)*

TAMBA: I know it will be difficult but it is our only path to peace. Other Liberians need only *accept* our transgressors, receiving them back into society. As

Christians, we must take that extra step toward forgiveness.

> *(Silence.)*

CONGREGATION MAN: I won't forgive Charles Taylor!

OTHERS: A*men!* / Never! / Satan on earth!

> *(Pause. Then TAMBA shrugs.)*

TAMBA: We are only human. At least we can forgive the rest.

> *(Beat.)*

MIRIAM: *(Eyes closed.)* We can forgive. We can forgive.

> *(OTHERS, except KOLU, gradually*
> *join the chant, eyes closed.)*

OTHERS: We can forgive. We can forgive. We can forgive. We can forgive. . . .

> *(In the midst of the chant, MIRIAM*
> *stops speaking, raises HER face, opens*
> *HER eyes.)*

MIRIAM: Kolu. Do you remember me?

> *(The chanting stops. ALL eyes on*
> *KOLU. KOLU startled and confused.*
> *SHE stares at MIRIAM. Slowly shakes*
> *HER head no.)*

MIRIAM: You took me in. You saw I was nearly starved, you gave me food, you were kind. God forgive me but I followed you awhile, you and those girls. Then I couldn't watch anymore, what you did. To others. I found escape, I took it.

> (KOLU, dazed, shaking HER head no again.)

TAMBA: Kolu. You must be humble before God. You cannot be forgiven until you confess your sins.

KOLU: I didn't *do* anything!

MIRIAM: I saw you, Kolu.

KOLU: And I *said* I didn't *do* anything! I was with some girls a time, how could anybody be alone, the war? *No*body didn't want to get killed could be alone! So maybe you saw me but I didn't . . . X-10. I bet you're thinking of X-10! now *she* did some stuff!

> (MIRIAM still staring at KOLU.)

KOLU: I said it wasn't me. You're confused. I can understand your confusion, all that... It was war. Who knew *who* – ?

MIRIAM: Okay.

> (MIRIAM has turned to check on the baby, an indication that SHE is through with KOLU. This confuses the OTHERS and KOLU. When it is clear MIRIAM will say nothing more:)

TAMBA: *(To ALL.)* I want you all to know I thank God every day for bringing me to serve your village. I have never felt so welcome, so at home. *(OTHERS: "Amen," etc.)* I thank the Lord Jesus to be acquiring a beautiful wife and a beautiful daughter all at once, *(the COUPLE smile at each other)* and it is with God's great mercy that I will share this blessed event with all of you. When I was originally summonsed to this village –

KOLU: *(To MIRIAM.)* What makes you think it was me? Why's everybody think it was me?

MIRIAM: Perhaps I was mistaken – *(Not believing SHE is.)*

KOLU: Well I'd just like to know why everybody keeps making the same mistake! *(To ALL.)* I didn't say I was innocent. It was war, I did what I had to. Not much! I didn't – I killed NO one! But plenty of girl combatants, easy to mistake me for someone else.

MIRIAM: I'm sorry.

KOLU: Don't say you're sorry! I didn't ask for you to say you're sorry! I just want to know why the mistake keeps happening! Okay? Okay, I did a *little, okay? Every*one – I'm sorry for whatever I did, it's just – It's not what you think.

(MIRIAM stands.)

MIRIAM: Whatever you did, Kolu, I love you, and I forgive you.

(KOLU is completely thrown by this, confused and terrified. MIRIAM walks to KOLU and lays HER hands on HER.)

MIRIAM: I love you, and I forgive you.

(Now the OTHERS, one by one, rise, go to KOLU, lay hands on HER.)

OTHERS *(not synchronized)*:) I love you, Kolu. I forgive you, Kolu. I love you, Kolu. I forgive you, Kolu.

KOLU *(trembling)*: Forgive me?

OTHERS *(uninterrupted)*: I love you, Kolu. I forgive you, Kolu.

KOLU: Forgive me?

OTHERS *(uninterrupted)*: I love you, Kolu. I forgive you, Kolu…

KOLU: FORGIVE *ME?*

(KOLU's outburst has stunned the OTHERS to silence, to giving KOLU space.)

KOLU: *They* got my mother! *they* got my mother then rape me. Many, many, many rape me, raping me, I think I'll die, soldiers for Taylor, I want to die take me, drug me, carry me with them rape me when they feel like it *often. Often,* then a rebel unit,

blows them all away! We're asleep and the shots
ring out, some run to get their pants, some run bare
butt no one survive, shot through, dead *good!* I feel
good, ready to die but *they* take me. Rebels take me
"No more!" Train me I'm a soldier, they don't touch
me I'm a soldier! But touch others, women, I watch,
I watch earn their trust their ammunition and one
day we come to an orphanage. Little girls, I don't
know what they're planning but *no*. No I blow
them all away, AK-47 *dead!* One tried to run I slash
him, cut him to bits my *ssssscythe,* and after I even
suspect a man looking at me my *sssssscythe.* And
one of these killings the girls witness, ask me to join
their all-girls, Yes! And we kill for protection and
we kill cuz Why not? And they don't know my
name but soon I'm out in front, never know my
name to them I'm X-10, notorious X-10 and tic
marks fill my rifle handle, tic for every kill and I
never even added in the ones I did before I met the
girls cuz I counted those I would've had to carve
"To be continued" and start on a whole other gun.

> (KOLU stares at THEM. THEY stare at
> KOLU. Then KOLU suddenly
> breathing heavy, suppressing a
> threatening torrent of sobs.)

TAMBA: I think Sister Zoe needs some time alone
with her granddaughter.

> (TAMBA gently ushers out ALL except
> ZOE and KOLU, MIRIAM carrying
> HER sleeping child. After the TWO are
> alone, ZOE gets a cup, goes to the

pitcher on the table and pours. Hands the cup to KOLU who drinks it down all at once. Then stares at ZOE.)

KOLU: Give me drink? After what I done?

ZOE: Always my grandchild. Right?

(ZOE then takes KOLU's cup, fills it again, hands it back to KOLU.)

ZOE: They say, "Do not look where you fell, but where you slipped."

KOLU: How I slip? They done it to me first.

ZOE: Ain't that war? *(KOLU stares at HER.)* Weren't all self-defense, were it.

(KOLU looks down at the cup.)

KOLU: Coconut milk. Long time since I had it. *(Beat.)* Think about you all the time, Mamada. See you in the fields, cutting the sugar cane.

ZOE: *(Eyes on the dusty scythe in the corner.)* Never touch it anymore. Combatants gave the scythe a bad name. They say rebels still hiding in the bush though, walk outside the village, you take it.

(KOLU shaking HER head a vehement no. Then:)

KOLU: Paying back. Whatever I done, I work for Firestone now. Break my back, I crawl. Crawl resta my life, tap trees all my life, slave for pennies 'til I die. Penitence.

ZOE: Penitence? *(KOLU nods.)* Penitence without reparation is *nothing*.

KOLU: *(Stares.)* Then *what?*

ZOE: Make amends.

KOLU: *How?*

ZOE: You the only one can find *that* out.

> *(Pause: KOLU tired.)*

ZOE: How city you got? *(KOLU stares at HER.)* We need women to pound the rice today, remember how?

> *(KOLU continues to stare. ZOE takes two long bamboo poles from the corner, turns them upside down, gives one to KOLU.)*

ZOE: Big barrel, the women stand in it. Filled with the rice, harvest, they prepare it to cook. Remember?

> *(ZOE begins to step forward and back with HER stick, a lively dance. KOLU joins HER with the other stick, facing HER, falling back when ZOE falls forward, then KOLU coming up to fall forward while ZOE falls back: pendulum.)*

ZOE: Very good. Very good, you remember. You remember, this is how we did it. Me, you, your mother, this is how we did it. You, me, your

mother; you, me, your mother; you, me, your
mother –

KOLU: *(Stops suddenly.)* They killed Ma, Mamada!
Make her sick, they make her die. Dying, dying
when I saw her last, years and years and years ago.
Dead now. Dead now.

> *(ZOE continues gazing at KOLU, then
> goes to the curtain along the back wall,
> draws it. Behind it, lying on a mat on
> the floor is a dying woman,
> MARGARET, AIDS sores prevalent on
> HER flesh, HER eyes closed. KOLU
> stares, stunned. ZOE gently touches
> MARGARET, and MARGARET's eyes
> open. SHE searches the room wildly,
> HER tongue white with liquid. Then
> HER eyes rest on KOLU. MARGARET
> is struggling, struggling.)*

ZOE: We been waiting for you, Kolu. Your mother
and me. *(KOLU continues staring.)* Go on.

> *(KOLU slowly moves to kneel beside
> MARGARET. With much effort,
> MARGARET finally speaks.)*

MARGARET: My mother, my mother.

ZOE: Only child, your parents have no more. Only
child also last child, last child son we call "father,"
last daughter we call "mother," the circle start
again.

KOLU: I know.

MARGARET: My mother.

ZOE: My daughter, my Margaret not die 'til she see *her* daughter once more.

> (*MARGARET's trembling hands lift HER top to slowly expose HER breasts.*)

MARGARET: I bring you into the world, Mother. Suckle me. I birth you. Now *you* mother.

> (*KOLU takes HER cup of coconut milk, goes to MARGARET and gently lifts MARGARET's torso, leaning MARGARET against HERself as KOLU gives HER drink, rocking HER gently. MARGARET sips.*)

Scene Five

> (*Late afternoon. KOLU walks down a paved road in Firestone. The turn-off into HER camp is marked by a Liberian flag hanging from a flagpole leaning at a 45-degree angle. MARDEA appears from the brush beyond the flag, HER arms behind HER back, startling KOLU.*)

KOLU: What's behind your back? (*Silence.*) You promised once you would not kill me in my sleep, nor while we work or eat. This is none of those.

MARDEA: (*Shows HER empty hands.*) Not today. But it *will* happen, guaranteed. Since you couldn't just say it, all I asked. I will always be the threat to keep your one eye open, I'm the poisonous fly that returns and returns until the day you own it, admit you killed my brother.

KOLU: I killed your brother.

> (*MARDEA taken aback. Then.*)

MARDEA: Knew it! Think I ever doubted? Your lies tricked me? (*Beat*) I appreciate finally at least the integrity to tell the truth.

> (*KOLU nods. As SHE turns away toward the camp entrance, MARDEA slugs HER, knocking HER to the ground. KOLU, a bit dazed, starts to stand.*)

KOLU: Okay we're even –

> (*MARDEA begins beating the crap out of KOLU. KOLU tries defending HERself against the blows but doesn't return the punches. A spectator crowd of TAPPERS starts to gather. SOME carry THEIR metal buckets. Finally MARDEA pulls away.*)

MARDEA: What's the matter with you?

KOLU: I don't –

MARDEA: Striking hurt *my* broke bones more than you, not even the respect to hit back? Fight! Where's all your so-called courage? Blowing-innocent-civilians-away valor?

KOLU: SORRY!

MARDEA: "Sorry"? *(To the TAPPERS.)* "Sorry"?! Look at her! How many of *your* relatives she slaughtered?

KOLU: MY MOTHER DIED!

> *(Beat: KOLU as surprised by the outburst as the OTHERS.)*

KOLU: I thought she died before. She didn't. She waited for me, last night. Last night she closed her eyes. They didn't come back open.

MARDEA: That's very sad. That's very heartbreaking *my* mother died. My *father* died. My *brother* died, how'd *that* happen? *(KOLU starts to walk away.)* "History." Say you know it. *I* know it. What side of my family brought progress, American! *(KOLU has stopped, looks at HER.)* What side took us out of the bush?

KOLU: What are you – ?

MARDEA: Who enlightened The Dark Continent?

KOLU: You don't know what you're talking about! *(DOUGBA enters.)*

MARDEA: Country! Fool!

KOLU: Leave me –

MARDEA: Kpelle bush monkey!

DOUGBA: Hey . . .

KOLU: Warning you –

MARDEA: You *and* your damn dead mother!

KOLU: KILL YOU!

(*MARDEA smiles.*)

MARDEA: Take the girl out of combat but never the combatant out of the girl.

KOLU: I ADMITTED IT! What more do you want?

MARDEA: (*Eyes stinging.*) I'm still figuring that out.

(*The sound of a truck pulling up. The TAPPERS look toward the rumble. A middle-aged man, BAIMBA, rushes onstage.*)

BAIMBA: What's going on here? This is no place for a gathering! Why aren't you at your camp? (*To DOUGBA.*) Aren't you the overseer?

DOUGBA: Yes boss, but –

BAIMBA: Why are these workers here? (*To TAPPERS.*) Do you need more to do? I can find more for you to do!

SMITH: (*Offstage.*) Looked like cat claws to me. (*Chuckles.*)

(*SMITH enters. HE is large and muscular and fair and American and white.*)

BAIMBA: This is Mr. Smith my – *our* boss. From America.

SMITH: *(To KOLU and MARDEA.)* There's more than one man out here. *(KOLU and MARDEA confused, which confuses SMITH.)* What else do women fight about?

BAIMBA: Overseer!

DOUGBA: *(Humble.)* Sorry boss, I just got here.

SMITH: What'd he say?

BAIMBA: Claims he just came.

DOUGBA: They good workers. Make their quotas.

SMITH: What'd he say?

BAIMBA: He says no complaints about their work.

SMITH: Liberia! We're all supposed to be speaking the same tongue, but they don't understand me, I don't understand them. How you call that English? *(Demonstrates a Liberian accent with great exaggeration.)*

BAIMBA: You have any orders for them, sir?

SMITH: RA RA RA RA RA RA RA RA!

DOUGBA: *(To BAIMBA.)* What'd he say?

BAIMBA: He said –

MARDEA: *(Eyes on SMITH.)* – "Tell them to get back to the trees."

SMITH: *(Pleasantly surprised.)* We understand each other! Educated? Don't see your kind in the camps.

> *(MARDEA shrugs. SMITH's eyes narrow.)*

SMITH: Don't *need* your kind in the camps.

BAIMBA: *(To DOUGBA.)* Get her out of here –

SMITH: Maybe someplace else.

BAIMBA: Sir?

SMITH: Superintendent staff. Definitely light in the female category.

BAIMBA: But sir –

SMITH: What? We'll trial run her, see if she has it. *(To MARDEA.)* What's your name?

> *(MARDEA staring hard at SMITH.)*

SMITH: Don't you want a job?

MARDEA: I *have* a job.

SMITH: A *real* job.

BAIMBA: Sir –

SMITH: Can you read?

MARDEA: Yes I read. *(Looks at KOLU.)* We *both* read.

SMITH: *(Turns to KOLU.)* *You* understand what I'm sayin'?

(KOLU stares at SMITH: silence.)

BAIMBA: *(To KOLU.)* Speak for the boss! He tell you speak, *Speak!*

SMITH: Forget it. *(To MARDEA.)* I wanna know about you. Who *are* you?

BAIMBA: Sir I just hope this is your own notion, that you're not just yielding to the pressure –

SMITH: I THINK I KNOW MY OWN MIND, BAIMBA! *(BAIMBA backs off quickly. To MARDEA.)* Well? *(Silence.)* You can read? Prove it. Write my name in the dirt.

> *(MARDEA takes a stick and writes "MY NAME" in the dirt.)*

SMITH: Funny. *Smith.*

> *(MARDEA writes "AMERICA" in the dirt.)*

SMITH: *(A quiet rage.)* I want you to erase that and this time make it right.

> *(MARDEA looks at KOLU. Then Xes over "AMERICA" and writes, much bigger, "AFRICA AFRICA AFRI" SMITH, furious, cuts off HER scrawling, grabs HER.)*

SMITH: Who *are* you? Spy! Human rights? Environmental?

KOLU: Who are *you?*

(ALL turn to KOLU. As SHE speaks, TAPPERS gradually appear out of the forest.)

KOLU: I thought colonialists only raped the continent 'til the natives exploded, then flee. Hit us 'til we take it no more, then when we hit back run, leave us to hit each other, no. No, guess you always stay, long as something left in the plantations or in the mines *Look at this!* "African debt," who's indebted to *who?* Africa provides for the *world* and the world takes: oil Nigeria, diamonds Sierra Leone, diamonds and gold South Africa, diamonds gold *latex* Liberia all the resources on earth Africa is RICH! Why we see only three pennies of it? The infrastructure decimated, no money to rebuild SOMEone getting the money! Why all *our* wealth go to *you?* LOOK AT THEM! *Most* precious resource *us!* African people! But tried to steal that too. Took black people, work them, whip them, rape them, *brainwash* them, turn them into *you!* Then they come back, inflict *your* slavery on *us*, does anyone ever *learn?*

SMITH: *(Eyes hard on KOLU.)* Not if you're black.

(In an instant KOLU has snatched ZOE's scythe from under HER clothing and holds it tight, quivering with emotion, at SMITH's throat. HE trembles, terrified, awaiting HER decision. After several moments SHE throws the weapon away, falls, hiding HER face, bawling.)

SMITH: *(After HE recovers.)* Get her the hell outa here! And the rest of you get back to work!

> *(BAIMBA moves toward KOLU but a couple TAPPERS block HIM.)*

SMITH: What the hell's the matter with you? Go!

> *(No one moves. KOLU, confused, looks up.)*

SMITH: You all gone deaf? Move it! *(Stillness.)* Think I won't let you go? You came to Firestone begging for a job, we gave you one! Not enough benefits? Didn't get the key to the executive washroom fine. Leave! We'll go out to the bush, replace every one a you today!

> *(No one moves. SMITH incredulous.)*

SMITH: I'll fire the whole goddamn lot a you! And where will you be then? What kinda skills you got? You're tappers, you know how to do one thing: tap. So go do it! Tap!

> *(One of the TAPPERS begins to tap HIS fingers on the metal tapping device of a nearby tree. The other TAPPERS begin to join in, SOME tapping THEIR buckets. It is a clean, clear rhythm, ALL tapping as one. The sound now comes from the woods. Louder, louder. KOLU, MARDEA, DOUGBA, BAIMBA and SMITH look around at the enormous forest: the sound, still beating in perfect time, coming from all around.)*

BAIMBA: *(Stunned.)* They're everywhere.
(Terrified.) They're everywhere!

ESTHER: *(Enters.)* KOLU!

> *(The tapping instantaneously stops.
> ESTHER, carrying the bag that held the
> fabric, walks up to KOLU.)*

ESTHER: I fear the fabric run out too soon. But just like Jesus' fishes and loaves, some things all it take is faith. And *will.*

> *(As ESTHER walks over to the flagpole,
> a TAPPER takes down the Liberian flag.
> ESTHER takes out of HER bag KOLU's
> new Liberian flag which ESTHER has
> sewn. ESTHER and the TAPPER raise
> the new flag. The tapping begins again,
> this time starting in the forest, even
> more thunderous than before, then taken
> up by the TAPPERS onstage; then
> ESTHER and the TAPPER next to
> HER begin tapping the flagpole; now
> DOUGBA; then MARDEA, smiling
> broadly, begins clapping. KOLU turns
> in a slow circle, staring at THEM all in
> wonder. Finally SHE raises HER hands
> high over HER head, joyously, making
> one clap in beat with THE OTHERS.*
>
> *Blackout.)*

End of play

Plunder, Plantation, Peace:
Two Weeks in Postwar Liberia

Rain

Its force and persistence are astounding. Ten minutes from now, when I think there can be no water left in the sky, the downpour will become incomprehensibly stronger. Ten minutes more: *stronger*. It is only the start of the rainy season so such grandiose cloudbursts are as yet rare.

It has awakened me, and I could just lie and marvel at its potency if it weren't for the cumulative effect of three circumstances: 1) the storm's formidable beckoning on my bladder, 2) pitch blackness – I can't see my hand in front of my face, let alone the floor I need to walk across en route to my private bath, having forgotten the flashlight my American contact back home had advised me to bring, and 3) a warning from this same woman: "Always check your shoes before stepping into them; there may be scorpions!" There would be no place for them to hide in the familiar five-and-dime flip-flops the family loaned me (everyone wears them around the house, calling them "slippers") but could they be somewhere on the *floor?* Despite my heroic attempts to withstand the agony imposed upon my urinary system, I am finally obliged, three times before the torrent is over, to pray, then lift the mosquito net and scurry to the toilet. (Days later it will become clear that the arachnid precaution did not apply to here, the city, but only to excursions into the bush.)

I am surprised how large my room is, and that I don't share it, nor the adjoined lavatory. I assume it is the master bedroom that the family has prepared for me as the guest. In my wide-eyed blindness between sprints to the john, I reflect on the rush of the last several hours: the chaos at the small Monrovian airport – confused travelers packed into what looked like an unkempt warehouse, stern customs officers, and expressionless onlooking Japanese soldiers of the UN peacekeeping forces; the friendly welcome of my host family; a billboard with realistic cartoon-like figures and the caption "STOP MOB VIOLENCE – CALL 911"; traditional African huts flying by as we sped along the two-lane highway, later passing a nondescript building identified as a "containment center" – a space provided for counseling of ex-combatants from the recent civil war (the ceasefire itself still in process); our entrance into the heart of Monrovia: numerous churches and no traffic lights and psychotic traffic. And this sign at the city center:

:

THE WOMEN OF LIBERIA SAY
PEACE IS OUR GOAL
PEACE IS WHAT MATTERS
PEACE IS WHAT WE NEED

Food
A mandatory hiatus: after nineteen years of eating nothing that walked, swam or flew, I have vowed not to impose my Western dietary idiosyncrasies on my good hosts. I was told by my American

contact the luckily employed may scratch out $35 a month for their families. I have vowed to eat whatever is put in front of me: no complaints. A mountain of white rice, and now Florence,[2] the mother of the family, spoons out generous gobs of "cow meat" in its greasy sauce, ground in no way familiar to an American, and plops the simmered flesh atop my grain.

Rachel Fay is my American contact – a white woman, the daughter of missionaries, who grew up in Liberia. As a young adult she taught at Cuttington University College in Bong County, the region of the country my host family hails from. She has lived in Florida the last twenty years but was still listed on the CUC website in the fall of 2003. (Perhaps in wartime, it is only the contacts outside of the country who are contactable.) When I spoke with her my decision to travel to Liberia was still only a few weeks old. Minneapolis' Guthrie Theater had been awarded a large sum of money through the Bush Foundation (not related to either president), and under the auspices of the grant had selected nine American playwrights to travel to the nation of her or his choice, then to write a play inspired by the experience. I didn't know any Liberians and faced herculean obstacles in connecting with anyone in a country still at civil war. It was the suggestion of my friend Naomi Wallace to investigate Liberian universities. Two years before Naomi had visualized, then actualized, six American playwrights (including the two of us) visiting Palestinian theatres on the

---

[2] All names of my host family are pseudonyms.

West Bank and in Gaza. But in Liberia, so soon after the latest unrest (an ironic word, as if terror and brutality and rape and mass murder were akin to a bout with insomnia), no Liberian schools were functioning. By late 2003 there had seemed to be a slow quieting on the front, however, and Cuttington had hopes of resuming classes for the spring semester. Rachel Fay's advice in preparing me for cultural differences, despite her two decades' distance, were invaluable, and one of the golden rules I ascertained by electronic mail was never to take second helpings. It is Liberian custom, I was informed, to serve the adults first and the children eat what is left, if anything.

Still, I immediately notice in this household that has welcomed me as a member for the next two weeks that the kids are clearly all well fed. It's difficult to determine a precise census because not all the youngsters living here are family members, but it seems there are seven offspring – twenties, teens, and the thirteen-year-old baby girl Ellen. As with adolescence in the States, the boys' bodies are slim and strong, and the girls' carry a few extra healthy layers of fat. (Of course in many African cultures heaviness, especially around the bottom, is a measure of great beauty in women.) From time to time the men sit around the table to dine with me, but for most meals I as the guest am served first and I eat alone, with mother Florence sitting by for conversation, the other adults, at their leisure, eating next. So yes, I would say the children were served last, but definitely not least. In the neighborhood I do notice some children with worrisome distended bellies but their limbs seem healthily baby-fatted – not sticks.

The enormous first helpings are mind-boggling enough. Later, having barely digested my several cups of rice and polite spoonful of meat, Florence would bring to my room a full plate of pineapple or mango, or several large hunks of a freshly baked loaf of bread, or once a large bowl of shelled peanuts, appearing indistinguishable from those back home, but when I crack them open and eat, the flavor, seemingly washed out until the aftertaste, is bitter. "I'm full," I tell Florence after a valiant attack on my mountain of rice or a few bites of dessert, "but it's delicious!" And smile gratefully, hoping I haven't insulted her. In the weeks before I arrived, I wondered about the availability of food: Could I starve in two weeks? Hardly: No lunch to speak of but always a breakfast that ranged from continental to large, with dinner and after-dinner snacks invariably gargantuan. Though the last several days of the trip, ironically, I would be quite hungry. For whatever reason, the fruit would disappear – I assume temporarily no longer available at the market – and, try as I might, I never could down much of the red meat.

My vegetarianism is so antithetical to their mindset that, in spite of my taking just a tablespoon of beef on top of my hordes of white rice, Toimu, the father of the family and my primary contact here, says, "Kia doesn't like rice. It's our staple."

Yes, I know. While America undergoes its periodic race riots, in 1979 Liberia was plunged into the infamous *rice* riots, when the price of the staple went through the stratosphere, with hunger already an issue. Dramatic changes would ensue, including the installation, via military coup, of the nation's first native African president a year later.

"Kia eats small," Toimu and Florence would occasionally observe. Well just put some vegetables on her plate and, believe me, Kia can eat big!

Infrastructure

In postwar Liberia, there is no electricity or running water. My bathroom has all the basic modern fixtures – tub, toilet and sink – but no working plumbing. There are holes where once were spigots. By the sink is an enormous plastic bucket of water, its lid even with my waist and a good yard in diameter, and this is filled daily from a public pump. Each evening I dip in a pail, set it in the tub, then stand in the tub, soap myself and rinse. (I would have bathed twice daily in the African heat if I weren't concerned about wasting water.) Sometimes I launder my clothes – I have three new dresses I bought for the trip at a 14th Street Manhattan discount store ($3.99 each) and three new similarly priced tops; the latter I wear mainly to conceal the money bag around my neck when we travel outside the house. (The cash I brought with me is all I have. There are no ATMs nor any credit card system.) Florence wants to wash my clothing for me. I refuse – I am embarrassed enough at her serving me at every turn – though ultimately her skill in this area may have made things more pleasant: by the end of the two weeks the deep sweat is embedded in the semi-clean cheap fabric and I can't stand the smell of myself. After my bath, I use the dirty water to flush the toilet. Though I fight the good fight, I never get it as spotless as Florence or the teen boy, and after a few days and the consumption of too much water in the attempt, I finally accept my failure and do my best to scrub the bowl respectably clean before the family comes in for the real spic 'n' span. At first glance the seat looks identical to those in American bathrooms but actually it has been constructed out of an exceedingly thin plastic: a cheap Frisbee with a large hole in it. I brought with me a water purifier, a yellow bottle with an odd-looking mechanism attached that raised the eyebrows of the post-9/11 airport security staff back home in New York. Rachel Fay suggested I be subtle about its use so as not to insult the family but my hosts have thoughtfully provided bottled water for me, with which I also use to brush my teeth, leaning over the sink. Even Samuel, Toimu's early 20s son, tries to avoid non-bottled Liberian water as it irritates his ulcer.

Because of the family's insistence on serving their guest, I have to forego politely requesting and simply declare one day that I am going out to pump my own water. (I don't even pretend that my independent act will last more than a day.) I follow sweet, ever-smiling Ruth, who I guess to be about eighteen, and Angie, about fourteen, who amuses me because her lips always seem sloped in an adolescent smirk. We have to go out the front door to get to the back, and now I understand why: the back of this house is partially connected to the back of another, though there is a back door leading to a small patio-like space between the homes. The two-foot high pump is public, serving several homes. Many neighbors come out to watch me, the stranger, at work. I assume the activity will require all of my physical strength, and am surprised that one easy lowering of the handle – I can do it effortlessly with one hand – brings up an enormous gush of water. In no time I fill all the family's buckets. A little toddler girl from another house comes up to me. Exhibiting none of the reticence of the adults in addressing the obvious foreigner, she hands me a teapot to fill for her. After all the kids who have been ogling my alien looks since my arrival, I am thrilled this child finds her container more interesting than me, her eyes locked on it, and I happily oblige.

The family's house, like all those in the neighborhood, is of the cement block variety, in deference to termites I assume, and the living/dining room space is a good four times the size of the large bedroom I am staying in. My guess is that the sizeable rooms allow any possible breeze to pass through more freely in lieu of air conditioning. When I first arrive, I eat my twilight supper in dimness, the only light source being a single bulb of maybe 75 watts, high on the opposite wall. The family has enough money for a little gasoline-generated electricity, used sparingly.

The kitchen, like the bathrooms (besides my private lavatory, there must have been another somewhere), is fully equipped with all the modern appliances, all nonworking. There is a round tray of hot coals upon which miraculously everything, including the delicious baked bread, is prepared. Florence and the daughters make daily trips to the market as there is no refrigeration to keep food. One afternoon I hear a sharp, angry "*Jesus!*" from Angie who'd burned her hand on the coals.

Cell phones, for those who can afford them and the generator for recharging, are operative in Monrovia and its close environs. The rest of the country is out of luck; mobiles do not function there, and no electricity means no landlines anywhere. Perhaps because postwar communication service is so new, or that the concept is a nostalgic link to a prior normal state of affairs, people are *obsessed* with their cells: constantly pushing buttons, taking calls at the most inappropriate moments, Toimu ringing me in my bedroom from the living room (while complaining about twenty-five cents for every local call). Once my sister Kara phoned from New York. I was in the middle of a meeting, interviewing the men of Theatre for Peace, who had convened especially to speak with me. I wanted to talk with my sis badly; I was feeling so lonely for home then! But I felt it would be rude and unprofessional so I got off quickly with a hurried "I love you!" I turned back to the artists to apologize and resume. They all stared at me as if I were insane. Initially I wondered if they were surprised by my verbal show of affection toward my sibling. Then I realized it was my rush that astonished them: Nothing and nobody keeps a Liberian from savoring to the fullest even the most mundane call.

There is always too much traffic. The combatants came from the bush, ravaging everything and everybody in their path, and many of the refugee country people, including my family, fled to Monrovia, swelling the city's population to many times its 1989 prewar size. In the night, the car lights cut through the blackness. Though I barely see them in the dark, I am aware of the futility of lampposts from day excursions. Beyond the lack of electricity, many of the lamps have been literally shot off the posts, leaving the odd picture of a giant, naked staff. Now, in the shadows, the road is lined with an endless snake of tables, people sitting on chairs behind them, thousands of lit candles on top of them. Romantic. Magical.

I don't want to be insensitive about the sufferings of a society whose decimated infrastructure has catapulted it back to the preindustrial age, but between once-magnificent buildings scorched to a black skeleton (on one such downtown high-rise, seemingly ready for demolition, a sign is posted advertising that within the building's crumbling interior is a new internet café), and an enormous mountain of burning garbage every mile or so along the highway, and the sickening odor of highly concentrated exhaust fumes overwhelming every drive, I feel compelled to remark upon the candles in the night, the only sign of any physical beauty on the landscape that I have observed. I mention it to Eunice, Samuel's fiancée, a slim, pretty nineteen-year-old college student. "Yes," she replies, rolled-eyed, "beautiful candles. If it weren't for all the house fires."

Language

"Those students are escaping assembly." Dr. Wamah's[3] phraseology seems much more accurate – escape: freedom! – than the mundane American "cutting class."

But for the majority of my stay I am not privy to these delicious idioms because I have grave difficulty understanding colloquial Liberian English, which sounds to me like muttering. Especially distressing is my communication gap with Florence, as I am so fond of her. I must have gradually developed some sort of ear for her accent, however, as my latter journal entries detail rather complex conversations, though I imagine an audiotape of our discourse would reveal an annoying multiplicity of my polite "Excuse me?"s. On the other hand I generally have little trouble comprehending professors and the college educated, including Toimu and Samuel, when they speak directly to me. Among themselves, of course they employ more casual Liberian English. (But for all I know, Florence may be equally educated. Her only email to me was written in near perfect American English, in stark contrast to the errors, from an American point of view, in the emails I'd received from the members of her family that I know hold university degrees.) In the car Eunice

---

[3] Pseudonym.

and the men speak quickly, and I recognize that it's English and not their tribal Kpelle because I catch a word here and there. I stare out the window, observing the hundreds of walking Monrovians doing their business, but now I turn back as they are addressing me: I know because suddenly they are speaking **LOUD** and slooooooow.

One evening a student of Samuel's is in the living room, trying to set up the brand new printer of the family's brand new computer, courtesy of Rachel Fay, that I had brought with me. The young man speaks with a flawless American accent. I have to ask if he has spent time in the U.S. He laughs, a certain embarrassment. "No." I can see he knows what I am bound to say next. "Because your accent sounds American." He laughs again. "You've been told that before?" He nods. I have no idea whether I have insulted him, complimented him, or simply tried his patience, repeating the same comment he's heard a thousand times.

English is the colonialist language, and the colonialists were Americans – cell phone is cell phone and bathroom is bathroom. But here and there a bit of Brit: cookie is biscuit.

I learn a little basic Kpelle. The phonetic spelling is mine.

Ya-ooon! – Morning!
Ee-say. – Thank you.
Ya toi? – How are you?
Mah-nee! – Fine!

One of the grown (early 20s) sons, college educated, who lives in Dbarnga (an American ear

406

only hears Banga), the bush home of the family, is here for a night. He tells a story about crossing a bridge, and a man asking him for ten dollars, and his response to the man. Everyone in the room explodes in laughter, and I smile, but I don't understand enough of his colloquial Liberian English to get the joke.

Literacy
"Eighty percent of the country is illiterate," according to Dr. Joseph Saye Guannu, who I quickly decide is a genius.

"So what would the rebels want with your books?" I ask Samuel one day. He has just lamented aloud that of all they lost when they fled Dbarnga, he grieves most for his texts.
"Toilet paper," he spats miserably.
Cuttington University College was built in Bong County, "the stronghold of our great rebel leader," the crossing-a-bridge joke son remarks at breakfast, his understated tone somewhere between irony and, even at this late date, utter disbelief. I will glimpse the deserted buildings of the institution later, '70s band Parliament's "Tear the Roof off the Sucker" absently floating through my mind as I am told this is what happened, literally, to the buildings of CUC when the rebels came trampling through. For now, the students and faculty inhabit the campus of a former high school in Monrovia, with administration housed in a downtown office building. No electricity means no elevators, so when we visit these offices my first full day, the men from our car have to carry Toimu,

by no means a slight man, in his wheelchair up five flights, seventy steps. When we are through they carry him down again.

I am sitting in Professor Dopoe's[4] office, which is a useless kitchen, once part of the cafeteria of the secondary school. There is no door, and students keep popping in to stare at me until the lecturer waves them away. All the professors I meet, generously volunteering their time for me, are Liberian but before the war, I am told, CUC boasted faculty from around the world.

> The Moon was shining
> But a terr was dark.

It takes a few stabs before I understand. "A terr?" Finally I get it – "Oh, *under!*" – and while I can grasp the gist of the Liberian metaphor, it floats somewhere out in koan-land for me without a more literal interpretation of its implications.

"*Under!*" repeats Dopoe, imitating my enunciation. Gregarious, given to guffaws and emphatic "*Yes!*"es, he rolls his head back in roaring laughter, the men of my host family following suit, albeit with the stiffer demeanor of cackling on cue. They think they are poking fun of my American accent. Only I know that it is actually my unique Kia voice they are mocking. I've had *Americans* ask me what country I'm from – I believe somehow related to my rapid speech – others commenting that I sound like a child. Now, in Africa, I force laughter over my glare. Ha ha! You're all *so funny!*

---

[4] Psuedonym.

Dopoe is articulate and fluid with his information – I fill pages of notes – and it is a relief because earlier I had been given a book proposal by a professor that read like an eighth grade composition. I ponder my own ethnocentricity: passing judgment by the only means at my disposal – standard American English. But then every literary reference I come across here is American. Dopoe recommends a Ben Franklin essay I don't know: "Too Much for the Whistle.[5]" Then he begins discussing Toro, "when he was in thee boosh."

Toro. Toro.

"Walden Pond?"

"Yes!"

Very late in my trip will be the first day (actually evening) of graduate school for Toimu and Samuel, father and son. While they go off to their business courses, at the invitation of Dr. Wamah I sit in on his Educational Psychology class. The study is designed for aspiring teachers, its goal "To enable the student to acquire the basic and necessary skills in explaining the psychological theories and principles that form the fundamental rudiments of the educative process." There is the requisite Pavlov and Skinner and Freud, and I'm pleased to see Noam Chomsky under the heading "Language Development" (his linguistic theories rather than the political analyses I devour). In addition there are fully fifteen listings under "Textbooks and References" – *Educational Psychology of the Gifted* and *Perspectives in Behavior*

---

[5] The title is actually ~~simply~~ "The Whistle."

Modification with Deviant Children and even *Feeling Good: The New Mood Therapy*. This is no cake course, even if many of the titles have decades' old copyrights, owing to the postwar economic slump. Correction: *Pre*war there was an economic slump. *Post*war the nation is an economic catastrophe.

One morning I come out of my room and all the adults are gone, my breakfast left for me, a towel sealing in its warmth. No use asking the kids where everyone is; we barely understand each other. I peruse the sporadically filled bookshelves: *Nursing, Organic Chemistry*, children's storybooks with animals. I pull out a reading book, very contemporary American, with the drawing of an Asian kid, a Latino kid, a black kid and a white kid all in the same class. I've seen no one here who looks like any of them, even the brown African-American child several shades lighter than any Liberian I've met. This is the type of textbook with photographs, profiles of popular singers and, in the drama chapter, what looks like an actual page from a Broadway *Playbill*:

FRANK LANGELLA[6]

in

DRACULA

Dir. By Edward Gorey[7]

Walter Beck Theatre

402 West 46th St.

---

[6] Renowned stage actor.

[7] I looked it up. The production was actually *designed* by Gorey and directed by Dennis Rosa.

Drive

I keep thinking we are pulling over because the driver, and it's taken me awhile to decipher that he is a hired employee and not a member of the family, will suddenly swerve wildly to the right, onto the shoulder. (Driving is on the right here like back in the States.) But in the next moment I know we are not parking because he instantly swerves back so far to the left as to be in the oncoming lane. Potholes. Almost the size of the car. The roads shot to bits during the war.

The main drag seems to have been smoothed over, at least enough to prevent major accidents. Filling stations are frequent along this route, all looking old and rusty and filthy with no posted price information anywhere. We stop for gas. At this particular station, and they are all different, the front half cover of the pump is missing so we can see inside. Two wheels, one at the top, the other directly beneath, and a band figure-eighted between them. The station attendant rotates a handle bar in a circle, the band then moves around the wheels, and gas is pumped into our car.

We are late to every appointment, often by two or three hours. Toimu was chastised in front of everyone by Dr. Wamah for our tardiness the first day (perhaps only forty-five minutes that time) to the Cuttington faculty meeting. Toimu is never behind the wheel – I imagine cars designed for disabled drivers are not readily available here – but as my host I suspect the responsibility for my punctuality is considered his. I feel bad for him.

But later I only wish he had taken that little humiliation more to heart. Our penchant for arriving late is especially astounding considering that on the open road our speedometer always hovers around 135. The gauge reads mph, *not* kph.

I feel like an honorary man on all our travels, usually the only woman in the car, and everyone I have been scheduled to interview is male. Exploiting my guest status, I always snatch a back window seat, more to avoid being smashed between two men in the perennially sardine-packed sedan than about getting next to the air in this a.c.-less transport. There is a lot of bitching that happens while we drive, chiefly from Samuel and chiefly about other Monrovian drivers. As our chauffeur pedal-to-the-metals, my dancing pupils seem to be the only indication of concern in the car, everyone else quite satisfied with the ride. One day on a quiet street, an old man walking with a child and a cart suddenly crosses in front of us, and when our driver slows to let the pedestrians pass, the other men fly into a rage. "We were here first!" "Don't slow down for them, let them run!"

During one jaunt there is talk of an accident. I don't understand the details but it sounds to me like some major event in the news. "Did anyone die?" I ask. I find out from Florence the next day that one of the young grown sons had been the victim. He came to the house the day after, miraculously in one piece given, as I had ascertained, that two tires suddenly flew from his moving car, and the vehicle flipped, landing on its roof.

Work

As the official stamps my passport upon arrival, he
informs me that I must go to the customs office in
downtown Monrovia within forty-eight hours.
Two days later I am driven there, and I follow
Samuel through the building, a rather precarious
journey without electricity as I find myself
undertaking narrow staircases in complete
darkness. I sense people everywhere. We finally
reach the proper office. Samuel, who knows the
older man behind the desk, is polite and humble,
constantly grinning. The customs man blatantly
relishes his power in the situation, small-talking for
the fun of delaying his decision as to whether he
will serve us and (as I discover later) if so at what
price. At last he takes my passport and summons
someone outside of his office to process it. I get a
call from New York on the cell phone I bought here
and am happy for the distraction from the cat-and-
mouse the man is playing with Samuel. A few
minutes later my passport is returned, I am
charged twenty American bucks, and Samuel and I
make our way through the blind maze again. We
now stand outside in the sun.

"He's my student," Samuel says.
Apparently if they hadn't recognized each other
my passport would have gone through many
hands, each one requiring a bribe to move it on to
the next level. When people earn twenty dollars a
month, he says, such extortion is the only way to
make a living.

This is considerably less than even the thirty-five a month reported to me by Rachel Fay. And the cost of living is not necessarily correlated to the official earnings. When I went to purchase my phone, my only means of communication with the States, I was not surprised to see a model for $10.00, as this would be in keeping with circa per capita incomes of $240. On closer examination, however, I realize there was no decimal point: $1000! The cheapest brand was $90. I took $150 Nokia, which was what Toimu was pushing for (though originally he was eying the $1,000 model!) and what everyone I've seen here who can afford a mobile seems to have. Immediately after my purchase, Toimu eagerly suggested that when I depart Liberia, I leave the phone with him, and it would be there whenever I came back to visit.

I also purchase a $50 phone card. With communication to the other hemisphere, it is exhausted rapidly, and I will need to buy at least two more $25 cards. Samuel remarks with distaste that he once bought a phone card from a Mandingo, and when he got home the card was empty: zero minutes. He is distrusting of Mandingo merchants. My readings had made reference to Mandingoes, a Muslim people who are generally traders, and who are often considered outsiders by other Liberians (even those Mandingoes whose families have lived in Liberia for generations), the antagonism theorized to be in part related to history: Mandingoes did business in the trans-Atlantic slave trade.

On my arrival, we had taken a sharp left off a main thoroughfare onto a dirt road, with a tall wooden fence on the right and houses all along the left. Toimu's home is at the end of the lane. Maybe a quarter-mile on the other side of the fence is the Agriculture and Industrial Training Bureau, where Toimu has been employed the last three months since his transfer from the transportation department, both government positions. Once I will hear Toimu describe his address as "in the AITB housing," so I wonder if all the household heads on this street are also employed at the Bureau. Late in the afternoon of my first full day, we pull into its small parking lot. I am exhausted from the earlier meetings with the Cuttington University College faculty and administration, followed by the drive to the campus where I was one of the speakers at a school-wide assembly – my formal address to the entire student body I knew nothing about until, ushered into the outdoor makeshift auditorium, I was seated on the stage. Now, at the AITB, the men carry Toimu up the flight of stairs to his office. He gives me a brief tour and, as this activity seems pretty low-key, I begin to relax. Unfortunately a few minutes later I am escorted through swinging doors into another room where I hear spontaneous applause. Damnit! This reception is for *me*, the guest speaker, the large space filled with AITB students. Toimu and I are led to our seats on the platform. The institution director makes a long speech detailing all the items the school needs and doesn't have, similar to the oration by one of the CUC speakers this morning, and it occurs to me that perhaps the reason for my honored guest status, and why Toimu was able to fill all the slots on my itinerary, was that my visit gives each of these institutions the opportunity to take a crack with the hard sales pitch at the visiting wealthy American. I *am* comparably wealthy; I could easily part with $100 for the AITB, which I hope would go a much longer way here than in the U.S. But the administrators of these organizations seem to be under the mistaken impression that I could just as easily scribble off a check for thousands. Hours before, I had concluded my CUC speech by extending an invitation to any of the students who may be interested in conversing with me privately about life here. In response, a young man spoke to me after the assembly: "What benefit to a student is there in talking to you?" I replied, feeling lame, that if the play I write would ever be produced, it could bring attention in the U.S. to what is going on here, and that hopefully could lead to struggling Liberia being assisted in some way. He turned away irritably. Obviously he would only talk for cold hard cash. The young women just stared at me.

The students I face now at the AITB are not college kids. They are ex-combatants. Active participants in the brutal civil war who are now enrolled in this vocational-technical center as part of their reintegration process back into a society at peace. Toimu's job transfer seems to have corresponded with the school's opening. Toimu introduces me with much fanfare as he had done at CUC, and I'm beginning to see the man lives for the spotlight. Not so Kia, at least not *on* stage, and I quickly scramble to remember and repeat the words I'd uttered in my earlier gig of this touring show: 1) This is my first visit to Africa, and 2) I am here through the Guthrie Theater's grant providing for my travel and a play commission. Both revelations, I am learning, unfailingly arouse enthusiastic applause, the latter because the nation is desperate for any attention by the outside world, the former as a sense of national pride: In 2004 Liberia doesn't exactly make the top ten list of continental tourist favorites.

One day in the car I ask Samuel about a Liberian adage I'd heard him use.

The bus is the bus.

I try to decipher what he is trying to say about public transportation. But he is going on about employers, that they are always right, and I'm not sure if he believes this or is just sarcastically expressing the common oppressed worker wisdom and then I get it:

The boss is the boss.

Christopher,[8] the 25-year-old filmmaker and family friend who is traveling with us, and using my video camera borrowed from the theatre to record our travels, asks now if I've seen *Animal Farm*. I'm still focused on the implications of Samuel's proverb, and am momentarily disoriented by the

---

[8] Pseudonym.

question. "I've read it," I say. He stares at me. "Oh – you mean the animated movie?"

"Yes."

I think I have seen it, or parts of it, but I've certainly read the novel, and I take it Christopher is commenting on the dictatorial nature of the work ethic to which Samuel has referred.

"Four legs good, two legs bad. Four legs good, two legs better!" I say, and we're both laughing, the others smiling politely, confused, and I'm happy, for once, to be the one in on the joke.

Nightlife

Toimu put together an amazing itinerary of day meetings, emailed to me just prior to my departure from New York. Early on he would arbitrarily announce in the evenings that we were about to go someplace not on the schedule. In my head I would sigh; I wanted to rest and have time alone. On my face I would smile. "Okay."

Thursday night, after my first jam-packed day, we take a short drive, a car full of males and myself, then pull off the road onto a dirt parking lot. Strangely everyone including Toimu stays in the car while only Samuel and I get out. The building seems to be some sort of improvised nightclub. I hear music from inside. On an outdoor table Dr. Wamah sits with another man, and we join them. The professor is quite witty, and clearly has an innocent crush on me. Right now, he's plastered. "I only drink between wars!" he announces with a hearty laugh. Samuel and I order orange sodas. I glance around at the other tables. I am stunned that no one smokes in Monrovia, not even in this public social space. My second day in the country I had observed a gas station attendant puffing away, and I would see two other men over the course of my stay on the busy downtown streets with their smokes, and that would be it: three cigarettes in two weeks in Liberia. When I return home and call Rachel Fay, I will convey my astonishment – a nonsmoking country! (Trumping even the smoke prohibition in the bars of New York.) As I wonder aloud as to whether such collective anti-vice is religious-based, she begins to laugh: "Well it's probably because no one has any *money* for cigarettes!"

Wamah's companion, a younger gentleman, is a Liberian journalist who has traveled much of the continent. At one point the professor, in a moment of semi-seriousness, declares that I need to meet all kinds of Liberians, not only the professionals and students but also "the riffraff." The word unnerves me. Still, before I judge, I wonder if there are cultural variations; perhaps here the expression isn't elitist and condescending in the way it is back home.

We hang no longer than forty-five minutes. Then Wamah generously pays for all our libations, unrolling a wad of Liberian cash several inches thick and leaving a healthy portion of it.

Two nights later I am told we are going to Old Georgia Estate. Is this another club? Who knows – No one tells me anything I think irritably, and get into the car. We are talking about the war, and turn off the well-peopled main route to a deserted road. Given the discussion at hand, and all mysterious blackness beyond our car lights, it feels creepy. But within seconds we pull into a large black-topped lot. The space is empty save for a group of six adults and a little girl sitting around a table. No candles, only the luminosity from inside the nearby house and moonlight. I am pleased to see one of the grown-ups is Dr. Wamah, who I can always count on for a good joke, and one I comprehend. On closer inspection it's clear he's sloshed again. This time both Toimu and Samuel accompany me while the others, all young men, stay, sitting on the car hood at a distance but still within earshot. Because this is Toimu's and Samuel's crowd and they were just along for the ride? Because there is drinking and they are under age? (Probably not all of them.) Because there aren't enough chairs? Periodically I exchange smiles with them.

Eventually I ascertain that this is a private residence, that this huge asphalt terrain is actually the family's back yard. I smile at the child, who looks about ten. Her two plaits stick straight up, pointing to heaven. For most white people to attempt such a feat with their own tresses would be to undertake a losing battle with gravity, and blacks in the U.S. have mimicked this hang-down quality. When an African-American child's hair sticks out horizontally (never ever shooting vertically to the sky, God forbid), it is generally a mistake and something that will have the little girl bearing the other children's taunts until she runs home bawling. And here in Africa I find a lot of the women, including all those of my host family, have chemically straightened hair. My long dreadlocks (which *do* hang because of their weight) make me an absolute anomaly: the utter absence of the style reminds me of its Western Hemisphere origins, a product of the Caribbean. So I am happy to see a style embracing African hair, and I tell the girl her hair is pretty. Her mother, the woman of the house, responds: "Say 'Thank you,'" and the child does.

Directly across from me sits a bald man, his scalp so clean that, even in his late middle age, it appears to be shaved. In the darkness I can only make out his profile – not a single facial feature distinguishable – yet it is clear his eyes are trained on me. "The Americans said they were going to help Liberia! Where did the money go? What can we do? After the war we have no electricity, we have no roads. No communication, we can't even make calls in the bush! How can we start from nothing?"

Professor Wamah to my left holds up his beer, and speaking in the effected tone of a candidate at a debate, says, "I'd like to reiterate that Kia is a playwright from America, and not a politician," then laughs his head off.

I laugh too, as do Toimu and Samuel. But I tell the ranting man, "I'm glad to hear what you have to say," which sounds patronizing in retrospect, but was anything but at the time. It was rather an invitation for him to continue, and continue he did. Until then I had felt my host family had been reserved in its criticisms of the

U.S. (something that would change). When it would come time to write the play, I would want to know what Liberians say about Americans when our backs are turned, and I was grateful for this gentleman in helping me start to scratch the surface.

The hostess and mother, whose look and dress remind me a lot of women back home, seems tired and long ready to draw the gathering to a close, especially eager to say her good-byes to the chatty, hammered professor whom she refers to as "Doc." But now he opens up a new topic for discussion. "What do women prefer? Guinness?" And another brand I'm unfamiliar with.

"Yes," the woman replies wearily. "A milder beer."

"Thank you for proving my point!" Wamah exults. "Those are imported. You should be drinking Club – the local beer." Thus ensues a discussion among the men, some more serious than others, on the subject of sending money out of the country, as apparently all the hard liquor is imported.

Dispute over, Wamah now announces that tomorrow is the woman's (and, to her right, her husband's) tenth anniversary.

"*Twelfth*," she corrects.

I congratulate them. Then the professor asks that she show me around the house. The prospect sounds rather dull compared with the intermittently interesting chitchat around the table

– How different could it be from Toimu's home? –
but when she stands, I don't refuse.

We walk around to the front. The first thing
I notice through the sliding glass door is a fully
furnished home with a huge screen TV. About a
dozen kids, most apparently neighbors, lounge
around the living room, the majority stretched out
on the floor, watching the program. As I enter the
house I see that it is a Hollywood movie, and on
my initial glance a man is shot in the face.

There are beautifully crafted wood banisters
and paneling. The woman takes me around the
single-floor dwelling to the master bedroom, the
bath, the kitchen, the place enormous, the décor
exquisite. "This is a *mansion!*" I say, stunned.

"It's more than a mansion," she replies
dryly. Toimu's house has large rooms but for the
most part they are empty, as the family are
refugees in the city who plan eventually to return
to Dbarnga, their hometown, hopefully in the
coming months. The people who own the dwelling
I stand in now are not just evidently well off, but
settled Monrovians, who at some point in the war
like everyone else were forced to abandon their
home in defense of their lives. Though I only see
two physical manifestations of assault. One is the
condition of the kitchen cabinets: broken, falling off
hinges. "We've been wanting to fix things up," my
hostess tells me. "We were waiting to make sure
peace will stay." In New York most fixtures are
decades old so, from my perspective, the cabinets
don't seem to be in such bad shape, but their

disrepair is blatantly out of whack with the flawlessness of the rest of the place.

"It seems like you *will* be able to start fixing it up soon."

"Yes." Her first hint of a smile. "Next month."

The other mark the gunslingers left is a bullet hole dead center of one of the sliding glass doors.

As we walk out she points to a smaller building on their property, a few yards away. "Is that a guest house?" I ask.

She seems momentarily confused. "Africans have big families. For relatives."

Back with the others, I express how impressed I was with the tour. When the woman, who had become sidetracked on the way out, returns to her guests, the Doc reiterates my description. "She said your house is a mansion!" It's incredible how I can comprehend his every word even through the alcohol.

"Yes," she answers, flat. "She told me."

Wamah comments that it is time to leave, that Kia needs her rest. (Kia thinks someone else needs to sleep things off.) I imagine this winding down must come as a relief to the lady of the house but the prof still isn't quite finished. He begins to expound upon Toimu's qualities. "He's a candidate for the master's degree in business management. He is a handicapped person who has never let his handicap become a barrier. He's never been a beggar. He makes his own way."

Toimu and Samuel continue to smile. Toimu can move his legs a little, and one of them, and one of Samuel's, sway uncomfortably.

Minutes later we are headed for our cars. Samuel will ride with Wamah since they live in the same house. Wamah insists on driving. Is he kidding? I think, and repeat it aloud. Neither Toimu nor the young men from our car answer. Wamah is so tanked he can't figure out how to get the key into the door. Samuel does it for him, then walks over to the passenger side.

We follow them down the busy Monrovia road. Their vehicle freely swings to the left and right of the lane, stopping periodically for no apparent reason. Had it not been us behind, I'd have laid bets on its being rear-ended, which is nothing compared to what may happen even now as the car perilously crosses the center line. Toimu, always in the front passenger seat, calls on his cell phone, sounding like a cop on a loudspeaker ordering someone to pull over: "You are leaving your lane. You are leaving your lane." (Mobile conversations I understand best because the speakers here always enunciate dramatically into the receiver.) The young men chuckle, as does Toimu. As Wamah crosses over once again, horns from oncoming cars blare. Finally their sedan pulls over, and we follow suit. Samuel gets out and runs to our car to express his disgust with the situation and to report that he's going to take over the wheel.

I have heard countless laments since my arrival as to how the war's decimation – mutilating the roads; obliterating electricity, plumbing, mass communication – has regressed Liberia by decades. But nothing to American me feels so much a throwback to an earlier era as the simple truth that no one had the guts to take the car keys from that drunk in the beginning.

History

We sit on the screened front porch of Dr. Guannu's beautiful home, its style, coupled with the trim front lawn, feeling very American suburban. I feel privileged to be the private audience to this lecture. The professor is brilliant, and worldly – surprising and delighting me at one point by wryly making a reference to Fulton Street in downtown Brooklyn, a place where few tourists have ventured, and almost as few white Manhattanites. I had digested several books before coming to the country, and much of Guannu's information is either a confirmation or refutation of that material, but there are a few new surprises as well.

Unlike other colonized African nations, the settlers of Liberia did not represent a country but were sponsored by a private organization: the American Society for Colonizing the Free People of Color of the United States, or the American Colonization Society. The ACS, a white boys' club established in the early 19th Century, attracted a few conflicted abolitionists and Quakers – and Francis Scott Key, Henry Clay, Daniel Webster, and Supreme Court Justice Bushrod Washington, nephew of the first president – but the bulk of its membership were Southern white planters. Though President James Monroe was not officially a member, he supported the ACS to such an extent that the capital of the colony, and later the country, was named after him. The organization was *not* about manumission; it professed no official political or moral opinion on the subject of humans in bondage. Rather, it was concerned with free blacks – in specific, their emigration out of America. At that time the area west of the Mississippi seemed a foreign enough land for a black colony in the eyes of many of the ACS members – except, it was argued, the settlers may harbor escaped slaves; except they may join forces with Mexico, Canada or Native America and make war against the United States of America.

So the ACS bore the expense of transport to Africa, as well as food and supplies to support the settlers in their initial months. The legacy of this Americanized colonization is evidenced geographically in Liberia: in addition to Monrovia, there is Maryland County, the former "Mississippi in Africa" settlement, the Old Georgia Estate home I visited. In an America where the slave trade was outlawed but slavery itself legal as ever, the colony also served as a location to "return" abducted Africans "rescued" by the U.S. authorities from slave ships. Of course no one knew where in Africa the kidnapped had come from; sending them to Liberia was *not* sending them home. These people as a group were dubbed "Congoes."

As it turned out, the frugal of the Society needn't have fretted too considerably about the extravagance of the cross-Atlantic excursions because 1) the ACS reneged on much of their promised support to the colonists, and 2) the travel costs themselves remained at a minimum since, after the initial push, emigration was so sporadic. Despite the ACS' big dreams, only a relative handful of free blacks were willing to leave the U.S., some naysayers (including Frederick Douglass) acknowledging the flesh and blood of themselves and their ancestors buried in American soil, others simply preferring to stick with the devil they knew. At the outset the ACS demanded that the colony be run by white men. It took the death of the last one in 1841 before the black colony was finally black-governed.

And it took from that point until 1980, upon the death of the nineteenth consecutive Americo-Liberian president, this executive demise *not* of natural causes, before the African nation was finally governed by someone of pure African heritage.

Because the great irony and tragedy of Liberia, an African state colonized by *blacks*, descendants of former Africans, is that those settlers came from a slave-master society, a race-defined oppressor-oppressed society, and therefore they began to institute upon the African majority the only rule of law they knew – from fines against any native not "properly" attired (meaning any questionable body parts showing; the colonists themselves enduring the tropical heat in the antebellum dress of their former tyrants) to mandatory indentured servitude. And there were, of course, the textbook practices, mimicking those perpetrated in hundreds of treaties in America coined by the slick Great White Father, of swindling natives out of their land. In 1930 Liberia, so named as a harbor of freedom for immigrants from a slave country, was officially investigated by the League of Nations regarding accusations of forced labor, specifically citing Liberian workers coerced by the government for toil on the cocoa plantations of Fernando Po island, a Spanish colony.

The republic of Liberia, established in 1847 as the first such political system in Africa, was at an extreme economic disadvantage from the outset, given its composition of a majority robbed of its self-sufficiency and a minority self-appointed aristocracy abandoned by its sponsor and devoid of self-sufficiency. This coupled with bad luck: the coffee export, the sugar export – hopeful enterprises that finally couldn't prevail over Latin American competitors. And other detrimental factors: descendants of settlers were considered "citizens," the pure Africans "subjects" of the state not even eligible to vote until 1946 (nor could any women until that time), and almost all money and power were concentrated in the hands of the elite, with the elite identified by nativity. When in 1979 the price of the staple rice suddenly skyrocketed like gold, it was the last straw. Uprising, and in 1980 by virtue of a military coup General Samuel Doe of the Krahn tribe was installed as the new head of state.

Here's something my books didn't tell me: "How did the people feel about the first native African president?"

Dr. Guannu smiles. "There was dancing in the streets."

But unfortunately, he goes on, Doe was a military leader, not a diplomat, not a statesman, and his fear of enemies, real and imagined, political and clan, kicked in. Repression, executions.

In 1984 Charles MacArthur Ghankay Taylor, a bureaucrat in the Liberian General Services Agency who challenged Doe, was imprisoned in a Massachusetts penitentiary after allegedly stealing $900,000 in Liberian government funds and fleeing the country. Later he and a few well paid fellow criminals successfully implemented a Hollywood knotted-sheets jailbreak, and he escaped the U.S., eventually landing back in West Africa, entering Liberia from the north, and stirring up enough terror – most infamously via his drugged and armed to the teeth child soldiers – to catapult the entire country into an intermittent fourteen-year state of catastrophe.

This is obviously the outlandishly abridged version. Dr. Guannu, I am sure, would be the first to say there are no easy answers but when I ask for one regarding the tensions that ushered in the 21st Century, he tells me without hesitation that the origins may be traced to the animosity that has always existed since the Americans began settling nearly two hundred years before and started making the rules: the divisions between a) the haves and b) the have-nots.

Religion

It seems there are two airlines serving the Liberia airport. One is an African local, flying intracontinentally several days a week, if not every day. The other is serviced by an enormous craft out of Brussels that makes this run only once a week over an eighteen-hour triangular Wednesday-Thursday schedule: five hours from Brussels to Monrovia, one hour to Abidjan, then the return to Brussels. This was my carrier. The arrival flight is packed, the vast majority Africans. The rest, at least the ones I account for, are either European U.N. workers or white American Christian missionaries. I converse with one of the latter, a middle-aged woman who would be spending her two weeks on a refugee camp. I imagine they have brought food and money but the donation she speaks to me of is toys. "We want to help bring back the idea of 'play,'" she tells me. "For children who have gone through war and may have forgotten how to be children."

When I enter the heart of Monrovia for the first time I am fascinated by all the churches, everywhere. A century before the influx of white missionaries, Rachel Fay's family among them, Christianity was of course proselytized by the black settlers. It comes as no surprise to me that my host family, recommended by the daughter of missionaries, are Christians. Very Christian. Toimu is a minister. Every morning his family engages in devotions – a time for worship, prayer and singing together. I miss almost all of these, not waking until I would hear the neighborhood rooster crowing around six. Toimu's church is quite new. The congregation meets Sunday mornings in a large room of the AITB facility where he works; he must have garnered permission to borrow the space on Sundays when no one else was in the building. Toimu leads the Sunday School, which seems directed more to the adults than to the children, in exactly the same vein as the subsequent church service, another man presiding as the senior cleric. It feels very much like my hometown black Baptist church (I grew up in a small Appalachian valley city of western Maryland, walking distance to West Virginia): the sermon, the frequent audience response, even the music, African instruments accompanying here, the unrecognizable words interspersed with a familiar "Hallelujah!" I am a bit skeptical of the preacher at first, mainly because he looks to be well into his 50s at least, his pretty fiancée *very* young. But she has a toddler daughter, her marriage eligibility then entering into question many scenarios: Young widowhood (the war)? A rape victim (the war)? Or simply a single mother? (The one circumstance I rule out is that the little girl is the minister's "love child.") So I let my judgment of the minister go (and come to be fond of the couple), for how could I fairly judge such a choice given the complications in this country by the complications in mine?

Cuttington University College is an Episcopalian institution. My first full day in the country I am invited to have a private conference with the bishop, who serves as head administrator of the college. Everyone seems to regard this

432

meeting with a certain reverent awe, as if I am
about to tête-à-tête with Jesus Christ. In truth I *am*
honored: the bishop's secretary, a lively elderly
woman, is funny and open and warm and I feel as
if I am in the company of my adored and long-
deceased grandmother. The meeting with the
bishop himself is less exciting, though he is
certainly polite. And he may not be the Messiah
but his office is heavenly: the first air conditioning
I've experienced anywhere in Liberia, the outer
office space of his sweet assistant cooled only by
periodic brief bursts of relief when the minister
opens his door on his way to the toilet.

Speaking of air conditioning, on the
Wednesday marking the halfway point of my stay I
am promised that today we would finally get the
a.c.-complete rental car for which I (meaning the
theatre grant) wired big bucks days before my
arrival. I'm not sure who owns the clunker that's
been carrying us around thus far. The rental does
finally appear, a surprise to me, but without a.c.,
less of a surprise. It doesn't look new or especially
clean. It does boast a sound system, cassette and (I
assume) radio. Someone sticks in an African
gospel tape. When it is over, it plays again. And
again. At one point a particular song, belted out by
a woman, is rewound and played numerous times,
and while I want to run screaming from the car,
everyone else, judging by their fervor in singing
along, seems to find each subsequent play even
more inspiring than the last. Near the end of the
ditty the woman begins to repeat-sing "He is my
savior" about two hundred and fifty times, and

Christopher the 25-year-old filmmaker says, *"Yes,"* and 20-something Samuel concurs. I am told the singer converted from Islam to Christianity, along with her whole family, and as there is blatant pride and approval from all for this decision, I suppress my urge to ask why and surely cause great offense in this "saved" car.

Before colonization the Vai and Mandingo peoples of Liberia practiced Islam. Their participation in the slave trade goes in part to explain why, contrary to the popular belief that African-American Islam originated around the time of Elijah Muhammad in the 1950s, there were Muslim slaves in the U.S. In a nation of Christian slaveholders, of course those faithful to Islam usually worshipped in secret. We will visit a large refugee camp, a sign by the road identifying it in English and Arabic. But there are numerous refugee camps in the country, and the Arabic script at this particular sight seemed to be an exception.

I had read about traditional religions, about Poro (male) and Sande (female) pubescent initiation rites that even some professed Liberian Christians have chosen to undergo. These tribal spiritualities are apparently still alive and well and prevalent, most notably in the bush, but traveling around with my Christian family I never heard anyone speak of such customs. In *The Mask of Anarchy: The Destruction of Liberia and the Religious Dimensions of an African Civil War*, Stephen Ellis observes that

> born-again Christians..., reflecting on
> the awful experience of the war, are

434

attracted by the Christian belief that all evil is the work of the Devil. This enables them to consign the actions they themselves took during the war, now considered evil in the light of their new Christian faith, to the work of another self, the one who 'died' when they were born again in Christ.[9]

I have noticed how the commandment about not taking the Lord's name in vain is so subjectively interpreted. In the U.S. many older Christians I know find nothing blasphemous in an occasional "Oh Lord!" And when I show Toimu the Free Cell game on his new computer, he quickly waves off my tutorial, then quickly loses, staring at the computer in amused disbelief and uttering "Jesus!"

Music

The night I arrived in Liberia Toimu Jr., the firstborn, pulled out his guitar and sang a welcome song he'd composed for me. A couple of nights later he and his singing partner Peter performed for us in the living room, and gave me a copy of their CD. Toimu Jr. looks fifteen. Actually he is married with a baby (I find this out *much* later); has degrees in physics, chemistry and music; and is one of the directors of a school in Dbarnga.

Some music software samples are built into the new computer – five pieces including

---

[9] Ellis, Stephen. *The Mask of Anarachy: The Destruction of Liberia and the Religious Dimension of an African Civil War.* New York, NY: New York University Press, 1999, p. 268.

Beethoven's Ninth, the top of the second movement, and a David Byrne song. Every so often in the evenings, I hear one or the other of these playing, making me feel like I'm part of a movie being scored with the wrong soundtrack.

And then all the Christian fare. The African instruments in the morning family devotions and the variations on African-American gospel in church. My last weekend we will take a car trip of several hours and I will deliberately choose the music-less rental car, even after the other was traded for a properly air-conditioned vehicle, and I have made the right choice: we make a stop and as soon as the doors of the tape deck car swing open I hear the *ad nauseatic* "He is my savior!"

The radio music Ellen and the teen boy are listening to on the porch today is decidedly *not* Christian. Rap/hip-hop – and, although strange to me, the DJ seems just as likely to play white American/European pop rock. The first song sounds like Jamaica by way of Brooklyn, the second also male New York, the third identifiable as rapper Eve. When the words "motha fucka nigga" are uttered in the middle selection, I know these adolescents understand the American English because they instantly look up at me, wide-eyed, hands caught in the cookie jar.

Toimu calls Theatre for Peace to tell them we would arrive at 11 AM rather than the originally scheduled 10, so when we roll in around 1:30 we technically are only 2 ½ hours late. The organization emerged during a lull in the war, mid-'90s. It was closed when hostilities resumed, their space in Dbarnga damaged. They have recently resumed work but, like everyone else, they have been displaced, crashing in this slum. The complex, numerous conjoined small houses seem comparable to housing projects back home. The temporary theatre space – no signs, no posters – is two tiny rooms.

But good news: they'll be moving back to their own offices in Dbarnga next month. Still everyone seems pretty morose. One man wears a red AIDS awareness ribbon, just like in the States. The organization records music and performs dramatic pieces, mostly for social educational purposes. Their major foci are disarmament, AIDS, and the literacy and vocational training of women. (As always, I am the only woman present.) I am happy to hear them speak of "the grass roots," and now I'm certain Wamah's "riffraff" remark was as offensive as I'd imagined. I ask many questions. "Yes." "No." Little elaboration. They aren't being rude. Just the doldrums – not really a lot to say. Boring boring but now I'm thinking about the other room. "Can I see the studio?"

Everyone transfers into this makeshift space, a good ten of us including Toimu and his wheelchair gathered in the cramped room already packed with sound equipment. One man pulls in a cord from outside a window, plugging in something and I hope it's not just a fan. Someone turns on a boom box connected to a soundboard, and *music!* All of us moving! Most of it upbeat African, and jazzy. There is obviously a trumpet on one of the tapes. Except it's not: Samuel explains that the musician makes the precise sound with his mouth. Then a beautiful hymn:

> God bless Liberia
> My home sweet home

Despite the approximation in lyrics, I hear *no* resemblance to any similar American tune.

Stopped at a filling station, I ask about a song on the radio. Toimu says the singers are talking about Judgment Day, and how God will be making decisions then.

"Are they really talking about judgment against Charles Taylor on earth?"

I am answered with polite chuckles, which I seem to get here whenever I make any statement that seems remotely astute, as if this embarrasses them. "Yes," Toimu says, "like 'Go Papay Go.'"

This was the one melody I had heard in the presence of the family adults that, as far as I could tell, was completely nonreligious. I wished I could understand it, its apparently biting satire, the title a reference to Papay[10] Taylor, the name the child soldiers were compelled to call their commander. I could hear a few odd "ahem"s in the midst of the singing. Samuel said that it was a mannerism of Charles Taylor to always clear his throat before making a speech.

Children
Jeremiah, the youngest child in the house, is a hyper boy of about eight. As I eat breakfast and

---

[10] As in Pappy.

Florence talks, I smile at him as I often do (he sometimes returns the look but never the smile), watching him fly about the rooms, and my distraction finally prompts the mother of the house to comment. "He is troubled son."

"Excuse me?" He's emotionally distraught? An "at risk" youth? Then why is her mouth turned up in a smile? Then I hear. "Oh – *troublesome!* Yes!"

But this was a rare discussion about children. Several times I would remark on something funny the boy was doing, and the adult with whom I was conversing would politely smile in recognition of my having been entertained, but otherwise the child could be doing back handsprings in the living room and the grown-ups, if they noticed, would just stare at him, expressionless. Kids are everywhere here; as the Old Georgia Estate woman said, "Africans have big families." And the children are ordered about by their parents, and they obey. But other than that not much attention is paid, neither fawning over them nor yelling at them.

In my readings I came across an interesting Liberian practice of unofficial "adoptions": orphans, and there would certainly be a plethora of them postwar, who exchange household chores for room and board. Unlike traditional notions of formal servitude, however, the children are treated as if they are a part of the family. Could this be the case with Jeremiah? Neither he nor the teenage boy who cleans my room were included in the family introductions my first night here. And what about all those little ones who seem to share the house with post- middle age Dr. Wamah and childless Samuel and Eunice? As for the two boys in the house I stay in, if they are in fact adoptees, I wouldn't say the older boy has any more chores than the blood offspring of the house, all of them lounging together when the work is done, and the little boy's only job appears to be to get into mischief.

There is discussion of thirteen-year-old Ellen emigrating to Florida to live with Rachel Fay. Rachel is concerned about the safety of a girl coming into her pubescence in today's Liberia. Thus far, however, red tape with U.S. Customs has stalled the plans. But the family seems hopeful their youngest will soon live in America or, alternatively, Europe. I ask Ellen if she wants to move so far away, imagining such a proposition would be terrifying to a child. She smiles, and nods.

On the porch one day I watch a couple of little girls walking down the road. Their toddler brother comes bawling after them. One of the girls carries him back home, then the sisters resume their stroll. The little boy comes crying again. The little girl brings him back. The chain is repeated. Sisyphus but with the patience of Job, the girl smiling every time she carries her brother home.

Next to our house I see little boys yelling and playing. They've taken a plastic bag and rolled it into some kind of ball, and are engaging in a team sport. After the discussion with the Christian woman on the plane, it's a relief to see children who haven't forgotten the concept of "play."

Ellen had finished her basic chores, including carting five full buckets of water on her head to refill my large pail. Toimu now tells her to boil water for his tea. (The family has one kind: Lipton's.) Ellen puts the water on to boil, then goes to the porch to hang with the other kids, forgetting about the task. Eventually Florence discovers the bubbling water and pours Toimu's tea. Toimu calls, "Ellen! Why didn't you tell me my water is ready?"

Ellen calls back from the porch, not budging or missing a beat: "Your water is ready."

Women
Toimu's Sunday School sermon my first Sunday (I wonder if it's for my benefit) is about respecting women. He stresses in what apparently would be locally considered a progressive homily that a woman is not a "slave," separating the "natural" tendencies of the sexes – women: understanding, tenderness, love, patience; men: courage, dignity, strength – but clarifying yin-yangy the equal importance of all these qualities for a beneficial, functioning society.

The men-strength thing is a joke to me since, by my observation, all the physical work is being done by the women. A couple of evenings into my stay a table and chair arrive. Toimu has thoughtfully arranged this as a desk for me. (Though in fact I write sitting on the floor as I do at home, reserving the table for the after-dinner

441

snacks Florence brings into my room.) Florence starts to pick up the somewhat heavy table to carry it to my space. I jump to grab the other end but she shoos the guest away, summonsing Ellen for the job. Meanwhile all the men and teen boys are gathered around the new computer a few feet away, it never occurring to any of them to assist. I think about Western Hemisphere macho: At least it means we can count on men to *lift* things. On the street the women carry all manner of heavy items. I saw a modern six-seater kitchen table balanced atop one woman's scalp: no hands! Which is astounding to me both in terms of brawn and, even more so, engineering.

Leaving the house for our appointments, I bid good-bye to Florence, to the girls – so tired of being the only woman for the rest of the day! But, as it turns out, it's not just a man's world. Two weeks before the first postwar elections, October 11th, 2005, only two of twenty-two parties will have publicly stated their platforms. One of these, the United Party, will be represented by Ellen Johnson-Sirleaf as its candidate for president and, as history will show, she will ultimately reign triumphant, the first elected female head of state on the continent. She has an extraordinarily impressive résumé, including former positions as Liberian Minister of Finance and Senior Loan Officer of the World Bank.

In a civil conflict such as Liberia's, the term "war" itself seems illegitimate, eliciting images of similarly armed adversaries but not the rest of the picture: brutes carrying heavy artillery raping and massacring civilians, frequently women and children. It is not surprising then that it is the ladies who tend to take the reins in the initiatives toward peace. In addition to the sign mentioned earlier, I saw one other small billboard designed toward this effort:

> THE WOMEN IN PEACEBUILDING
> NETWORK SAY
> LET US LOVE ONE ANOTHER
> WAR IS NOT THE SOLUTION
> TO OUR PROBLEM
> PEACE IS THE ANSWER

Toimu tells me his father was a chief with four wives but, as a Christian, Toimu has to limit himself to one. He says he calls Florence "Mommy," that women are really mothers to their husbands. The concept is certainly familiar given its recurrent application in my own country but I'm still irritated. I hear young Samuel and his fiancée Eunice discuss issues, and while I can't make out all the words, by the tone it is clear that if *any*body backs down it's Samuel. And for all her fervor for service, I would be hard-pressed to describe Florence as "subservient." In church she surprises me when she stands and makes a passionate, assertive speech about her fears upon hearing of her son's car accident, and while this maternal concern may fit well within the purview of a traditional-roles society, her unapologetic stealing the show from the men did not. Sometimes I notice she and Toimu privately whispering and laughing with each other, an endearing indication of a long, healthy marriage.

As for the children Florence actually gave birth to, they all seem to be respectful enough, though I suppose they take parents for granted in the same way parents seem not to notice them. One evening moody Samuel sits away from me on a smaller table. Because I'd been served my dinner first I'd finished first. Now he says, "Thank you, Mom, for the naaaaaaaas meeeeeeeeel," the exaggerated enunciation obviously to ensure I heard him. I am profuse in my appreciation to Florence after every meal, nice or not, and Samuel has finally been shamed into showing some acknowledgment of his mother's endeavors. She is always grateful for my manners but now she rolled-eyed waves him away, knowing it's just a show for me. Later in the week, Samuel will accidentally smash his mother's finger in the car door, and she will screech in pain. I'm sure he feels badly about it but he only frowns. I wait, listening carefully, but to my knowledge an apology never comes.

Identity

There is a moment in our evening at Old Georgia Estate when someone asks if my name means anything. I tell them that my mother, with the help of an aunt, made it up (I was second born after my fifteen-month-old sister Kim, and my mother was looking for something alliterative), that it wasn't a common American name back then but that there seems to be a fair number of little black "Kia"s running around now. "Black parents in the U.S. tend to be creative with names. White parents tend to be more regular."

Everyone stares at me, blank.

Somewhere in my subconscious I understand their confusion but I still nurture my denial until the next morning. Sunday, hours before church, I am sitting at the breakfast table with Toimu while he phones someone we'd briefly run into the day before to set up an official appointment. "Yes, you met her yesterday. Remember the white lady?"

I stroll out to the porch. I was warned by black friends from home who'd traveled to the continent that this would happen. There are tears in my eyes that I suppress; with all the horror and its aftermath in this nation, I am *not* going to cry because someone called me white. But I'm *black*. When I wrote to Toimu to describe myself for the pickup at the airport, I said I was a light-skinned *black* woman with long dreadlocked hair. My favorite James Brown is "I'm Black and I'm Proud" but this is not pride; it's just *fact*. I have spent my entire American life enduring all the trials and tribulations of being black. It is a dominant part of my identity. But what am I here?

I know the history. Someone looking like me in Liberia would likely be a part of the elite. But, then again, I see *no* one here who looks like me. The adults all glance at me, the children stop and stare, often smiling. I don't want to disregard the privileges I would have been afforded by virtue of my obvious birthright had I been born here, but I wasn't. Later Eunice, who I have come to consider a friend, will surprise and unintentionally hurt me when she refers to a colleague nurse at the hospital where she works: "You'd like her. She's another white lady." She is in a car with me days later when I finally say, "You know, in my country I'm black. Both my parents looked like me and had to go to the same segregated school as all the other black kids." This startles them.

Toimu had mentioned that his cousin Rita, who works at the airport and had met me there upon my arrival, wanted to know if I was interested in joining her women's group. I was touched and replied affirmatively but now I'm annoyed: I just found out the ceremony marking my inauguration is happening after church today (noon – then rescheduled to 2:30) and I was supposed to finally have a day off. I try to take a brief rest before we leave but here's Toimu knocking on my door. He hands me a list that he has printed neatly, remarks for me to make at the gathering. Oh God. Another speech. Then he begins chattering about what I would need to do in the event of this or that at the meeting, and I appreciate that he's trying to fill me in on what's culturally proper so I don't screw up but Alright, Toimu, *got* it!

Points to talk to on May 30, 2004
Bellemu Women's Program, 2:30[11] PM

    1.   Thank them for their invitation.

---

[11] Make that 4.

2. Tell them that it is a wonderful thing for people to honor a person they did not know before.

3. Tell them that you are happy that you came to Liberia without knowing anyone personally besides Toimu, whom you got to know him by e-mail introduction. Say you are happy to be considered member of such a wonderful Women Organization in Liberia.

4. Tell them that you will reach to see the village of Bellemu.

5. Tell them that you too will remember the group.

6. Tell them that you will also tell the good news to your family and other friends.

7. Prepare your email address and give it to them and tell them to use it at any time they wish to write you.

So we're on our way to this thing which I have ethnocentricified in my imagination as a quaint little ladies' tea party, and I'm pissed because Christopher, the young family friend, has taken the camera again. Perhaps he didn't hear me before: I WANT TO USE IT *MYSELF*. It's fine when he records my long question-and-answer sessions for the sake of all the progeny who are yearning to be bored out of their minds but what he regards as everyday dull stuff and not worthy of videotape – the UN trucks everywhere, the woman with the kitchen table on her head – *I* find interesting. We make one stop and the family exchanges maybe twenty dollars of the American currency I gave Toimu for zillions of Liberian bills. Everyone seems giddy with anticipation of this affair though I'm too focused on Christopher and MY CAMERA (well, the theatre's, but it's mine here!) to take much notice.

We make a turn and Christopher says, "I'll get out of the car now" and, as our vehicle slows, he steps out. In the distance I see some African dance ceremony in procession, women in full native dress. Now *there's* a picture! and I'm glad for once Christopher has the wherewithal to spot it. We're already so tardy for my little event that a little later won't make much difference.

Then we pull over and park, and everyone leaves the vehicle.

OH MY HOLY GOD.

This *is* my ceremony! All those dancing women – It's for *me!* There must be two hundred people here! I wanna turn around! Oh God. I wanna go back!

As we walk closer, a few women come dancing up to me, putting their arms around my back and shoulders, leading me. I can't African dance! I had always planned to learn, to take a class but… Their amazing steps, their brilliant colors, their bare feet. And me, sneakers and backpack and Dee & Dee discount dress, trying to move with them, swinging my arms, grinning! grinning!

We are seated now, me, Florence to my left, then Samuel, then Toimu in plastic chairs (Toimu in his wheelchair) with the clear subtext that, for this afternoon, we are the royal family, this lounge furniture our thrones. A woman fans Florence and me from behind (*Hate* it), and in the large circle before us the other women perform incredible movements, which I would enjoy so much more as an anonymous spectator. Occasionally a woman bends way over, her torso parallel with the ground, and dances in front of us by our knees and, as I had been instructed by Toimu, I place my hand gently on her back, an indication to her of a job well done. Toimu and the others give the dancers the Liberian money, flinging it at them by the fistful. One tall woman has twelve toes, six on each foot, but it takes me awhile to grasp this, to decipher what is unusual about her long feet. She dances in a way to bring attention to them, as if they were a source of great pride.

Now it is time for speeches and, for no reason that I've earned, the women offer me their love: that's the word they use. They give me a gorgeous traditional ensemble – head wrap and top and skirt. I put them on at their urging. They're *heavy*. *Hot*. How can they wear clothes like this in Africa? They hand me a kola nut as part of the ceremony, and I remember the warning pamphlet from the nurse practitioner who'd given me my travel shots, then take a great big Centers-for-Disease-Control-be-damned! bitter bite. Florence brings awkward me into the big dance circle and makes me move a few steps, then off to dance by herself. She's wonderful! Her sons toss much money at her and everyone laughs.

Now it is time for my speech. I struggle to remember Toimu's talking points now that I have been shocked into the understanding of why he so painstakingly wrote them all down.

"Thank you so much! I'm so honored that you have done this for me!"

Enthusiastic applause!

"I'm so glad I came to Liberia! It's my first trip to Africa!"

Enthusiastic applause!

"When I get home I'm going to tell my family and friends about Bellemu."

Enthusiastic applause!

"And if you want to stay in touch – " I turn to Toimu, panicked. "Should I tell them my email address?" Ridiculous!

"Yes," he replies with conviction.

I turn back to the crowd: "You can email me at C-O-R-T-H-R-O-N-at-hotmail-dot-com!"

Silence. Someone blinks.

A man in a Western suit finally asks, "What was the address?"

Toimu mutters, "You can get it from me after."

My light-skinned black face is red. Stupid Toimu! Stupid Kia!

The dancing continues, me seated and observing. A woman hands me an infant girl. I am happy for the distraction, and I coo at the child. No one else seems interested. I am not clear who the mother is.

A couple of hours later we are at Samuel's house. He pulls out a homemade board game, the markings crudely drawn on with colored felt tip pens, and I instantly recognize it as Parcheesi. (He calls it something else.) I feel like a fool in my fancy African garb, and I'm sweating like a pig, I want to tear it all off! But I don't: respect.

"I'm gonna win I'm gonna win!" I tell the children near me, the ones who mysteriously seem to live in the house with Wamah, Eunice and Samuel. They had been staring at me but now, not understanding my words or intentions, they back away. Playing against a man, being competitive – all part of my American self that I suddenly cling to. Samuel wins the first game. On the last play of the second – I need to get a 1 on one of the die for a victory – I say, "Here's what we do in the States." I blow on the dice and toss them. 3 and 3. "Doubles!" By the rules Samuel has laid out, I get another turn. Blow. Roll. 4 and 1. "*Yes!*"

I did not come to Africa to trace my roots. When I was offered the travel grant in early 2003,

Liberia was not the first destination that came to my mind. Iraq was, Baghdad having just "fallen," the staged celebrations for the benefit of the American media implying an end to the war when of course it actually only marked the beginning of a new phase of what came to be the longest American conflict save only Vietnam and interminable Afghanistan. I also considered Haiti. Cuba. Rwanda. Vietnam. Palestine again. Then that summer the combatants descended upon Monrovia, and Liberia, in brutal bloody turmoil for thirteen years, was finally deemed worthy of American news. Actually it was the BBC version of the events that I observed, my eyes locked to the screen. I made my decision. Drawn to the political ramifications: I write about injustice, not identity. But here I am, a mighty confused African-American woman who in the course of a few hours on a Sunday in June went from being mistakenly identified as white (But I'm black – just like you!) to being ceremoniously reborn as an African (But I'm an American – nothing like you!).

In the evening Florence brings me plantains, and the three girls accompany her into my room. Ruth, the oldest daughter, gives me lessons in African dance (as Angie and Ellen sit on the floor next to each other, giggling), African dress, and the Kpelle language. After all my excursions with the men, it is very nice to have a little all-female time.

Christopher had said earlier with no small admiration that I looked like "a beautiful African woman" all decked out in my new duds. Ruth now says I looked "beautiful" this afternoon when

I was wearing the headdress (I'd removed that part of the outfit) and, more significantly, that I looked "different." She clearly wants me to confirm my sense of cultural transformation.

Except I don't feel different. All I feel wearing the African clothes is awkward.

But it's not just some bull she's throwing. So maybe my "Africanization" made *them* feel differently about *me*. Now Ruth says: "You are one of us. Our family."

I imagined I would be huge in Liberia but, as it turns out, I obviously weigh less than most other adults here. The Kpelle name the women at the ceremony chose for me is Negbarn (nay-*bon*). Toimu tells me it means "slim."

Thank God it doesn't mean "white."

Charity
My guess is, by Liberian standards, my host family is in the middle of things economically. They are not among the hundreds of thousands of desperately poor, living on refugee camps inside or outside of the country. They are educated, many of them with college degrees, which certainly gives them an advantage with four-fifths of the nation illiterate. Toimu, in a land where there are not even simple wheelchair-accessible ramps (though making any broad judgments about sensitivity would be unjust given that the postwar to-do list could fill the Manhattan phone directory), has miraculously managed to stay governmentally employed while preparing for his master's studies. Samuel is also a master's student while teaching at

the college level. Toimu's bare Monrovia house certainly seems shabby compared to Old Georgia Estate but, for all I know, their real home in Dbarnga may have been equally "estate"-worthy, though undoubtedly looted to nothing when the rebels came roaring through. Still, I look around and see a family of obviously healthy eaters. They are also subsidized by an American donor, a family friend. I realize this as I wait in the car on the Western Union parking lot while Toimu and Samuel go in to pick up the cash. Simultaneously I'm giving subsidy cash, a few American dollars, to a man with one leg, supported by crutches, who has just come up to the car. I don't remember seeing other Liberians with limbs missing. Liberia is not Angola, the country of land mines. In Liberia there was only raping and killing, with creative variations on technique.

By my arrival day the family had received U.S.$4,300 in funds paid them by the theatre grant through me, no small potatoes in this land of $240 per annum for the minority few who find a job. My last full day I'll buy African gifts for my family back home. "A thousand dollars," the vendor will say. As my pupils explode out of my eyeballs and I prepare to decide which items to put back, Samuel will translate into American terms: "Twenty dollars." Of course. I drank a twelve-ounce can of Orange Crush with a $30 (Liberian) price tag. And the bankroll Wamah pulled out to pay for our drinks that night. The exchange rate is astronomical. The $20 for the gifts, I will understand later, is a rounding off; the precise math is $56 Liberian = U.S.$1.

One day Toimu asks if I like fish. "Sure," replies vegetarian me who never touches the stuff. (I will come to love it here, especially when other food gets skimpy later on. Unlike cow meat, the fish is quite tasty.) That afternoon we see two little girls selling fish alongside the road, and we stop the car. Toimu asks the children, "How much?"

The girls: "One twenty-five."

Toimu briefly considers. "I'll give you one."

The children say they have to ask their mother, and run off to do so. They return with the permission, and Toimu counts two hundred Liberian dollars for both girls' loads. Each child holds a bunch of about a dozen large fresh fish, and they now hand them over to Toimu in return for the cash. These slender children, I presume, are not standing on the shoulder of the road vending seafood to strangers to supplement their family's middle-class income. They are poor, the mother perhaps widowed in the war, and are trying their best to get by. I'm thinking about the $4,300 I gave to Toimu. I'm thinking about the 56:1 exchange rate. Toimu just negotiated these little impoverished girls down from the U.S. equivalent of 4 ½ cents per dozen fish to 3 ½ cents. No one seems bothered by this, sulky Samuel having come to life in describing the many delicious ways the fish could be prepared. And, yes, I know that it's a part of African culture to bargain, but as long as they've adopted western Christianity anyway, couldn't they consider the concept of Christian charity?

We will make two visits to refugee camps – actually camps for "the internally displaced" since these refugees are still in the country. Toimu's brother, his wife and their family live on the first, near the town of Harbel and the airport, outside of Monrovia. The sister-in-law will speak at length about the hardships she has endured, and at the end I will take Samuel aside and ask if it would be alright to give her U.S.$20, as I wouldn't want to insult her. "*Yes!*" he will bark, as if I were a moron for even asking the question, as if I had been selfishly holding back from his relative and should have offered long before the conclusion to our twenty-minute visit.

Late in my stay, we will travel to the hinterlands, *the bush*, coming to Totota in Bong County, the location, I am told, of the largest camp for the internally displaced in the country. Indeed, the rows of metal huts seem to extend endlessly. A pathetically thin woman comes up to sharp dressed Samuel, asking for a little money, her voice so humbly low I can barely hear her. I stare at her, my mind on my wallet in the trunk of the car. But I see in the faces of the other family members and Christopher, most turned away, that for me to ask someone to open the trunk for my backpack would ignite a small riot amongst my car mates, as the sight of American cash would result in our being bombarded by hundreds from the camp. There is an embarrassment in their eyes, not unlike that of guilt-ridden New Yorkers who don't pull out their purses for panhandlers. Except for Samuel who furiously snaps at the begging woman, "No! I don't have enough for myself!"

I remember the day of my women's ceremony, when Samuel was one of the most enthusiastic money hurlers, laughing as he pitched gobs of Liberian dollars as if they were confetti.

Throughout our excursions, he and Christopher have repeated to me patronizingly, "You're going to see things you've never seen before," as if they've known me my whole rich, spoiled, carefree, naïve, American life. They said it again just before we entered this camp, always stressing how much Liberia has suffered, a phrase they use interchangeably with "how much *we* have suffered."

By no means do I wish to trivialize the horrors Samuel and Christopher have endured, and at such a young age. But, like everywhere else, some people are suffering infinitely more than others.

Wildlife
Sunday night, after the women's ceremony, after the gathering of family women in my room, late and alone, my initiation into African life is complete: a cockroach in my bathroom the size of a Volkswagen beetle.

I go through scrupulous planning to use the minimum amount of water that will leave me reeking as little as possible. I wear short-sleeved blouses under my jumpers but I've come to realize I have to wash the outer garment as well every day or I'm going to be stinkier than I already am. It is Monday, the night following my surprise visitor from the tub, and I prepare to wash my hair. I forgot to pack shampoo so I have to use the Irish Spring -type bar soap the family has provided for me. According to my experience here, the most efficient use of H_20 is: 1) shampoo, 2) use the dirty water to flush, 3) wash myself, 4) use the dirty water to flush, 5) wash my clothes, 5) dirty water to flush. I don't have diarrhea – yet. It's just that I'm pathetic at this manual flush business so it takes every bit of secondhand water I can drum up to make for one good ol' American flush.

You know that metal disc on some tubs directly below the spigot and above the drain? The cover on mine is gone so it's an open hole. As I put my pail of water in the tub for Step 1: Shampoo, out of the corner of my eye I notice movement in the hole. I try to calm myself. Time spent at a writing retreat in Key West trained me to regard little salamanders as the harmless creatures they are and now, against all logic, I try to convince myself that a friendly little amphibian has come to call. I am about to walk into the tub, naked, when out comes *La Cucaracha Grande* in an encore performance. I let out a yelp. I imagine giant cockroaches are probably harmless but no matter: no way I'm sharing the tub with that thing! Insanely I grab gobs of water, throwing it on the insect, big as a large mouse. It flips, confused, but has no intention of drowning. (Though I regularly don't eat or wear animals, when they enter my territory, it's WAR.) I realize it is useless, then turn around to see, to my horror, the floor covered in all the water I've just wasted. Now I turn back and my alarm regarding the flood is trumped by the image of part of the insect's body separating from the rest. Wings! But they settle against its "torso" again. A warning: I may not fly right now, Kia, but just so we understand each other – I *can*.

Rapidly scrub my head, knees on the floor, hair hanging over the tub. Take the bucket out. Flush the toilet. Refill bucket to clean my body. Empty the dirty water into the toilet: flush. Use the plunger: nothing seems to clean the damn john! I am starting to employ my dirty underwear to soak up the saturated floor when I hear a knock on my bedroom door. Grab clothes and go out to answer.

It's Florence, not surprisingly; she seems to come by every hour to bring me something to eat, or to have an extensive, challenging lost-in-translation discussion about what she plans to bring me to eat later. She has fresh rolls. Now for some thoughts on tomorrow's menu. I keep my bathroom door closed so she doesn't see the disaster area. I smile. "Yes, that'll be *great!*" I'm a little hungry, and feel the need to calm down, so after she leaves I eat the smaller of the two rolls, saving the other for the next day. Back to the crusade in the w.c.

Where the hell's that bug?

There. Headed for my toiletries bag. God Almighty. I quickly finish soaking up the water, then close the door.

As the evening of the next day rolls around, I become increasingly nervous. Thinking of delaying my bath until the following morning. But so far no sign of uninvited company. I pray the thing has gone away.

I approach the bathroom. Something moving. So gargantuan from outside I can *hear* it walking around in there.

And now I see it. Them. There are two.

First thing after the cock crows daylight I stuff the hole with a plastic bag I'd brought with me. I don't want to complain to the family about the cockroaches from hell but I *sure* don't want someone tidying my space to remove my peacekeeper. So I show the hole stuffer to the teen boy and explain its imperative utility. Minutes later Florence enters my bathroom and I hear, and smell, the spray of household insecticide. I look in and see she's applying it directly into the hole. She doesn't use much, which relieves me both because I don't want the family to waste it on me and because I appreciate my oxygen not being *too* contaminated. In truth I don't see how anything short of someone putting on a radiation protection suit and going in there with a hose would disturb my steadfast friends. But I am wrong: even after she removed my plastic blockade (which initially horrified me) I won't see the beasts again.

There never would have been a hole had there been working plumbing, and perhaps this is why Kia's Battle of the Bath has left me feeling especially empathetic for the Liberian people, for Liberian *women*, having 21st Century housecleaning standards to live up to with, suddenly, early 20th Century facilities.

War

Upon the confirmation of my travel plans to Liberia, I had no clear idea what sort of situation I was walking into. Africa's sporadic appearance on American news is certainly not because nothing's happening. In the days prior to my departure from New York, I had ascertained from Liberian web resources that the United Nations peacekeeping forces had just entered the country, and that seemed a good sign. It wasn't 'til perhaps a year after returning to the States that it dawned on me: all the frustration during the months it took to find a Liberian contact possibly saved my life. Knowing what I know now, an earlier arrival into the thick of it all would have exponentially reduced my chances for survival. (In 2007 I met an American aid worker in Kenya who had also worked in Liberia, and who seemed stunned that I risked being there even in 2004.)

Sitting in my room in Monrovia, I listen to the BBC radio news. They speak of rebel eruptions in the Congo. At home, sympathetic as I may have been, the central African nation would have felt like another universe. And it still is the better part of two thousand miles away, yet the threat feels close. And closer: Someone was killed in Monrovia the day my plane landed. Sounded like it was an American – I caught just the end of this report – shot dead in front of his hotel. With guerilla civil warfare the delineations of war time and peace time are even more obscured than with state-declared ceasefires. But, for all intents and purposes, most Liberians consider the war to be over. It has had its ebbs and flows and while, certainly, this isn't the first time in the last decade and a half for this rumor of withdrawal to become widespread and then refuted, there is something convincing in the sentence that I keep hearing: "Everyone's tired of fighting." There is weariness in just the uttering of the statement; not a morsel of the elation that should accompany such a long-awaited peace. The general feeling of the country is, on the contrary, mass despondency. It's the lack of plumbing and electricity; it's former public buses sitting idle, burned black, while people walk miles along a highway in the African heat (we'd picked up a few such pedestrians, acquaintances of the family); it's streets so shot up that potholes have become more accurately potcanyons; it's billions of dollars needed to restore minimum basic civil function and empty pockets all around.

As I gaze at the thousands of candles flickering along the road in the night, I ponder aloud, "So these streets were completely empty during the war." It is a question but I am certain of the answer.

"Not a soul," Samuel confirms. He used to live here, downtown, until last summer when the brutal rebels came raining down on Monrovia and he knew to get the hell out of his place, doors away from the Executive (Presidential) Mansion.

I don't tell Samuel how much I admire Kofi Annan when I ask what he thinks of him. Samuel seems to be pretty critical of everyone, and I'm curious if he may feel differently about the first black African UN Secretary General. He shrugs irritably: Too little too late. Easy to bring in the UNMIL (UN Mission in Liberia) now that the nation is basically at peace. Where were they when we needed them?

On the porch I ask Christopher if, when the war first started, people thought it was something that would quickly blow over. In '89, he tells me, the beginning, Charles Taylor entered Liberia from the Ivory Coast and began to train kids as combatants. People in the hinterlands began to see a few brutalized corpses but these were presumed (or hoped) to be ritual murders – as in religious-based human sacrifice.[12] Gradually rumors about rebellion began to spread. By 1990 the populace was certain that a rebel militia led by Charles Taylor was in the bush. President Samuel Doe sent an army to suppress the insurgents but the soldiers weren't prepared for people used to surviving in the forest. And the rebels were hard to identify since they dressed like civilians. (In years to come the infamous cross-dressers would appear: men wigged, nailed, lipsticked and semiautomatically armed.) The guerilla troops gradually divided into various splinter rebel groups. Sometimes a combatant would fight for one group, leave, then join and fight for another group. Prince Johnson ("Prince" is a common Liberian name, not a title) had been Charles Taylor's partner but, Christopher tells me, Johnson was opposed to training children, and he wanted to depose Doe without killing

---

[12] Which still happens occasionally (and not necessarily in the bush) and is always fervently condemned by other Liberians.

civilians, so he and Taylor parted ways.
Christopher mentions a few typical combatant
activities: cutting the babies out of pregnant
women; plunging a machete into an infant, then
parading the dead baby and forcing civilians to
salute the "flag." Mandingoes were killed just for
being Mandingo. Taylor's follower kids chanted

> You killed my ma
> You killed my pa
> And I will fight for you!

and these killings were not poetically figurative,
but literal. According to AllAfrica.com, the war
claimed the lives of one out of every seventeen
Liberians. Though it was Johnson who ultimately
removed Doe, Taylor was elected to the presidency
by an antagonistic constituency who only hoped
allowing him to fulfill his ambitions would finally
put an end to the horror. His supporters, or those
who claimed to be, cheered

> You killed my ma
> You killed my pa
> And I will vote for you!

After his election, Taylor continued his dirty
dealings in Sierra Leone, trading guns for
diamonds. He owned a tiger, an alligator and a
snake, and it was the common wisdom that he fed
them human flesh. Hungry Liberians were killing
people to eat them.

"We hoped America would help us,"
Samuel says bitterly, remembering the hostilities'
beginnings, when two thousand U.S. marines on
four warships entered the coast of Monrovia,
evacuated some Americans and foreign nationals,
and left. A U.S. military presence, had the troops
lingered long enough to provide any sense of
defending civilians, would have nipped the war in
the bud, he believes. The people held out hope for
it. But in August of '89 Iraq invaded Kuwait, and
Liberia disappeared off the American-drawn map
of significance, if it ever was there.

There are legitimate reasons for an
expectation of U.S. aid. Of course it was American
colonization that fundamentally informed the
nation's social divisions. American corporations,
such as the Firestone Tire and Rubber Company,
have exploited the country's resources,
astronomically more to the economic benefit of the
foreign company than the citizens of the land they
employ. During the Second World War, Liberia
permitted the U.S. to build a modern airport,
initially used as a base to transport American
soldiers. During the Cold War Liberia remained
steadfastly anti-communist. On a drive Samuel
points out the towers of a radio system the
American military had set up at that time,
overriding the local radio communication. When
the Cold War was over and Liberia no more of use
for the time being, the Americans packed up and
left, leaving their abandoned materials behind and
never mending the infrastructural damage they'd
wreaked. During the Reagan years, in exchange for

economic aid, Doe's government was at least as sycophant as the previous Americo-Liberian administrations in jumping to please the White House: reducing its Soviet embassy staff, establishing diplomacy with Israel and, most delightful for Washington, facilitating the CIA's covert operations against another African nation, Libya, and its president Muammar Qaddafi. With all such good political will nurtured between Liberia and the U.S., whether or not Liberians agreed with all the policies, the populace was completely baffled and bewildered at America's abandonment when its assistance was needed most.

Toimu, Christopher and I wait in the parking lot of a large shopping center while others from our entourage run errands. Toimu in the front seat tells me in the back that the whole complex is owned by a famous Liberian footballer – George Weah, who will prove to be Ellen Johnson-Sirleaf's key competitor in the future presidential elections. Eventually I get out to speak with Christopher, who leans against the car. There are people *everywhere*, shopping, busy: Life. Christopher says, "If you'd seen the way it was before."

Last summer when all hell broke loose on Monrovia, Christopher had been abducted – snatched and pulled into a car by what looked like eighteen-year-olds – because he carried a cell phone and a camera, booty that were naturally confiscated. The kidnappers called him a "dissident collaborator" – Christopher believes

they didn't even know what the words meant –
and a machete was thrust against his torso. He
instantly reared back, blocking his chest with his
hand. The blade pierced his palm, cutting through
the flesh and pushing through almost to come out
the other side of his hand, and I see by its position
as he unconsciously re-enacts the defensive gesture
that this would have been at least the depth of the
cut into his heart had it not been for his quick
reflexes. For whatever reason there was no second
attempt on his life, and the thugs released him.

"I saw the guy there," Christopher says,
pointing to the entrance of the parking lot. He is
referring to a recent confrontation with his former
assailant. "I asked him, 'Do you know me?' He
said, 'No.' I reminded him of that night. 'Yes,' he
said, 'I tried to protect you.' 'No, you *stabbed* me,
you tried to kill me.' 'No,' he said, 'I was there.
But I tried to *save* you!'"

Refugees
Toimu asks if I've ever been to a refugee camp.
He's obviously certain I haven't. "Yes. In
Palestine." He is startled. Then: "Oh, those are
fancy refugee camps."

He has a point. Palestinians have been
internally displaced in their homeland for
generations now, much time to have constructed
houses – nothing extravagant but at least the basic
functions: working kitchens, working bathrooms.
Far worse off than Toimu's family in plumbing-less
electricity-less Monrovia are those confined to the

new refugee camps: a cramped box and a roof and nothing left to furnish even such humble quarters.

We walk into the refugee camp with the English/Arabic script entrance sign: Samuel, Christopher carrying the camera, and I. It is quite a hike over rugged, muddy ground, too arduous for anyone to manage the wheelchair, so Toimu stays in the car. The camp is operated by the UN. Hundreds of tiny newly built identical one-room metal shacks.

Samuel is looking for his uncle, who lives here now. We find the uncle's young wife. She and I don't understand each other. She speaks long monologues to Samuel, never looking at me, with Samuel translating: the NGOs (international nongovernmental organizations – a frequently uttered acronym in Liberia) promising food that never comes; her husband out looking for day work, hoping to bring home U.S.$1 today. The small hut houses the couple plus their four small children. Samuel's little cousins have sores up and down their legs – ant bites, their mother says. The children stare at me, grin at me. I recognize this scene from late-night Save the Children infomercials but the info the TV never conveys is that, before the war, the starving or ailing depicted on the screen were middle class. The young aunt follows us back toward our car and continues her nonstop soliloquy. When I hand her the twenty-dollar bill, she looks at me for the first time, beaming, thanking me, and I hate taking credit for the theatre grant's involuntary generosity but know it would be ludicrous to try to explain so I simply smile, I am happy to have made her happy if for only a short while.

One evening at dinner Toimu mentions that at 9:30 the next morning we are scheduled to meet with the second in command at the Liberian Refugee Repatriation and Resettlement Commission, referred to as "the L triple R C." (The top official is at the Totota camp – the one identified by the family as the largest in Liberia. We will run into him when we go there in a few days, he rightfully wondering who we are and what the hell we are doing there.) In a radical effort towards punctuality, I ask what hour we would need to leave the house in order to make the 9:30 appointment. This brings about a startled pause, and befuddled expressions, as if actually planning a time to depart in order to be prompt for an engagement had never occurred to anyone, and I sense I am considered a bit pushy for suggesting it. Finally Toimu utters "Nine," and Samuel concurs. We don't leave by nine but are only twenty minutes late, impressive by the standards that have been set thus far. But it's not good enough. Employees of the LRRRC office are barking at Samuel, Toimu and company while I stand by the car. I can't comprehend most of the rapid, confrontational Liberian English but I keep hearing "9:30" which pretty much clarifies the rest. When my hosts return to the car, Toimu tells me the commissioner had another meeting to attend but rescheduled ours for 2 PM, never owning up to the fact that the man left because we were late. I wonder how student Toimu and student/teacher Samuel ever make it to class on time.

Toimu has work obligations and can't come to the afternoon postponement so Samuel and I return for our 2 PM – at 2:05. Luckily the commissioner is running behind so he is never apprised of our second strike. When we are led into his office, his first order of business is to chastise me for the morning's infraction. It isn't my fault. I'm not the driver. I have no idea how to get around sprawling public transportation -less Monrovia on my own; this isn't my continent. I wait for Samuel to explain this, that I have no control over his family's tardiness, but he says nothing. So I apologize, accept the blame.

The commissioner proves to be a complete prick, responding sarcastically to my every question, critical of my queries in his replies.

> Kia: Do you have estimates of the number
>   of refugees?
> LRRRC commissioner: *Estimates*? We
>   don't have "estimates"! We have
>   exact numbers! 300,000, 75,000,…
> (Kia in her head: Those are estimates,
>   jackass.)

When another man in the office answers a question clearly and respectfully, I smile and thank him, which irritates his supervisor. (Incredibly the latter will end the meeting by telling me, genuinely, what a pleasure it has been making my acquaintance and how he'll look me up the next time he's in New

York. I won't be home.) Sifting through his derision, I am able to ascertain that *every* Liberian has been a refugee at one time or another during the war, and that this office, in conjunction with the UN, is charged with the daunting task of rehousing both the internally displaced and those refugees who have fled Liberia's borders and want to come home. He describes a road leading out of the country overflowing during the height of the war with throngs walking, walking.

This was my second Thursday, one day past the halfway mark, and that morning I'd finally made it to a family devotion. Throw on my dress and walk into the living room in time for the second and final melody. Hearing the singing from my room, I'd always pictured everyone standing. All sit in a circle, the kids slumped, dazed, sleepy. Toimu has the gourd. I notice Jeremiah is missing but there's another kid I don't think I've seen before. Every day it seems for a few hours, or over night, a new person appears. The singing over, now it is time to "Praise God," everyone taking their turn, and when it comes round to me I say I am thankful for the past week and hope the coming one would be as wonderful. Now Toimu begins to talk about ex-combatants who still haven't surrendered their weapons nor their violent mindset, then on to a few other topics and I think he's going to preach a whole damn sermon, the youngest teen boy asleep in his chair. Finally Toimu arrives at the last item on his list: he has "news." He had seen somebody yesterday who apparently everyone in the family knows. This person had told Toimu his "Mommy" had died in Guinea, on a refugee camp for Liberians. The only person who openly reacts is Florence, visibly upset, groaning in shock and disbelief, but obviously holding back greater emotion as Toimu speaks generally about trust in Jesus and in God's plans. The eight kids, now all awake, stare at Florence.

At breakfast a few hours later I ask her about the woman who died. Was she a good friend?

She was Florence's little sister.

She and her family had lived on the Guinea refugee camp, and she had died the day before giving birth to twins.

Now I'm the one staring in disbelief. Why the hell didn't Toimu tell you yesterday? Why'd he wait 'til this morning, and give you the news in front of everybody? Including me, a stranger!

As if she can read my thoughts, she replies, "He told me last night there was bad news but he said if he told me then I'd start crying, so he said he'd wait 'til devotion."

She rails about the hospitals in Guinea. "They don't care about the refugees!" The night before the day of the death, Florence had had a dream that she had taken out her suitcase, pulled out a garment, and put it over a dead body, so she knew somebody was going to die. I remember reading about the significance of dreams as premonitions in Liberian society and I listen, silent, staggered by the accuracy of this dream in substance and timing, respectful of this outpour being Florence's first expressions of grief, incredulous that someone she has known only a week has become the only recipient of that grief. Then Toimu, Samuel and another son come to breakfast, chattering on a different topic, and Florence goes to serve them: subject closed.

Eunice will later tell me how a few years ago, when aggressions reconvened, she ran thirty miles through the bush to cross over into Guinea. Toimu's family's entrance into that country to the north, as will be reported to me by Rachel Fay after my return to New York, was paid at the border patrol with Toimu's wheelchair. He crawled across.

Peace
Every day the announcers on the UN radio station, FM 91.5, report the count: "Today seven hundred twenty-six combatants turned in their weapons."

The UNMIL trucks are white with black block lettering, like generic canned peaches. They are everywhere. We have an appointment with the radio station set up on the enormous temporary military compound, wire fences, high security. We are required to present i.d. – mine is my passport – which they keep for the duration of our visit. We, but not our camera, are permitted entrance.

I never thought I'd be writing this: I'm happy to see white people in Africa! Europeans. Foreigners like me! In Toimu's crowded and friendly house I, the only non-Liberian, feel lonely, alone. And I'm tired of being stared at! Look at that blond Norwegian woman. Stare at her!

The offices are trailers, like a TV production lot. Samuel bossily orders me to write down the questions he wants to ask the UN reps himself, about their sluggishness in coming to help, etc., but when a European woman leads me into the space where I sit with a well dressed Liberian woman (and I can understand her every syllable!), there is no room for Samuel's agenda: *she* is asking the questions, and the interview becomes about me and why I've made my journey to her country.

We have driven to a beach. Palm trees. A few buildings by the seaside. This is the home of Flomo Theatre. I am impressed by their founder, a slender man perhaps in his 60s, soft-spoken and articulate. I am astonished by the performance, apparently prepared especially for me. Two weeks to put this forty-five minute show together. No set, no lights, but the writing, acting and dancing is meticulous and inspired, the work easily stronger than most of what I see in New York with professional artists and budgets. The play, performed by youth, is a social teaching tool but it is also enthralling drama, compelling and complex.

> *Scene 1:* The protagonist, a teenage combatant, tries to convince another combatant to lay down his gun. The second boy expresses concern that if he surrenders his weapon but his enemy doesn't, then he will be left defenseless and an easy target.

> *Scene 2:* The most gripping segment. A teenage girl recognizes the protagonist as

the killer of her brother. The protagonist doesn't remember her or her sibling but takes responsibility, expressing his regret. The girl is not willing to let him off so easily. A third party, another young man, enters the picture and intercedes in the confrontation. He reminds the girl that the healing of the country demands both the ex-combatant's rehabilitation and her acceptance of his reintegration as a part of the civil society they will now share. She is not wholly convinced but offers, reluctantly, to try.

Scene 3: The protagonist returns home to his family. His mother and sister welcome him but his father is not pleased, imagining the atrocities he surely committed during the war. The other family members address the patriarch's bitterness and, like the girl from Scene 2, with great reservations the father agrees to allow his son back into the family.

The United Nations' process for facilitating peace is the DDRR: Disarmament, Demobilization, Rehabilitation, Reintegration. It mirrors the Rwandan model. In a nation where the civil violence is so far-reaching across the population, the only way to a ceasefire is to discard prosecution and retribution, and to ask only that combatants turn in their weapons (D_1) and disperse from their rebel groups (D_2). Next is counseling (the containment center that was pointed out to me on arrival), and education and/or vocational training such as that at Toimu's workplace (R_1), all leading to the return of the ex-combatant to society (R_2). Of all that I have seen in Liberia, most mind-boggling, coming from preemptive strike America – punishment before any crime has even been committed (eg, the Iraqi WMD fiasco) – is the idea that a society can *forgive*.

But make no mistake: nobody wants to forgive Charles Taylor.

On another beach stand the remnants of what was once the Liberian Cultural Center, with stages dedicated to music, dance, and theatre, comparable I imagine to New York's Lincoln Center. As we turn onto the entrance road Samuel points to the bareness where there used to stand sixteen sculptures, attributes to each of Liberia's original sixteen tribes. Much of the area has now been sold to private investors. Lumber companies it seems, as I am told of their habit of cutting down trees and letting the unused parts rot on the beach. There still is a lovely amphitheatre, however, and a man who refers to himself as Mr. Culture runs a children's dance program here. To bring meaning back into their lives, to provide an alternative to violence. Shirtless in the heat, Mr. Culture is well built with a major outie navel that I've noticed on other Liberian men. He presents a program of traditional dances performed by the local kids, displaced from the bush. I've seen African dance numerous times in the States. It is nothing compared to what I witness today. I am awestruck by the skill, the unbelievable movements of their legs. One boy, appearing to be no older than nine, looks at me, his sly eyes speaking knowledge no child should have. But then these children have seen, and undergone, what no child, or adult, should ever experience.

I try to tell sweet daughter Ruth, with whom I have a major language communication gap, that one day I'd like to go with her and her mother to the market, that I am always riding around with the men, that I would like to spend a little time with the women. She smiles at me, having no idea what I just said. Then she expresses what is on her mind: "We have peace!" And her face, unlike the "Everybody's tired of fighting" fatigue, is bright. Has there been some new development?

"Did you hear that on the news?" I ask.

"We have peace!" she repeats, grinning ear to ear, and I see for the first time since my arrival the joy that *should* accompany that statement. I grin back: "Peace!"

Plantation

When Toimu and I were conversing by email before my trip, I had mentioned my interest in seeing the area where, according to my books, the U.S. Firestone Tire and Rubber Company had once exploited the local labor pool. This seemed to excite Toimu, who set up a meeting with the Firestone Labor Office. Surprising me on a number of levels: I wasn't even sure that the company was still functioning in Liberia, and if they were I couldn't imagine why they would want to meet with me. But then the offenses about which I had read (tribal chiefs, through the federal government, collecting taxes – and keeping a commission – then forcing those who couldn't pay their taxes into public labor projects, including work for Firestone; very little profit being seen in Liberia in contrast to the original stated motivations behind the Firestone venture in the economically strapped nation) all happened in the '20s and '30s so perhaps there is now a pride in the company's progress and reform since those less enlightened days. I pictured photos on the wall, a sort of gallery where we would be given a glimpse into the "before" in order to be more duly impressed as we look around now at the happily ever, or at least union-sanctioned, "after."

According to the original itinerary I was to visit Firestone my first Saturday, three days after my arrival. A Firestone official called Toimu in the hours before my plane landed, requesting to reschedule for Tuesday afternoon because, as Toimu was told, the people who would be most helpful for me to meet would not be around on the weekend. Toimu agreed. He tells me now he believes the real impulse with respect to the delay was the company man's knowledge that Toimu had provided me with a tight schedule, and his presumption that a postponement might have forced us to cancel.

The magnitude of this meeting's implications, in the eyes of my host family, is manifested to me when we arrive for the appointment three hours *early*. It is located outside

Monrovia in Harbel (so christened for Ohio tycoon *Harvey* Firestone, who oversaw the conversion of the natural forest into his rubber plantation, and his wife Ida*belle*). We use the extra time to make the visit to Toimu's sister-in-law, her refugee camp just a mile or so down the road from one of the Firestone entrances. After I give her the $20, we get back into the car and drive to the Firestone security gate, then move through it to our destination, single-floor offices. Still a good ninety minutes to kill before our rendezvous. We go into a large building. Supermarket. I've seen nothing like it anywhere else in Liberia. Huge and clean and bright and *American*. The food choices are staggering, especially having just crossed the road from hordes of hungry refugees. An aisle with all manner of first aid and over-the-counter medicines (though even here I can't find the insect repellant for which I've searched the city over, having forgotten to bring mine from the States – my fear of malaria driving my obsession – so Toimu must be right: there really isn't any available), an aisle with large plastic toys, an aisle with thirty brands of American cold cereal. The people at the top echelon on the acreage on which I stand are *my* countrymen. We purchase snacks. Samuel complains they are exorbitant. The driver tosses a soda can on the ground and the others immediately snap, demanding he pick it up. I saw Jeremiah chastised for throwing something in the family's front yard once, a sweet garden planted there, some effort at adornment. But outside of home and powerful Firestone, litterbugging seems to be the

479

norm, the men always pitching trash out of the moving car. No garbage pick-up, public receptacles rare, and those mountains of burning rubbish back in Monrovia – What's the use?

It is finally time for our three o' clock but uh oh: the Firestone administration claims we have no appointment. While Toimu and Samuel quarrel with the plant managers, I stare out at the afternoon downpour. A few tired workers are just outside under the roof's edge, and a sad little girl wearing a faded, undoubtedly U.S. consignment shop -provided T-shirt featuring a bare-bellied Brittany Spears.

Three-quarters of an hour later I am sitting in the office of a manager, a middle-aged man who tells me he just started working for Firestone this week, and as it is Tuesday I wonder if this is only his second day. Toimu, Samuel and the other men line up in the chairs brought in for them, against the wall behind me. The official's hands are folded in front of him, and he seems cautiously willing to answer my questions, though his replies are brief. I ask how much land Firestone owns. The answer, I know, I can find in my research materials back home but I have forgotten the details and, anyway, it would be interesting to hear his response. He says he doesn't know but that I should talk with the main man – I'm not certain if the man he refers to is the head of labor or of public relations – who has worked here for many years. He keeps referring to this gentleman, saying he could give me a tour of the plantation so that I can see where the tappers work, and he converses with another man in an effort to have me transferred to the more experienced executive. Have there been any grievances against Firestone regarding environmental issues? "No, no complaints," the man answers. He says that the school system has just been upgraded for the children of employees – that previously they only provided education to the eighth grade but students may now continue through the twelfth. He explains that there are regular worker camps, and other camps for "contractors" in forests of older trees that no longer produce much sap.

> Kia: How many trees does each tapper have to tap?
> Official: About five hundred a day.
> Kia: Five hundred a day?! *Each* tapper?
> Official (a chuckle): It's not as much as it sounds!

He says that they just completed union negotiations. "Oh, was there a strike?" "No, friendly negotiations. This is the president of the union." I turn around and see a man, sitting on the left end of the family line, a goofy grin on his face, waving at me. I smile, confused. "So... what were the terms of the contract?" "Oh, wages and benefits," the official utters vaguely. The man who had been sent off returns and whispers to the official, who tells me, subtly relieved, that the executive to whom he had been referring is ready to receive me now. The family and I get back into the car but the next stop turns out to be just a few yards around the bend.

When I enter this building, I am told by a young man to wait in an area just inside the door. I peek around the corner, down the corridor where he'd disappeared, and see him looking back at me, then instantly closing a door. Something feels strange, a little more precarious than the previous situation but, before I have a chance to pursue this line of thought, the young man returns, the closed-door meeting having lasted a minute or less, and I, with Toimu *et al.* in tow, am ushered into an office.

The eyes of the well fed Liberian behind the desk are decidedly different than his semi-cooperative predecessor; this man is *ready*. He immediately introduces Mr. Somebody, "He sits in on all our important meetings," an enormous, muscular white man so blond I think he's a Swede. He's an American. The first American I've met in Liberia, and I am *not* pleased by the sight of my fellow countryman. He stares at me, confused and nervous. He offers his hand. After a week of the Liberian handshake (a clutching instantly followed by a smooth sliding of each hand away and into a snapping of the fingers) I am momentarily thrown by this simple American version, and while my muddling obviously comes out of the new habit I've fallen into, I speculate on whether it is also something subconscious on my part regarding alliances.

I face the heavy official, my car load lined up behind me as before. The American man sits two feet directly to my left, his chair facing my profile, his eyes edgily searching me the whole of the interview, and the sense of apprehension I try not to show does not come out of any manifestation of hostility from him but rather I am discomforted by his own sense of threat, fear, *incredulity* that anyone would question Firestone. How much land does Firestone own? My interviewee shrugs. "It varies."

For a moment I wonder if I heard right. I wait for him to elaborate. Silence. "From what to *what?*" is all I can think to ask.

He is generally arrogantly confident but for some reason this question catches him off guard, and he feels obliged to come up with an answer. "About eighty thousand acres." The freshman official I'd spoken with before now asks this executive about showing me where the tappers work. "No!" snaps the man of experience, "this isn't a tourist place!" Then, for the second time in the short interview: "We have nothing to hide." He claims that if we'd made an appointment ahead of time, all this could have been arranged. Of course we did, but neither I nor the family decide to get into an argument about this. As a matter of fact, the family has remained notably silent throughout these interrogations. The official now asks about my project. It had of course been detailed at the time Toimu set up the meeting but I reiterate: the grant, the option to go anywhere in the world, my choice to travel to Liberia – this decision having gratified every Liberian I'd met. Until now. "*Why?*" he barks, and the white man chuckles. Now I am taken aback. The Liberian union head, seated in the back as before, is silent as always, this affront to his country also garnering no response. I quickly recover with a cool and testy reply, refusing to let the official detect my uneasiness: "*Well* Liberia and the United States share history, and I was interested in exploring those common threads." The man then speaks to Toimu, asking about his job with a subtly intimidating tone, asking where he lives. Toimu grins and provides all the right answers with a vagueness, minimal detail.

As soon as our car pulls away from the building all of my previously mute travel companions are screaming at me, ever-indignant Samuel the loudest. "He's lying!" "It's *not* eighty thousand acres, it's a *hundred* thousand!" I nod, say nothing. Yes, I know they're lying. I try to sift through the information provided for me by the officials, their words and, perhaps more importantly, under their words, in their tones, gestures. I try to sift through the information the family is conveying now, their feverish need for me to comprehend the deep deception of this place.

Near the offices is an area of handsome homes, for those in supervisory positions the family tells me, such as the men we just met and their families. We drive a good forty minutes without a turn or a curve on a smooth paved road, surrounded by endless Firestone forestry. Tap mechanisms hang around the trunks of the trees. Finally we turn off to the right onto a dirt road so rugged and poorly managed that, in the back seat, I feel the floor under my feet ripple, the vehicle apparently having dropped into a ditch and the floor rubbing directly against the ground. This disconcerting ride goes on for several minutes. Then suddenly: a clearing. We turn into a grassy area, a village of metal shacks so dilapidated as to make the refugee camp look five-star. Half the slats of roofs are missing, and it's the rainy season. An uncle of the family used to work here, which clarified for me how they found the place: hidden deep in the woods, no one driving along the main road would ever sense this community. Which is evidently what the official counted on when he refused to show us around, assuming that without his assistance the workers would remain invisible to the naked eye. Strangers are clearly a rarity, as everyone comes out to inspect our party. By now it is six, late afternoon, and tappers are coming home from labor in the forest. Samuel, translating the Liberian English (I don't understand a word now), speaks to a man returning from the trees who looks to be in his 50s. He says he's worked here just five months. This solves the mystery of the missing uncle, whom we can't find: as a fulltime worker he must have been moved from this elderly forest, which has been converted into a contractors' area. Samuel asks the man how much sap he is required to tap. Reply: a ton a month. This astronomical figure, especially in light of trees that no longer produce to capacity, will be verified by my research later at home. In response to Samuel's queries the man states that there are no days off, that the water is not fit to drink. There is despair in the faces of all the adults. The children stare at me and grin. I have finally unearthed a way to put an end to this. I smile back, and point to Christopher and his camera. The children run to have their picture taken! and I am more than happy to fill tapes with their sweet faces. As we move back toward the car, a younger man comes hurrying out of the forest, asking who we are. Samuel explains. I think how I could never be an investigative reporter because my desire to gather, and dispense, such information is in direct conflict with my shame, that I am infringing on the privacy of others, people who have enough pain in their lives, and I assume this young man is about to tell us just that. But he says he is so happy that we have come, that he hopes *some*one will finally tell people on the outside what's going on here.

Who is the outside? The U.S.? Because according to the family, every Liberian has a relative working for Firestone, arguably the country's biggest employer (though at times surpassed by the public sector), so I imagine within these national borders the conditions are well known. My car mates say that quotas can't possibly be met without everyone in the tapper's family working, including children. I am cynical myself about the school business reported by the first official. Is education provided for *all* the workers' children or, in practical terms, only for the offspring of employees at the top of the hierarchy? Logistically speaking, how would the kids in this remote contractors' camp *get* to school? I see no vehicles here but ours. Christopher says he ran to hide on a Firestone camp during one phase of the war. The plantation, I am told, was always protected, even in the most brutal times; Charles Taylor saw to it. In 1997 six people who posed a threat to Firestone were shot on its grounds when Liberian government security forces in conjunction with the dubious ECOMOG (the ceasefire monitoring group of the Economic Community of West African States [ECOWAS]) opened fire on them. The six were Firestone workers on strike for better living and working conditions.

We rock and roll back out the bumpety road and onto the main stretch again. Drive a little further, then come to an enormous camp. There are thousands of workers and their families living on numerous camps scattered across the plantation. We have just entered a regular workers' facility, and it at least appears to meet the standard of the refugee camp. We speak to a 50ish man, an overseer.

Vocabulary: We stand on the Firestone *plantation*, and the immediate supervisor of the tappers is the *overseer*. Those terms may not instantly elicit whips and chains to the minds of Liberians but this company was built by *Americans*.

Regardless of Western Hemisphere connotations, this man charged with managing the quotas seems as miserably resigned as all the other workers. Six hundred fifty trees per worker per day, he tells us – up from the five hundred quoted in the offices. Four days off a month. Interestingly he tells us a new pump had just been installed, providing clean water. A zillion children stare at me! I point to Christopher. This time the kids follow my finger to the camera man. Look at him, blank. Turn back to me.

When I return to New York, I'll check my books. In 1927, in exchange for its aid in securing a five million dollar U.S. loan for the economically desperate African republic, Firestone leased one million Liberian acres to cultivate as a rubber plantation. The agreement specified the arrangement would be in effect for ninety-nine years at a cost of six cents per acre: $60,000 rent per year – and in 1943 alone the Harbel plantation brought in $35 million. The restructuring of a natural forest destroyed the habitat of its animals, and rubber processing has polluted the country's water sources, dumping ammonia and sulfuric acid into the rivers and creeks. In September 2005 the Voice of America (VoA) news online will report that Firestone had just extended its lease for another thirty-six years, adding sixteen more to the original date of 2026 before the land may be returned to the Liberian people. The negotiation, made without the consultation of the workers, is criticized for having been ushered in a month before the first legitimate postwar elections in October, and under the administration of the interim government, currently under investigation by ECOWAS for corruption.

In the hours and days following our plantation visit I ponder: Was *that* the big union negotiation mentioned by the first official I spoke with? After seventy-seven years the regular workers finally have clean water to drink? But perhaps not even this came from Firestone:

according to the VoA, it is the UN who installed the drinking water pumps.

And in these latter days of my Liberian journey I suddenly understand. The reason the regular workers' kids didn't run to Christopher to have their picture taken was because they'd never seen a camera before. Unlike the contractors who may have only been working here a few months, a regular worker is born onto a Firestone camp, may spend a lifetime tapping trees for Firestone, and die, never knowing a world outside of that camp, and that outside world, save relatives, never knowing the camp nor those workers exist.

But we certainly benefit. I ask the new-on-the-job official where the manufactured products go: to the U.S., to other countries? He is surprised by the question. "*All* the products go to the U.S." And what are the products? He responds, and now I am the one startled, his official confirmation of something Wynfred Russell, a Liberian professor at the University of Minnesota, had asserted to me months before. Tires of course. Rubber for tires, created out of the sap, which is latex.

And, most significantly, condoms.

Shipped to American drugstores, at a bargain price, right out of AIDS-ravaged Africa.

The Bush

My first Sunday, before church, Toimu calls me out into the living room to meet his cousin. The man works for the FDA – Forestry Development Authority. Toimu says the UN has put sanctions on timber going out of Liberia. The cousin remarks on the rebels still in the bush which is why he works in Monrovia. They speak more but I don't hear much after this. *Are* there rebels still in the bush? Cuz, according to my itinerary, this Friday we're headed into the bush.

Thursday night Eunice falls out laughing when she hears the next morning I'll be on my way to "thee boosh." "You better bring your mosquito net!"

We don't even come close to making our 6 AM scheduled departure. We take two cars and, as there is room, fun Eunice has decided to come which makes me happy, and Florence excitedly gets into the car, and they're both in *my* car, two other women besides myself! I am touched that Toimu is bringing Florence, her first trip back to their home since before the war. Then Toimu says, "We have to carry her with us so she can cook."

It is a good three-hour drive to Dbarnga in Bong County. About an hour outside of Monrovia we stop in Kakata for a bite, everyone purchasing little plastic bags filled with local water and boiled eggs off the street. I pass. But the driver has barely turned off the engine when Christopher jumps out of the car: "Take off that button!" Another young man, a stranger, wears a campaign button, and Christopher speaks to him for less than a minute before the offending item is removed. In Monrovia I had visited the Liberian Broadcasting System, a television and radio facility which once was obviously a modern, high-tech communications structure but, postwar, most of the buildings have been burnt out. We stood in the ashes of a previous edifice, a black frame, only the exit signs still in place, cruelly ironic and eerie now that anyone can exit right through the former walls. The one functioning building had just gone to darkness when I arrived, the generated electricity available just a few hours a day. The LBS signals, which at one time served the entire country, now may be picked up only in Monrovia. With the nationwide eighty percent illiteracy rate no doubt highest in the bush, and no television or radio or even phone service to convey information to most of the nation, it is a colossal concern that on election day, a year and a half from now, the first legitimate ballot since before the war, an unsavory individual, apparently such as the one depicted by the button, will go out to the hinterlands and trade a vote for a bag of rice, as had been done in the past.

As we approach Bong County we are stopped at a UN military checkpoint. I had seen plenty of checkpoints two years before in Palestine but this was the first I'd come across in Liberia. Then again, as Samuel's brother had said a week before, we were now entering "the stronghold of our great rebel leader." The armed and uniformed foreigners order us to get out of our cars and walk across the border, picking up our vehicle on the other side.

When we finally reach Dbarnga I am impressed by the charm of the small city, even after the plunder of the war. We drive straight to the REFAY School, coordinated by Toimu Jr. and the crossing-a-bridge brother. I now remember Rachel

Fay saying she subsidized a school – REFAY: Rachel E. Fay. We sit in the honored seats on the stage space at the front, the program before us – meaning we see it from behind. Songs and dances and plays and poems. There are small children in the audience, and palpably bigger students. The kids look to be third-graders; there are seven hundred enrolled. The brand new students, teens and young adults, eleven hundred of them and the vast majority male, are ex-combatants. They cheer when one of the speakers makes reference to them. I feel a great admiration and affection for these teacher sons of Toimu. Later I remark to Toimu Jr. that it seems a good sign that the formal rebels want to go back to school. He says the UN is paying them U.S.$2 a day to do so. Sitting next to me on the stage is a pretty smiling teenage girl wearing a gold-sprayed cardboard crown, the "queen of the school." Until recently she was a combatant.

We drive to dwellings that seem to be on the outskirts of the city, with much forest all around. One of these is the house Eunice grew up in, and I meet her kind mother. We also see another house which must be Toimu's, Florence's, and their family's. Now Florence is left behind to cook while we board the cars for the second trip today. The ride turns out to be *another* three hours, not so much due to distance – we were flying at 135 on the highway to Dbarnga – but because this dirt road through the bush is so rugged. It astounds me that we make it over the terrain in our small cars. In Monrovia the horrible streets had been decimated in the war. At Firestone the road to the tappers' camp was unkempt apparently because of the infrequency of anyone going in or coming out. Here the problem seems partly that it's an undeveloped country road and partly, again, trigger-happy rebels. We pass several villages along the way before we arrive at Bellemu.

This traditional African village which, at first glance, looks as if it could have preceded colonialism, is the birthplace of Toimu and the home of his chief father, the husband of four women. No Liberian English now; native Kpelle is the only tongue spoken. The people, not used to visitors, marvel at our arrival. Some remember Toimu and eagerly welcome him home; as always everyone, especially the children, stare at me. A Monrovian who came with us, a man I hadn't seen before today but whose intelligence and calm demeanor cause me to take an instant liking to him, shows me around the village, a parade of children and some adults following us. This is the building where food is stored (some in cans). This is the church, indicating the village's conversion at some point to Christianity, a hut like all the others but with a rough cross over the door. There's the river that served the village for centuries but now has become polluted. And there – two young women stand in an enormous pot with long sticks, smiling as they engage in a quick-paced, bizarre pendulum dance – there are the women pounding the rice for the village. Samuel points out a little girl who looks no older than three herself carrying an infant on her back. He beams: "Here women are trained from the beginning to be mothers." And some men are trained from the beginning to be babies I feel like telling him, but don't.

Toimu sits next to me, me next to Samuel, the others standing and staring at us, the requisite speech I feel approaching. But first: Toimu's mother is coming. Rachel Fay will laugh when I tell her this upon my return. "His mother died years ago! It must have been an aunt." Or one of his father's other wives? On our way home from the village Samuel and Christopher, engaging in their never-ending bitch session, will furiously condemn the colonialists for defining relationships, claiming that before the settlers' invasion the native people would call a daughter "mother," a mother "daughter," for examples. I read later about Kpelle tradition, referring to the youngest daughter as mother, the youngest son as father, which seems symbolic of these lastborn someday beginning the family cycle again. I agree with most of the charges leveled against America I have heard here but I can't say I get Christopher's and Samuel's foaming at the mouth over this issue. From my point of view, ethnocentric no doubt, I appreciate the specification of relations. Now the woman Toimu refers to as "mother," who must have been *like* a mother to him whether or not they actually shared blood, has been brought by car to us. The village is not large; I circled it in twenty minutes or less, and we were walking slowly as I was being given the tour. But the tiny, feeble woman who emerges from the sedan with the aid of younger hands required the transport. She looks easily to be in her

90s, blind from old age. They gingerly set her beside Toimu, and he speaks softly to her. She feels his face. She is overcome with joy! They have not seen each other in fourteen years, since the start of the war. Often in that time, as hostilities would reconvene, the village would be deserted, the people fleeing the terror. Samuel, gazing at his "grandmother" fondly, tells me that she is much thinner than when they had seen her last. She begins to sing a song that she creates impromptu, performing a weak dance from her seat, circling her fragile arms. Samuel translates from the Kpelle: now that her son has come home she can finally die content. It goes on for several minutes. Then, suddenly, she lifts her top to reveal her ancient breasts. I'm shocked! And I laugh with everyone else but unlike me their response is not embarrassment but simply the surprise of the moment. As I was told by other Africans, breasts on this continent are not sexualized as they are in the West but are simply functional. To show hers to her long-lost son was probably the most definitive and tender display of her maternity to Toimu, if not in body than certainly in soul.

In the oration segment Toimu speaks of my travel to Africa. (Though I can't recall now, he must have been speaking in Kpelle with Samuel translating for me.) Toimu says the fact that someone who looks like me would visit Bellemu is a sign that peace has finally come, which garners cheers from everyone and makes me feel sickeningly conflicted. He goes on: My ancestors came from Africa and now I have come "home,"

and he believes deeply in his heart that my
forebears were from this very village, Bellemu, and
I am suddenly overwhelmed, I don't understand
what I ever did to deserve such an honor, for
Toimu to say something so beautiful, for me to be a
witness to this wondrous reunion of mother and
son.

It's near dark by the time we get back to
Dbarnga. We eat dinner outside. I am to sleep in
Eunice's mother's home with the other women.
Back in Monrovia I loved being spoiled with a
room of my own. Here I am terrified but don't
want to say so. The combatants took *everything* so
not only are the houses bare, there is no glass or
any other protection in the windows, nor locks on
the doors. Like staying in a multi-room hut on a
refugee camp. "Now you are living like an
internally displaced person," Eunice quips.
Apparently even the toilets and sinks are gone; we
wash ourselves outside and pee in the grass. I can't
bring myself to do anything else in the company of
others, which is unfortunate because my body has
finally succumbed to my foreign ingestings: I have
diarrhea, and I hold it in. The women arrange my
mosquito netting – unnecessary I learn later
because it is the bloodsuckers who fly around the
urban waters that are most likely to carry disease –
and I wake in the night, staring at the blackness
through the open window, imagining combatants
appearing, then falling asleep only to have the pain
in my intestines wake me up minutes later to
repeat the terror. I could sleep if I could only

empty my system but that would require going outside into the shadows alone: NO.

By the next morning my system is backed up, and I feel dizzy. I sit to steady myself. Everyone seems so happy to be back home. Toimu asks me when my flight is on Wednesday. Three, I reply. It's actually 5:50. I had prepared this lie, and now I am torn between my guilt at telling Toimu the falsehood and my paranoia, given the family's tardiness record, that I should have lied better and said Two. Toimu picks up from the ground a dead critter. "Bat," he says. It is. He examines it, then tosses it away with a meticulously enunciated and strangely ominous "No life in it."

A couple of hours later I am ill and sleepless and am relieved to be on our way back to Monrovia. Except we're not. We stop to meet the Chief Education Officer and his colleagues, an appointment we missed when we arrived four hours' late the day before. The director of the local school system shows me around a burnt out high school which was obviously once a superb facility. At the end of the meeting Toimu tells them about my women's ceremony and my new name: Negbarn. The Chief Officer considers Toimu's interpretation – slim. He says that the word presents an image of slimness but, more significantly, it also means torch, light. That I could bring illumination to all this. I think about the play I'll write. I'll try my best.

Back into the cars and a few minutes later we stop *again*. It is the Dbarnga Theatre for Peace building. Apparently there used to be a beautiful, spacious theatre that was pulverized in the war. But the despondent men I had met days ago in Monrovia seem in much better spirits now that they are back home, getting things ready to re-open in a few weeks. We speak briefly, then say our good-byes, exiting out onto the front porch. On one end are several men, ex-combatants, glaring at me with a piercing hatred. Ridiculously I smile and say hello. All the Africans I have met claim to be full-bloods, though some have remarked bitterly that there are Americos still in Liberia, passing as pure Africans, now calling themselves "Congoes": their ancestors were *never* slaves. Still, judging by my anomalous appearance, it seems that the vast majority of American descendants had the means to get out of the country when trouble started fourteen years ago – ironic since, according to Dr. Guannu's haves/have-nots theory, they are the original cause of the trouble – leaving the Africans to turn on one another. (With some variations, this seems to be the general crude colonialist model: 1 – Settle and restructure so the natives are robbed of their traditional livelihood, 2 – Get out before trouble starts, 3 – The impoverished, frustrated and fuming natives take out their aggressions on themselves.) So after ten days of friendly, welcoming grins at the sight of me, it is my enormous pleasure (in the company of my party so I feel in no immediate danger), as someone whose looks are representative of the fugitive oppressor, to be the recipient of these figurative daggers.

The checkpoint exiting the bush isn't as daunting as at the arrival site. Evidently the caution is more related to the possibility of people going *in*to Bong County to reassemble and begin mischief again than to those exiting the nativity of the terror. When the UN security guards take my passport, they are thrilled. "America!" they exclaim, big smiles. I'm not certain if this is because they have any affinity with my homeland, or because an American is something they never see in this postwar nation of scarce foreign visitors so my passport simply broke the monotony of their jobs. Yes, America! I think. Homesick Kia smiles widely back.

Health

A long ride home, and my vague nausea. Plus a strange pain in my right leg since coming to Africa, flaring up harshly on long rides, and this one is torture. I don't speak of these infirmities – vastly insignificant in this suffering land – but my stomach and leg are relieved when we briefly stop the car, inertia and a stretch. As we finally approach Monrovia and the traffic begins to fill in, I glance at the meter: Why are we *dragging*? But as it turns out it is only that I've gotten used to jet-speeding the thoroughfare. The tortoise speed we've dropped to is eighty.

      The previous Tuesday morning close to nine, which always feels well into the day because of our early reveilles (rendering our compulsive tardiness all the more ironic), Florence and oldest daughter Ruth told me they had to go to the hospital. Ruth: "I am sick. I have typhoid." Trying to listen through Florence's accent, it sounded as though one of the sons has malaria. I'm not sure how serious either condition is. Samuel has said that, for Liberian adults, malaria is not considered life or death; it seems to be comparable to getting the flu in the U.S. But Florence will tell me that, on my last Sunday, their old pastor from Dbarnga died, that he had malaria and it went "to his head." (This will be the same day she and the teen boy will knock on my door, unsure how to break the news that my former president, Ronald Reagan, has died. "Oh," I say, thinking He was still *alive?*) There is no dispute, however, that malaria is a significant killer of children under five. I had seen billboards stressing the usage of mosquito nets for children, which reflected my host family's home: when I glanced in the children's room (and I was relieved that it was a mess, that the obsessive cleaning of my room was related to my guest status and not a pressure Florence burdens herself with regularly) there were nets over their beds, as well as over mine as the foreigner – whose system was used to all manner of genetically engineered American foods but not Liberian mosquito-transported microbes – but there was no net in Florence's and Toimu's bedroom. On my first day when we went to the Cuttington University College assembly, we arrived in the middle of a presentation given by the dean of the science department on POPs (Persistent Organic Pollutants). The professor condemned the prolific spraying of DDT in the country (explaining my surprise and relief my first evening to notice no bugs swarming around the porch light while Toimu Jr. sang his welcome song to me) and detailed the alarming, and ironic, consequences of having utilized an insecticide banned in many countries for its toxic qualities in order to suppress a local malaria epidemic. Apparently, given the regularly high mortality rate attributed to the disease, and DDT's astounding effectiveness against the insect carriers, the pesticide's condemnation and prohibition is still controversial in world (including Western) medical circles.

The day after our return from Dbarnga, Ruth knocks on my door, to let me know why she, the only other adult remaining in the house, would be away for a couple of hours.

"I'm going to the hospital now."

"Oh. Do you have to go there every day?"

"Yes."

"Because of the typhoid?"

"Yes."

"Oh. Do you feel sick?"

"Yes."

Had I questioned Samuel or Christopher in this way, the very first query would have been retorted with an impatient "*Yes!*" They have a habit of making most of my questions sound like dumb ones. Now I feel like I *have* asked a dumb question though the women are always calm and nonjudgmental. Eunice, the exception, can take on a sharper tone but she doesn't seem irritable so much as emphatic, as in her "*Yes!*" in response to my asking if AIDS was a big problem in Liberia. It's certainly an issue (I'd seen a woman with a T-shirt that read "SAY NO TO UNPROTECTED SEX / USE YOUR CONDOMS") but, according to my research, the death toll has not come close to the genocidal proportions of southern Africa. My dumb question to Ruth – "Do you feel sick?" – came out of my observation that she seems so healthy! bright! And now she smiles her big smile and turns to leave for the hospital.

Finally home after the long journey from the bush, I lie down. Then get up: diarrhea again. And there really isn't much in my system to come out. I can also tell that I have the slightest fever. I remember the considerate nurse practitioner's words, the young white man who'd administered my required yellow fever shot (as well as a few other immunization suggestions):

"If you get a fever, go to the hospital *immediately*."

But this seemed to directly contradict his warning of several minutes before:

"You don't want to get stuck with a needle in Africa."

He had printed out several pages from the internet on medical precautions for travelers to Liberia and from this decided I also needed shots (four in all) and pills to prevent hepatitis A and B, polio, typhoid, meningitis, malaria, and

NP: When was your last tetanus shot?
Kia (tears): Third grade.

Not knowing the state of affairs in Liberia, I seemed to have no problem walking into a country where I might get shot *at* but my needle-phobia kicked in regarding shots required to get there. In retrospect, I think the typhoid immunization was a pretty good call. Florence would make this cake-like treat; it sounded like she called it "saw" bread. Not only was it delicious but baked goods are among the WHO thumbs-upped foods for foreign visitors. Two nights before my departure I see ill Ruth's hands in a bowl, kneading the dough for the bread I'd been eating. (Though probably more significant was my physical proximity to her.)

I read and reread the label on the bottle of the medicine to be taken for "severe" diarrhea prescribed to me by the NP, trying to decide whether my condition is severe enough. My week-long trip to the Middle East two years before had resulted in a dangerous bout, not letting up for days after my return. Ruth walks in too quickly for me to conceal the bottle. Thus far I'd been successful in hiding my sickness from the family, feeling some embarrassment about it, my weak Western constitution, and what could they do anyway? But now I'm caught. She asks if she can look at the bottle, then studies it for an inordinately long period before speaking.

"This is gooooood medicine?"

"I don't know. I haven't tried it yet. It's supposed to be."

She studies it awhile again. Now she has decided. "This is gooooood medicine." I wonder if her fascination is a desire to cure her typhoid with it, and in my lightheadedness I consider giving her some, but then she says, "I finish high school. I want to be a nurse." As she seems to be about eighteen, in the moment I interpret that she has *just* finished high school. But, given the obvious school closings with the war, perhaps she meant *when* she finishes high school in the future. Her attraction to the prescription medicine, then, had been academic. Eunice is in nursing school, and every girl I meet here with aspirations of higher education wants to be a nurse. I'm sure they all will be needed. We'd driven to the hospital once, several flat buildings, looking more like a small college campus. Eunice said the Liberian hospitals are good, and I was relieved to hear it, but later I realized she has nothing to compare them with. In four days, the last hours prior to my departure, Ruth will terrify her mother when she opens her hand, her palm covered with numerous multicolored pills, bringing to my mind an AIDS cocktail. The teen orphan boy, who took my blood pressure for fun one day – Is he much older than he looks? In med school? Nursing school? – will confirm that the rainbow of chemicals is necessary, and he seems to know what he's talking about. Ruth's dazzling eyes and smile of the week before are gone, her energetic demeanor deteriorated to a deportment of fatigue and disease. I will inquire about her health in emails to the family after I return to the States but the question will go unanswered. So I will put my faith in Ruth's truckload of drugs, and in the probability that had there been bad news I would have heard.

But now, in my sick room, Ruth leaves for a few minutes, then returns with all the women, worried about me, doting over me. I feel so foolish! My God, Ruth has typhoid fever, and you're all concerned about me and my pathetic diarrhea? As they strategize among themselves about what to do for me, I look from strong, capable, caretaking Florence to optimistic, African-proud Ruth to educated, wisecracking, determined Eunice to adolescent Angie with her ironic wit and beguiling audacity to courageous thirteen-year-old Ellen, prepared to leave her home and life and cross the ocean to explore a whole new world and in this moment I decide the play I write will be about *women*.

Adieus

After returning from the bush my second Saturday evening, things start to wind down a bit. The minor fever had broken overnight, and I wake Sunday morning feeling much better, though the diarrhea has not gone away and I will ultimately decide to take the medicine. The mangoes and pineapple that had been filling my stomach have mysteriously vanished, I assume because the market has run out, and between that and the runs I am hungry all the time, but the resultant weakness is balanced by the eager energy generated by my anticipation of going home. It takes me awhile after returning to sort out that my loneliness was not homesickness per se, but more related to much emotional information and no fellow American to bounce it off of.

A big soccer game today: Liberia vs. Mali, here in Monrovia, evidently the first postwar contest. The family tries to get it on the TV, a small set which I assume is stored in one of the bedrooms because it only makes its living room appearance periodically, like the other night when the family watched videos of Nigerian sitcoms. Nothing but snow on the screen now so they go out to the porch and listen to the radio. Samuel tells me that some people who'd purchased tickets to the football match long ago couldn't get in because a number of ex-combatants arrived early and took seats without paying. There had been requests to remove them but the local police and armed forces are at this time *not* armed, and as no one was certain how ex-those ex-combatants really were, the latter won the battle before it had begun. This, Samuel claims, would never have happened under Charles Taylor and his brutal elite ATU (anti-terrorist unit), and a denied ticket-holder, interviewed on the radio, waxed nostalgic about the old ATU days. Samuel and I giggle. He says Liberia must win (intimating certain peril for the players if it doesn't) so as not to be eliminated in the quest for the African Cup. Two hours later, as I sit on my floor writing, I hear the radio through the window, and the silence from the porch is deafening. At last, in the final minutes, an uproarious cheer. Liberia the victor: 1-0. In July they'll face their next opponent – Senegal.

Eunice laments that I won't be around for her capping ceremony as a nurse in ten days. I'm also disappointed I'll be missing such a monumental event for her. She is infuriated with the other students, ludicrously electing that they each purchase some fancy mail-order cap: U.S.$20. I empathize with her, and want to kick myself later as it doesn't occur to me until she's gone to give her the money. I wonder now if it was because, for the first time since coming here, I heard someone complaining about an expense without the subtext being for me to cover it. (Between the family and all the organizations and people to whom they had introduced me, nearly always with much pressure to immediately contribute financially, I had had very real worries early on, given no ATMs, that I could be run flat broke – something I did *not* want to happen, at least until I had safely arrived at the airport to come home.) And because I consider Eunice a friend, an equal, I had forgotten as such that we lived in entirely unequal economic worlds.

On Monday we return to Talking Drum Theatre, which we had visited during the first days of my trip. The shockingly spacious, full-functioning, air-conditioned and, by outward appearances, undamaged studio produces television and film dramas with an antiwar emphasis, including a soap opera – *Today Is Not Tomorrow* – and a children's program. The director of the organization ponders aloud why more black Americans don't travel to Africa. I reply that the vast majority of blacks in the States can't afford it, that the American blacks most Africans meet on this continent are at least somewhat well off, a minority, and as I say this it suddenly becomes clear to me why Africans assume all Americans, with black Americans no exception, are rich and spoiled. I tell the director that I came from a working class family, that my father (who died nineteen years before) worked in a paper mill and my mother is a homemaker living on a miniscule fixed income, so as a working artist (and one exceedingly grateful to be able to make her rent), I have no nepotistic wealth to fall back on. I am glad that the male members of the family and Christopher, with all their assumptions about me, are present to hear this.

Tuesday, naturally, a big going-away event – complete with one-page photocopied programs – is planned for me. The setting is the family's large living room; chairs are brought in especially. I know I'll have to make a speech and, happy to be home soon, I am finally ready. The place is packed. (I imagine there aren't many interesting social affairs for Liberians to attend these days.) Samuel, whose arrogance has rubbed me the wrong way on more than one occasion, is now quietly polite, and rather humbly melancholy at my farewell. I am touched that several of the women from my ceremony have come. The senior minister and his young betrothed are here. Tomorrow she will drop by again with a gift for me (an African outfit and shoes) in the hours before my departure. In our struggle to understand each other, I will tell her how the rings of my cell phone (and everyone's ring is the same) had begun to drive me mad. She will show me how to change the ring, as well as a few other tricks, obviously handy with a mobile. "Do you have a phone at home?" I ask, assuming she does.

"No," she says.

"Does your mother have a phone?"

"No."

I'm puzzled. The only other people in her household are her mother and her toddler daughter. "There isn't any phone at your house?"

"No."

Upon my departure, I had planned to give my phone, purchased with the grant money, to my host family, just as Toimu had suggested. But I remember one day when Toimu answered his cell in the car. It was Florence calling, telling us we were late, and she wanted us to come home so she could feed me. That means there are at least two phones in this house, and Samuel has his own at his place.

"Do you want this phone?"

"Yes." Her usually beaming face is now serious, staring at the phone, not looking at me, as if she is afraid I am not serious. Then I hand the mechanism to her, and the instruction box, and she breaks into a broad smile. In the living room a few minutes later she will dial her fiancé, the minister. "Sister Kia gave me a phone!"

My speech at the event is brief and ever so grateful for the kindness and hospitality everyone has shown me. I cite Florence in particular for the meals and conversation, and I end with "Eesay, eesay, eesay!" Either my accent is way off, or I just surprise everyone with the Kpelle thank-you, because there is a confused moment of silence, then all cheer.

There are greens! I gorge. No vegetables in two weeks, and it dawns on me, the irony that I never told the family I was a vegetarian so as not to trouble them: they prepared the meat for me, the guest, and saved the second-class collards for themselves.

Christopher naturally has videotaped today's affair. He plays it back on the monitor. I see myself and am stunned. After two weeks in Africa I look so thin. And so *white*.

Tired, I go to bed early this Departure Eve but just before sleep I hear what sounds like an approaching army. Not now, I selfishly think. Hostilities can't resume *now*. But I realize it's just the TV. Blasting seems to be the only volume setting.

Wednesday. My mother, a gifted sketch artist who reserved her talents for the delight of her children and their activities, taught me how to fold a piece of paper into a box. I ask Samuel to give this tiny cube to Eunice, a gift for her capping. They thank me by email later for the folded $20 bill contained within.

Hot-footing to the airport our driver passes two cars at once, flying in the left lane in the face of an oncoming UN truck. We safely make it back to our side in time, and as we approach the UN vehicle a European arm, the driver's, wags a chastising finger at us, and I am gratified to know I'm not the only one who thinks Liberian drivers, and passengers, are a little insane.

I am about to go into the airport. In a few minutes I am going to be surprised. Small, but the space will appear like any modern facility, clean and painted and a.c., and even sundries shops and a bar filled with smokers, all laughing white men as far as I will see. They'll irk me somehow. I can only guess that the night and day difference between this and the dirty garage feel of the arrivals section is due to international standards regarding security – the metal detectors and x-ray machines perhaps subsidized by outside funds and as long as these technical safety items are up to snuff, the other furnishings may as well be.

But at this moment I turn around to wave at the family: Florence and Samuel and Toimu. And as they smile sad waving back, I notice for the first time that Toimu's knees are charcoal black, hard. Some history. Toimu and I have had our differences but now I remember yesterday afternoon, he and I waiting in the car for Samuel to purchase books for their graduate classes that had begun the night before. Toimu pulled out his syllabus, eagerly rereading the schedule for the coming semester, and the image moved my heart. Rachel Fay, in her introduction of Toimu to me, wrote that this paraplegic had miraculously managed to get his entire large family through the war unscathed – no small feat. Here was a man who crawled across international borders to save his family, and now he was undertaking postgraduate studies, expanding on an already remarkable life, and disability and middle age and a calamitous war weren't enough to stop him.

Go, Papay, go.

Biographies

KIA CORTHRON's plays include *A Cool Dip in the Barren Saharan Crick* (Playwrights Horizons co-production with The Play Company and the Culture Project), *Trickle* (Ensemble Studio Theatre's Marathon), *Moot the Messenger* (Actors Theatre of Louisville's Humana Festival), *Light Raise the Roof* (New York Theatre Workshop), *Snapshot Silhouette* (Minneapolis' Children's Theatre), *Slide Glide the Slippery Slope* (ATL Humana, Mark Taper Forum), *The Venus de Milo Is Armed* (Alabama Shakespeare Festival), *Breath, Boom* (London's Royal Court Theatre, Playwrights Horizons, Yale Repertory Theatre, Huntington Theatre and elsewhere), *Force Continuum* (Atlantic Theater Company), *Splash Hatch on the E Going Down* (New York Stage and Film, Baltimore's Center Stage, Yale Rep, London's Donmar Warehouse), *Seeking the Genesis* (Goodman Theatre, Manhattan Theatre Club), *Digging Eleven* (Hartford Stage Company), *Life by Asphyxiation* (Playwrights Horizons), *Wake Up Lou Riser* (Delaware Theatre Company), *Come Down Burning* (American Place Theatre, Long Wharf Theatre), *Cage Rhythm* (Sightlines/The Point in the Bronx). Awards and fellowships include the Rockefeller Foundation's Bellagio Creative Arts Residency (Italy), Dora Maar Residency (France), MacDowell Colony, Playwrights Center's McKnight National Residency, Masterwork Productions Award, the Wachtmeister Award, Columbia College/ Goodman Theatre Fellowship, Barbara Barondess MacLean Foundation Award, AT&T On Stage Award, Daryl Roth Creative Spirit Award, Mark

512

Taper Forum's Fadiman Award, National Endowment for the Arts/TCG, Kennedy Center Fund for New American Plays, New Professional Theatre Playwriting Award, Callaway Award, and in television a Writers Guild Outstanding Drama Series Award and Edgar Allan Poe Award for *The Wire*. Kia is currently a member of the Dramatists Guild Council and of the Writers Guild of America, and an alumnus of New Dramatists.

MICHAEL JOHN GARCÉS is the artistic director of Cornerstone Theater Company, a community-engaged ensemble based in Los Angeles. He has directed several plays by Kia Corthron, including *Light Raise the Roof* at New York Theatre Workshop, *Snapshot Silhouette* at The Children's Theatre and *Force Continuum* at The Atlantic Theatre. Other credits include *Oedipus El Rey* by Luis Alfaro at Woolly Mammoth and *the break/s* by Marc Bamuthi Joseph at the Humana Festival, the Walker Arts Center and A Contemporary Theatre. His play *Los Illegals*, created in residence with day laborers and domestic workers and presented by Cornerstone, will be published in Yale School of Drama's *Theatre* in the summer of 2011.

KARA LEE CORTHRON's plays include *Julius by Design* (Fulcrum Theater, 2011; Penumbra, 2012), *Etched in Skin on a Sunlit Night* (NEA Access to Artistic Excellence Grant; InterAct Theatre, 2012), THE GERM PROJECT: *AliceGraceAnon* (New Georges, 2011), *Holly Down in Heaven* (Princess Grace Award), *Spookwater* (O'Neill Conference

Finalist), and *Wild Black-Eyed Susans* (Helen Merrill Award). Other awards/honors include: The Vineyard Theatre's 3rd Annual Paula Vogel Playwriting Award, Lincoln Center's Lecomte du Nouy Prize (three-time recipient), an E.S.T./Sloan Commission, the Theodore Ward Prize, the New Professional Theatre Writers Award, residencies at MacDowell, Skriðuklaustur (Iceland), the Millay Colony, and Ledig House and she was twice finalist for New Dramatists membership. Current commissions: South Coast Rep, New Georges, and Naked Angels. Play development: African Continuum (D.C.), ACT Seattle/Hansberry Project, Ars Nova, CenterStage (Baltimore), Electric Pear Productions, Horizon Theatre (Atlanta), Naked Angels, New Dramatists, New Georges, The Orchard Project, Page 73 Productions, Penumbra, PlayPenn, The Shalimar, TheatreWorks, the Vineyard Theatre, and Voice and Vision among others. TV: staff writer for NBC's KINGS (2008-2009). Kara is a Juilliard alumna, instructor at Primary Stages' Einhorn School of Performing Arts, and member of the 2010 Ars Nova Play Group, 'Wright On! Playwrights Group (co-founder), Blue Roses Productions, the Dramatists Guild and is a New Georges Affiliated Artist.

NoPassport

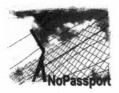

NoPassport is a Pan-American theatre alliance & press devoted to live, virtual and print action, advocacy and change toward the fostering of cross-cultural diversity in the arts with an emphasis on the embrace of the hemispheric spirit in US Latina/o and Latin-American theatre-making. **NoPassport Press'** Dreaming the Americas Series and Theatre & Performance PlayTexts Series promotes new writing for the stage, texts on theory and practice and theatrical translations. www.nopassport.org

Series Editors: Randy Gener, Jorge Huerta, Mead K. Hunter, Otis Ramsey-Zoe, Stephen Squibb, Caridad Svich (founding editor)

Advisory Board: Daniel Banks, Amparo Garcia-Crow, Maria M. Delgado, Randy Gener, Elana Greenfield, Christina Marin, Antonio Ocampo Guzman, Sarah Cameron Sunde, Saviana Stanescu, Tamara Underiner, Patricia Ybarra

NoPassport is a sponsored project of Fractured Atlas, a non-profit arts service organization. Contributions in behalf of [Caridad Svich & NoPassport] may be made payable to Fractured Atlas and are tax-deductible to the extent permitted by law. **For online donations: https://www.fracturedatlas.org/donate/2623**

Selected titles available from NoPassport Press

Antigone Project: A Play in Five Parts
by Tanya Barfield, Karen Hartman, Chiori Miyagawa,
Lynn Nottage and Caridad Svich, with Preface by Lisa
Schlesinger, Introduction by Marianne McDonald.
ISBN 978-0-578-03150-7

Migdalia Cruz: El Grito del Bronx & other plays
*(Salt, Yellow Eyes, El Grito del Bronx, Da Bronx rocks: a
song)* Introduction by Alberto Sandoval-Sanchez,
afterword by Priscilla Page.
ISBN: 978-0-578-04992-2

Envisioning the Americas: Latina/o Theatre & Performance
A NoPassport Press Sampler with works
by Migdalia Cruz, John Jesurun, Oliver Mayer,
Alejandro Morales and Anne Garcia-Romero, Preface by
Jose Rivera. Introduction by Caridad Svich, **ISBN: 978-0-578-08274-5**

Catherine Filloux: Dog and Wolf & Killing the Boss
Introduction by Cynthia E. Cohen. **ISBN: 978-0-578-07898-4**

David Greenspan: Four Plays and a Monologue
(Jack, 2 Samuel Etc, Old Comedy, Only Beauty, A
Playwright's Monologue), Preface by Helen Shaw,
Introduction by Taylor Mac, **ISBN: 978-0-578-08448-0**

Karen Hartman: Girl Under Grain
Introduction by Jean Randich. **ISBN: 978-0-578-04981-6**

Kara Hartzler: No Roosters in the Desert
Based on field work by Anna Ochoa O'Leary **ISBN: 978-0-578-07047-6**

**John Jesurun: Deep Sleep, White Water, Black Maria –
A Media Trilogy,** Preface by Fiona Templeton. **ISBN:
978-0-578-02602-2**

Carson Kreitzer: SELF DEFENSE and other Plays, (*Self
Defense, The Love Song of J Robert Oppenheimer, 1:23,
Slither*), Preface by Mark Wing-Davey, Introduction by
Mead K. Hunter.**ISBN: 978-0-578-08058-1.**

Matthew Maguire: Three Plays: (*The Tower, Luscious
Music, The Desert*) with Preface by Naomi Wallace.
ISBN: 978-0-578-00856-1

Oliver Mayer: Collected Plays: (*Conjunto, Joe Louis Blues,
Ragged Time*) Preface by Luis Alfaro, Introduction by Jon
D. Rossini, **ISBN: 978-0-6151-8370-1**

Chiori Miyagawa: Woman Killer
introduction by Sharon Friedman, afterword by Martin
Harries, **ISBN: 978-0-578-05008-9**

Octavio Solis: The River Plays (*El Otro, Dreamlandia,
Bethlehem*), Introduction by Douglas Langworthy. **ISBN:
978-0-578-04881-9**

Saviana Stanescu: The New York Plays
(*Waxing West, Lenin's Shoe, Aliens with Extraordinary
Skills*), Introduction by John Clinton Eisner. **ISBN: 978-0-
578-04942-7**

The Tropic of X by Caridad Svich
Introduction by Marvin Carlson, Afterword by Tamara
Underiner, **ISBN: 978-0-578-03871-1**